PENGUIN BOOKS

THE RECKONING

Sue Walker is a television journalist who has worked in the industry for twenty years. She started out in her native Edinburgh, eventually moving to London to work in BBC TV's News and Current Affairs Department. For the past fourteen years, Sue has concentrated on documentaries specializing in crime investigative work and miscarriages of justice, mainly for Channel 4.

Her debut novel, *The Reunion*, is also available in paperback and her latest novel, *The Dead Pool*, will publish in Autumn 2007.

The Reckoning

SUE WALKER

PENGUIN BOOKS

PENGUIN BOOKS

Published by the Penguin Group
Penguin Books Ltd, 80 Strand, London WC2R ORL, England
Penguin Group (USA) Inc., 375 Hudson Street, New York, New York 10014, USA
Penguin Group (Canada), 90 Eglinton Avenue East, Suite 700, Toronto, Ontario, Canada M4P 2Y3
(a division of Pearson Penguin Canada Inc.)
Penguin Ireland, 25 St Stephen's Green, Dublin 2, Ireland (a division of Penguin Books Ltd)
Penguin Group (Australia), 250 Camberwell Road, Camberwell, Victoria 3124, Australia
(a division of Pearson Australia Group Pty Ltd)
Penguin Books India Pvt Ltd, 11 Community Centre, Panchsheel Park, New Delhi – 110 017, India
Penguin Group (NZ), cnr Airborne and Rosedale Roads, Albany, Auckland 1310, New Zealand
(a division of Pearson New Zealand Ltd)
Penguin Books (South Africa) (Pty) Ltd, 24 Sturdee Avenue, Rosebank, Johannesburg 2196, South Africa

Penguin Books Ltd, Registered Offices: 80 Strand, London WC2R ORL, England

www.penguin.com

First published by Michael Joseph 2005
Published in Penguin Books 2007
1

Typeset by Rowland Phototypesetting Ltd, Bury St Edmunds, Suffolk
Printed in England by Clays Ltd, St Ives plc

ISBN: 978-0-141-01751-8

To Susan Allen and Martin Farrow
Friends indeed

Acknowledgements

Great thanks to my editor, Beverley Cousins, and my agent, Teresa Chris, for their superb work and support.

The wipers couldn't keep up with the downpour. His head-lights barely cut through the blackness of the wretched night. One more turn and he should see it up on the head-land. Yes, there it was. A single, dim, yellow light trying to beacon its way across the heaving waters of the Firth of Forth. The jeep fishtailed dangerously as he took the final bend.

'Damn it!'

His curse was aimed solely at his own bad driving. Not at the vehicle. Not at the weather. As he changed down the gears he noticed that the shaking in his left hand had deteriorated into a violent palsy. His right would be the same if it hadn't been clamped, white-knuckled, to the steer-ing wheel. Despite the hermetically sealed state of the jeep, he could still feel the freezing air outside. Could still hear the bansheeing whine of the wind as it attacked anything upright, the jeep included. The roar of the sea was loud and near. The approach to the building was via a cliffside, tarmacked road, gushing with the night's rain.

His headlights swept the brown and white wooden sign. 'St Baldred's Hospice'. He'd always known of the place's existence. Since childhood. But it was a place to be ignored. Denied. An invisible place. A place for adults to talk about in whispers. A place that elderly neighbours had occasionally disappeared into. And never returned from.

The nurse must have heard him, even through the howl-ing of the wind. She was standing grave but welcoming by the door, her silhouette marking a ghostly outline against the barely lit entrance area.

'Mr McAllister?'

She led him into a small, carefully furnished reception room, blissfully overheated. Only now did he notice what she was wearing. She was in civvies. No cold, formal, clinical garb here.

'. . . and if you'll just sit here. I'm Nurse Lizzie Henderson. We talked a couple of hours ago?'

She was sitting by him, close, but not too close. Keeping a comforting but professional distance? She seemed to be waiting for something. He just wanted to get in there.

'Mr McAllister. I'm so sorry. Your father died forty minutes ago. We thought he was going to last a bit longer. As I think you know, he'd been unconscious with the morphine for the past day or . . .'

He drifted away from her.

Relief.

Yes, relief was his first reaction. But relief from what exactly? And then the shock. The reality of it. The permanence of it. He was gone. Absolutely, utterly, forever gone.

'. . . see him? Mr McAllister?'

'I . . . I'm sorry?'

She'd moved closer to him. He could see the concern on her face. 'I said, perhaps you'd like to see him now?'

He managed a nod and followed her out. Nothing was stirring. Any lights seemed to be the dimmest. Just enough to lead the way. He risked a glance into the few darkened and silenced rooms he passed as he made his way along the lino-floored corridor. But not a sound from anywhere. This wasn't like a hospital. It was a place of death. Of quietude. Of peace? For some, maybe.

Without realizing, he'd followed her into the last room.

She was standing at the end, next to fully closed curtains. He kept his eyes focused straight ahead, aware of perhaps two, maybe three other beds on either side. But there was only one area where the faintest of lights glowed.

Without a word, she parted the curtains, bowing her head as if in benediction, and let him enter. Then, silently, she stepped back and he was alone. At first he thought there had been some ghastly error. A hideous mistake! This . . . this . . . skeletal shell was not him. Not his father! Where was the tall, muscular frame he remembered so well? One that he himself had inherited. Always an uncomfortable reminder of his lineage.

'But Christ no, this isn't . . .'

Christ, yes. It was like a negative. Or one image superimposed on another. He knew by the eye sockets. Always wide and deep, like his own. And by the skull bones about the temple. Prominent yet delicate, like his own. But it was the hands. The slim, almost feminine fingers. Like his own. He was his father's son all right. But this, before him? This collection of bones inside a yellowing bag of . . . of . . . you could barely call it flesh. He pressed a palm to his mouth. To staunch a wave of nausea. To stifle a cry of horror. And pain? He allowed himself to inch forwards and touch the back of a hand. Cooling but not yet death-cold. Strange. Just as if he'd been out on an autumn day, without gloves. On the boat, raising the sails . . .

Then he stepped back. For the first time he noticed what they'd done. Perfectly laid out. They'd given him fresh pyjamas. Fresh sheets. And someone had laid a rose on the pillow by his left temple. A lush, oddly out-of-season red rose.

That's what did it. He stumble-sprinted to the front door, his sobs and spittle unstoppable. The rain was more than welcome on his face as he ran to the jeep. Skidding down the lane, he half grimaced through his sobs. The thunder had started its whip-cracking overhead, lightning flickered between the clouds. The storm was on its way.

'Bring it on! Bring it all fucking on! Go on, damn you!'

As he reached sea level, the heavens obliged. He risked one final look at the hospice, now strobe-illuminated in blue and silver. The building's Gothic, threatening silhouette lowered out over the sea. A place of darkness, fear, suffering. He nodded his approval.

It was the perfect place for his father to die.

'Treasure Island'

Fidra in the Firth of Forth is one of a group of five small islands dotted along Scotland's East Lothian coast. It is commonly held to have been the model for R. L. Stevenson's 'Treasure Island'. However, this joyful connection to one of the world's favourite children's stories cannot and should not permit us to ignore the island's historical treasures.

Historians, archaeologists and local folklore have created a rather colourful picture of this little island. Fidra has seen immense activity over the centuries, much of it spiritual. There is evidence of what was thought to be a medieval monastery. There are also the ruins of a chapel, built by the monks and used as a place of pilgrimage for local nuns. The monastery building is believed to have served as a hospital during times of plague. Unsurprisingly, given its history, there are tales of the island being haunted by a hooded figure – 'The Dark Monk of Fidra'.

These are all distant echoes of bygone times, and largely forgotten. However, the twentieth century has brought a more disturbing and bloody reputation to the island.

Fidra – said to be Norse for 'Feather Island' or 'Isle of Feathers' because of its abundant breeding grounds for aquatic birdlife – is now held in the collective memory of locals as a place to be shunned, and is considered by some to be haunted by more than the ghost of an eight-hundred-year-old monk.

Extract from *Fidra – an Island History*, by Duncan Alexander, Whitekirk Publishing, 1st edition, 1978.

I

June 1973

'Is it true, Dad?' He was having to shout above the noise of the sail flapping and the waves splashing against the sides.

'Is what true, son?'

'About Fidra? That it was the *real* Treasure Island?'

Miller saw rather than heard his father's laugh as he hauled on the wheel, squinting into the sun, vigilant, as the boat made its approach to the landing point. His dad raised a hand at him.

'Hah! Well. You'd be better asking Dr Buchan here. He's the expert on Robert Louis Stevenson. Isn't that right, Forbes? Or what about you, Catriona? You're a bit of a scholar on the subject too, aren't you? Probably know more than your dad, eh?'

Despite the pipe hanging from the corner of his mouth, Dr Buchan managed a big smile. 'Oh, aye, my lassie knows all about Stevenson.'

Miller watched Dr Buchan as he moved up the boat towards him, cupping Catriona's face in his big hand as he went past. He didn't look like the family doctor today, all relaxed in shirtsleeves and casual trousers. He stopped to ruffle Miller's hair and offer him another cheery grin. Miller liked Dr Buchan. He didn't feel scared when he had to go to the surgery. Dr Buchan was always nice to him. He'd brought him comics and sweets when he'd had chickenpox and measles. Anyway, he was a friend of Dad's, and Catriona

7

was his daughter. So Dr Buchan had to be all right, didn't he?

Catriona was looking pretty, *really* pretty today. Very grown-up too. What was she now . . . fourteen? Just three years older than him. The same age as his brother, Greg. But she looked almost as old as their big sister, Mhari, who was just about to leave school! Catriona was certainly taller than Mhari, and more sure of herself, though Mhari tried to make up for that by acting the bossy-boots.

Catriona had appeared by his side, smiling and shouting over the wind to his dad.

'That's right, Mr McAllister! I know a fair bit about Robert Louis Stevenson and Fidra. After all, that's why I'm called Catriona. I told you that yonks ago, Miller. *Stupid! Catriona* was the name of the sequel to *Kidnapped*. And yes, Fidra is the basis for *Treasure Island*. That's right, Daddy, isn't it?'

He hated being called stupid. Most of all by Catriona. But Miller knew she didn't really think he was stupid. She was still smiling at him. Catriona was always nice to him when she was invited to the island. Every summer she said how lucky he was to have a family that owned an island. An island with a lovely house on it. He liked it in the winter when she was at his house on the mainland. She would stare through the binoculars at Fidra, counting how long until the first trip of the summer over there.

He sneaked another look at her. She was staring at her dad, waiting for his reply. Dr Buchan looked funny, trying to shout above the wind and keep the pipe clamped between his teeth at the same time.

'Oh, aye, Miller. Cattie's right. You see, Stevenson used to have family holidays here in North Berwick, so he had plenty of time to think about what he saw and use that amazing imagination of his. *And* Catriona *was* the name

8

of Catriona Drummond. She's the sweetheart of David Balfour, the hero of *Kidnapped*, and the sequel's named after her.'

Mhari was pushing her way past Dr Buchan.

'Yeah, yeah, but we've heard it all before, Miller, you know we have. Why d'you always ask the same questions? Every time we make the first trip of the summer. *Eejit!*' He felt Mhari's punch on his upper arm as she lowered her voice to the merest whisper. '*Erse!* You just want bloody Catriona's attention. Well, she's far too old for you, *wee* brother. So there!'

He hated it when his sister was like this. It was happening more and more. Probably one of the reasons why their mum hadn't come over this weekend. Mum had been grumpy for days. 'Snippy and snappy', Greg called it. Mum could be that way sometimes. But she'd been like that loads lately and had quarrelled a lot with Mhari the past week. And, to top it all, Mhari had some sort of huff on today. He thought she was a bit jealous of Catriona, to be honest. Her being pretty. That was what Mhari didn't like. Mhari was quite vain, always looking at herself in mirrors and shop windows. And she was a bit two-faced with Catriona. Pretended to like her. He caught Greg rolling his eyes at Mhari and gave him a wink in return. He really hoped this trip was going to work out okay.

'All right! We're going to land in a few minutes. Mhari, will you take hold of Bella for a minute, please?'

His father was busying himself for the landing but still found time to stroke the ears of Bella, his chocolate-coloured Labrador, whose tail was going twenty to the dozen at the thought of being out of the boat.

'Gregor! Miller! Come and help with the sail!'

His dad's orders rushed past him on the wind and Miller

made a thumbs-up sign to indicate that he understood. It was one of his favourite things, helping with the boat. As he moved up towards his father, he took a long look at Fidra. It was particularly green, lush and sparkly today, the sun glinting off its various rocky outcrops. A perfect little island. Not so small that there was nowhere to hide, and not so big that you got lost. It was a funny shape. Long skinny tail with a lump at the top. Its crowning glory was the lighthouse. He loved the lighthouse. And there was the house! Their house. High above but in a sheltered nook to the right of the jetty. Dad had had it newly painted inside and out during the spring. It looked fresh, crisp. A plain square white-washed building that had once been a weather station.

The house's outstanding feature had to be the two huge sliding glass doors that led out to a metal viewing platform, also painted a startling white. Panoramic views. To the sea – down the Firth of Forth and across to the fishing villages of Fife. To the shore – to spy on the entire East Lothian coastline. He couldn't wait to get there. But before that he wanted to be first out of the boat. That way he could give Catriona a helping hand on to land.

Yes, it was going to be a good trip.

2

Miller booted a stray rock out of his path. He felt a bit deflated. The two grown-ups, Catriona and Greg were all fishing on the other side of the island. Dad said he could go for a wander but he couldn't take Bella. She had to stay with Dad, just for the first couple of hours on the island. In case she worried the birds.

Dad had seen him off with a smile and the usual lecture he gave at the start of every summer. '*Don't go too near the cliffs or the old ruins.*' The cliffs were scary anyway – a huge drop into the Firth of Forth – so he'd be keeping clear of them. And the old chapel ruins at the north-west of the island had always been out of bounds. Dad said they'd been unsafe since the year dot and were permanently blocked off, buried underneath a hollow. There wasn't any actual building left. Just some crumbling walls, unsafe foundations. He and Greg had once tried to have a closer look. They'd removed some stones from a dry-stane dyke that surrounded the area. But all they could see was what looked like a wooden fence and maybe another wall. Dad had caught them before they'd done much damage and gone mad, saying that they could have been crushed by falling rubble. A bit dramatic, Greg had said, but one telling off was enough with Dad. *Stay away*.

So, bird watching it was today and he wasn't the only one. Mhari had gone off in a sulk to look for puffins, *with his binoculars!* She said that she'd forgotten her own. Within half an hour of landing she'd started whining that she was bored and that she was too old for 'these juvenile trips'. But

Dr Buchan had sorted her out. He'd said, in that case, it made him definitely too ancient at the grand old age of . . . well, whatever he was. Too old to remember! He said he'd better be getting off home then, and made to take off his sandals and socks, pretending that he was going to swim back. Everyone had laughed. Except Mhari, of course. She couldn't take a joke. Not nowadays. Greg agreed. He said that he'd had enough of her 'bossy ways' and wished she'd 'bugger off' to university. But Mhari wasn't going anywhere for a while. There was the whole summer to get through before she went to uni.

He scuffed another rock out of the way and threw his head backwards to catch the full blast of the warm wind. It was really hot today and so clear. It lifted his spirits. The first visit of every summer made him feel more than just happy. Different. Another Miller. The island did that to him. Free and completely safe. He could do what he liked on this pretty little place without anyone to bother him. Each day he could and would lie down on the soft bouncy moss, his face to the sun, and listen to every bird call, every gull cry, mentally cataloguing who and what was up there in the skies. By the end of the summer everyone – his brother, sister, Dad, the Buchans, and Mum too when she came along – would look well, tanned, smiling, happy. The island made them all a bit different. Different in a good way. Even Mum and Dad would be spotted holding hands now and again. That *never* happened on the mainland! Catriona would be more relaxed and friendlier to him. Mhari would forget about being a bossy-boots. Yes, Fidra made everyone behave differently. Behave better. Like a magic spell. A real treasure island after all.

He was tempted to lie down now and catch the sun but thought better of it. He just wanted to check everything was where it should be. Stupid really. There was only moss, grass and rocks to check on and they weren't going anywhere. Still, good to do a quick patrol. Say hello to Fidra.

He smiled to himself. He liked being alone but he'd have preferred it if Catriona or Bella had come with him. Still, he knew where everyone was, except Mhari, and she was most probably up the other end of the island if she was looking for puffins. The Puffin: *Fratercula arctica*. A lovely wee bird with wings that worked like clockwork when you saw them airborne. And then he heard it. The familiar sound of the herring gulls. *Larus argentatus*. A rather stern-looking bird. Always an annoyed expression on its face. *Damn*, he wished he had his binoculars. Trust Mhari! He scrabbled down the slope from the main path and followed the cries of the gulls. It sounded like they were laughing, and some-times – he often heard this type of call when he first woke up in the morning on the island – they sounded like cats miaowing.

He slipped halfway down but managed to break his fall on the spongy grass below. The gulls' laughter had turned funny. It was more a screeching now and he could hear a fluttering coming from behind a big boulder to his right. As he inched round it, he saw what was making the noise. Two adult male gulls were locked in battle. One was in a bad way. It was bleeding heavily from its head and chest and it was trailing a hurt wing. Grey and white feathers were strewn everywhere. Without thinking, he hurled himself forwards and the victorious gull flew off with a wail and a majestic flapping of wings. But its victim was hopping, trying in vain to take off. The wing looked broken and the poor creature was making little squeaking noises. The tears came in a moment as Miller spun round frantically. He had to get Dad. He'd be able to do something. Maybe take it to the mainland.

Dad had done that before with injured birds. Slowly, Miller backed off.

'It's all right, it's all right. I'm not going to hurt you. I'm going to help you . . . I wish I had some fish or some bread to give you. You poor thing . . . poor, poor wee thing.'

'Who the hell you talking to, Miller? You're crazy. Crazy. Cuckoo. Mental.'

Miller spun round again. Above him, on the same slope he'd descended, was Mhari, his binoculars slung around her neck.

He pointed behind him. 'It's a gull. It's been in a fight and's in a bad way. I'm going to get Dad.'

He watched Mhari slither down the grass and approach the injured bird. She gave a twisted moue at what she saw. 'It's going to die. If it's broken its wing, it's fucked.'

He hated when she used that sort of language. It embarrassed him. Dad (and Mum!) would be livid hearing her talk like that.

She had turned away from the still-struggling bird to look at him. 'I think we should kill it. Put it out of its misery.'

'No! No, no! We've got to try and help it. I'm going to get Dad.'

She was standing hands on hips, shaking her head. 'There's nothing we can do. Look at it! Dr Buchan's right, you know. I heard him saying to Catriona when they visited before, that when you're in a wild habitat like this, you have to learn *not* to interfere with nature. It can be hard but wild things should be left alone. I agree, except I think we should help it along. Hurry along the inevitable.'

Before he had time to respond, she'd picked up a heavy rock.

'*No, Mhari! No!*'

But she'd moved away from him, raising both hands,

ready to strike with the stone. He turned and ran, fingers in ears to stop the sounds, tears streaming into his mouth. Overhead, soft, downy feathers from the dying bird floated past him on the warm breeze.

3

'The boy's very upset. He's a sensitive lad. Very sensitive.
I worry about him sometimes. I mean he's awfy young for
his age, in some ways. That's not necessarily a bad thing but
can be a curse as well as a blessing. And he's bright, too
bright maybe.'

Hidden at the top of the stairs, he peered down through
the wooden banister. His dad, Bella fast asleep at his feet,
and Dr Buchan were sitting together in the study. Both
were nursing part-filled tumblers and a bottle of posh whisky
sat on the floor between them. Dr Buchan was raising his
glass.

'There's nothing wrong with having a bright child. Your
Miller's a great laddie. And he loves nature. He's a bloody
budding ornithologist, in case you hadn't noticed! That's
why the gull incident shook him so deeply. Truthfully,
though, it sounds like your Mhari did the best thing, in the
circumstances. Quite a gritty thing for a lassie to do.'

'Aye, she's a sensible girl. I'm sure you're right. Anyway,
speaking of the girls, how's your Catriona doing? She looks
blooming and so bonny. You've done an amazing job with
her, Forbes.'

Miller inched back from the banister, frowning. He
couldn't remember anything about Catriona's mother. He'd
heard his dad say that she'd been 'an absolutely lovely lady'.
She'd died of cancer or something horrible when Catriona
was young. And Dr Buchan's mum had looked after her
sometimes. She said her granny was nice. He didn't see

much of his grannies and granddads but at least he had a mum. It must've been hard not having a mum. Poor Catriona. Imagine if Greg or even Mhari died. Terrible.

'*Hey you!*'

He felt the tug on his pyjama sleeve. Mhari. 'You should be in bed, you little eavesdropper. Go on, off you go. I'm going down to watch some telly.'

He wriggled out of her grip. 'Get *off* me. I'm going, all right!'

She was obviously in a better mood than earlier. 'Okay. G'night, Miller . . . and . . . I . . . I had to do that thing with the gull. It was suffering. One day you'll understand.'

He turned and wandered towards his room but within half a minute he was back at the top of the stairs. He wasn't tired and Greg was asleep, so he couldn't read. Greg went spare if he tried to read by torchlight. It always woke him up. Out of the blue, Bella appeared at his side, tail wagging. 'Hello, girl, what you doing here?' He kissed her soft head and put his arm around her neck as she settled down on the top step, sitting up but leaning into him. Downstairs, Mhari had switched on the TV. The news was drowning out anything the grown-ups were now saying.

'. . . *and Lothian and Borders police said that the hunt for missing fifteen-year-old Eileen Ritchie from the village of Garvald was intensifying, including a wave of door-to-door inquiries. Eileen was last seen walking her dog on the edge of the Lammermuir Hills last night. Police have conceded that it is "very likely" that her disappearance is linked to those of two other girls from East Lothian in the past four years. Today, Eileen's distraught mother, Mrs . . .*'

'Mhari! Let's turn that off, shall we! It's hardly suitable viewing for a holiday break. And it's too loud. You'll wake the whole house!'

Miller jumped and, simultaneously, felt Bella stiffen, as

she pricked up her ears. It wasn't usual for Dad to be so short-tempered. Mhari too looked astonished as he marched across the room, switched the set off and then went back to the study, closing the door firmly behind him.

Five minutes later, Miller was in Mhari's room. 'So why's Dad suddenly in such a bad mood?'

She shrugged, picking at a stray thread on the blanket covering her bed. 'Haven't got a clue. You're the spying little eavesdropper. What were they talking about at the time?'

'Nothing really. Just stuff.'

Mhari shook her head. 'Dad's been snappy a couple of times the past day or two. Something's going on.'

He awoke to the sound of the screeching gulls, a depressing reminder of the day before. But by the time they'd all had a swim off the jetty, he was feeling a lot better.

'C'mon, Miller! Time to load up the boat. Mum's meeting us at the harbour.'

His dad was back to normal. Everyone seemed okay today. He helped lug the bags down to the jetty.

'Thanks, son. We'll be back soon, and next time we can stay longer. You'll be on your school hols then, eh? It's already been lovely weather of late. Let's hope we're going to have a scorcher of a summer!'

Miller nodded, returning his dad's smile and slinging the bags on board.

The sailing didn't take that long, though the town always looked deceptively nearer than it was. Still, it was early and so once they were home he could stay out in the sun for a few hours yet. He and Bella and maybe Greg could climb Berwick Law. Have a race up there – all 613 feet of it. Bella always won that game, though, and Greg usually cheated by tripping him up. Still, with the binoculars, the view would be fantastic today.

He looked over at Catriona. She was chuffed because his dad had invited her to pull on a halyard to raise the sail. She was doing quite well, her slim hands hauling on the rope until the sail billowed out. Shame he hadn't seen much of her this short trip. He'd sort of hidden away after the gull thing. He knew she understood. She'd seen him at teatime and said that she was sorry.

There was a flurry of jobs to do as the boat pulled in to the harbour. Miller paused to check the quayside. Where was Mum? Bella saw her first and started up a manic barking. They all waved at Mum but she didn't look that pleased to see them. She lifted her hand in a half-hearted way. Not another grumpy bad mood? Oh well, if she *was* in a mood they could expect eruptions between her and Mhari for the rest of the day. Those two just weren't getting on.

He and his dad let everyone off the boat before them. They were just about to begin unloading the bags, when two men who were dressed oddly for the harbour area – in suits – walked over from a nearby car.

'Mr McAllister?'

He watched as his dad turned round smiling, one foot on the harbour steps the other still on the boat. He pushed himself on to land and turned to the men. Maybe they'd come through from Edinburgh. From his work at the bank.

'Aye, hello there, gents. What can I do for you this lovely day?'

The taller of the men took a step forwards and spoke something very quietly into his dad's ear. Before the man could say any more, it happened. As if in slow motion, his father turned back towards the boat, doubling over as if in pain. His face had gone pale, like he was going to faint, and he'd lowered himself on to the harbour steps, head in hands. Then, one of the men put a hand on his dad's arm, and began dragging him to his feet like he'd done something wrong.

4

Late September 2005

The conspiracy of the elements had come as no surprise to him. The storm that had started the moment he'd left the hospice had held out the whole weekend, causing havoc to the shoreside buildings below him. Now, all was leaden, with low rain clouds meeting the sea, and the haar obliterating the horizon. The sun hadn't and wouldn't show its face this afternoon. Today had seen an all-day twilight. Fitting.

He'd forgotten how his father's house offered an eyrie-viewpoint of the harbour at North Berwick on one side and an equally dramatic view of the fourteenth-century fortress, known as Tantallon Castle, to his right. Once the stronghold of the 'Red' Douglases, like his own more modest family home, it stood atop a cliff, further up the headland. The old ruined castle, albeit dramatically situated, towered over the often roiling waters of the Firth of Forth. He remembered as a child charting its daily moods. Some days it seemed bigger, more brooding than ever. On others – usually blissful sunny days – it seemed far less threatening. But Tantallon's moods were all a trick of the light, of course.

If only all buildings could confer that sense of protection and security, including the one he was in right now. A plain yet solid stone, detached Victorian villa. Three floors, six bedrooms. And, in a neat match to the observation platform on the island house, panoramic views of sea and coastline were provided by a once-tempting balcony. Always satisfying the need to look outwards. Endless possibilities. How vast it had all seemed in childhood. How empty now. He'd last set foot inside the place two years ago, after his mother's death. What a day. Then, the change in this house had really affected him. This house, once a place of joy and security. A long-distant memory. He took a final look at the darkening outline of the castle ruins and moved back into the heart of the room. He shivered. The heating had been on for hours and there was a coal fire burning, but still he couldn't get warm. He didn't remember the house being particularly cold when he was a child, nor especially dark, either physically or in its atmosphere ... not until later. But today, the late-afternoon greyness had leached the light out of the living room despite its sizeable windows looking out towards the Firth. He really needed a lamp on but at the same time he enjoyed the feeling of being able to hide in the encroaching darkness. Like turning back into his shell. If only it were that easy.

He wandered down the hallway towards what had been the old television room. The two beaten-up leather settees were still there but the tartan rugs had long gone. God, he'd loved it in the winter, snuggling up and watching kids' telly. He and Greg used to race each other back from school. That trek on the train to and from their school in Edinburgh! Amazingly, it had been a daily adventure rather than the two-hours-a-day nightmare it would have been to most commuters. And once home on those dark winter afternoons, they'd wrestled over who got the best settee, the one nearest the TV. He slumped down on that one, feeling the soft leather give as he made himself comfortable. He needed to sleep but he was restless too. Not yet four. It would be completely dark soon. Good.

He forced himself back on to his feet. Time to roam the

house again. Between fitful sleep and periodic insomnia, the weekend had been spent patrolling the house. Hunting down favourite places from childhood. Foraging in the basement and attic for childhood memories. Sitting in the back garden. Trying, and failing, to edit out recurring images of his father. And staying, wherever possible, away from the sea views. Keeping Fidra out of his sight.

He wandered through to the kitchen. The vodka bottle was half empty. Last night's attempt at oblivion. Foolish. He snatched it up, jammed it in the freezer, and grabbed a handful of ice. Picking up a tumbler and family-size bottle of mineral water, he headed back to the living room, sloshing a few inches into the glass, drinking as he walked. He caught sight of himself in the hall mirror. *What a state!* Haggard and unshaven, crumpled clothing, like someone living on the streets. But he knew the rot was deeper than anything a sleepless weekend and a recent bereavement could cause. Bodywise, he was definitely losing it. His jaw had lost its razor-sharp tautness and would hint at a jowl before long, *and* there was a slight but definite thickening around his middle. His former fitness regime had gone. Slowly, by increments, but it had gone. Not good. *For heaven's sake man, get a grip!*

The landline rang. He'd deliberately run the mobile out of juice. No intrusions. Who the hell was this? He let the machine take it.

'Miller? It's Mhari. Aren't you at the house by now? Thought you were travelling up at the weekend? For goodness' sake, where are you? I'm assuming you got my letter before you left London? The house should be habitable. Mrs Watt has been in to clean and air the place. She always does it before I come to stay. I'm arriving Wednesday afternoon. We've got to be at the solicitor's at three on

Thursday. Frankly, I think it's a bit unseemly to meet with him before we've even cremated Dad. But he says he wants to see us all as soon as poss. Predictably, Gregor's not sure if he can make it. But he *will* make it for the funeral, so he says. I wouldn't hold our collective breath, though. I take it *you are* going to the funeral? Surely? Oh . . . shit! I wish you were there, I hate rambling on like this. Y'know, I left Dad on Friday afternoon, thinking he'd make it through the weekend. The staff seemed to think he might. But I had to get back up to St Andrews. Work's fine. The uni's given me as much time off as I need. But the kids, you know, they need me and I've been trying to deal with their loss of their grandfather and all that. And that's complicated, as you well know. And . . . and . . . well I missed Dad. Him dying, I mean . . . he died alone . . . well there were the lovely staff but . . . oh shit! Where *are* you, Miller? Call me as soon as you arrive.'

Typical bossy Mhari. No, 'Hello, how are you?' or, 'Look forward to seeing you.' Not even a bloody, 'Goodbye.' Just the usual self-obsession.

Moving over towards his half-unpacked bags, he brought the envelope out. He took a seat by the window but the gloom had won. He switched on a lamp and spread the letter out before him. He'd read it umpteen times. But why not sharpen his anger once more by reading it again.

Dear Miller

Following our phone conversation today, I really feel that I must put my thoughts down on paper. I feel that you have misunderstood me — perhaps wilfully. You know that our father is dying. The cancer is very aggressive and in its final stages. He's going to be allowed to spend the last period in St Baldred's, thank God. At least there's some compassion and humanity left in the world. The director is a saint and has persuaded the authorities to allow Dad this final dignity.

You can have no idea how our father has suffered. As you know, the diagnosis came out of nowhere. Absolute bolt from the blue. Yet Dad has been so very, heartbreakingly philosophical and stoical about it. He says that at the age of seventy-five life's had enough of him (and maybe he's had enough of it?) and it is obviously time for him to go. He mainly fears pain but he's been told that he will just become progressively more tired and will be able to do less and less. His form of cancer's like that, apparently. Also, the hospice assures me that any pain will be dealt with in the most humane way possible.

Miller, I beg you. Please, please visit Dad. It would help him, help him face his death. Can't you find some common humanity, for God's sake? I know you and I fundamentally disagree about Dad, but you wouldn't treat a dying dog like that. This must be a time of pain, suffering, and sheer terror for Dad, despite the smile he still puts on.

Think on that and do your duty as his youngest (and, I've always suspected, his favourite) child.

Mhari.

He nudged the last page of the letter away and drained the remaining drops of icy water from his glass. Well, he'd done her bidding. He might have left it to the very last minute – and arrived too late – but he'd come. Why, he wasn't absolutely sure. Perhaps because his mother would have wanted it, had she been alive to tell him so. Perhaps because he *did* want to behave decently. Whatever the reason, he'd pointedly avoided analysing it.

He slugged straight and carelessly from the water bottle this time, deliberately boorish in his manner, rivulets sluicing down his front. Mhari would disapprove. That made him feel just a little bit better. Christ, she was pushing it! *'Pain, suffering, and sheer terror?'* No doubt. But why the hell shouldn't his father have experienced these worst elements of the human condition? No, there was a karmic appropriateness about it.

He had deserved it.

5

He opted to take the train to the meeting in Edinburgh. It meant he could fall into the nearest pub, if necessary, depending on how the meeting went. A sad admission but true nevertheless. There was no doubt that his general deterioration had intensified. That at least he could recognize. And the symptoms were far from pleasant. He sat back in the deserted carriage, silently cataloguing them to himself.

Chief among them, and surely the saddest, was that his once fanatical exercise regime now left him indifferent. He allowed himself any and all excuses to avoid it, using 'overwork' to himself and anyone else who asked. The exercise issue, which on the face of it could be dismissed as superficial, was in reality far from that. It symbolized a worrying loss of control over his life. He'd always needed regimes and routines in his life. Welcomed the external ones that work imposed and created others for the rest of his life. They gave him the appearance of being in control, no matter what the inner truth might be. Fitness had been a long-standing one and its wilful loss had left him more worried than he cared to admit.

Instead, he'd developed a substitute. Wandering the streets of central London, sometimes stopping at one or two carefully chosen darkened and anonymous bars, sometimes seeking the solace of a visit to his favourite art-house cinema to lose himself in another world. Whatever he did, it inevitably meant arriving home too late to see his wife and children. The 'I'm sleeping in the spare room so as not to wake you' cliché was now his well-embedded reality.

But his deterioration had multiple causes. Of course it wasn't just this business of his father, though that had been the catalyst for some very low periods lately. The news of his father's terminal illness three months ago had been deeply unsettling, and he'd recognized an escalation in his withdrawn behaviour around that time, since he knew there'd have to be some sort of reckoning. He'd tried to shove the matter to the back of his mind – a well-worn habit – but this time it hadn't worked. He knew he'd have to come back here and deal with it. That thought had terrified him. Where would he find the reserves to manage it? He was already emotionally exhausted.

But that wasn't all. It was his problems back home that were niggling away at him. Could it be that simple, that selfish? Was the real spur for his coming back here to avoid his life in London? Nikki was pretending not to notice his obvious dysfunction. Leaving things, important things, unsaid was her way after all. In that respect, if in no other way now, they suited each other. Part of him had been waiting for her to suggest that he rejoin that silly men's group she'd bulldozed him into attending after Mum died. How he'd allowed that to happen, God knows. She'd caught him at a vulnerable moment, perhaps the *most* vulnerable in their entire marriage. More emotionally exposed even than when he'd found out about her affair. Nearly a year it had lasted, and he hadn't so much as caught a hint. It showed just how little attention he was paying to her, was Nikki's – to an extent accurate – justification. They'd never properly gone over the reasons for the affair before Mum died. Then he'd lost the space to even think about it. Nikki had packed him off to the men's group. And he'd been unable to shake off the suspicion it was so that *she* didn't have to pick up the pieces.

The men's group. It had been excruciating! Worse than his most cynical expectations and he'd left after a handful of sessions. He'd hooked up with another escapee and they'd pretended to their respective spouses that they were still attending, but instead had a pint and a game of pool at a nearby pub. In some ways, it had provided a childish satisfaction. A poke in the eye to Nikki for trying to force him into something she must have known was entirely unsuitable. The weekly outings had only stopped because his friend's work had relocated him outside London. Shame, since their nights out had done more for him than any group. There'd been a couple of occasions over the years when his doctor had sent him to see someone, and they'd been a hundred times more competent than the men's group counsellor. Why he'd never told Nikki about them was, of course, part of the issue. It was all to do with the father thing, and he didn't want to discuss it with her. She, for her part, was content not to go near the subject either. Vicious bloody circle of merry dysfunction. Maybe he couldn't blame her for the damage she'd done to their marriage. He'd certainly been carrying his own wrecking ball around for years, using it largely on himself and, consequently, those foolish enough to care about him.

But one thing had surprised him about Nikki once he'd told her of his father's diagnosis and, most recently, of his intention to visit the family home. To his astonishment she'd said that she wanted to come with him and bring the kids! He'd had to put his foot down. What on earth was she thinking? What was she going to tell them? He didn't want them to be around death, funerals. Certainly not those linked to a grandfather they never knew they had, and never would. Unbelievable!

He sighed and glanced out of the window as the train pulled away from North Berwick station. He kept an eye on the coastal scenery, enjoying the autumn sun shimmering off the waters of the Firth of Forth. He stared at the gentle waves until the island of Fidra came into view and then he looked away. It was more difficult to avoid the view from the house, since the whole west side looked out on the island. But he'd stayed away from that part of the house since he'd arrived.

That had been one of the reasons he'd refused to come back before now, even when Mum was alive, even when Mhari had begged him to visit Fidra with her kids and his. They could go to the island, just like when they were children, she'd kept saying. And that was the whole point. How could she forget their last, happy-bloody-families trip there *and* what happened subsequently? She had determinedly chosen to wipe out the memory, since she'd visited at least once a year when her kids were younger. Mum hadn't gone out there. She might have been bloody-mindedly determined to stay put in the area, had kept the boats, but she wouldn't set foot on Fidra. She too had seared into her memory that last day, waiting at the harbour for them all to return. Smiling, laughing, sun-kissed, exhausted from the day, happy, until . . .

He wasn't particularly comfortable being back in Edinburgh. Too many memories of adolescent hell, adult frustration and professional failure. Yet here he was, in a bloody lawyer's office. An Edinburgh lawyer's office. Just like the one he used to have until . . .

'Mr McAllister? I'm Russell Sinclair. Many thanks for coming in at such short notice. I really wanted, *needed*, to see you on your own prior to the meeting with your siblings on Thursday, for the formal reading of the will.'

Miller shook the man's thin, papery-skinned hand and took the offered seat, watching as Sinclair rearranged papers on his desk. He was elderly and looked frail.

'Mr McAllister, I knew your father for over forty years. Douglas and I were friends before all this happened. In fact, I remember meeting you several times when you were just a wee boy. And, if I may say so, you very much have the look of him. It's uncanny.' He paused, seeming thoughtful, as if unsure how to go on.

'Now, let me see. Somewhat unusually, your father asked me to deal with his estate. Although probate is not my field, I've had enough time and *very* specific instructions from your late father. I also took specialist advice. Everything is in order. But . . . this is very difficult. Let me start again. Your father has left a . . . a rather, for you certainly, surprising will. In fact, this might be quite a shock.' He paused again, letting out a polite, preparatory cough. 'Mr McAllister, your father has left you the mainland house, the Fidra house, and Fidra itself. Oh, and one of the boats.'

Miller sat up, suddenly aware of the silence. *Damn it*. He hadn't been paying attention. Had drifted off thinking about his days as a lawyer in Edinburgh. Only now he'd become aware that the old man's slightly droning yet soothing voice had stopped.

'I'm sorry? He's left me one of the boats? Right. Well, that's *some* joke.'

But Russell Sinclair was cutting back in on him. 'No, Mr McAllister. Your father's left you *everything*. Well, all the property anyway. The mainland house, the Fidra house, and the island itself. It's all yours.'

Miller half rose out of his chair, almost toppling it over. '*What!* But that's mad, absolutely insane! I hated him. *Hated him!*'

He was aware of Russell Sinclair standing up and moving to the other side of the office. 'That may well be, Mr McAllister. I do know of your . . . your *position* on things. But whatever you may have felt, your father clearly loved you.'

He'd allowed the solicitor to force a cup of over-sweet tea on him, though he'd have welcomed something considerably stronger.

'*I just don't get it! Why? Why me?* Why not Mhari and Greg? They always protested his innocence. I, as you well know, and as my father well knew, have always been convinced of his guilt. *Jesus!* Mhari will go spare! She'll probably contest it anyway.'

But Russell Sinclair was shaking his head. He'd seemed to grow more tired and his voice was weaker. 'Then I'm afraid she'll be on a hiding to nothing. I know you originally trained as a lawyer in Scotland, Mr McAllister, but I wonder if you remember your probate law? I suspect not. Under Scottish law, children are not entitled to just walk away with everything of their parents'. It's not as simple as that. I won't bore you with the detail but, in short, Mhari and Greg will be getting considerably more from what your *father* has provided than if they were to contest the will and settle for what the *law* says they can have. I will be pointing that out to them. It's a matter of simple arithmetic.'

'*Brilliant!* Just what I need! Another family feud!' Miller clattered his cup down on to the desk, noting the solicitor's impassive expression. 'Well, Mr Sinclair, I've no choice. I'll clear both properties and sell them off. The mainland house will be worth something. Spectacular outlook to the sea, massive gardens to the rear. A grand Victorian family residence like that is surely still desirable.'

He got to his feet and shrugged at the solicitor.

'And the wretched island and its house? Actually, I doubt anyone will want the island with its history. Maybe I can give it away to the RSPB! Anyway, I want to get rid of everything immediately. Split whatever proceeds three ways. There's bugger all the law can do about that, I'm sure. Will you organize that for me please, Mr Sinclair?'

'I'm afraid not, Mr McAllister. I'm about to retire. Poor health and old age. This week is my last as a practising solicitor. A rather sad week as it happens, having to deal with your father's affairs. You see, I believe him to have been innocent. I just couldn't prove it. As I said, I knew your father fairly well, eventually *very* well, and I can honestly say that he was incapable of the crimes for which he was imprisoned.'

Sinclair stopped and began rearranging more papers, as if giving himself some time to think over what he was going to say next.

'I . . . I just wonder why you hold such a firm belief in his guilt since you were only what . . . eleven years old, I think, when he was arrested? What has made you so convinced? Douglas always maintained his innocence. To everyone, you included. Do you know something none of us do?'

Miller was aware that the solicitor's tone had gone from mild and polite to slightly hectoring. Or was he just getting emotional? Hard to judge. But what did it matter? He wanted out. Out of the stultifying office. Out to make plans for the disposal of the estate.

'Look, Mr Sinclair, up until the time of his arrest, my father was the single most important influence on my young life. I worshipped him. Adored him. Admired him. To say I felt betrayed by him would be something of an understatement. But deceiving a child is easy, up to a point. However,

I was a perceptive child, and once my father's mask had slipped, there was no going back. As modern forensic psychology has shown us, the deadliest psychopath can fool their nearest and dearest. And fool us, *me*, he certainly did. Until his unmasking. Of course I don't know something that you or any of the others never knew. What I *do* know is that the case against him was strong. Circumstantial but strong. And the only defence he offered was to repeat, "I didn't do it." Far from convincing. No, he did it. I *am* convinced of that.'

He accepted the farewell handshake from the solicitor, whose expression was now far from impassive. He looked sad and solemn. 'Goodbye, Mr McAllister. I'll see you and your siblings the day after tomorrow for the formal reading of the will. Another member of the firm will be able to help you with anything else you need after this week. You'll no doubt be wanting to know about various ancillary matters, inheritance tax and such like. Safe to say, your father was very canny in protecting his assets for you all. Anyway, I'll tell you about that at our next meeting. But in the meantime, I'll be sending you some of your father's legal effects, if that's all right. Tomorrow morning, shall we say?'

Miller nodded his assent and then headed for the front door, one thought hammering through his head. *Fine, send what you like. They'll all go straight in the fucking fire.*

6

The place was a disgrace. So was he. He'd fallen asleep on the favourite settee in front of some mindless TV programme, a half-emptied lager can propped in the crook of his elbow, a congealing mass of foil take-away dishes littering the floor.

He'd been beyond shock when he'd left Russell Sinclair's office yesterday. Had floated back down to Waverley Station, waited patiently for the next train and, at the other end, sprinted all the way back to the house, locking himself away in the TV room in a partially successful attempt to obliterate all thought. He'd awoken with a heart-stopping jump to the sound of battering at the door. The delivery driver had given him a quizzical, possibly disapproving look, demanded a signature, and left the document storage box at his unshod feet.

He'd cleared up well enough but the abiding feelings of shame and disappointment wouldn't shift. No doubt it was the visit to the solicitor's that had been the catalyst, the tin lid. But he was too old and too weary to even begin to blame anyone else for this ... this adolescent party mess he'd made. Utterly shameful.

The box was still staring at him from the table by the windows. He felt marginally better after a shower but no shave. He wasn't in a clean-cut mood. Mhari would have a go at him about it when she arrived. Accuse him of looking scruffy. Good. He'd give her no argument against that. But he didn't feel like brooding over his sister just now. He had a couple more hours before he had to face her. He sipped at his coffee, and ripped the taped envelope from the box lid.

Dear Mr McAllister

Please find with this delivery one document box – the entire surviving legal archive of your late father's case: *HMA v Douglas Cameron McAllister*, held at Edinburgh High Court, October 24th to November 15th, 1974. There is a master inventory of the box's enclosures inside, though as you can imagine after this length of time, it is far from complete. Many papers and suchlike have been lost or misplaced over the years, some I believe wilfully so by the authorities.

I have to trust that you will find it in yourself to have a look through what is left. I beseech you to do so and reiterate what I said to you yesterday – after a lifetime working in criminal law, I am certain of your father's innocence. Furthermore, I am also certain that, were he put on trial today, he would be acquitted. The evidence did not warrant his conviction, though I must shoulder some of the blame as I was your father's instructing solicitor after his arrest. I may not have been, objectively speaking, the first or best choice for such serious charges, but I was his friend, and no trouble on my part and no expense on your family's part were spared in securing the best advocate and legal team that money could buy. But we all failed him. Though, may I say, your father, as was characteristic of him, never laid any blame at my door or the rest of the legal team.

How he got through all these years I will never know. As I am sure you are aware, the criminal justice system is ferociously punitive to those who fail to settle down and acquiesce to their punishment. As long as your father continued crying, 'Innocent!' there was never a hope that they would let him out. In my eyes, that fact adds to the grievous wrong done to him.

I have sent you everything – including material you may not, strictly speaking, be entitled to see, even now – but there is nothing else I can do. I am happy to speak with you on any aspect of the case if you wish but, like your dear father, I too have fallen victim to seriously failing health, so I suggest you be quick if you decide to have further contact with me. I expect before long to be apologizing again to your father for my professional failings, but this time in the peace of the next world.

Please do not destroy this archive without examining it. Douglas told me that, among many other fine qualities you possess, you are nothing if not highly and intelligently inquisitive, with a strong sense of justice. Qualities noticeable from an early age, and which perhaps prompted you to turn to the law for a profession?

Use your enquiring mind well – <u>your father was innocent</u>.

Yours

Russell L. Sinclair

So, Russell Sinclair's final professional act, it seemed, was to continue to plead on behalf of a dead and universally reviled client.

Miller sighed, dismayed. Despite his exhaustion, despite his frustration at himself and his anger – nay, fury – at having to deal with all this, it was going to be very hard to ignore the wretched archive. Did common decency mean that he should take a look? Or, was he perfectly within his rights to dispose of it without further debate? Wasn't he entitled to dismiss the pleas of Russell Sinclair as the sad, valedictory musings of someone consumed by guilt for a lifelong professional failing?

He flicked the top off the box. Four lever arch files faced him, spines upwards: *Trial File I, Trial File II, Trial File III, Trial File IV.* Slipped down the left-hand side of the box were some loose papers. The master inventory of contents. And something else. A photocopied sheet of A4 with a scrawled handwritten annotation at the top – *Sentencing, Trial Judge Lord McLeish, 15.11.74.* The first words sucked him back to that quivering moment, sitting bolt upright, between his ashen mother and two statue-like siblings.

'Douglas Cameron McAllister, Scottish criminal history has rarely, if ever, seen the likes of you. We can only be thankful for that . . .'

He smashed a fist down on the paper, unable to read any further. Those icy, compelling words from the judge had run around his head week after week following the trial. They had marked the absolute end for him. There it was. His father unequivocally guilty. The weight of that moment had seemed to erase the memories of all the 'happy' times. They'd gone. Rendered meaningless. From that hellish day at the harbour steps his father had brought untold misery to them all. His mother, sister, brother. Not one of them had known a genuine moment of happiness throughout the rest of Miller's childhood. His mother had spent years trying to put on a false smile for him and his siblings. But he hadn't been fooled. No, he'd vowed never again to be fooled by either parent.

Miller threw the photocopied paper to the floor. Why had he come back? Why had he attended any lawyer's meeting? Why, after the hell he, they all, had been through? Thanks to the nightmare that was his father.

7

'C'mon, Miller, son. Time for a bite to eat, eh?'

Reluctantly, Miller took his seat next to Greg and sneaked a look at him. But Greg was staring down at his plate of runny beans on toast. Then he tried to catch the eye of Mhari, sitting opposite. But she was looking at Dr Buchan, her voice strangely high-pitched.

'*Why? Why's* Dad gone with the police? And why's he been taken to Edinburgh? Is it something to do with his work? Has something happened at the bank? If so, why's Mum gone with him? *What is it?*'

'It's okay, Mhari. Okay.'

Miller watched as Dr Buchan gave her a gentle smile that included both him and his brother. He tried a half-hearted smile back, followed by a forkful of beans. They were too hot. He dropped his cutlery and lowered his right arm, softly patting his lap under the table. As hoped for, Bella obliged by sitting next to him, putting her warm muzzle to his fingers. He laid his palm on her head for comfort. Dr Buchan was sitting forward, hands clasped together, his unlit pipe held between them.

'Look, kids, your mother's asked me to stay with you until she gets back. It might be late but she said she'd phone when she could.'

'*But what's going on?*'

Mhari had banged her teacup down. She looked on the

39

verge of tears. Miller recognized the facial signs. What was less familiar was that his sister looked not sad, not huffy, not about to have one of her tantrums. No. She looked . . . looked . . . *afraid*. Her voice was almost at screaming pitch now.

'*Tell us, Dr Buchan! Something's wrong.*'

He felt Greg tense up beside him. He too reached for Bella's soft head and their hands touched as Greg gave his a reassuring squeeze.

Dr Buchan was clearing his throat and began fiddling with his empty, unlit pipe.

'Okay, Mhari, lads, I'm not entirely sure what's going on myself. I think there's been some sort of mistake, which I'm sure your dad will sort out, but he's had to go to police headquarters in Edinburgh. Now, don't any of you worry. C'mon, eat your tea and maybe we'll play Monopoly or something after, eh?'

Miller felt heartened by the reassurance. If Dr Buchan said that things were okay, then they must be. And Monopoly wasn't such a bad idea. He stuffed a forkful of toast and beans into his mouth and nodded his head, mumbling through his food.

'Aye, Monopoly's a good idea. We've not played this summer. Can Catriona play? Where is she?'

Dr Buchan was trying another smile. 'Catriona's at home, son. She's got a biology project to write up. In fact, I've no doubt that you and Greg have homework still to be done, but we'll forget about that for tonight, okay? But don't tell your mother. Our wee secret, a'right?'

Miller was relieved to see Greg smiling and even Mhari's face had relaxed. They ate on in silence until Mhari creaked her chair backwards and stood up.

'Right. That's me done. I'm going to my room. I don't fancy Mono—'

The ringing of the phone cut across her and made Bella give out a single deep bark. Dr Buchan moved surprisingly quickly to beat Mhari to the receiver.

'Hello . . . yes . . . yes, they are . . . right. Oh, okay . . . see you then.'

Miller expected Mhari to start interrogating Dr Buchan again, chivvying him. But there was no need. His face gave it away.

'Your mum's on her way back . . . but . . . but . . . I'm afraid your dad's having to stay. Stay the night.'

Mhari was at him again. 'Stay where? With the police? *You mean at a police station? Why?*' She really was going to cry this time.

Miller watched as Dr Buchan moved towards her. He too recognized the signs. 'Your father . . . look . . . I'm sorry. The truth is, your father's been arrested.'

Mhari's sobbing filled the silence. Miller knelt down to kiss the top of Bella's head and hold as tight as he could to her solid neck.

8

Miller couldn't remember the last time he'd been in a taxi. The police had taken Dad's big car away. Mum still had her Mini and he couldn't understand why she hadn't driven them. She'd hardly said a word on the train from North Berwick to Edinburgh, and when she had she'd been snappy. So, by common consent, he and Greg had followed Mhari's advice as she put her finger to her lips, and stayed silent. Like Mum, who was pretending to read a women's magazine, Greg had his nose stuck in a football comic and didn't look at him once, despite being given two sharp elbows in the ribs.

Now Mum was leaning forwards to talk to the taxi driver. 'If you'd just drop us off here, please, that'll be fine.' She paused to turn round, her face sour. 'Mhari, get the boys out and wait on the pavement while I pay the fare. Go on now, quickly please.'

Mhari was tugging roughly at his sleeve. 'C'mon, stupid, get out. Greg, move it!'

Greg was stuffing the rolled-up comic into the back pocket of his jeans. He looked in a bad mood. And sounded it. 'What's going on with Mum? Where the heck are we? What we getting out here for? We're not even there!'

Miller saw his mother fiddling about in her purse, tut-tutting under her breath as she scrabbled for change to pay the driver off. Mhari was whispering. 'She doesn't want the driver to drop us at the prison gates. Too embarrassing. Now shut up! Here she comes.'

'Okay, kids, just a little walk along the main road and then it's on the left. Hurry up!'

Miller brought up the rear, amazed as Mhari uncharacteristically put her arm through their mother's and gave it a tight, comforting hug.

'The four of you go through and sit at a table in the visiting area. See, where all the other visitors are? I'll take these bags of things. In future, will you mark all things you're bringing in for your husband "Prisoner SG5567". All prisoners are dealt with by their numbers. I thought you'd have known that.'

His mother was about to remonstrate with the fat, unfriendly prison officer but Mhari was gently pulling her arm. 'C'mon, Mum, this way. Look, there's a little tea counter. Let's get a cuppa.'

Two minutes later he and Greg were sent to buy a big pot of tea and five Caramel Wafers, including one for Dad. Miller was glad there was a queue. It gave him a chance to ask Greg what had been on his mind all morning. 'Well, did you find out? Mhari'd tell you but never me. What's going on? Dad's been here since Monday. *Three days!* He wouldn't be here if he hadn't done something wrong. What's he done? Robbed his bank?'

But Greg was giving him a sarcastic half-laugh back. 'Oh, aye! I doubt that. Mhari never tells me anything either, not anything important. But y'know last Sunday, when they came to the harbour for Dad? When we went home, I saw Dr Buchan hide this under the settee. He must've forgotten about it in all the fuss. I had too, until this morning when I was looking for Bella's tennis ball. I've heard Mum telling Mhari that we mustn't have any of the papers in the house. That's why she's kept us off school too and kept us away from the news. I heard her and Mhari going on about it. Here. Don't let Mum see you with it. I'll stand behind you. Shield you.'

Miller was glad the queue was slow in being served. He took the ripped-out newspaper cutting, placed carefully between the pages of Greg's football comic, and began reading.

He shuffled forwards as they reached the tea counter. 'So? This isn't anything to do with Dad being here. Don't be daft. He's here because of something to do with the bank, surely?'

But Greg was shaking his head as he paid for the tea and biscuits. With the laden tray he made for the table where Mhari and their mum were sitting. 'No. It makes sense of what I heard after they picked up Dad. I was going to tell you but Mhari said I mustn't, though you might as well know now. I heard Mum talking to Dr Buchan. She said, "They've found the dog leash. In the garden." This is serious, Miller. And it's not about the bloody bank. I mean it.'

Just as they reached the table a bell rang. A line of hard-looking men in single file, all in uniform shirts and trousers, came trooping out of a side door. His dad was eleventh through the door. He was thinner and looked tired. His mum moved forwards to give him a quick peck on the cheek but pulled away from a fuller embrace. Silently, his dad hugged Greg and Mhari, who clung to him like they'd never let go. But Miller held back.

'Come on, Miller, son. Your old dad's been missing you. Give's a cuddle.'

Instead, Miller threw the football comic at his father, the ragged cutting fluttering face-up on to the tabletop. He heard his mother's intake of breath. And then he swiped the back of his hand at the nearest full cup of tea, spraying scalding liquid over everyone, including himself.

'*Why! Why! Why!*'

He turned and ran from his father's grasp towards the exit door, only to be plucked off the ground and held tightly in mid-air by a giant of a prison warder. A few yards away, he was aware of his father shouting after him. He wriggled out of the warder's grasp and twisted round to see what was going on. Within seconds, his father had been bundled from the room, kicking and punching, every eye on him. His mother and big sister, arms round each other, had been left sobbing, inconsolable, while Greg stood motionless, his face a pale, blank mask.

There it was. The family in ruins.

The Fateful Sunday

The early summer of 1973 saw the end of Fidra's rather modest reputation as a place of obscure archaeological, ecclesiastical and ornithological interest, and its high-profile entry into the annals of Scottish criminal history.

By 1973, Fidra had been owned by a local family for generations. The then owner, Douglas McAllister, was a respected financier with a senior banking job in nearby Edinburgh. Married to a committed charity worker, Ailsa, and with three children, Mhari (then 17), Gregor (then 14) and Miller (then 11), the family were well liked throughout the locality.

One Sunday in early summer, 1973, the father, his children and some friends sailed back from a short overnight stay at the McAllister's island house. Waiting for them at the harbour was Ailsa McAllister. A few who were present have said they feared something was wrong, given Ailsa's gloomy demeanour. But none could have known what was to come, except Mrs McAllister who had that morning, prior to a visit from the police, been reading the latest on a disturbing local story in her Sunday newspaper:

POLICE 'DETERMINED' TO SOLVE RIDDLE OF MISSING GIRLS

A source close to the investigation into the disappearances of three young girls from East Lothian, dating back to 1969, have told *The Sunday Herald* that police are 'determined to make headway on this case'. The comment follows yet another disappearance which bears all the hallmarks of the previous two.

Eileen Ritchie, 15, disappeared near Garvald village on the

fringes of the Lammermuir Hills last Friday evening. She had been walking her golden retriever, Angus. When the dog returned alone to the family home, Eileen's parents initially looked for their daughter themselves but failed to find her. It was then that they alerted police. The two previous disappearances occurred during the winter and police have expressed some surprise that an abduction has been made during the summer months, a time when local beauty spots are often busy. The two other missing girls are Jacqueline Galbraith, 14, who went missing just outside Dirleton in February 1972 and Alison Bailey, 15, who disappeared from Yellowcraigs beach in November 1969. Like Eileen, both had been walking their dogs. In all three cases, the dog leashes were missing.

The police source continued, 'After four long and distressing years for the families of these girls, we are determined to discover what happened to them. Already the response from the public over Eileen has been tremendous and we are continuing our door-to-door enquiries.' The source also claimed that there had been an early and significant breakthrough but declined to give details.

What Ailsa couldn't know as she sat reading this with the deep empathy of a loving mother, was that in a handful of hours her life would be turned upside down by the arrest of her husband in connection with the disappearances of these three young girls.

An event that would shatter a previously close-knit family.

Extract from *Fidra – an Island History*, by Duncan Alexander, Whitekirk Publishing, 1st edition, 1978.

9

She couldn't remember when she'd last seen Miller. Eighteen months maybe? Yes, once, since Mum's funeral. A rather awkward, unsatisfactory Christmas visit she and the family had made to London. He looked a good bit different now. Not only did he seem somehow older, primarily because he was so obviously exhausted with black smudges under his eyes, but where was the exercise fanatic – the muscular, fit man, who so reminded her of Dad? Greg had the delicate willowy frame of their mother. Something she wished she'd inherited. Truth was, she looked like neither of her parents. Fair where they were dark. Dumpy where they were tall. Plain where they were handsome. Her mother *had* been a handsome woman but also nervy, bordering on the unstable at times, giving her strong features a strained, tense appearance. Thank God she hadn't inherited that trait. But overall, her differences made her the proverbial milkman's child. Still, she was the brains of the family, thanks to Dad. You couldn't have everything in life. Miller may have inherited his dark good looks but he wasn't preserving them as well as he used to. He still looked better than most men of his age and he wasn't flabby yet. But he'd lost that crisp, super-fit air of animal vitality and well-being. And he'd not even bothered to shave for what she judged was the best part of a week. Disgusting.

Mhari took her chance to scan the room as Miller busied

himself in the kitchen. There was no way Mrs Watt would have left the place in this state. Dirty coffee cups, glasses, a couple of plates. And the bins!

'Miller! That recycling box. The cans? Was that you? It's not me! Or Mrs Watt!'

Silence. Maybe he couldn't hear her. Well, there was no way he behaved like this at home. Nikki would tell him to shape up or ship out. She was a fitness freak herself. She might not be much of a wife, but she was a responsible mother. Most of the time anyway.

That reminded her, she hoped Neil was coping. He was pretty useless when left to his own devices. But at least the kids were a bit older now. They were probably enjoying his lax, or rather non-existent, discipline. She'd call them all later. She heard the kitchen door being kicked open as Miller came back into the living room clutching two mugs of coffee.

'So what if I've been having a drink? I'm a big boy now, Mhari. I'm allowed to. Though five cans of beer across a weekend hardly constitutes hard-core alcoholism. I imagine your Neil sneaks more than that when he's "working" in his studio.'

She was going to ignore that. They had more important matters to think about, now that he'd deigned to come back into the living room.

'Well? You heard from Greg yet? Is he coming over and . . . and is he bringing that . . . whatever his name is . . . that architect guy who was there at Mum's funeral?'

She knew Miller always enjoyed her discomfort at talking about Greg and his partner. Knew full well she didn't like him. His half-smile said it all.

'You mean Guillermo. He's not just "that architect guy". He's Greg's partner of eight years. And no, he's not bringing him. Hardly likely, considering the set-to you had with him after Mum's funeral. A heated discussion about the situation of the Basques isn't really recommended wake fodder, is it? And yes, Greg's getting a flight over first thing. Apparently the flights from Bilbao were all full, so he won't be here until lunchtime.'

She gave him a curt nod. 'Good. In plenty time for the solicitor's.'

Miller watched as an already drunk Greg popped open another bottle of red, slumped back on the living-room sofa, and shut his eyes. The will reading had taken it out of them all. And the wine and travelling had just about done for Greg. Miller turned to look out at the sea. The Fidra lighthouse was blinking its warning. The wind was up, doing a bit of window rattling, and whistling through the slats of the balcony. He sipped at his wine. Surprisingly, though presumably in compensation for Greg's state of drunkenness, he'd stayed sober and alert. Couldn't let Mhari loose on both of them when they were completely incapacitated. She'd opted for an early night, thank God, having spent most of the after-noon and evening on the phone in what had been their father's old study. Bitching to Neil no doubt.

He knew he'd been wrong not to tell Mhari about the will before the solicitor's meeting. It had nagged at him throughout an uncomfortable dinner the night before as she talked about her career, her children, her husband. She'd punctuated that with the occasional barb at 'how very tired' Miller was looking. Meaning, he'd let himself go. He couldn't argue with that, instead he'd ignored the needling and put away even more wine, just to annoy her. However, she had, sensibly, stayed off the topic of Nikki, the kids and his job. The latter, corporate lawyering, was no doubt boring to

Mhari. Dr Mhari McAllister, the specialist on the Brontës, who was invited to lecture far and wide on the subject, who was expecting to be offered a chair, 'in the not too distant future', by St Andrews, that most 'now' of the Scottish universities, as she liked to put it, and her alma mater. *And* she'd talked excitedly of the offer of a professorship in the US.

Miller smiled to himself. That may well have been true. But the perennially insecure Mhari would never leave these shores for good, even though it might change her life for the better. Everything had to be so controlled, so close at hand in her world. Christ, she couldn't even leave that useless Neil and her spoilt kids for a couple of nights without a list of verbal (and no doubt written) instructions on what to eat, how to cook it, when to go to bed, when to take a bloody breath! As for Neil? He was a leech, a freeloader, a more useless husband it would be hard to find! His job? *'I'm a sculptor. Just consolidating my body of work. Hoping to show soon.'* What tosh! He'd been spouting the same pretentious rubbish for years! Neil was essentially a fraud. Minor public school, parents who had frittered their money away on greed-fuelled, ill-advised forays into the stock market, leaving a spoilt only son, incapable of living in the real world. He doubted if Neil had ever earned enough from his 'sculpting' to keep his children in shoes. No, it was Mhari who'd brought home the bacon. Mum had helped out hugely too, certainly in the early years. Mhari had definitely been given more than her fair share of financial help, compared with Greg and himself. A fact she seemed to have forgotten a long time ago.

'Wassup, Mill?'

He thought Greg had passed out.

'I'm not bothered, Mill. 'Bout Dad's will. You know that. I'm just bothered 'bout Dad. Him dying, I mean. I wished

I'd been there. I mean, I know you . . . you felt differently 'bout him but . . . I think it's sad anyway. Horrible way to go. The illness, pain. I saw enough AIDS-related terminal cases in the Eighties to know that. Life really is shit sometimes. *Fuck it!* Come here. Let me fill your glass. Y'know, I reckon Dad knew what he was doing with this will thing. Didn't want that tosser Neil getting his mitts on things. And me? Well, I don't think he got his head round me and Guillermo. Nor my work. All my massage and complimentary therapy stuff that took fucking years and *years* of training. But Dad never had a go at me. Just didn't talk about anything to do with my life in his long, rambling letters from prison.'

Greg was struggling to sit upright.

'Anyway, Mill, it's not as if he *hasn't* left anything to me and Mhari. We get a fair whack of cash and investments. I know she's seething about it. But, I don't care. I'd rather he was still alive than have a penny of his money. And, know what else? I don't think you should sell up and split everything three ways. By all means sell up. It's all yours. But I think you should keep the money. Neil-the-leech will just spend all Mhari's share, making them buy an even bigger house and him an even bigger studio, in inverse proportions to his artistic ability. And me? I don't need the money. Guillermo's rolling in it, so I'll just sponge off him, eh!'

Miller shook his head as Greg sploshed red wine uncaringly down what looked like an obscenely expensive shirt, and leaned his head back against the sofa, eyelids drooping. It looked like he'd really had enough this time.

'Greg, Greg, you never could take your drink, laddie.'

Miller padded over, gently easing the glass from his brother's fingers and shifted him on to his side, head downwards in the recovery position. No movement. Comatose. He took a rug from the back of one of the easy chairs and spread it across the long, lean body. Finally, he fetched a glass of water and a bucket from the kitchen, and put both by Greg's head. *God almighty!* How many bloody years had he been doing this for Greg? Little-brother-acting-like-responsible-big-brother syndrome. Still, Greg was Greg. He'd never change. Unlike Mhari, with Greg what you saw is what you got. There was some uncomplicated comfort in that. Always had been.

Switching off the only remaining light, Miller took himself and the wine bottle back to the table by the windows, refilling his glass as he walked. He could speed up the drinking now, relax, with Mhari in bed and Greg out of it. He sat back, enjoying the perfectly choreographed moans of the gathering wind and the rhythmic crashing of the waves below. As ever, the Fidra lighthouse blinked its eternal warning.

All told, it had been a wretched day but could have been worse. Uncannily, Russell Sinclair had somehow sensed immediately that he'd told neither sibling of the will's contents. The unspoken pact had even extended to Miller feigning surprised horror at the disclosure. Quite a convincing double-act they had made. Neither Mhari nor Greg were stupid and they processed what was being said rapidly. Still, Mhari had asked for the key parts to be read again.

'Are you serious, Mr Sinclair? When on earth did my father draw up this . . . this farce? I simply cannot believe that he was in his right mind. I just cannot.'

Greg had remained resolutely impassive . . . well, not quite, there was the hint of a smirk.

Old Russell Sinclair had picked up on Mhari's implication and was giving as good as he got.

'Your father, who, as you are aware, I had known for

very many years, was perfectly aware of what he was doing. The death of your mother was the catalyst for my chiding him to make provision. Previously, she had been your father's sole beneficiary, he assuming that he'd die first and with good reason. Remember, your father couldn't have hoped for release until he was well into his dotage. Apart from any other consideration, his steadfast refusal to admit his guilt ensured that the authorities would keep him locked up. In short, your father was far from convinced that he would leave prison alive. He assumed that your mother would survive him and that she, in turn, would make provision for you all. However, the unexpected death of your dear mother changed all that.'

Mhari's face was livid as she tried to cut across Sinclair but he'd raised a shaky hand to silence her.

'What I *can* say is that your father spent a long time after her death thinking through what kind of will he wished to leave and this included lengthy discussions with me on my monthly trips to see him in Peterhead prison. We were, by then, firm friends rather than solicitor and client. I must tell you, whatever you think of his decisions, and they may seem difficult to understand, I can assure you . . . and please don't think me presumptuous . . . I can assure you that he loved, he *adored* you all.'

At that, the old man had faltered. Was it his own loved ones he was thinking of, who were soon to lose him? Or did the memory of those monthly confidences with their father remind him of his failure as lawyer and friend?

Mhari, typically, failed to pick up on the old man's emotion.

'But why Miller? Look . . . I'm sorry, Miller, no offence, but you cut Dad loose practically from the minute he was arrested. But we, me and Greg, stood by him. Always. Why on earth would he do this? It's . . . it's a . . . betrayal of the worst sort! It's not the money. We're all comfortably off, but it's the *symbolism* of it. The houses, the island. These are cherished things. Christ, they've been in the family for what? Generations! I'm sorry, Miller, I think it's outrageous!'

'Look, Mhari.' He'd reached the point where he'd been unable to curb his anger or his tongue. 'I wouldn't overplay the laird o' the manor theme as if we're old money or bloody aristocracy! You know fine well that Fidra was won by one of our forebears – a local merchant, no more, no less – in a card game. The sad thing is that it was effectively stolen hundreds of years ago from the monks who originally owned it. Stolen by those *with* money, before being used as a mere gambling chip! Fucking disgrace. But that's all in the past. As far as what's happened now, I'm not clear about our father's motives but you can rest assured that you and Greg are not going to lose out. I'm going to sell up and you'll get your share.'

She hadn't seemed mollified by the offer but he'd ignored her dismissive shrug and rattled on.

'Everything. The two houses and Fidra *will* go. They're places of hell anyway. Though frankly, I don't know who'd want to buy the bloody island, under the circumstances. Oh, I know you, Mhari, always made a point of visiting it, including with your kids. But, frankly, I never knew why Mum didn't move us all to Edinburgh or even further away. Maybe it was just her bloody-mindedness. We can all remember how adamant she was that we weren't going to be hounded out of the place, the area she, and we, loved. But now I'm going to do it, and the proceeds will be split three ways . . .'

A drunken grunt from Greg as he kicked a leg from under his blanket roused Miller out of the recent memory. He checked to see if his brother was still more or less in the recovery position.

Very little else had been said after the solicitor's meeting. Mhari had announced frostily that she'd be making her own way back after doing some shopping in Edinburgh. He and Greg had gone to the Café Royal, had a couple of whiskies just like they used to do when they were younger, before rolling down to Waverley to catch the train. Interestingly, Greg hadn't really dwelled on the will. He defined himself as being fairly remote from their father, although he had written sparingly but regularly to him in prison, and had visited him when he was in the country – which was about every two or three years for the occasional Christmas with Mum.

The rest of the evening had been spent catching up on their personal lives. Greg's, blissfully happy; his own, far from it. He sensed that there was more, much more, to come from Greg about Dad and the will. But tonight wasn't the time for either of them. Perhaps Mhari had sensed that too and retreated to their father's old study, the phone, and an early night.

He smiled at the thought and checked the sea and weather outside. It was an unconscious act. A comfortable and comforting habit. Ever since he was a child, he'd loved to sit by this window, or the one in his bedroom, or any of the windows in the Fidra house, and check 'his' sea, 'his' weather, 'his' castle. Tantallon was invisible at night-time, except if there was an exceptionally bright moon over it. Then, he could pick out its brooding silhouette using his binoculars. A pair of his mother's old binoculars sat on the window ledge. There was always a pair to hand in both houses. To check the birdlife, the sea conditions, the weather, or just to stare aimlessly into an impenetrable grey haar. Tonight there wasn't a lot to see but he had a peer anyway. Only the faint spangles of some ship's lights far out in the Firth of Forth.

He was dreading tomorrow. The funeral. Sheer hell. *And* there would have to be, as Mhari had ominously put it, 'further conversations'. That meant a row. She was expert at bringing out anger in him and he was tiring of being an angry person. Anger and resentment at his father had percolated through everything, even though he'd done his damnedest to hide or manage it. Now he doubted he could face another scene with Mhari. But he had to give the *appearance* of standing up to her, of seeming in control, though God knows that's the last thing he felt.

And what of the archive? Russell Sinclair had said nothing about it at the will reading and the box had been safely hidden since Mhari and Greg arrived. Should he just burn its contents? Or should he go through it and offer the same facility to his sister and brother? He pulled the now crumpled paper from his back pocket. He knew the answer didn't lie there but he felt the need to re-ignite his anger, his resolve. Why the hell was he even thinking about doing anything other than selling up and getting out?

Sentencing, Trial Judge Lord McLeish, 15.11.74
'Douglas Cameron McAllister, Scottish criminal history has rarely, if ever, seen the likes of you. We can only be thankful for that. The terror and suffering that you caused these three young women is unspeakable. In my twenty-three years sitting in the Scottish courts, never, <u>ever</u>, have I come across such a litany of diabolical deeds.

'That you managed to evade the authorities for so long, masquerading as a responsible citizen, a respected member of Edinburgh's financial industry and, worst of all, as a caring, loving husband and father to three children, only compounds your depravity. In one fell swoop, no fewer than four, <u>four</u> families have been destroyed by your actions. Those of your pitiful victims and your own family. Some would say that is the least you deserve. I can only feel the greatest sorrow for your wife and children. They have become your final victims. Having seen your family in this court and studied background reports on them, it is testament to your wife that she has brought up three such excellent children. I hope that the local community will take note here as to where the blame should lie for these wicked and appalling crimes. Only with you, Douglas McAllister. <u>Only</u> you.

'To add to your crimes, you have not once in this court or anywhere else, it seems, shown one iota of remorse or offered any admission. You have consistently run a defence case which claimed that the evidence against you was circumstantial. That was your, frankly, incredible defence, but the jury have found themselves unanimously dissatisfied with that. So be it.

'It is my recommendation that you serve a sentence of no fewer than forty-five years for the untold misery that you have perpetrated. Fifteen years per young life may seem woefully inadequate to the victims' families, but, at your current age, I think we can rest assured that if you are ever released, then the world in general, and young women in particular, need no longer fear you. Take him down.'

How many minutes, how many hours, days, weeks, months, years had she spent looking at Fidra from this bedroom? How many blinks of the lighthouse had she witnessed? How many ... and here she was once more, a 49-year-old wife, mother, professional woman, playing that childish game again. Looking over to that most lovely of places. The childhood idyll whose radiance had been so suddenly and savagely extinguished that beautiful June day. Now it stood as a blighted, contaminated lump of rock. Reviled, detested, feared even. Contrarily, the view never lost its beauty, no matter the weather, the time of day, or her mood.

And her mood right now? She felt absolutely alone tonight. The jovial voices of her brothers had faded away an hour ago. Probably both passed out. How could they be so jolly at a time like this? Inappropriate behaviour. They'd both been guilty of it since childhood. Not enough discipline. Mum and Dad had always been too soft on them. Miller had got away with anything. His wild, gamin charm managing to melt hearts most of the time. As for Greg. He just seemed to float through his childhood without attracting Mum's or Dad's notice half the time. Invisible Greg. But together, the boys had been as thick as thieves, happy to exclude her. No change there.

Despite his protestations, maybe Miller was in celebratory mood. Such good fortune and so unexpected! In fairness to him, yes, he had offered to split any sale three ways. But that was only right and proper, surely? Besides, that wasn't the point. It would be wrong of him to let the properties go, given how long they'd been in the family. Of course they, particularly the island, held their own memories but everyone, *everyone* else in the family had spent the best part of thirty years trying to overcome all of that. For pity's sake, she'd taken her own children there summer after summer to make that point. Mum had drawn the line at setting foot on Fidra again, but she'd certainly had the guts to stay put here *and* protect her children while they were growing up. Whether it was stubbornness – and her mother had had loads of that – or defiance, or determination, or all three, Greg and Miller owed Mum a lot. As they did their big sister – especially Miller, in the light of current events – for her hard work in looking after this house since Mum's death. Though, she had to admit, the place had been left largely untouched, like some childhood museum. Even the ritual redecoration every few years had left it unchanged – the dated wallpapers, the dark carpets, the dull, samey furniture. Essentially conservative Seventies. All so different from the clean lines and bright freshness of the island home. That house had more the appearance and feel of something to be found in a Greek fishing village. How differently those two properties had made them all feel and behave.

It wasn't that the mainland house was depressing. Just very conventional, sober, proper. Kind of like Dad's image at the bank. Real, but not the whole story. Without doubt, three boisterous kids had brought the house alive, giving it some of the vibrancy that the Fidra house had without even trying. Though what the house must have been like for Mum during the long days when all three children were at school in Edinburgh, she couldn't imagine. Situated just outside North Berwick, there were all the benefits to be had of living near a lovely Victorian seaside resort that boasted just a few thousand inhabitants now and presumably much fewer then. A place that could be heavingly but pleasantly busy in summer. The promise of so much fun to be had on your doorstep. But the much quieter and sleepier periods out of season, with children at school and husband at work, must, at times, have led to a lonely existence. Maybe that was, at least unconsciously, one reason why their mother had spent so much time out and about on good works.

Mum had kept the mainland place the same, presumably for her own reasons. Which were? Pop psychology might say it was denial. That one day things could be returned to 'normal'. Ludicrous. Wholly understandable, however, for any wife and mother in such a nightmarish predicament. But why had *she* followed her mother in that? She'd had two years since their mother's death to modernize, spruce things up. Indeed, hadn't Dad said on one of her prison visits soon after Mum had gone that she should 'do something nice' to the mainland house? Yet she hadn't. Analysing it now, she recognized the signs of her own denial. Part of her had thought, presumably like Mum, that maybe it could be left, stuck in some kind of time warp until Dad had got out. But they'd all known how unlikely that prospect was. No, it was simple. Since Mum's death, she hadn't wanted to dig deeper into that house. The memories were all too painful. As long as it could function, in a superficial kind of way, as a second, occasional home for her, Neil and the kids, then that was fine. Any deeper excavations to sort the place out could be left to Miller. It was his responsibility now. He was welcome to it. She felt an undeniable relief at that prospect. Anger, too.

There was no escaping her own self-interest in keeping this house habitable since Mum died. As the eldest and most clearly responsible of the children she had been certain, yes certain, that she'd be left the house or at least half of it, along with Greg. So there was an extra motivation for her to care about it. Similarly with the Fidra house, which, in any event, had needed very little looking after. It seemed to withstand anything, just needed regular weatherproofing and painting. The most recent work she'd organized herself. There you had it. She'd always taken on family responsibility. It was second nature. Even at the beginning of the nightmare.

Granted, things had been marginally easier for her, since she was packed off to university before the trial even started. Although she had insisted on supporting her mother and being with her during those hellish three weeks in court, not helped by Miller's tantrums and sullen silences and Greg's air of detached nonchalance. She wondered now, as she did then, at her mother's wisdom in gaining permission for someone as young as Miller to sit in court. Granted that only happened on days when the evidence was not going to be graphic. But still, it had always struck her as a misjudgement, given that Miller, of the three of them, undoubtedly suffered the most serious disturbance by the arrest and conviction of their father. Perhaps unsurprisingly, since he was the youngest, and probably Dad's favourite child. And that favouritism had so obviously been returned by Miller, which made it all the more difficult to fathom why he had so taken against Dad. Prior to Dad's arrest, Miller had seen him as a towering, indomitable figure. A supreme protector in life. Even despite the appalling shock of events, why hadn't Miller been Dad's most fervent supporter? Everyone's reflex action had been to say it had all been a ghastly mistake, and then, as matters escalated, to stand by Dad in his protestations of innocence. But not Miller. It was as if, overnight, his father had turned from saint to devil.

Of course Dad knew it and was devastated by it. God, that scene at the prison! Then there were all the other worrying incidents: the nightmares, bedwetting, night terrors, the brooding silences, occasional tantrums, leading Miller, ultimately, to the child psychologist. She pressed her forehead against the cold glass of the bedroom window. What a job they'd all had with Miller. His distress had infected the family with nearly as much anxiety as their father's conviction. She lifted her head wearily to look at Fidra again and thought back to all the effort the family and professionals had put into her youngest brother.

Those dreary phone calls every Sunday night to Mum from the payphone at the university halls of residence, listening to Mum detailing the psychologist's findings. He was working with Miller, attempting to reconnect him with his feelings of love for his father. The task was to banish the fear and hatred and, if not regain trust in his father, then at least try to find some middle ground. But Miller, always a creature of emotional extremes in childhood – as he was in adulthood – had resisted that aspect of the therapy.

Where there had been some success was in getting Miller's day-to-day life on the rails again. Eventually settling him down at school. He'd seemed to enjoy life again and grown into, on the surface anyway, a reasonably stable adolescent and young adult. Their mother had been relieved beyond description, although the psychologist had cautioned that her youngest son's emotional scarring ran deep. It seemed that Miller had developed a kind of amnesia. Of course he knew what had happened with his father. It's just that he couldn't remember a lot of detail or accurately recall his exact feelings. The psychologist had said that this was normal, a self-protecting strategy and reaction to trauma, while stating the blindingly obvious: '*This can store up trouble for the future.*

64

In his adulthood. A kind of emotional/psychological time bomb. One can only wait and see.'

And there was the sticking point. The years of therapy had undoubtedly helped Miller to live a successful life but never to *really* face the cauldron of emotion about his father. After all, if you couldn't remember what you really felt about a traumatic event, how could you treat its effects? To that extent the therapy had failed. From the earliest point Miller had resolutely turned his face away from Dad. Forever. The episode at Mum's funeral only two short years ago had reminded them all, if any reminder were needed, of the strength of Miller's complete emotional defection from his father. She could still recall, word for word, the tale she had told to her bereavement counsellor . . .

'. . . Miller was like a volcano that day. He's so muscular and strong anyway. Y'know, one of those big men you look at and think, God, he really could kill with his bare hands. Anyway, he was white, I mean white with anger. He came up to me in Mum's kitchen, closing the door so we were on our own. He was ranting. "I fail to see why he's being allowed out. I don't want him anywhere near me and he's not coming anywhere near Callum and Emma! They don't even know he exists, for God's sake! Jesus, this is going to be torture! Pure torture!"

'But Miller was wrong. It wasn't torture. Just sad. Sad and moving but strangely comforting too. A lovely service. Mum was Catholic and she was being given a beautiful requiem mass. And that's when the trouble started. After the service. You see, they'd brought Dad in at the last minute, handcuffed to a warder with another one, ever-watchful, by his side. As if a 73-year-old man was going to somehow do a Houdini, throw off his handcuffs and sprint away. Ridiculous! Anyway, they'd kept him at the back, away from us, the chief mourners down at the front, while the mass proceeded. Dad wasn't going to be

allowed to join us for the cremation afterwards and maybe that's what started it off. He was really upset. I mean, imagine, losing your wife after all those years of marriage, and having spent most of them in prison, and not being able to say your final farewell. It's barbaric! He was choked and Greg and I were just bubbling away and hugging him. And then I felt him tense up. He was looking over my shoulder. He'd seen Miller. Mill was bundling his kids and his wife into their car. She and the kids were going on ahead to the wake and we siblings were going with Mum's coffin to the crematorium.

'I think it was the sight of Miller's children. I mean, Dad knew that Miller was married and had two children, one of them just a baby. Mum and I made it our business to keep him up-to-date, take in photos, all that. But it was the actual flesh-and-blood sight of his grandchildren that did it, along with all the other emotions that day. He called over. "Miller! Miller, son! Please, come here, let me see you, let me see the kids! Please, son!"

'I tried to shush him. The warders were already beginning to pull him roughly away from me and Greg. Then, the next thing I knew, Miller had booted the car door shut, denting it, and his wife had screeched away. He sprinted up and grabbed Dad by the collar. He slammed him – a 73-year-old man, mind – against the church wall, despite the two warders and me and Greg all trying to pull him off. But Mill was just too strong. He spat the words at Dad. "How dare you! I'm not your son any more and they're certainly not your grandchildren! And you ... you're nothing! Or rather, you are. Something vile! A killer and a rapist! Vile! It should be you in that coffin. Not Mum. You cunt!"'

She slumped back against the uncomfy bed and wiped the beginnings of tears from her eyes. 'A killer and a rapist ...' Her father. Never. But why had he rewarded the only member of the family who'd never stood by him?

'Why, Dad? Why?'

Slowly she turned on her side, not bothering to wipe away the fresh tears.

'Gregor, son, c'mon help me with this.'

'Dad? Where are you? I can't see you!'

'Here, son, here! Near the chapel ruins!'

'Where? It's too dark, Dad. There's only the light from the lighthouse! You know it doesn't reach down to the ruins. Come here, Dad! Please!'

'Okay, son, coming!'

'Dad, that was scary. Don't do that ag——. But what's that you've got there?'

'Oh, just something, Greg, son. Just something.'

'But . . . but, is it Mhari? Is she not well? She's sleeping, it looks like. But no. It's not Mhari. Oh God, no Dad! Who is it? Look! Look at her throat. It's all red . . . all red. Help her! Help her Da——'

'Wha——! Jesus!'

The roar of what must've been an exceptionally high wave battering itself against the rocks below had him jumping up, half on, half off the sofa, the blanket tangled round his feet. He saw the bucket and the pint glass of water, conveniently nearby on the floor. Miller. What a gem. Greg flopped back, letting out a long slow sigh, trying to calm himself. It wasn't so much the fiendish hangover that was taking a grip on his heart rate. It was the dream. He was surprised. He didn't normally dream, or rather didn't remember dreaming when he was drunk. Especially not the Dad dream. The dream that Miller had planted in his mind so long ago.

'God!'

He sat up and took a swig of the water, kicking the blanket on to the floor. The sea sounded weird tonight.

Overloud. He checked his watch. Twenty past bloody three. He could remember opening that last bottle of red. Then, nothing after that. He stumbled over to the table by the windows, glass of water in hand. Not much to see outside; the faint silhouette of the cliffs, the invisible but noisy black sea, and there was Fidra. Or rather, there was the lighthouse, giving out its billion, trillion, trillionth wink of warning. Remember that game! Mum's old binoculars were on the ledge. Not a lot to see. The rain was obscuring everything. All was an inky mass.

He put the binoculars down and rubbed his face and eyes hard with both hands. He couldn't for the life of him recall when, as an adult, he'd last been over there. An afternoon trip maybe, years ago, with Mhari and her brood? Funny, he couldn't remember much of it. In truth, Fidra had been a lovely place, a dream playground for kids, but he'd never reacted to it with the same passion as Miller and Dad and the rest of them. It did have a special feel, maybe it was just the isolation. No one could get to you. But that was it, sometimes that very isolating quality had left him dissatisfied, especially after a few days there. Claustrophobic and stranded. Like being on a boat and unable to get off. Also, he'd liked hustle and bustle. Enjoyed mucking around a busy Edinburgh city centre after school, enjoyed living now in a busy city. Fidra had been calming, peaceful but maybe too much so for his liking, as a child and certainly now as an adult.

He dearly wished he was back in the apartment in Bilbao. Relaxed, comfortable, yet in the centre of things. Humanity, civilization on his doorstep. But no, it was right he should be here. Mum would've wanted it this way. He just didn't know how much more of Mhari he could take. There was absolutely no doubt that she was incensed by the will. It wasn't really the money. If Miller was serious about selling up then he definitely would do the three-way split. Mhari knew Miller was a man of his word. No, she'd spent the evening huffing in Dad's old study because of the power thing. For once, she wasn't, and couldn't be, in the driving seat, though God knows she'd tried to be at that bloody solicitor's. The cheek of her! She'd been very rude to Miller too. His restraint had been commendable. But probate was probate, the law was the law, and that old solicitor had put her in her place. Priceless! Her bossing days were over as far as what she could do with Miller was concerned. Or with himself, for that matter. She had no hold or claim of seniority over them any more. Those days were long gone.

But their father's decisions over his will were a surprise. If he'd thought about it, he supposed Dad would have left an equal division. Unlike Mhari, who he knew was expecting either *all* the estate, or for her and him to share it. With her as executor, of course. Yes, he had believed Dad's sense of fair play would have prevailed . . .

He'd been about ten, there had been some sort of row and Dad had told him off. But half an hour later Dad had found him crying in the TV room, feeling hard done by. Then he'd said the words. '*I love all my children equally.*' They'd always stayed with him. He believed then as he believed now that Dad had meant them. But were they true? He doubted it. Miller had always been Dad's favourite. And Mhari, Mum's? Maybe. Until Mhari was older anyway. And he, the second child, was stuck there in the middle. Emotional no man's land. Classic stuff.

Maybe that was why he'd coped better than Miller or Mhari with Dad's conviction. Maybe there was less at stake for him. Miller had idolized Dad and Mhari had worried so much for Mum. Christ, he'd worried more about Miller than

Dad, at times. It had been the end of Miller's world. He'd never really recovered. He'd had all the love in the world for Dad but, it would seem, none of the trust that went with it. He was just too young. Whatever the truth about their father, the cruellest by-product of everything had been, not to their mother, not to Mhari, not to himself, but to Miller. The shattering of an ideal.

But he'd not shared Miller's tendency to idealize – and that was probably one of the reasons why Miller had set his face against Dad – because a toppled idol is hard if not impossible to resurrect. Dad had been a good, caring father. But not perfect. He could be overly authoritarian. With his admonitions and house rules during visits to Fidra: no going near the cliffs, or the ruins, or letting Bella run free. *And* there had been a solitary, introspective, unreachable aspect to him. Much like Miller, come to think of it. Dad had spent a lot of time on his own, tinkering with the boats, going to the island, taking long walks with only Bella for company. And he and Mum had never seemed to be love's young dream. But Dad's shortcomings were those of any normal family man. He certainly was no killer. Just the victim of catastrophic bad luck.

And there you had it. In a strange way, Dad's misfortune had been for him a positive thing. He'd pledged to try and be as happy in life as possible. It didn't make him feel guilty. Just grateful that he'd been able to take this 'lesson' from Dad's life. What *did* cause him guilt was that Miller couldn't react in the same way. In that respect they were polar opposites in their approach to life and, by God, he wouldn't want Miller's life.

Greg finished off the water, took a last look at the lighthouse and moved silently through the house to find a bed, an inexplicable anxiety eating away at him.

Unseen at the top of the stairs, Miller nodded, drew back from the wooden banister and retreated to his bedroom, gently closing the door behind him.

11

June 1973

'There will be absolute hell to pay if we get caught, Miller. I'm telling you. I promised Mum I was taking you to the East Bay to go swimming and maybe watch me do some fishing off the point. Under no circumstances were we to go west and she certainly wouldn't want us to take the boat out. It's too big for us.'

Miller scowled his disagreement. 'Well I'm going, Greg, and I'm taking the rubber dinghy with the outboard, stupid, not the sailing boat. I can manage that myself. If you don't want to come, then fine. No one'll see us this early. Mum's gone into Edinburgh and Mhari's obviously having a lie-in. I'm going. Before they get here.'

He quickened his pace towards the harbour, Bella at his heels, Greg bringing up the rear. As he waited for his big brother to make up his mind, he played back the previous night's eavesdropped conversation. Mhari to Greg. Voices low.

'. . . Miller seems to be over that scene at the prison. Y'know, he seems much chirpier. I think Mum made a mistake taking him to see Dad. He's too young to be going into a prison. But I don't think he's taken against Dad. That's not really possible, is it? I think he was just scared by the whole prison thing. I'm pretty sure that he hasn't really understood about the newspaper story. You know, you shouldn't have shown him it, Greg.'

'Why not?'

Mhari was getting annoyed.

'Because, *stupid*, before long, it'll just throw up a thousand questions in his head. You know how nosy he is. How much he thinks. Question after question, after question. But he does seem to be getting back to normal. Well, "normal" for Miller.'

But Greg had stuck up for him.

'There's nothing wrong with him being nosy. It's because he's very brainy. His teachers have said that lots of times. Miller's just a bit different, that's all. You're right about one thing, though. I think it's just as well he's not been his usual self, otherwise he would've been asking all sorts.'

Mhari had nodded back. 'Oh God, what a bloody mess! You don't have to be a genius to know that everything's become really, really serious now. I mean, I just don't understand why the police can't see they've made a mistake? It simply doesn't make sense. And this searching of the island tomorrow, that's just so . . . so . . . *excessive . . .*'

They'd reached the deserted harbour. 'See, Greg. It's a Sunday. I told you there'd be no one about. The police told Mum that they were going over about eleven, so that gives us plenty of time to get there. Tie up on the other side of the island.'

'But they'll see the boat, and what about the tides?'

'No, they won't see the boat and I told you, I checked the tide tables. We can put the dinghy into the north cove and ground her there until high tide which is ages away. The police won't be interested in that side of the island. I heard Mum tell Mhari that they're mainly interested in the house.'

He made for the dinghy, Bella bounding in front of him, picking up the air of urgent excitement. But Greg was shaking his head.

'Look, Mill. If Mum comes back or Mhari suspects, I'll just tell anyone that you're swimming or birdwatching or something. So you'll be not be missed.'

Miller stopped and turned round. Silently looking Greg in the eye. Disappointed. 'Fine. At least help me untie the dinghy and see me and Bella off. It's bad luck if you don't see us off.'

That Greg was a coward had hardly surprised him. Again and again his 'big' brother had let him down. This was just one more example. The trip across to the island had been uneventful. He'd done it on his own twice before to see the birds. One occasion Dad had found out about it and gone mad, though he thought he'd been secretly proud too.

Miller heaved the light rubber craft on to the sand and tied her up around a stout rock, well inside the cove. She was invisible now. He put a leash on Bella and they clambered out of the shadows into the sunshine. He didn't know why on earth the police thought any of these girls would be on the island, but he wanted to help Dad. Especially after that prison scene. It was just that he'd felt . . . scared, and Dad . . . he'd looked strange. The whole place was strange. He'd hated it and didn't want to go back. But he needed to help Dad. If the police thought that somehow these girls were stranded on Fidra, he'd get started searching first. After all, he knew the layout of the island better than any policeman. He wasn't hopeful, though. Surely only one of the girls might *possibly* be there. The one who'd gone missing most recently. The others had been gone for donkey's years. Run away from home maybe. It wasn't unheard of. If this most recent girl was on the island, though goodness knows how she'd got there, then he'd find her first and all would be well. In fact, if she had somehow made her way to the island, she was probably loving it, having a great time and didn't want to come back. Maybe she was dozing or sunbathing on the moss, enjoying the sunny day. Who could blame her? She probably wanted to stay here always, just like he did.

He headed straight for the house. It was never locked. Once inside, he let Bella run free as he wandered through all the rooms. No one there. Just as he'd expected.

'Right, c'mon then, girl. Let's try outside. I'll keep you off the leash, but stay close.'

What a waste of time. It had taken him less than half an hour to scour the small island. Nothing. Just birds. It would be the same for the stupid police. The girl wasn't here. He sat down on a soft, grassy patch and gently lay back, arms stretched up to meet the sun.

'C'mon, girl, lie down for a while. It's a lovely day. Let's count the birds.'

With that he shut his eyes and began listening to the various bird cries that pierced out above him over the whisper of the warm breeze.

Twenty minutes later he was lying on his belly, Bella by his side, binoculars scanning the landscape, impatient for the invaders' arrival. Now, finally, his luck was in. He focused on an approaching boat, cutting its way across the calm, deep blue water. Here they were. One, two, three . . .

'There's *eight* of them, Bella! Eight police! Why so many?'

That was going to be a problem. He and Bella would have to stay up at this highest point, near the lighthouse, if he wanted to see what everyone was doing. He counted them all off the boat and then he noticed a ninth man who had been below decks. He held a bulky black case in one hand, and wore a bright orange fluorescent waistcoat, with the words 'Police Surgeon' emblazoned across the back. As he turned round, Miller gave a gasp of surprise as he recognized the man, unlit pipe in mouth.

'Dr Buchan!'

What was he doing here and what did it mean, 'Police Surgeon'? Dr Buchan was the family doctor. What did he have to do with the police? He ducked, pulling Bella down with him, his fingers grasped tightly around her collar.

'Right, we'd better stay put for now. Just wait until they're finished.'

At some stage, he knew some of them would come up this way. They needed to search the lighthouse. Oh no, but they couldn't. The doors were always locked. Twice a year a special boat came out with two men on board and they checked the lighthouse. But that was it. It was out of bounds like the old chapel ruins. But maybe the police had keys to the lighthouse? Yes, they *would* come up here. He and Bella would have to watch for that and hide elsewhere. In fact this whole spying thing wasn't turning out how he'd imagined. He thought there'd just be a couple of policemen. But eight *and* Dr Buchan. They'd soon be swarming the little island!

The sense of being trapped, of *him* being the hunted, was growing with every minute. He'd had the devil's own job in keeping Bella still and quiet, especially when she too had recognized Dr Buchan, *and* she wanted to chase the gulls. He'd put the leash back on her and dragged her away as he skirted around the two policemen who had been despatched to the lighthouse area. They didn't spot him, thankfully.

Now there was a fresh worry. Through the binoculars he could see one officer heading for the cove. If he kept going there was absolutely no doubt that he'd find the dinghy. These policemen were being far more thorough than he'd expected. Still crouching uncomfortably behind a mossy boulder, Bella tethered by her leash around his wrist, he watched the policeman's stumbling progress towards the cove. He had to be just yards from it when Miller saw the magnified image stop dead and turn around. For a heart-stopping moment it looked as if the officer had seen him, was staring right up the binocular lenses at him! And then he heard what he must have missed the first time. A shout. Bella was trying to wriggle out of his grasp, excited. He swivelled the binoculars to his left and saw two officers and a very grim-faced Dr Buchan waving. Within seconds, the remaining policemen had appeared from all corners of the island and were hurrying to where Dr Buchan stood.

'C'mon, girl!' Carefully, staying crouched, he made his approach. He still couldn't make out what everyone was saying. The whistling wind and screeching gulls made that impossible. But he could now see the looks on their faces with his naked eye.

'You'll have to stay here, girl. Be good.'

He tied Bella to a thick gorse root, patted her, and put a finger to his lips. 'Ssh, quiet.' She knew what that meant. He continued down the slope. He could see exactly where they were now. At the out of bounds, old chapel area. It was very dangerous there. Maybe someone had fallen down into the ruins. But Dr Buchan would have warned them about that. Still, things looked serious.

He was within only a few feet. Must stay out of sight. All the police were down in the chapel area, except Dr Buchan who was standing back, as if waiting for something. Then suddenly, the group parted into two lines, like a guard of honour. Dr Buchan was being beckoned through by the officer in charge, who, oddly, was holding a big white blanket.

Got to get closer. There it was. A twisted pale leg. A girl's. He moved a couple of feet to his right, and then saw it. Not dozing in any sunshine. Not sunbathing. She was lying on her back. With no clothes on. Marks all over her body.

A gaping gash of reddish black at her throat.

12

Late September 2005

Miller's eyes were locked on the draped coffin. There was no way in the world that this day, this place, wasn't going to remind him of that last time he'd stood here. It was the same crematorium chapel from which they'd said farewell to their mother. Then, he'd have gone through anything to be with her on her final journey. This time he wished he hadn't come. And he nearly hadn't. Only a few hours before, there had been a row with Mhari at breakfast as he'd tried to back out.

'I'm not going, Mhari, and that's it!'

Her face had turned puce with rage, rage at more than his eleventh-hour decision not to attend the funeral. She'd been waiting to tear into him over the will. An evening on the phone to the dreary but poisonous Neil, honing her fury, had just about guaranteed it.

'You can't simply duck out of it like that! Our father's funeral! The father you may have disowned but who has bequeathed a fortune to you materially, and more symbolically! It's utter hypocrisy! *And* who's the one who's had to make all the arrangements as you've offered no help nor shown any interest in any of it? *And* with your brother doing his out-of-sight-out-of-mind act in bloody Spain, only deigning to come over at the last minute. Me! That's who. *I'm* the one who's had to make intricate arrangements with the crematorium to keep the gawping public and bloody media away from our father's funeral, and make equally strenuous efforts to ensure that those who remained behind Father all his life get a chance to pay their respects. The least, the *absolute* least you can do, is spare us, him, them, me, an hour or so of your precious time! You . . . you bastard!'

At that, she'd fled the room, sobbing. Greg, who he'd forgotten had been in the room, swigged down the last of his coffee.

'She's right, Mill. About one thing. There *are* people who have helped this family over the years. Mum was always good about keeping in touch with them. Some of them were at her funeral, though you didn't meet them because . . . well, because of that thing with Dad.'

Greg moved towards him and put a friendly hand on his shoulder.

'Think about it. *This* funeral could have been a fiasco. I daren't even think what the papers will say. "Evil Psycho Dead At Last", that sort of thing. Mhari has done well to organize everything discreetly. We *need* you there. Come with us. Please, Mill.'

Now here he was, at the front, in the chief mourners' row. Mhari was openly weeping as the coffin, a simple bouquet of white lilies on top, headed for incineration. Next to him, Greg was holding a handkerchief to his eyes, shoulders trembling. The heartbreaking strains of Palestrina's 'Sanctus/ Benedictus' – Greg's delicate choice – sang out from hidden speakers. Miller examined his own emotions. Only an un-feeling monster could fail to be moved by the ceremony of a funeral. Any funeral. But his overriding sensation was of claustrophobia. He desperately wanted out of here. So much so that, more than once since arriving, he'd fantasized suddenly scrambling out, sprinting for the door. And now, here he stood, immobile. Unlike the other two, he had resolutely refused to turn round to see how many people were here. He'd noticed Mhari do it several times, and mouth silent and exaggerated hellos and thank-yous over her shoulder. Greg had risked a couple of glances backwards, his face impassive. A certain familiarity about the situation hurtled Miller back decades. Sitting three abreast, in age order, left to right, at some formal gathering or other. Mhari, firmly in charge. Greg, unreadable. And himself, today? There was the difference. Not nosy. Not inquisitive. Merely tolerating the intolerable.

Ordeal over, Miller had to admit that Mhari had done a good job with the arrangements for the wake. The hotel was along the coast between Edinburgh and North Berwick but not near enough for them to bump into anyone who knew them. Mhari had made the booking in her married name. To the proprietors it was just another overpriced reception.

He stood in the garden, sipping his first drink, looking out at Gullane Bay. He'd allowed Mhari to bully him into some meeting and greeting. He'd kept up appearances but escaped outside at the first opportunity, feeling sick, depressed and overwhelmingly tired.

'A bit cold to be out here, don't you think? It certainly is for me.'

Miller turned round to see Russell Sinclair standing a few feet away. He looked paler and thinner than at their last meeting, even under an oversized coat that had once presumably fitted him.

Seeming unsure, he took a tentative step forwards. 'May I have a word? Somewhere inside?'

Two minutes later, Miller found himself reiterating his

position, for what he hoped was the last time. He was aware that his irritation, bordering on anger, was disproportionate. This sick old man before him surely deserved more respectful treatment. Miller sighed to himself. He simply couldn't find any tone other than irritation. The fact that he felt like sitting down and sobbing in despair at every bloody thing only added to his need to cover that despair with something else.

'I've told you, Mr Sinclair. I've been through the box. Read, twice, the judge's summing up. There's nothing there to change my mind. I may not be a criminal lawyer any more but I *am* a lawyer all the same. I understand court papers, rules of evidence and suchlike. The case was circumstantial but strong. Agreed, the court didn't have the benefit of the most sophisticated scientific techniques available today *but* we have this.'

He began counting off the points on his fingers for emphasis. 'Firstly, my un-alibied father out "for a walk" at the crucial time of the third girl's disappearance, *without* his dog Bella. Absolutely unheard of. Those two were inseparable. I was second best for Bella, *if* he wasn't around, but there is absolutely no way he'd have gone for a walk without her. *And* he was out for an inordinate amount of time, given what he claims he was doing. It was apparently after my bedtime by the time he got back. My mother must have been worried sick. Odd behaviour, to say the least. Secondly, we have two respectable, credible eye witnesses identifying my father near the locus of the third disappearance. Thirdly, the dog leash. Found in *our* garden. No fingerprints of his. No fingerprints anywhere in fact. But that didn't matter to the jury then and I doubt it would now. It was clear that everything, including the site of the interments, had been wiped clean. What did trouble the jury was that there was no reasonable explanation as to how the leash got into the garden. None. Fourthly, the defiled body of Eileen Ritchie found on my father's island *and* the remains of the other two poor souls buried nearby, bound with lengths of halyard rope, rope used by sailors, like my father. And finally, a point raised at trial but not rammed home, given the wealth of other evidence available, though to my mind it's a point as compelling as any. Namely, that there were no similar abductions, disappearances or killings *after* my father was arrested. I mean, *please*. I disagree with you, Mr Sinclair. I believe a jury today *would* still convict.'

Miller waited for some impassioned defence from the frail man sitting opposite. Silence. He could hear the sounds of the gathering next door, Mhari's overloud bray carrying through to them in the quiet anteroom. Russell Sinclair stirred at last.

'I didn't expect you to go through those papers and magically see an escape route that no one else had. I suppose I hoped ... hoped, well what did I hope? That I could *connect*, yes connect your professional mind with some sort of residual feeling for your father. Your father had good reason for being out alone that evening. He had troubles at the time that you never knew of. The identification evidence is laughable. Two witnesses who were together, who knew each other well, had undoubtedly talked about the case again and again, who saw what they saw in *fading light* and from a considerable distance. As regards the dog leash. It *had* to have been put there deliberately. As for the bodies? Think about it. Why would your father be so ... so *stupid* as to have used his island, the family playground if you like, as a disposal ground. Was your father mad? And as for the lengths of halyard. The rope was of a generic type and never matched to anything found on your father's sailing boat, though, God knows, the police tried to make enough capital out of it.'

Sinclair took a deep breath, now clearly exhausted from the conversation.

'Finally, the absence of any further similar abductions and killings is far from being without precedent. There are countless cases the world over where killers have stopped forever. The true killer in this case may have died, quite possible given the time-span, *or* thanked his lucky stars for your father's conviction and got his perverse pleasures elsewhere. No. It's not as convincing a point as you wish to make. And again, strictly speaking, it is purely circumstantial. Please, Miller. Think again.'

The old man had paused to take a sip of his tea, an unsteady hand returning the cup to the table. 'Look, I don't think we'll ever know the truth of what went on. All I had hoped . . . wanted, for your father, would be for you to think again. I'm going now.'

He seemed reluctant to leave and Miller frowned as the old man struggled to pull something from his breast pocket.

'I'd like you to take this. I promised your father that I'd give you this after . . . after he passed away. I should have given it to you the first time we met. But I hoped . . . maybe once you'd thought over things, you might, you might, *soften*, without seeing this first.' He nodded towards the envelope. 'These really are a dying man's last words and, as such, should be taken heed of. Goodbye, Miller. I'll see myself out.'

With some sense of shame Miller allowed the old man to leave without so much as a handshake, the door clicking softly behind him. He fingered the envelope. His father's writing was more or less the same, or did he see or imagine a new shaky quality to it? That fine script from another age.

84

Those two words on the front: 'For Miller'. They threw up images of every birthday card, every Christmas tag, every occasional little present when he'd done well at school. 'For Miller.' And later? On scores of unopened letters sent via Mhari or his mother, no doubt containing precious, ever-hopeful but wasted visiting orders. The temptation to do with this what he'd done with the past thirty years' worth was barely resistible. He took it between both hands and twisted it. A bit more force and it would rip in two.

'Miller! Mill?'

Without a knock the door was shoved open with a bang, bouncing back on whoever had tried to enter. Miller jumped at the sudden and unexpected noise. He didn't know how long he'd been in here since Russell Sinclair had left the room. Their encounter had left him in a vague and depressed daydream, trying to ignore what had been said. And failing.

'Ah, there you are, Mill. You look like you're hiding. Mhari's on the warpath, wanting you to do the honours with drinks and things.'

Greg, the inevitable glass of red in his hand, was flushed and beaming away good-naturedly at him. Miller stood up, desperately wanting to escape, to leave them all to it.

'C'mon then, Mill. It's okay out here and there's someone you've got to say hello to.'

Greg had pushed the door fully open. Just behind him stood a tall attractive woman, a quizzical, unsure look on her face.

'Miller?' Her voice was hesitant.

'Oh c'mon, Mill!' Greg's tipsiness had led to his usual boyish over-excitedness, Miller tried to back away as his brother put a friendly arm round his shoulder, dragging him towards the woman.

'Greg, please. I need to g—.'

The woman took a tentative step forwards, her face still unsure. 'No, please, Miller, it's my fault. I've just introduced myself to Greg.'

Then she smiled.

'I'm Catriona. Catriona Buchan.'

13

'It's funny how just a few miles up or down the coast can make all the difference. Everything. The topography, the atmosphere, even the smells are different!'

He watched her, in half-profile, as she stood on the hotel's vast open lawn, looking out over the gentle expanse of Gullane Bay, coffee cup in hand. Her head was tilted slightly upwards like a hound on the scent, the breeze ruffling her hair. In truth, although his childhood memories of her were like those of yesterday, recollections of Catriona in her late teens were less clear. After his father's conviction, he saw less of her, indeed less of most people outside the family. Then she went to university and that was that. But today he'd have walked straight past her in the street, never seeing the likeness. Her height, yes. She'd always been tall. Same dark, almost Mediterranean colouring, not unlike his own. But as for everything else? Not in a million years. The hair was cut short now, in a deliberate and no doubt expensive, messy style. To some, a risky decision for an older woman, but one she carried off with her strong, sensual features. And she looked young and fit considering she was a few years older than him. She obviously looked after herself.

If he'd come across her as a stranger he'd probably have been slightly wary of her, despite her initial warmth and openness. She had the striking though somewhat intimidating look of the super-efficient. Switched-on, hyper-aware, never fucked-things-up. A bit like many of his female colleagues back in London, except without the hardness and brittleness that made them insufferable. Or was it just because he *had* known her, *had* harboured a puppy-dog crush on her, that he saw her through a softer lens?

'*Bugger!*'

Her unexpected expletive made him take a step back. 'I'm sorry?'

She turned round smiling, one hand in her coat pocket. 'Bloody vibrating mobile. 'Scuse me.'

She wandered over to the edge of the grass, and he watched as she nodded and mumbled her way through a brief conversation, never taking her eyes from the sea view. Within two minutes she was walking back over to him. 'Apologies for that. Work. There's a patient I need to do a home visit on straight away. Thought this might happen. I *am* on call today but I wanted to . . . to pay my respects to your father.'

He sensed her loss of composure rather than saw any physical evidence of it. She, of course, knew his views on his father and probably thought that she'd committed some *faux pas* in talking to him of 'respects'. But she'd recovered within a millisecond, jangling her car keys and disposing of her cup and saucer on a nearby garden table.

'Perhaps we could catch up another time? You said you'll be staying up here for a while?'

He nodded. 'Eh, yes. Things to sort out, y'know?'

'Okay. I'll call you at the house. I have the number. You probably know I met up with your mother from time to time. 'Bye, then.'

He hadn't known that. Quite possibly his mother had mentioned it but he'd tuned out of so many of their telephone conversations over the years, unable to bear another pleading mention of 'your poor father'. That aside, he dearly hoped that his mother had found some comfort in meeting

Catriona. Someone to talk to. Someone to share things with.

He watched as she hurried to her car, revving the engine in a surprisingly boy-racer kind of way, and disappeared down the drive. He moved over to the spot where she'd taken her phone call. The sea was mill-pond calm for the time of year. But grey. Freezing battleship grey. He sipped at the last of his drink. She may have changed in every other way but one quality had remained with Catriona Buchan.

When she left, you felt it.

14

She pulled away from the hotel feeling relieved. Miller McAllister was pretty much what she'd expected in the flesh. His proud mother had shown her enough photos of him, from childhood to adulthood, during the occasional lunches and coffees they'd shared. *And* she'd managed a good look at him at Ailsa's funeral a couple of years ago, though she hadn't spoken to him thanks to the incident with his father. Yes, he'd turned out very well, physically. He'd never actually been nerdy-looking back then. She half smiled. Nerdy by nature certainly but he'd had a bit of a wild look as a child. Almost feral at times. Just him and Bella, more often than not, by his side. His love of the birds, the island, nature. Then there was that other, almost unnerving aspect to him. Forever vigilant, silently observing so much. Appearing wise beyond his years. A benign Midwich cuckoo.

That was it. The reason she felt relieved to get away. He still carried that unsettling air of being all-seeing. As if there was always much more bubbling under the surface. Just like when he was young. That big brain working overtime. She knew some release had come out in the periodic tantrums and dark moods of his childhood – particularly after the arrest of his father. And, in adulthood? She wondered what he did now with all that ferocious cerebral and emotional energy? He'd been a strange boy and to some women he'd be a strange but intriguing man. To her? Hard to say. Her memories of him were all as an odd, vulnerable little boy . . .

'. . . D'you think he'll be okay? About the gull, I mean.'

She watched Greg crouched up on his bed, eyes glued to the binoculars. 'Hey, Cattie! I can see the mainland house really clearly tonight. There's one hundred per cent visibility. Can almost see Mum making her supper!'

It was Greg's way. Not answering immediately. She'd wait him out.

He was transfixed by the outside scene, talking to the window. 'The gull thing was nasty. I don't agree with what Mhari did. And I'm not sure if my father did either, though he wouldn't say it to your dad. Your dad's a doctor. I think doctors are . . . well, they're different. They're used to things dying.'

She'd had to laugh at that. 'Hardly! My dad would be a pretty crappy doctor if all his patients died! No. Dad is realistic. Miller's very sensitive, don't you think? He's not like you or Mhari at all. He's sort of young for his age and yet not. It's weird.'

Greg was still talking to the window, refusing to meet her eye. 'He's got a crush on you. You must see it?'

'Don't be daft. He's definitely too young for that. All Miller cares about are birds, boats and this island. He knows everything about all three.'

She'd smirked to herself at Greg's suggestion. Well, yes, she knew Miller liked her. But it wasn't something she really gave much thought to. He was far too young. And Greg? Nearly her age, so still far too young.

The door burst open without warning. Mhari. Looking grumpy as ever.

'What you two up to? Dad's looking for you, Greg. You're to help with the dishes. Now.'

Christ, the last thing she wanted was to be alone with Mhari. She'd got up to follow Greg out the door but Mhari was blocking her way. Not much choice but to stay back. Mhari was older, much heavier and she had that troublemaking look on her face.

'What did you say to Miller at teatime about the gull? I had to do *it. There was no alternative. Mill's got to shape up, you know. Grow up. He'll be going to secondary school after the summer. He's got to get tough.'*

She wasn't having this. 'Listen, Mhari. You like playing the bully but you're not going to do it with me. I said I was sorry about the gull to Miller. What I meant was that I was sorry he had to be there. It wasn't about you killing the gull. It was about you doing it in front of him. Pretty bloody insensitive. You know what he's like about those birds.'

Mhari was looking furious. 'It wasn't in front of him. He ran away. That's what I mean. About toughening up. I'm going to uni soon so I'll not be around to protect him, and Greg's a joke at that. So, is he going to run away every time some arsey second-year hard-nut has a go at him?'

Mhari was wagging a finger now. 'You know what I think? I think you like the fact that silly little Miller has a crush on you. You, years older than him! He, who doesn't even know what a crush really is!'

She was about to get up and leave this time but Mhari was opening the door for herself. Though not without a parting shot.

'He's just goggle-eyed every time you appear or your name's mentioned. It's pathetic. You shouldn't encourage it. But I think you like leading him on. And I tell you, no good's going to come of it.

'Not now. Not ever!'

15

He was relieved beyond words to be on his own at last. He stuffed the last few items into a rucksack, picked up the legal box, and headed out the door. He'd walk down to the harbour. He had to shake off the habit he'd acquired of avoiding walking through the town. This wasn't thirty years ago when fingers pointed and tongues wagged. No one knew who he was. Besides, summer had gone and the whole area was quieter. He wasn't going to encounter a raging lynch mob. If his mother could stick walking out and about – which she had for three decades – then so could he. The few people he'd encountered in the streets and shops so far hadn't given him a second glance. Most had offered a friendly smile and greeting. Locals knew the house, knew that family still came to stay there, but no one knew *him*. He had to stop hiding away.

As he walked down to the harbour he shook his head at Mhari's increasingly irritating behaviour. It had started out okay. He'd made the offer. Insincere. But he'd made it.

'I'm going to the island. For a couple of days. I don't know what either of your plans are, but if you want to come, be ready by midday. But remember about the tides. At this time of year we'll be effectively stranded. We won't get off until late tomorrow.'

'Why you going there? Why now? Are you up to something, Miller? Are you going to have a valuer there or something? If so, I think you should let us know.'

He'd brushed past her with the breakfast dishes. 'Don't be ridiculous. My God, paranoia really is getting a grip on you, Mhari!'

'Well I hope you're being truthful with us. I want to know if anything's changed from what we've previously discussed. I saw you disappear into that room with Russell Sinclair. What's the big secret?'

'There's no secret, Mhari. Nothing's changed. The old man's ill and he just wanted a few words with me. That's all. On second thoughts I don't think you'd better come over. You need to calm down, get a bit of perspective. I'm going over because I want to. That's it.'

Her ability to infuriate him was draining. It was using up so much of his feelings. And again, wasn't his anger a bit disproportionate? Just as with Russell Sinclair? It was all too easy to get fired up but, in truth, his anger at Mhari conveniently left little or no room for any other feelings. He had to get a handle on himself. Anger was destructive. To others, to himself. Though Mhari *was* the limit sometimes.

Well, she wasn't coming anyway. If she wanted to continue her rant, tough. With no landline at the Fidra house, and by screening his mobile, he could happily avoid her. On second thoughts, she probably would leave him alone for a while. She'd made it plain that her children and her job needed her, implying that *he* should be looking to those things as well, especially his family. Interfering cow! Greg had tried to dampen things down or at least distract her attention by asking if she'd drop him off at Edinburgh airport. He'd said he needed to get back to his life.

The two days since the funeral had got them all down. The mood was made worse by Mhari's insistence that she clear Dad's clothes – the ones Mum had kept for God

94

knows what reason – and sort them for charity. She'd given up in tears after ten minutes and Greg had had to sit her down with a cup of tea, promising that he'd finish the job for her, which to his credit he had.

And she'd swiftly been developing another obsession since the funeral.

'. . . and I don't see why you had to spend so much time outside in the garden, the freezing cold garden, mind you, with Catriona Buchan. What was wrong with being in the main room with everyone else? First, it's private chats with Russell bloody Sinclair, then it's an audience with Dr Catriona Buchan. She gave you her life story, did she? I never knew what Mum saw in her. She turned out to be exactly what I'd have expected. Remote and snooty. But she's good at pulling the wool over. Mum *and* Dad adored her.'

At that, Greg had made a rare and forceful intervention. He'd obviously had enough of her. 'Perhaps, Mhari, that's because they felt they owed her and her father. You know fine well that Forbes helped with overseeing the mainten-ance of Fidra. Even when he was infirm, and right up until his death. All out of the goodness of his heart. He knew Mum would never set foot on the island again but someone had to keep an eye on the bloody place. And Forbes didn't exactly ask for a factor's fee. Not that any local would've touched the job, and that's the point. Mum, and by default Dad, had few trusted friends around here. Forbes *and* Cattie Buchan, when she came back to live here, were two of them. You know it's true, Mhari. I don't know, or rather I *do* know what you've got against Catriona. Same as when we were kids. It's called the green-eyed monster . . .'

Greg's impassioned defence of Catriona and her father had taken Miller aback. The very fact that Greg could assert himself when provoked was impressive and surprising. But at least they'd all parted on reasonable terms following the breakfast spat. He sighed as he saw the harbour coming into sight. On waving the others off, he'd yet again found himself promising that 'no irrevocable steps' would be taken without consulting them both. Indeed any thoughts of wholesale disposal of the estate *were* suspended. For the moment. That had been his one big lie of the morning. Something *had* changed. Maybe.

He cleared the harbour and lined up the boat for Fidra, sitting back, thankful for the break in the weather. The crossing was going to be a bit choppy but that was okay by him. He still spent a lot of his spare time sailing, much of it in rougher waters than these. The day was fine and clear, offering almost the hint of warmth, though that would fade by late afternoon.

He'd tried his best not to admit it to himself, both last night and that morning, but the anticipation of going over to Fidra had taken its grip. Here he was, repeating that last journey, this time alone, no Bella, no hopes of meeting some girl that he could rescue. He shook his head at the memory. Typical Miller childhood naivety. The price he'd paid for that, and was still paying now, was beginning to look incalculable.

He raised his head to check the wind. Visibility was excellent. There was Fidra! Oddly, deceptively close and distant at the same time. One of those optical illusions of being at sea. He always felt his spirits lifted by being on open water. And being so close to Fidra? When he'd last been up here, after their mother's funeral, he'd come down to the harbour for some badly needed air and sense of freedom. The family boats were there. Tempting, inviting. The feeling had taken him utterly by surprise, after all his cursing about coming back. The truth was, he'd been a hair's breadth from leaping into the dinghy and zooming out to the island. Until the image of his ashen father collapsing on to those very harbour steps obliterated the desire. Instead, he'd turned on his heel, sprinted back to the house, and began packing for his return to London.

His heart rate was up now. The jetty was in sight. It looked just the same! Somehow he'd expected it to be a pile of rotting planks, barely serviceable for landing. But no, all was in good order. The lighthouse was ... well, the lighthouse. It never changed. And there was the house. High up in the nook of the cliff, its clean white lines a reassuring reminder of all those previous happy visits.

What a moment! His first step back on to the island in thirty-two years. A watery sun had come out for him, and the breeze that had made his crossing mildly choppy was picking up into a proper wind now. But it was welcome. The cries of the gulls that had drifted over to him long before landing seemed deafening. He secured the dinghy, slung his bag over his shoulder and made his way up the steps. The boxy structure of the house was shimmeringly white even in the weak sunlight. The massive windows and metal observation platform – also painted a blazing white – looked just the same, though the lack of any smiling face or waving hand up there added to the overall impression of desolation and emptiness.

He could've sworn that the front door was still the exact same shade of blue as thirty-odd years ago. The metal knocker in the shape of a bulbous fish head with bulging eyes was just as hideous as he remembered it. Though he'd always wondered why a doorknocker was needed at all. No chance of anyone just dropping by. It was a slightly twee touch, and all the more unusual for it, given the simple taste of the rest of the place. Maybe it had been a gift from someone. The Buchans perhaps, Mum's neighbour Mrs Watt? Whatever, it added a rather sinister touch. He'd remove it when he got the chance.

He pulled out the big stout mortice key which Mhari had, ever so reluctantly and resentfully, handed over to him that morning. Another reason for her bad mood? The smell as he entered the inner porch flung him back to that last day. The house had its own odour. Mainly the smell of the sea. It was never musty and, miraculously, never smelled damp. The power was working and he was relieved to see a strong wattage bulb lighting up the porch but he immediately switched it off again. No need. Natural light was flooding through. The second door, giving on to the main room, was wedged open. It was like being outdoors again, except this time insulated from the wind and the plaintive cries of the gulls. The room seemed made of glass. Sky, sea, and birds whirling around. One glance was enough. The same spartan furniture, the same old wireless, and what looked like the same binoculars hanging on the wall hook. Another museum. He shook his head in disbelief. He didn't like to admit the feeling, not at all. But there was no escaping it.

He was home.

16

As Mhari had promised, there were plenty of fuel supplies at the house. It didn't take him long to have the fire roaring, occasional smoky and sooty plumes coughing themselves down the chimney, thanks to the freshening wind outside. The hip flask offered the promise of inner warmth, and he settled himself, archive box and letter by his side.

His hand hovered over the letter. Taking a slug from the flask, he put the envelope down on the coffee table and opened the box. He knew its contents off by heart now and knew what he wanted to look at. He felt no guilt whatsoever at not revealing its existence to Mhari or Greg. He most certainly didn't want Mhari prying, squealing her miscarriage of justice arguments in his ear. He wanted, needed, time to think. The photocopied A3 sheet lay in his lap. The lengths to which his mother, and others, must have gone to prevent him and Greg seeing this. It was the front page of *The Scotsman*, Saturday 16 November, 1974. His father's photograph stared out. It was obviously an official head-and-shoulders portrait from the bank. The head turned slightly to the left, unsmiling but amiable-looking. Solid, a man to be trusted – that was a joke! – in perfectly knotted tie, brilliant white shirt and formal suit jacket.

Senior Bank Executive Guilty of Triple Murder and Rape

Judge: 'The terror and suffering you have caused is unspeakable.'

The end of a five-year hunt for the murderer and suspected rapist of three East Lothian girls reached its conclusion yesterday in dramatic scenes at Edinburgh High Court, when their killer was sentenced to a record 45 years' imprisonment.

Lord McLeish, one of Scotland's most senior judges, handed down the sentence with strongly worded comment. He told Douglas Cameron McAllister, 44, a married bank executive with three children, who lives near North Berwick on the East Lothian coast, 'In my 23 years sitting in the Scottish criminal courts, never have I come across such a litany of diabolical deeds.' He then went on to hand down the 45-year sentence, explaining that he was giving 15 years for each victim.

Family of the victims, Eileen Ritchie, 15, Jacqueline Galbraith, 14, and Alison Bailey, 15, were in the public gallery as the sentence was handed down. Some cheered, others wept. Later, the girls' parents were said by friends to be 'relieved and very satisfied' at the outcome of the trial and the exceptionally severe sentence.

Following the third abduction, police sources had intimated that there was a feeling of 'despair' within the investigating team who were said to be 'frantic' for a breakthrough in the case. After the previous abductions, a number of theories were being considered, including the possibility that there was more than one person, even a gang, involved in the disappearances. However all leads, which included appeals to the Scottish criminal underworld, led nowhere. It was only with the abduction of Eileen Ritchie that the police achieved early success when they uncovered evidence implicating McAllister.

The jury took less than a day to weigh up what it had heard and reach a unanimous verdict of guilty. The prosecution offered four main planks of evidence against McAllister.

The dog leash: found in garden

The case has puzzled police since November 1969 when Alison Bailey first went missing while walking her dog on Yellowcraigs beach, followed by Jacqueline Galbraith in February 1972, who went missing as she too was walking her dog outside Dirleton. Finally, Eileen Ritchie went missing in June 1973 as she walked her dog near Garvald village. Curiously, while all three dogs were either found or made their way home, their leashes were missing. An initial clue as to McAllister's involvement came on the day following Eileen's disappearance. Police had quickly publicized the missing leash, and the evening following her disappearance, a visitor to the area reported seeing one matching its description in the garden of McAllister's home. Police rapidly established that the leash belonged to Eileen and this triggered an investigation into McAllister's background.

Alibi: 'I went for a walk'

Police soon discovered that McAllister's behaviour on the evening of Eileen's disappearance had been unusual. The court heard McAllister claim that he had returned from work in the evening, found his wife and children were out, and decided to 'drive towards Tantallon Castle and Dunbar to get some air and go for a walk'. Exhaustive searches failed to find anyone who saw McAllister or his car on that route. When challenged over the unusually long time he'd been on his walk, McAllister claimed that he'd lost track of time but admitted that he must have been out 'for a few hours' returning only after dark. Further evidence was offered to indicate that it was practically unheard of for McAllister to go walking without his chocolate-coloured Labrador, Bella. He admitted that Bella had been in the house that evening when he returned but claimed that 'for once I wanted to be absolutely alone'. The prosecution maintained that McAllister had had more than enough time to abduct Eileen and transport her to Fidra.

Further checks were made into his whereabouts on the evenings when Alison Bailey and Jacqueline Galbraith disappeared. The court heard of more unusual behaviour. It was revealed that on both nights in 1969 and 1972 McAllister had used his car to drive to and from work in Edinburgh. This was established by checking the detailed records of all those who used the bank's executive car parking spaces. McAllister's car registration appeared on the records on the dates of both girls' disappearances. Challenged in court on this, McAllister admitted that he 'mostly' took the train to work but that he had 'probably opted for the car on those dates as it had been the winter and trains were likely to be running late'. Further checks revealed that McAllister had only taken his car to work a handful of times during both winters.

Eye witness: 'I am certain I saw him'

A local couple gave evidence of having seen McAllister up on the fringes of the Lammermuir Hills beyond Garvald village, close to where Eileen is thought to have disappeared. Lena Stewart, now 20, and Andrew Blackford, now 27, were in the area that evening and drove past a man they believed to have been McAllister, who they said was further up the hill and heading for some trees. Mr Blackford, a member of the local coastguard who knew McAllister said, 'I am certain I saw him. It was Douglas McAllister.'

Fidra: 'An archive of horror'

The final and most damning plank of evidence was discovered on the island of Fidra, situated off the East Lothian coast. The island has been in the McAllister family for generations and they have a house there, where McAllister's children and friends would frequently stay during the summer months.

The island also has a lighthouse, medieval chapel ruins, and is known for its colonies of gulls and puffins. But beneath this idyllic exterior police found what a senior investigating officer described in court as 'an archive of horror'. During a search of the island police discovered the body of Eileen Ritchie.

This discovery prompted a further search that led to the final pieces of evidence being uncovered. Eileen's body had been found at an out of bounds area near the ruins of an ancient chapel. This area was excavated. There, the remains of both Alison Bailey and Jacqueline Galbraith were found. The court heard from both the senior investigating officer and the local police surgeon, who stated that the remains had been 'expertly interred' in sealed graves, and could have lain undiscovered 'indefinitely'. Poignantly, for the victims' relatives, both girls' remains were found with their dogs' leashes beside them. The court heard that formal identification of the remains had to be made by reference to dental records.

Rape: 'Strong suggestion of sexual interference, probably rape'
Medical evidence put forward by the prosecution indicated that Eileen Ritchie had been subject to some form of 'sexual interference, probably rape'. The jury was satisfied with this evidence and found McAllister guilty of the rape of Eileen Ritchie as well as the triple murders. The remains of the other two victims were not in any condition to support an allegation of rape or sexual assault.

Despite the catalogue of damning evidence, throughout the trial McAllister denied every accusation put to him, claiming that all the evidence was 'purely circumstantial'. Lord McLeish dismissed his claims as 'frankly incredible' and remarked that with his removal from society, McAllister would never again be a menace to young women. In an unusual and pointed addition to his closing remarks, Lord McLeish urged the local community not to lay any blame at the door of McAllister's family.

Miller allowed himself another pull from the hip flask, the nearby envelope nagging away at his peripheral vision. He laid the cutting down. The counter argument was to hand. There, in that twisted, crumpled but untorn vellum envelope. This wasn't the first time he'd read the thing in the past forty-eight hours. Far from it.

The day was going but he didn't want any artificial light yet. Picking up hip flask and letter, he moved towards the sliding glass doors that led out on to the vast observation deck. Outside, he had a clear view of the coastline from the headland at Tantallon to his left, the castle standing proud as ever, along past the mainland house to the stunning golden strip that was the sand-duned beach at Yellowcraigs nature reserve. He'd have liked to sit out on the deck but at this time of day he'd be frozen and/or blown away in moments. Instead, he pulled an easy chair over to the window and settled down.

17

My Dearest Miller

My great friend and long-time solicitor, Russell Sinclair, will have, I'm sure, given you this as soon after my death as he could. Please don't be surprised at the handwriting. It is not mine. Only that on the envelope and the 'top and tail' of the letter is. Since I am now very weak, I have asked one of the hospice staff to write this as I dictate. A lovely nurse called Lizzie. Lizzie and the other staff here have been my salvation these past weeks. It's odd. The process reminds me of my work at the bank, dictating endless letters in those days to my trusted secretary. How far I am from that now. Also, I suspect that this letter will take a few days to get down, as I can only concentrate for short periods.

It did cross my mind that once you knew of my death you might cut yourself off from the family. Take no part in this next stage of what we must all eventually go through, namely probate, funerals and the like. But you could have done that after your mother's death two years ago and you didn't. You have kept in touch with your siblings and they tell me that you are a good, if distant, brother to them. Even that hard taskmistress Mhari recognizes your innate decency and cites you as also being a good uncle to her children. An admirable feat, as I understand from your late mother (and from Greg) that Mhari's children can be 'difficult'.

And you and Greg? It was always a source of great happiness to me and your mother how close the two of you were as children. Greg, although older, so often seemed to depend on you as if <u>you</u> were the elder brother. I don't know if that's how you saw it at the time but I do know that Greg recognizes that he owes a great debt to you. He loves you. That makes me so happy, especially at this time.

I am almost certain, from what Mhari has said, that you didn't read the letter I sent you after I received my devastating diagnosis those few short months ago. My first or perhaps second thought on being given my death sentence was to write individually to each of you, my beloved children. I must admit that, initially, the thought of you tearing up or burning or in some other way destroying a mere handful of last loving words from me, broke my heart. But now, three months on, and very near the end, I don't feel that kind of pain any more. I'm so far away from that now. In a way, I feel I have already left this world.

First of all, I want to explain my will which Russell will have told you about and which will have shocked you, no doubt. But there are sound practical reasons for me doing this. Much as I love Mhari, I despair, and always have, at her choice of husband. Your mother and I initially disagreed on this but over the years she came to agree with me. Mhari is what I believe is called these days a 'superwoman' – a model professional, mother, wife and breadwinner. There's the rub. Neil would fritter the estate away, one way or another. I have made sufficient cash provision for Mhari and her children from my savings and investments. Her children cannot get their share until they are older. Perhaps by then Neil will be a divorcee, with any luck. Greg is also given an equal share of the same. Sweet, gentle Greg. I feel he was always a rather semi-detached member of the family. But, as I understand it, he is happy and prosperous. I can rest at that. Finally, on this, you'll note that I have left a substantial cash amount to the hospice. It is the least I can do after these past few weeks.

I am entrusting the properties in the estate to you, since I know how much you loved where we lived, especially our wonderful island. I have never known of a child so sensitively attuned to place, to nature, from such an early age. Fidra _is_ you. The sea around it _is_ you. The birds _are_ you. You were always so at one with the natural world that, for a time, I had fond fatherly fantasies of you ending up as bird warden on an island far more remote than Fidra!

Dear Fidra. It has helped me beyond description to be here and to have been able to look out at the little island's beauty. We have such a superb view of it from the hospice. Breathtaking! I don't know if it's the medication, but some days, I've sat looking out at her and imagined that I've flown over, just like any old herring gull or little puffin and then I make my way round the island, surveying her every contour. Some days I feel I'm more there than here. Here in this aged, failing body.

Despite its subsequent contamination by events, I believe that you _can_ reclaim Fidra. Mhari, to her credit, has tried with her family visits, bless her heart. Your mother never would return and for that I am deeply saddened. But she had her limits, as do we all, in what we can cope with.

What about you, my son? I have followed and vicariously enjoyed all your successes, professional and personal. That you have a wife, and two children, makes me happier than I can tell you. Here it is fitting for me to apologize for my hysterical behaviour at your mother's funeral. I have passed on my profuse apologies to you through your siblings but I offer you them again. All I can say is that it was a bad day all round.

Now, if you are still reading, I thank the gods. I come on to the most difficult part of this letter and I ask that you stay with me.

My conviction. Unlike your mother, I have never had a strong, unshakeable religious faith and these thirty years of incarceration have put me in the company of many who might call themselves religious. The prison chaplains, the newly converted zealots, the true believers, the self-deluding, and the outright charlatans. But in here, this hospice, this place of peace, where the deepest of believers do the most difficult of work, I can begin to understand, to _feel_ close to something 'other'.

Popular belief has it that a dying man tells the truth. To make good with his maker? Perhaps. But I think also for another reason. There is no point in lying. What would be the point of any more effort, when all one's efforts are spent in getting through the next minute, the next hour?

I will say it baldly. I was wrongly convicted. Maybe it was just meant to be. I'm not the first and most certainly will not be the last. I long ago gave up hope of any legal exoneration. It is just too late. But, it is my last dying wish that you believe in my innocence. I was fortunate enough to have the unerring support these past three decades from everyone else in the family. Except you, my little Miller. Strange, I still remember you as that, whatever your age. My little Miller – that most beautiful of children – with a wild, untameable look about him. It breaks what's left of my heart to have you believe me a monster. In one final effort to make you see, I want to guide you through the evidence against me and tell you some things you could not have known as a child and which, since you never spoke to me or allowed me to contact you, I will tell you now.

Being a father, I feel certain that you will understand the lengths a parent will go to, to protect their children from distress, insecurity and worry. That early summer's evening in 1973 I returned home with a heavy heart. I had expected your mother to be out at her usual church activities but I had hoped that at least some of my lovely children would be at home. No one was there to greet me with either a smile or a scowl (as was Mhari's habit at the time). Either would have been welcome. No, you were all out enjoying the first hint of the summer. There was Bella, of course. Her customary frantic welcome momentarily helped me. Why you or Greg hadn't taken her with you, I cannot remember.

Anyway, finding that I was effectively alone, I made an instant decision. I too wanted to blow the day's cobwebs away and, if not enjoy, at least be part of that summer evening. I dumped my briefcase in the vestibule, apologized to Bella for not taking her with me, and drove the car east along the coast. In my rear-view mirror I enjoyed seeing Fidra, Lamb, Craigleith, all the little islands, nestled peacefully in the gloaming, the golden sky telling all that summer was here. How I, and you after me, so loved that part of the coast. But, as I approached Tantallon, I was far from peaceful within myself.

I pulled into the castle car park and got out to stretch my legs. The place was shut but I walked on, clambering over the gate and heading for our favourite view. I drew the line at climbing the battlements and made for the castle close, with its magnificent views of the Firth and the Bass Rock. Your childhood wonder and joy at that view, which so chimed with my own, often moved me to tears on our many visits. It did that evening, as its memory has so often, these past thirty years. I sat on the bench near the sea gate until the sun went down, and pondered our family's future, a future I had been agonizing over for days.

Ever since your mother told me she was leaving me, leaving us all.

18

The last sip from the flask had caught in Miller's throat and prompted a fit of coughing and spluttering that left him feeling nauseous. That and his poleaxing tiredness were bringing on a thumping headache. He shoved aside the doors to the observation platform. The whoosh of the invading wind as it made its way to the coffee table, stirring his papers into a swirling vortex, was suddenly deafening. He grabbed the remaining pages of the letter and stepped outside, closing the doors behind him, his boots clanking along the platform's metal flooring. The roar of the sea had joined the wind but he was enjoying the cacophony. Always had. Immediately he felt better, his head and lungs clearing.

He moved to a more sheltered corner where the light from inside would allow him to read these last few pages. He knew what they contained. After all, this was his fifth reading. The gut-wrenching sensation he'd experienced on the initial readings had long since passed. With a final glance and approving nod at the twinkling lights on the mainland, he read on, the wind tugging at the pages, threatening to suck them down into the churning waters, a sickening drop below.

> I have always loved your mother. Your mother had
> always seemed so surprised and honoured to be loved by
> me. Perhaps because I worked so hard to woo and win
> her much against my own parents' wishes. They'd wanted
> someone further up the social scale. We agreed to differ

but it left an unbridgeable gulf between us. No, there never was anyone else for me except your mother, so her news knocked my world from beneath me. We all know how difficult, waspish, impatient she could be at times. But she had boundless physical and emotional energy and needed an outlet for it. Maybe in these modern times she'd have been a career woman like Mhari. But then, the way we lived, where we lived, being a wife and mother was the done thing. That's why she busied herself with so many activities, I'm sure. And I know I annoyed her sometimes with my enthusiasms, for the boats, for Fidra. But I thought she was happy. As fulfilled as she could be. Obviously I was wrong.

At first I thought there was another man. That would have been devastating enough. But no, it was far worse than that. Unbeatable. She said that, after a year of hard and tortured thinking, she had decided. She wanted to leave us, renounce her former way of life and join a religious order.

The implications I was only beginning to see, after the initial shock. We had agreed to talk through the future, what to tell you all, what it would mean for her and us. We'd planned to do it that coming weekend, on the Sunday when I'd brought you all back from Fidra. Strangely, the trip there eased my mind. I almost forgot my troubles, suspended the shock. I was going to talk to my great friend, Forbes Buchan, about it. I knew I could trust him and he would offer sound counsel. But, on reflection, I felt it better to wait until your mother and I had talked.

Then out of the blue came my arrest and when I was on remand I was attacked by two prisoners. I was pretty badly hurt and they even delayed the trial because of it.

But I recovered more quickly than any of us thought and, once I was well, your mother and I <u>did</u> have a talk. She said that my arrest must be a sign that her decision was wrong, that she should stay with her family after all. I think she was very, very confused at that time and I had nothing to offer her. I was dealing with my own absolute disbelief at what was happening to me. I do know, though, that she somehow blamed herself then, and I believe forever. If she had not delivered that news to me, would my behaviour have been different that evening? Perhaps. But how much of a difference would that alone have made? I don't know, but I have been pondering the question daily for thirty-two years.

You know that your mother always had a deep religious faith. There was no doubt in my mind that coming to the decision to leave us must have been tearing her apart throughout that year. However, I think her faith led her to some strange places. I know that her feelings of guilt about leaving us escalated to such a degree that she felt that what happened to me was some sort of punishment. On her as well as those she loved – her family. That somehow the sin of pride had overtaken her. How could she really think that she could be 'good' enough to join an order? I believed all that thinking to be highly self-destructive and deeply saddening. But, whatever else, your mother stood by me and loved me in her own way for the rest of her life. I could never have asked more of her.

So, that was my state of mind that night when the unfortunate young girl went missing. After Tantallon, I drove on towards Dunbar and then turned back home again. <u>At no point</u> did I go anywhere near Garvald or the Lammermuirs.

What of the two people who said they saw me near there? They were simply wrong or worse. I know Russell went to considerable lengths to try and re-interview those witnesses. He was pursuing a theory that the man, Andy Blackford, whom I knew a bit, was, through his job with the coastguard, <u>very</u> close to the police and may have exaggerated his certainty, or simply lied outright. Russell also thought that he might have allowed his fiancée at the time, Lena Stewart, to be influenced. (Interestingly, to Russell anyway, those two never got married and split up soon after the trial.) I thought these all long shots.

I have no explanation, no theory about the dog leash. It could have been tossed into the garden at any time in the short period between when the girl went missing and the phone call to report the leash. <u>And</u>, if I was guilty, why, <u>why</u> would I have left such incriminating evidence there, of all places? Why didn't I just take the thing out to Fidra and drop it in the Firth of Forth, when I was supposedly taking the body over? Or, keep it as some sort of trophy to be interred like the others? If, as was suggested, it was some sort of panic reaction, it was remarkably stupid for someone who'd been organized enough to get not just one but <u>three</u> bodies over to the island during four years.

In relation to that, I have left the worst to last. I have absolutely no explanation for the bodies of these poor girls. The thought that two of them were secreted on our island, where you, Mhari, Greg, Catriona played, still chills me. My defence team made a brave effort at this. Yes, anyone could have access to Fidra. It wasn't as if we lived there all the time. Approaches could be made there at night unseen, especially if one berthed in the north cove. The interment and concealment were expert, and included taking materials over to the island to essentially make, open and seal the tomb. All this would have taken time. And what of the uncovered body of that poor last girl? The prosecution was adamant that she had lain there well hidden inside the blocked-off ruins as we picnicked over the weekend. A fact that undoubtedly assisted the jury to their verdict. But if I was guilty would I really have risked this? Taking an overnight picnic party out there? Also, when and how was I going to inter her? Not on an island teeming with visitors, surely? The truth was that your mother and I talked about having some breathing space from each other. It was urgently needed after the week that had just passed and a trip to the island seemed the best thing. We rang the Buchans on the Saturday morning to ensure that they'd come along, to make it a busy and fun-filled time for you and your brother and sister. So that you wouldn't notice my dejected frame of mind, I suppose. On balance, it was a good idea, if what followed on our return had never happened. If we'd 'only' had our marriage to worry over, not my arrest for multiple murder.

The prosecution postulated that I'd taken the body over on the Friday night after dark. Then, apparently my plan was that once I'd returned everyone to the mainland that Sunday, I would have made an excuse to return to inter her. They said that I frequently made trips to Fidra on my own to 'check' or 'make repairs' (including taking building materials) to the house and stayed the night there on my own, making it easy to suggest that this is how I could have disposed of the other bodies. It's true I did make frequent visits. A house like that doesn't look after itself. And, the tides often made return the same day impossible and sometimes I just wanted to be on my own there. Surely you, Miller, of all people, who adored that place as much as if not more than I, can understand that? Fidra was – is – part of me. I felt viscerally attached to it as I'm sure you did, and I hope you once again will.

To this day, I shudder at the thought of your presence on the island that day of the search. That you had in your own marvellous, bold, adventurous way, gone there to help me, to find the missing girl, as you thought, safe and sound. And then to see that. My poor wee lad. Forbes told me how you'd been spotted and that he and another officer had held you as you screamed and screamed and screamed. Then, over the next few weeks and months he and your mother had to get help for you. The psychologist said that you responded well, up to a point. But I wonder. Wonder how you could have recovered from such an experience? I think it was that incident that somehow settled my 'guilt' in your mind. All the rest of the family stoically stood by me, none, not one of them, saw any truth in what I was being accused of. But you did. Maybe it was just too much. In your young mind I'd also betrayed you in the worst possible way. I'd contaminated, ruined, forever spoilt your sanctuary, your playground, your island. I suppose it's no surprise that a firm belief in my guilt made a permanent home within you.

What of my case after half a lifetime's imprisonment? I've been over everything an infinite number of times. Driven myself mad with it. Had hopes raised and dashed as Russell, good man, pursued some theory or other. But for so many years it has been far too late. All appeals processes ran dry, evidence was destroyed or lost, aeons ago. Indeed there was precious little forensic evidence for modern science to tackle. No real physical evidence. All circumstantial. It was impossible to fight.

I slid into reluctant resignation many, many years ago. I suppose it became less reluctant as I fully accepted that I would never be released. My continual protestations of innocence sealed my fate, ensuring that the authorities would do anything they could to keep me. Through all this, it was your mother and the knowledge that my three wonderful children were out there thriving that kept me from losing my sanity. I have been living vicariously through you all, which, of course, is what any loving parent does.

But, alongside the death of your kind-hearted mother, it is *you*, Miller, who has caused me the most heartache. If I'd known that you believed in me, it would have made my hell so much more bearable. I can't say any more than that.

As I dictate the final words of this letter, I know I will never see you again. My only hope is that you have a change of heart somewhere, somehow.

Whatever you finally think of me, know this.

I love you. I have always loved you.

And I am,

Aye Your Loving Father

Aye your loving father. That archaic Scottish endearment appended to all of Dad's notes and cards to him as a child. Straight from another age. Sometimes it would just be 'Aye Yours'. Always yours. In contrast to the neat, clearly legible hand of the nurse taking the dictation. He remembered little of the nurse, Lizzie. Other hellish memories of the visit to the hospice had overshadowed any true image of her. But he did remember her being gentle with him. No doubt she had been that to his father.

Miller laid a finger to the last page of the letter and noticed again that these last words had been scrawled in the shaky, indeed barely recognizable handwriting of his father, as had the opening, 'My Dearest Miller'.

Aye your loving father. His last written words ever? Probably.

He was aware that the light had almost gone and he was freezing. He touched his cheek. Tears. Standing up, hunched against the wind, he stumbled back into the warmth of the main room, closing the doors against the growing gale and the crashing of the sea. Taking a last look outside before the indoor lights would only cast back to him his own reflection, he saw it straight away. A boat approaching! Quickly, he made his way to the front door and hurried down to the steps leading to the jetty. Fuck! Whoever was coming here would have a hell of a job landing, and worse, if they did, they'd be stuck here until the morning! Who *was* it? He didn't recognize the boat, so it couldn't be Greg or Mhari suddenly changing their travel plans. He'd forgotten the binoculars hanging up by the door, but at the rate the boat was careering in, he'd soon be able to see its pilot.

He squinted through the twilight. One person. Silhouetted against the fading sunlight. Standing erect, body leaning at a forward angle, like a living figurehead seeking landfall. And no! Surely not? He watched closely as the wind plucked at its clothes, billowing them out, like an extra sail. He peered again. The clothes? The cowl, struggling to stay on the head as gust after gust tugged away, threatening to dislodge it and reveal the hidden face. There was no mistake. The man was wearing a monk's habit.

Miller shivered. The visitor cut an eerie figure, and, were it not for the modern boat, Miller thought the image would have been much the same eight hundred years ago, when the medieval brethren came to what had then been their island and chapel. Childhood ghost stories of 'The Dark Monk of Fidra' crept into his mind as he watched the boat's rapid approach. Was this real?

Suddenly the figurehead came to life and waved an all too human hand, indicating he'd need some help to come in.

A few moments later and Miller had secured the ropes. He grasped the man's outstretched arm and heaved him on to terra firma. His visitor shook his hood down. He was shaven headed with a kind though weather-beaten face, the age impossible to judge within fifteen years either side.

He held out a huge hand. 'Abject apologies for intruding on your peace and quiet here but I wanted to see you. My name's Duncan. Brother Duncan Alexander. I don't know if you'll remember me. It's nigh on thirty years since we last exchanged a word.'

'. . . and as I said on landing, I'd heard that you were back. This is a small community. Word gets around. I can't tell you how sorry I was not to attend your father's funeral. I was in seclusion until yesterday. I'm sorry about the tides. It was foolish of me. I should have checked. It's just that I saw the family's boat on its way over here an hour or so ago, assumed, *hoped* it was you, and decided to come over.'

Miller scrutinized the face yet again. '*Dunc-the-monk*.' He smiled to himself. Greg, forever the wit, had come up with that particular nickname. And it had stuck. The robed figure, who would occasionally visit the house for a cup of tea with their mother, had been a constant source of wonder to them. Simultaneously exotic and yet sinister, like nobody else they'd ever seen, he'd always brought them some treat. Chocolate bars, bags of boilings, a book on some interesting topic: birds or wildlife for Miller, sport or science for Greg. Some plant cuttings from the abbey gardens for their father. They'd all come to like him. Their father, who had always been unfailingly polite to visitors, would be overjoyed at the gifts for the garden. Although too young at the time to make full sense of it, a solemn and know-it-all Mhari had informed Miller and Greg that this was significant.

'. . . You know how Dad can't stand the Catholic Church. "The height of hypocrisy", that's what I've heard him call it. It caused ructions when Mum "re-found" her faith. But it seems okay now and he and Dunc-the-monk get on all right. They sometimes have a sneaky whisky in Dad's study and y'know how Dunc's researching some book on Fidra? Well he's always asking Dad things about it, which Dad loves, and asking permission to land there . . .'

Although heavier, balder and thirty years older, Miller could still see vestiges of that keen and bright-eyed young monk. How old would he have been then? Hard to judge. In his twenties? Possibly older. He'd been tall, especially so to an eleven-year-old child, well built, and – a shocker at the time – allowed to have hair! No shorn head, no pudding-bowl cut with tonsure. No, he'd sported 'groovy', longish, Seventies hair. Not much trace of that now. The voice was much the same, though. Rich Borders lilt.

What of his appearance here? The surprise of it apart, Miller had at first been unable to suppress his annoyance. He hadn't quite realized just how much he craved being alone here. But the man's natural warmth, accompanied with his sense of urgency, had forced him to put his irritation aside and behave – for the first time in what seemed like an age – in a civilized, hospitable manner. The feeling wasn't altogether unwelcome.

'No, please, Brother Duncan. There's no need to apologize again. As you can see, we're not short of spare rooms here. Let me top up that whisky for you? Thanks for bringing it. Glad to know you're allowed a dram.'

Duncan was struggling to put his finger on what had changed about the McAllister boy, as he still thought of him. Over the years, Ailsa had shown him photos of Miller's journey from boy to man. The last ones only a few years old. She'd emphasized the boy's fanaticism with fitness. In adulthood, Miller had looked the epitome of super-fit masculine health. Ailsa had also spent countless hours, these past years, relating her despair at how her youngest refused to visit his father in prison, or read any letters from him. In later years, she'd stopped talking about Miller altogether, although he knew it was an abiding source of sadness to her.

He accepted the refreshed drink and sneaked an appraising look at Miller. The spit of his father. And the lad was young for his age. No lines or grey in that black hair. But he looked worn out. Dark shadows under the eyes, an almost sickly pallor. Clearly under significant strain and misery. He'd spent enough years observing visitors to the abbey's retreat, with all their worries and woes, to recognize the signs immediately. Well, it was time to add or to take away from them, depending on which way you saw it.

'I certainly don't make a habit of intruding into others' solitude but, since I heard of your father's death and that you were here, I wanted, *needed* to come and talk with you. I thought about trying to get in touch with you after your blessed mother's sudden death to see how things were but . . . I . . . I couldn't, I'm afraid. I was in seclusion.'

He took another sip of his drink, biding his time before going on and nervously clearing his throat with an over-loud cough. This was turning out to be more of a challenge than he'd anticipated. But it was too late to go back now. Wasn't it?

'Anyway, I visited your father now and again when he was in Peterhead. I always thought it was so unfair of the authorities to keep him in a prison that far from your home. I know Russell Sinclair tried again and again to have your father moved back to Edinburgh and into Saughton. But no. Their answer was always that his category of prisoner warranted the highest security and they were keeping him there. It's a miracle that they actually allowed him into St Baldred's at the end. And that's what brings me here.'

He glanced at Miller who was staring into his drink. He prayed that the boy would be okay with what he was about to tell him.

'You see, our order has strong links with the hospice. Many of the staff come to our retreat to recharge their batteries, including the nurse who met you there on the night of your father's death. Lizzie, Lizzie Henderson. Through this and work I myself have done at the hospice, I've come to know her quite well. We have had many discussions about what I'm going to tell you. And I made it my business to contact Lizzie as soon as I came out of seclusion. When I saw her she was deeply troubled. In fact, she was and *is* in despair. Can I ask you? Have you received the letter from your father? The one Lizzie wrote for him?'

He returned Miller's puzzled nod.

'Well, Lizzie described to me what taking that dictation was like for her. An act, she said, that was so touching to her but also so disturbing. You see, some weeks earlier she'd had a crisis. The announcement that your father was to be a patient had been discussed in detail at staff meetings. All were agreed that the fact that your father was a convicted killer would have no relevance for his care. But things weren't quite so straightforward for Lizzie. She had a private meeting with the hospice director. The director had been instrumental in persuading the authorities to release your father into the care of the hospice on compassionate grounds. Such grounds many outside the hospice felt were undeserved. There was considerable local opposition when word got out, as well as steely resistance from the authorities that almost scuppered everything. However, the director is well connected and your father was admitted to St Baldred's to be treated with the same care as any other patient. But in Lizzie's mind he wasn't exactly like any other patient. She had a personal connection of sorts to your father. Or at least to his case.'

He acknowledged Miller's raised eyebrow and went on.

'Lizzie's aunt is Lena Stewart. Lena Stewart, as I'm sure you recall, was a key prosecution witness who said that she saw your father near to where the third victim went missing that night in June of seventy-three. Lizzie had, from time to time over the years, heard various tales about your father repeated within her own family, and wasn't sure if it was appropriate for her to remain at the hospice while he was a patient. The hospice is a small, intimate place and all staff and all patients mix. So, she was considering taking a leave of absence until ... well ... until your father's inevitable death. But, after talking at length with the director, Lizzie agreed to stay.

'During the next few weeks, what can only be properly described as a transformatory experience overwhelmed Lizzie. She became closely involved in your father's day-to-day care, leading eventually to her taking down the dictation of that final letter to you. Now, that letter was and *is* absolutely confidential between you and your father. I don't want to give you the impression that Lizzie has discussed its contents with anyone. She hasn't. What I think I *can* safely say, is that what your father said to you in that letter, he had earlier said to Lizzie in the previous weeks. It was clear that as he grew weaker, and felt iller, he wanted to talk. And the issue, the *only* issue close to his heart, was his conviction. Through this, Lizzie became increasingly convinced of your father's innocence. I should say that at no point did Lizzie divulge her family connections. She felt, rightly, that it would be unfair and unnecessarily stressful to a dying man. But she certainly went away and thought about it all, in particular her growing belief in his innocence. At some stage she mentioned this to her aunt. This was breaking no ethical boundary. As I said, it was common knowledge that your father was a patient at St Baldred's.

'Lizzie and Lena Stewart had a few heart-to-hearts about your father until . . . well . . . until her aunt eventually broke down and admitted that she had given false testimony to the court. Although she had thought at the time she had good reason for believing your father to be guilty, she had not in fact seen him on that fateful evening.

'In short, she lied.'

'An Archive of Horror'

Following the conviction of Douglas McAllister, the island for-ever changed in the minds of locals. As described earlier, the label introduced in court – 'an archive of horror' – now took firm hold. To date, a mere handful of years after the grim discoveries on the island, the local community remains in a state of disbelief. Some have said that they wish the island could be obliterated from the horizon. Others, more charitable to the McAllister family, prefer never to talk in public about the events.

As for the family, the period immediately after the conviction was far from happy. Ailsa McAllister had pledged never to return to Fidra, although it remained in the family's estate, and a close family friend took over responsibility for its management. But Ailsa was determined to remain in the part of the world that she and her children loved, and she hoped that life would return to some semblance of normality. Meanwhile, the children were being helped to get over the shock. The eldest, Mhari, left to attend university and the two boys, Miller and Gregor, returned to school in Edinburgh.

Ailsa continued her work for local charities but others dis-pensed with her services. The priest at her local church con-tinued to welcome Ailsa but many in the congregation shunned her. So she took to going on retreat to a nearby monastery that housed male and female visitors in guest quarters.

Whitekirk Abbey (where this author is a member of the brethren) is situated along the coast near Tantallon Castle. It has been the site of a monastery since the eleventh century. Indeed, it was the order there who set up a monastery, chapel and plague hospital on Fidra in medieval times. And so it was with some irony that Ailsa McAllister became a regular visitor to the abbey.

Extract from *Fidra – an Island History*, by Duncan Alexander, Whitekirk Publishing, 1st edition, 1978.

20

According to the postman there were drifts up to two feet high on the A198. The snowploughs had cleared a route through but the guest-house office was getting call after call cancelling bookings.

'Brother Duncan? I've made up five rooms in the men's quarters and one in the women's. That'll be okay, won't it? Everyone who's coming is here now, except one and she's on her way, isn't she?'

Duncan Alexander looked up from his clipboard and nodded as the housekeeper vanished out the front door. He was alone now, at last. The phone had stopped ringing. The relief! He stood up, stretching his stiff shoulders and moved round the oversized desk to make his way outdoors.

The late afternoon was spectacular. The lowering sun had turned the previously blindingly white landscape into a glittering array of golds and purples. Fifty yards in front of him where the land stopped, the Firth of Forth was now a deep, constantly shifting mauve. To his right, the snow-covered battlements of Tantallon Castle sat, reassuringly solid, in the coming evening light. Behind him, far in the distance, the gentle peaks of the Lammermuir Hills offered their glistening goodnights as the shadows engulfed them. No chance of a brisk constitutional up there now. Too late, too cold, too much snow.

He rubbed his eyes in tiredness. He'd been on the phone

all day, taking cancellations, rearranging bookings. Might as well be working in a travel agent's! But not quite. On occasion, it still amazed him how many were so eager to come here. It certainly wasn't for the material comfort. The rather crudely converted old infirmary building, though younger by centuries than the original abbey building up the road, was far from being hotel standard. Still, those keen to be here didn't seem to care.

But precious few of them were going to make it this week thanks to the weather. He felt for those sorry souls, in extremis, who so needed the seclusion of a retreat. The period after Christmas and New Year was always a busy one for the guest house. It was the season when so many were depressed. Those with no resolutions left to make that hadn't already been broken, those going back to the routine of drudgery and depression, those who'd experienced one of life's monumental events and simply couldn't cope a minute longer. No, the guest house had an important function. All that was expected from those who came to stay was to help with the household chores and share a meal every evening. Even in that he allowed exceptions. The guest house came, after all, under his purview at the abbey. Guests weren't even expected to attend prayers and masses. Indeed, their faith wasn't interrogated or questioned. The only truly unbreakable rule was that guests didn't bring alcohol on to the premises. Too much of a temptation for the significant minority of recovering alcoholics who used the sanctuary of the guest house to help them with their battle. It worked. Most of the time. Yes, Whitekirk Abbey's reputation as a peaceful, healing place was well known. Also, if he was to be brutally truthful, he knew only too well that some of the better-heeled guests were *very* generous in their donations and bequests, and that helped the abbey in its other work.

He wrapped his arms around himself against the biting cold. He felt utterly exhausted. More exhausted than the past sedentary handful of hours warranted. But wasn't it always like this when he came out of seclusion? That strange re-growing of an outer skin. His defence against contact, *any* contact with the outside world. And that included the sheltered world of the abbey. Sheltered way of life or not, he still found readjustment after seclusion something of an ordeal. But it was different this time. This time he'd welcomed the release into the abbey. Welcomed the space on offer outside a solitary's cell. Then today's snowfall, though beautiful, had brought the threat of disappointment. He knew many guests wouldn't get through. Not if they were coming a distance of more than a mile or two. Most of them were. Some from Edinburgh and environs, usually less than an hour by car. The three coming from the Borders didn't stand a chance and cancelled before even trying to leave, as did those from Fife.

Maisie, the housekeeper's little Jack Russell, heard it first and started her manic yelping as she scampered past him, brushing the hem of his habit. He peered through the twilight and the beginnings of another snowfall, the flakes falling heavily on his face and prickling his cheek. He pulled his hood over his head and eyes. Two dim headlights and a scrunch of tyres. The Mini struggling up the ice-encrusted driveway, had him sighing with relief. And concern.

She'd made it.

The top floor of the female quarters was in darkness, save for the dimmest glow-worm bulb hanging from the hallway ceiling. On either side of the hall were three bedrooms, each door wide open, showing identical iron-framed beds with single mattresses and a simple bedside table by each.

Through every window he could see the heavy snowfall as the abbey's exterior lights caught the flakes on their way to the ground. There were occasional interruptions in the steady falling pattern. Swirls and flurries would appear each time a particularly vicious gust of wind seemed to whip up the snow, shaking the building to its core, causing a creaking and howling every couple of minutes.

As he padded along to the end room he was aware of committing two transgressions. Firstly, by being here when any females were in residence, and secondly, the bottle of single malt he was swinging in his right hand. Still, not all rules had to remain unbroken. Not all sins were mortal.

The seventh bedroom door was closed. He tapped gently with the bottle. The door opened immediately.

'Wee nightcap, Ailsa?'

She was looking gaunter than ever. Her tall frame would soon be approaching emaciation at this rate, and he doubted if she'd eaten more than a forkful at supper. Although a good deal older than him, she'd always had an air of energetic youthfulness. But it was fast being extinguished.

Her face was stern. 'You shouldn't be here, Duncan.' It was hardly a warm welcome but she pulled the door wide for him. 'I could do with the company, though. The dram too. Might help me to sleep more than I have of late. Come away in.'

He offered her the only chair but she shook her head, seeming irritated, and indicated that he should have it. She scurried around for a minute and came back with a couple of ill-matching tumblers which she put down on the bedside table. Beside them, two flickering votive candles offered the only light in the room, leaving it darker than the hallway outside. She perched on the edge of the narrow bed, waiting, sneaking a furtive glance out the window at the falling snow and flinching as the wind rattled the casement. Rather than irritated, she was anxious.

He tried to ease himself into the uncomfortable, too-small chair. 'How are you, Ailsa?' He raised a finger against any precipitate reply. 'I mean, how are you *really*? Not what you tell them at church and the few decent folk that still talk to you around these parts. And don't tell me you're doing fine. I can see you've been crying.'

She'd dropped her head and was staring at her hands, accepting the over-filled glass of whisky without looking up. The candlelight, as it played in her hanging hair, cast long shadows over her face, making it impossible for him to see her expression. Her voice was low, a near whisper.

'I saw Douglas yesterday. He's not doing at all good. He looks very unwell. Not sleeping and getting a lot of stick, well stick's too mild for it. Not as bad as that episode on remand but he *is* getting a lot of threats and things from other prisoners. And for goodness' sake, Doug's . . . well . . . he's *useless* at that sort of thing. The last man who knows how to stand up for himself. His advice to the kids was never to be afraid of running from a fight. But there's nowhere to run to in a prison. A couple of warders have had a go, too. One of them got him alone in his cell. Punched him in the kidneys and stomach, saying that he knew one of the girls' families and that his days were numbered in this place. Actually, it looks like the authorities are moving him from Edinburgh and sending him to Peterhead. They say Saughton's not suitable. Peterhead's got a special high-security wing and, well . . . he'll be in with other . . . other notorious . . . *hated* prisoners. So it might be a blessing in disguise.'

He shook his head at the news. '*Peterhead*. But that's at least a hundred and fifty miles away! How do they expect you and the kids to be able to get there regularly?'

She looked up. 'The authorities don't care about that sort of thing. He's just a number. All they care about is how to manage him with the minimum of trouble.'

'I'm sorry, Ailsa. I really am. And the children? How're they?'

She sipped at her drink with a grimace, obviously not enjoying it. 'Mhari seems quite used to university life now. St Andrews suits her. She's still by the sea, is enjoying the course and has made . . . or . . . is beginning to make some friends. I don't know what she tells them of her background. If they've put two and two together, recognized her name or whatever. I don't know. She mentions a boy's name quite a lot. That might be a good thing. She never really had herself a proper boyfriend at home. Not very confident in that way. Always thought all the other girls were prettier. So, hopefully things will go all right for Mhari.'

'And the boys? How's wee Miller?'

He watched as the twitch of a frown crossed her face before she hid it again. She'd resumed her head-down posture, this time fidding with her glass and swilling the whisky round and round as if in some meditative ritual, the candle flames picking out golden sparkles on the moving liquid.

'I'm at my wits' end with him, Duncan. Greg's okay. He's doing fine at school although I've had quite a few meetings with his teachers. To discuss what's best under the circumstances. But Greg's got a very calm, *detached* way with himself. Always has had. He cares so much about his wee brother, even if he doesn't always show it.'

He asked the question again, sensing her reluctance to fully answer the first time. 'And Miller?'

She slid her glass on to the table and covered her face with both hands. 'He keeps wanting to go away in a boat and sail around the Firth. Just him and Bella! It's like some nightmarish "Owl and the Pussycat" tale! He says he just wants to be with Bella, his sea and his birds. That's how he puts it, his birds. I've had to get the harbourmaster to secure both our boats *and* Forbes's one too or Miller'd be off. He's gone out on his own in our dinghy before now.'

She paused to swallow back tears. Her tetchy veneer was dissolving. 'I think Miller's . . . I think the laddie's very disturbed. I've been talking to Forbes, y'know Forbes Buchan? Forbes is speaking to his medical contacts and we're going to get someone to see him. A specialist who's used to dealing with disturbed children. But I don't know. I just don't know about these things. I'm keeping him off school at the moment. He went up to the big school, where Greg is, in September, and that seemed to go okay. Then there was the trial and you know how nightmarish that was. Then Christmas. That was so depressing. Now this . . . this alone at sea obsession.'

He refilled his own glass, not bothering to offer her any more. She'd given up on her nightcap, the need to talk clearly vital to her.

She looked up at him, hands still pressed against the gaunt face.

'Oh Duncan, it's the living end. I mean . . . who knows the workings of a child's mind? Especially Miller's. He's always been an unusual boy. Very bright. More interested in animals, the natural world, than people. In fact he's so much his father's son. There have been times when I've felt that Doug would've been happy taking off and just sailing around day and night. On his own except for his constant companion, Bella. *Silly man!*' Anxiety flitted across her eyes. 'And Miller's definitely inherited those traits, so, Lord help us all.'

She took a deep calming breath, obviously on the verge of tears again. 'I can't get through to Miller now but . . . but

Greg's been helping. He was marvellous with his wee brother over the Christmas period. Just there for him. Mhari found him a bit of a problem. She used to play the bully with Miller. Always needling him. I think she was envious of his braininess. She wanted to think she was the brightest. But she's over that phase now, really growing up. But Miller's prolonged silences and dark moods, this staring for hours through the binoculars at the sea, had her a bit unnerved. Although she did make one good suggestion and said we should invite Catriona Buchan over. Miller's very fond of her and she's a lovely girl. So we had Catriona and Forbes over a good bit at Christmas. I think it helped Miller . . . though there was one very bad evening but . . . overall, I think it did him some good.'

She stopped suddenly and flashed him a doubtful, fearful look.

'At least, I pray it did.'

21

24 December, 1974

'Tantallon's not open at this time of year, Miller. It's a waste of time. We should've stayed at home with your mum and my dad and played Monopoly. In the warm. With hot chocolate.' Catriona sounded annoyed.

But Greg was winking at him behind her back as they stacked their bicycles against the car-park fence. 'Ah, but Mill knows a secret way in. Don't you, Mill? Lead on!'

Miller shrugged. 'It's not exactly secret. Just common sense. This way.' He led them round to the low entrance gate padlocked for the winter, and in two swift movements he was on the other side.

He watched Catriona, gloved hands on hips, half smile and shake her head. 'What? Is that it? Just over the gate? Not very exciting. I thought there might be secret tunnels!'

But he'd turned away and was trudging across grass that crackled underfoot from an overnight frost and dusting of snow. He was glad to be out of the house. Glad Catriona was here. Glad Greg was here too. Though he suspected that neither of them really wanted to be. Still, he'd rather be outdoors any day. He heard the other two, yards behind him, muttering in low tones – probably about him.

He trotted up to the top of the mound where the ground flattened out into a vast open expanse of short grass, with the bulk of the castle ruins straight ahead. It might be freezing but it was one of those very still, blue-sky winter days. No wind.

Perfect for a trip to the top of the battlements! And that was why he was here. He quickened his pace, leaving the others further behind, passing through the main gate, always a rather dark and claustrophobic area. On the other side, the castle ruins opened out into another vast expanse of grass called 'The Close', and before him lay a panoramic view of the Firth of Forth, the pale guano-covered hulk of the Bass Rock squatting in the sea, off-centre to the left. No matter how often he came here, the moment when he passed through the gate, and the view hit him, always took his breath away. He moved forwards to the wooden bench that stood at the edge of The Close, where the land stopped and cliffs took over.

Through the stillness he could hear Greg's voice before he appeared through the castle gate. 'Hey, Mill! What's yer hurry?'

Half a minute later, Greg and Catriona had jogged over to him. Catriona looked pleased.

'It's brilliant here on our own. When Dad's brought me here, it's usually in the summer and there's been too many tourists. It's just so different when it's quiet.'

He was relieved that she seemed to think the trip worth it now. Time to do the best bit. 'D'you want to climb up to the battlements? All the way up there!'

All three of them were craning their necks following his pointing finger.

Greg answered first. 'I'm going to look at the dungeon and things. Maybe I'll be up later.'

With that he skipped off. Miller nodded after him. Greg didn't have much of a head for heights, but he wasn't going to tell Catriona that. 'He means the pit-prison. It's in the basement of the tower there. You've probably seen it before. Horrible place. Anyway, let's get up to the battlements. The west stairway's always open.'

The spiralling climb, holding on to rope banisters as the

way grew narrower and steeper, took them a few minutes. Then they were there. He allowed Catriona to go ahead of him and watched her smile in wonder.

'Wow! I've not been up here in years. It's fantastic! You can really see how cleverly they built this place. We're just teetering on the edge of the cliff. The sea must be, what? A couple of hundred feet below. Unbelievable!'

She sat herself down on the stone floor of the battlements and gestured for him to do the same. He felt the cold through the seat of his jeans but didn't care. He was surprised to see her bring out a packet of cigarettes and shook his head as she offered him one.

'Don't, whatever you do, tell my dad. He'd go fucking mental. Anyway, tell me. About you and this place? How often have you been coming here and how did you know you can just climb over the gate? I'd have thought it'd be much harder to get in after closing.'

He was sitting too near to her and inched away to his right. 'My . . . my dad always liked this place. He brought me here after closing sometimes. You can get great photos at sunset. The colours, you know? And with the binoculars you can see all the gannets on the Bass Rock. We used to come h—'

He had to stop. He could feel the tears starting. He pulled his woolly hat further down over his forehead. He didn't want her to see his eyes. But he'd been too late. She flicked her half-smoked cigarette over the battlements and moved closer to him.

'I'm sorry, Mill. I didn't mean . . . look, have you been to see him recently? Your mum take you?'

'Don't wanna go.'

'Why not?'

'Just don't.'

*

Shit, she'd buggered that up. He hadn't said anything for about five minutes. She hadn't even wanted to come out in the cold – on bikes! – with these two boys. But her dad had insisted. She'd felt annoyed that Mhari hadn't been forced to come out too. She still had a bike somewhere in the garage. It had been especially galling since she knew the Tantallon outing had been Mhari's idea. They all hoped that it would 'take Miller out of himself'.

Well that wasn't happening. He was just sitting there beside her. In the freezing cold, staring directly ahead at the sea. It was spooky. He hardly seemed to be breathing. Only the trickles of vapour coming from his nostrils indicated that he was. Still, she wanted to find out more about what was going on with him. It was important.

'Mill? Miller? Listen, please don't be like this. Talk to me. Tell me what you think. 'Bout your dad, I mean. Do you . . . d'you think he did it? Is that it? Your mum and Greg and Mhari obviously don't. Other folk too. Dunc-the-monk. Mrs Watt. One or two other people.'

Nothing.

She tried again. 'Well? What d'you think?'

His reaction made her jump. He was on his feet and sprinting to the end of the battlements, smashing into the metal chain-link fence at the end. The top of it must have jarred him on the shoulder and hurt. But she could've sworn he'd run into it deliberately.

She'd caught up with him. 'What you doing? *Miller!*'

He was ignoring her. Just staring over the fence and down the cliffside to the sea, foaming hundreds of feet below. And then he turned to her, his face white against the dark stone of the tower ruins.

'*Of course Dad did it! Who else could have! I hate him!*'

Suddenly, he made a leap for the fence, the toes of his

wellington boots scrabbling and somehow finding purchase on the mesh.

'*Miller! Stop! Stop! Get him. Catriona, get him!*'

She spun round. Greg was hammering along the battlements towards her, slipping once on an icy patch but miraculously recovering his balance. He too slammed into the fence, both hands grabbing at Miller's duffel-coat hood.

'*Help me, Catriona! Get him down!*'

Miller, though smaller and lighter, was kicking against them, lashing out furiously. One leg was over the fence now. She saw Greg look down at the rocks and sea below, swaying slightly, his eyes closed against the sight. He was clearly terrified but kept pulling at his brother.

Two against one eventually triumphed. The three of them fell back in a heap, Greg taking the brunt of the impact on the stone, his wheeze loud as the wind was thumped out of him. She tried pulling herself up and away from the tangle of bodies but the low animal moan stopped her. Miller was rocking to and fro, Greg holding him tight, his arms around him, his head on top of Miller's, mumbling into his ear.

'It's all right, Mill. All right.' Greg looked up at her. 'What the hell happened? Why would he try to do such a thing? What were you talking about, Cattie?'

'I . . . I . . . just . . . I was talking to him about your dad, about what folk thought, what *he* felt. I thought it would do him good to get it out of his system. To talk about things. I'm . . . I'm sorry.'

But Greg didn't seem angry at her. Just puzzled. 'What did he say?'

'He said that he thought your dad was guilty. And that he hated him.'

22

'Are you sure you're comfortable? Here. Walking in these parts?'

Duncan waited as Ailsa climbed the last few feet and joined him, sitting on the stump of a long-felled tree, pulling a flask from his haversack. 'Let's stop for the view and a cup o' this soup. Brother Francis's best. That man would make a fortune as a chef in the outside world. Sometimes I think it's the main reason why half the guests come to the abbey. For his cuisine.' He caught her smile. She seemed in lighter mood than of late. With some relief he asked his question again.

'You okay, Ailsa? Being here?'

'I'm all right, Duncan, thank you. It's not as if this is the exact spot where she went missing. Nonetheless, I wouldn't have come back to these hills on my own. It's not just . . . because of what happened . . . it's in case I meet anyone who knows me or knows who I am. I mean it's nigh on eighteen months since they took Douglas away, so I'm used to the looks and comments by now. But I still don't like being on my own if there's any awkwardness. It's okay if I'm walking along a busy North Berwick high street. I just don't like being caught alone.'

She paused and he caught a flicker of worry crossing her features before she went on.

'The worst time was when I was walking Bella way way

beyond the West Sands, almost at Yellowcraigs. I usually wouldn't go that far but I was just lost in thought, a bit down, not noticing things. Thinking back, I *had* been aware of someone hurrying past on the track by the golf course. I remember thinking, I wonder why they're running. It wasn't one of the usual folk in their tracksuits, doing their training or what have you. This was a big man in a dark coat and cap pulled right down over his face.

'Anyway, just as I was passing a group of rocks he stepped out on the beach in front of me and crouched down as if to pet Bella. Well, you know what a friendly, trusting dog she is. She went running up to him and everything was okay for a few seconds. Then, as I drew close, I was aware of Bella squirming and then coughing and half yelping. It took me a second to work it out . . . I couldn't believe it! He had her by her collar and was twisting it, choking her! It was horrible . . . and then . . . then he shoved Bella away and she came whimpering back to my heel.

'I asked him what he wanted. He stood up and said that he knew Jacquie's, that's Jacqueline Galbraith's, family and that they were going through hell. That I'd better watch out for *my* family. I was absolutely shaking by this time. He was about to come closer towards us when a couple of dog walkers came into view. Then he ran off. I've tried never to be on my own like that again.'

He noted her unsteady hand as she took the cup of steaming soup from him.

'Did you tell the police?'

She stopped, cup midway to her lips. 'Oh *come on*, Duncan! D'you think for one minute they'd be bothered? Probably silently cheer whoever the bully boy was. No, it would be pointless. I've just warned the children not to get into isolated situations. Of course, I didn't tell them what happened.

I don't want them scared. But I do keep an eye on where they say they're going and who with.'

She was returning home tomorrow. He shifted uneasily, the surface of the tree stump rough underneath him.

'Look, Ailsa . . . I've been meaning to ask you this for a while and I thought it better to let a bit of time pass. But I do worry about you. Those boys of yours too. Especially wee Miller. It's just that you've never . . . never really talked about Douglas's conviction. I . . . I just wonder what you feel, I mean *really* feel about everything?'

In reply she handed him back the cup, still full, and stood up, wandering a few steps away to take in the view of hills and farmland rolling towards the sea, miles into the distance. 'What d'you mean, what I *really* feel? D'you mean, do I think Douglas is guilty? Is *that* what you mean, Duncan?'

The question had obviously been a blunder. Her mood was changing, the familiar touchy, defensive tone back again. He wanted to apologize for being clumsy but thought better of it.

She turned round to look at him at last. What was it in her face? Accusation? Anger? Fear maybe? 'It's simple. I *have* to believe Douglas is innocent. Otherwise, how can I go on? *How? Tell me how?*'

The outburst was bordering on the hysterical and she was making no attempt to hide her tears. But within moments she'd rallied, merely standing, arms limply by her sides, the silent sobs shaking her thin frame. Fury, fear, confusion, and impotence at her situation. It was all there. He knew to stay back. Let her take her time. She walked a few feet to her left and sat on a rocky outcrop facing him.

'There's no one else in the world I'd admit this to. No one I could trust enough. Of all the things that were against Doug . . . even the bodies of those poor lassies . . . I could somehow even explain them away to myself as being the work of someone else. No, it was the alibi evidence. The lad who worked for the coastguard, Andy Blackford, knew Douglas quite well and I knew him to say hello to. His fiancée as well. It wasn't just a nodding acquaintance between Douglas and Andy. I remember Doug was thinking of buying a boat off him a few years back. And Doug, in fact all of us, saw Andy out in the Firth on patrol quite often when we were toing and froing between Fidra and the mainland. The man even offered to let Miller come on the coastguard boat once, shortly before Doug's arrest. Doug's defence really tried to play down the relationship, making out he hardly knew Andy. It worried me because it was a lie. Watching Andy in court, I think it annoyed him. It made me furious with Doug and his lawyers. It was a stupid thing to do.'

'So, d'you think this Andy Blackford was lying, exaggerating what he saw?'

She was shaking her head vigorously. 'Not a man in his position. Being in the coastguard's a very responsible and respected job. And that's just it. If Andy Blackford thought he saw Douglas . . .' She tailed off and was looking down, picking nervously away at the finger of her glove. 'But I have to believe he was mistaken. I have to trust Douglas. I *need* to. I owe him that. Though I'm finding it awfy hard sometimes, Duncan, I promise you that.'

She stopped fiddling with her glove and looked directly at him, her expression challenging. 'And what about you, Duncan? What do you think? *Really* think.'

It was the question that he most feared but unavoidable if he was asking the same of her. He sighed deeply before giving a reply.

'Evil can be, *is*, found in the most unexpected places. Let's pray it doesn't reside in Douglas.'

That was no sort of answer and he could feel her disappointment. But her response surprised him.

'*Pray?* Well then, you're lucky, Duncan! I've not been able to pray since the day Douglas was arrested. *I'm in hell!*' She offered him a final bitter look before standing up and turning away from him.

He almost laughed out loud! If only he could tell her *his* truth. That he'd been unable to pray for considerably longer than that and wondered if he ever would again. Wondered how he could go on justifying wearing the robes of a holy man. But that was his hell.

His alone.

23

As Duncan drove away from the harbour he thought back over the previous night's events. He and the McAllister boy had shared the better part of a bottle of whisky, and he was feeling it now. Miller had looked none too fresh this morning either. It was odd, the lad . . . had what? *Under*-reacted for most of the evening? He would've expected the news about Lena Stewart to have had more of an effect. Instead, Miller had nodded, asked a few questions, and then gone silent. That was it. He either had superhuman self-control or he just didn't care. Impossible to know. The laddie had a morose, gloomy air about him. Depressed? Almost certainly. But then again, as a child Miller had always been hard to read. Especially once Douglas had been arrested. Ailsa had had the devil's own job with him. Was that it? Had the boy spent his entire existence drifting away into glum silences? In her last year or two of life, Ailsa had confessed that she'd given up trying to understand her youngest child. She'd hinted that she thought all was not well in her son's marriage, and his life in general, but didn't elaborate. 'He's married the wrong woman and he's made a lot of wrong choices, wrong decisions over the years. But only he can discover that for himself.'

That wasn't the whole story. Over time, Ailsa had catalogued to him her myriad failures at getting Miller to engage in any way in a discussion about his father's guilt or innocence. He'd refused all her implorings to visit his father, or at least write him a few lines. Recruiting Mhari and Greg to try and persuade him had also failed. Miller had caused his mother untold pain, there was no getting away from it, but she would never have let him know.

As for Douglas McAllister? Duncan sighed to himself. He'd done his best for Doug, hadn't he? Used his good offices as a respected member of a religious community to secure what small advantages he could for Douglas in the early days. But after his conviction? It was all change then. The distance had set in. Douglas had accepted the occasional visit. But there was no warmth of welcome. Well, he certainly wasn't visiting out of a missionary zeal to recruit a repentant sinner to the church. Doug knew that. No, there were other, more deeply felt reasons for his coolness . . .

'. . . It's bloody ironic. She confides in a monk more than she does in her own husband. I'm not going to rehearse my views on the Church here with you, Duncan. I'm sure Ailsa has given you chapter and verse on that. I do believe her retreats do her good. It's not the first time she's been on them. Didn't you put her on to that convent up the coast that she went to a few times? I never batted an eyelid at that, as long as she was happy. Nor her stays now at your guest house. If nothing else, they take her away from the staring eyes and poisonous gossip of some of the locals.'

And then he'd leaned forwards, gripping the table with a white-knuckled intensity.

'But I want to ask you something, Duncan. Exactly what part did you play in her decision, eh? You must have had some role? What did she tell you? That she cared so little for me and our children that she could walk out just like that without a backward glance. What kind of bloody God could allow, encourage that? Tell me. You're the expert, aren't you? Her spiritual advisor? Confessor? Did she ever

148

*discuss our marriage? Pah! Even if she did, I suppose you wouldn't
feel able to tell me. The seal of the confessional, eh?'*

*'I don't take confession, Douglas. You know that. But I am
Ailsa's friend.'*

*'But not my friend? I believe her when she says she's changed her
mind. That she'll stand by me in this . . . this hell! But let me confide
in you. Part of me feels I'd never be in this if she hadn't fucked up
our marriage. If she'd never had me in despair that night, driving and
wandering aimlessly around. Alone. No alibi, no defence. I try not to
think about it. But sometimes I can't help it. Can't help blaming her.
She has her share of guilt to carry over this . . .'*

It had been an uncomfortable visit. There hadn't been many
more. Until the end. Here at the hospice.

He found her in a corner of the empty tea room. 'Sorry
I'm late, Lizzie. I'm a bit slow in starting today.'

She looked very tired. Worn out. She shrugged. 'It's okay.
I'm just off the night shift myself. Bad night. Two patients
in a terrible state. Anyway, did you talk to him?'

He nodded. 'He was at the island. I went over there.
Stayed the night.'

'And? Did you tell him 'bout Auntie Lena? Cos if you
didn't, I'm going to. I know you w—'

He held up a hand to placate her. 'It's okay. I'm sure you
would have told him but I think it was better coming from
me. At least I know Miller. I told him about Lena. He took
it very calmly, considering. Anyway, he's going to be up here
for a while. I get the impression he's thinking a great deal
about his dad. He's got a lot to take on board.'

She snorted. 'Aye! Including a lifetime's guilt at not standing by his own loving father.'

He put his big hand over hers. 'Look, Lizzie. This is exactly
what I meant before. About not jumping to conclusions.'

The look was belligerent. 'What?'

He sighed, shaking his head. 'You know what, Lizzie? I think I should speak to Lena before she talks to Miller. I said it before and I'll say it again. Just because Lena lied doesn't mean that Douglas McAllister was innocent.'

24

'What d'you mean you're staying up there? I thought you were just going to get the estate valued and get the sale moving. What the hell's going on? We need you back here, Miller. It seems like you've been away for bloody ages! The kids keep asking when you're coming back. They're missing you.'

'And you, Nikki? Are you missing me?'

'What? Of course. Now come on back.'

He wasn't sure if the momentary pause had been in his imagination. He thought things were okay now but there was something about . . . about what exactly? Her tone? Distance? Whatever. He'd decided.

'Look, Nikki, I'd like you and the kids to come up here next weekend. Come and stay on the island.'

There was no doubting the pause this time. He thought she'd hung up.

Then she was off. 'You *are* joking! What the hell's come over you? I made the offer to come up before but you bit my head off. You've always said that you'd never tell Emma and Callum *anything* about your father. Christ, it's been hard enough on the rare occasions when they've mixed with Mhari's kids to monitor any conversation in case it strays into grandparent territory. Christ, the grandparent nightmare runs in the bloody family! You never saw yours and our kids only saw your mother down here once in a blue moon. Thank God I've got a normal family! Now suddenly you want to take our kids to the island! What's going on, Miller? Have you lost your mind? Jesus! This is all I need. I'm up to my eyes with the business, you've buggered off and . . . and what about *your* office? *Your* work responsibilities? They'll want you back. *For God's sake!* You can't bunk off work, just leave me with a two- and a six-year-old *and* a full-time business to run *and* think that's okay! Look, get home, Miller. *Now!*'

The terse phone conversation buzzed round his head as he stood looking over towards the mainland house. As usual, he felt she was being unfair, exaggerating. Her 'eco-tourist' travel company was doing just fine. Small but lucrative. It could run itself. Or rather, the hard-pressed but remarkably good-natured assistants in her office ran it with super efficiency, despite having a boss like Nikki. No, she was being deliberately unreasonable with him. Spoiling for a fight. He'd won, though. She and the kids and the dog would be here in a few days' time.

The wind was biting but the day was as clear as you could wish for. Better to do what he was about to on a lovely day. Duncan Alexander's visit had more than unsettled him. Truth be known, he'd spent the last two days trying to find some way of denying the implications of what he'd been told. But whether or not one had any religious beliefs, a monk, a hospice nurse, *and* a key prosecution witness were all saying the same things. And further, his father's letter, among all it had said to him, had left one, niggling aspect in his mind. Namely, that his sight of the body that dreadful day on this island had somehow transformed how he saw his father from that moment onwards. There had to be some truth in that notion. No doubt today some smart-arsed shrink could lay it all out before him just as his childhood one had. But right now he didn't need that. He'd always recognized that event as the crystallizing of his belief in his father's guilt, or rather, the end of his idyllic childhood innocence. Crucially, the end of his, until then, inviolable sense of his father's protection. At that moment he knew that he'd wanted someone to pay for what he saw that day, and somehow it had been the easiest thing in the world to blame his father. He'd got his wish and his father had been taken away from him. For ever.

Yet here he was, still reluctant to let it all go. What he held in his hand was the worst part of the legal archive. He'd given the police photographs no more than a cursory glance when he'd first taken receipt of the box from Russell Sinclair. He'd eventually looked a bit closer. But only after some Dutch courage. You had to have some sort of crutch to be able to look at these things. Prior to Duncan's disclosures the photos helped to convince him. Spur him on into effectively saying goodbye and good riddance to this family's hellish past. And so, he'd try it again. In glaring daylight and sobriety. With the knowledge he now had.

The whistling of the ear-aching wind, and the screeching of the ever-present herring gulls added to his tension as he scrambled the last few yards to the chapel ruins. Then, miraculously, he was in near silence, cocooned by the surrounding hillocks, safely hidden from the elements. The dry-stane dyke around the ruins was in good order. Something Forbes Buchan or Mhari had seen to over the years? That reminded him. He'd picked up a message Catriona had left on the machine at the mainland house. He should ring her back. The idea made him nervous. He pushed the thought away, settling himself into the sheltered nook.

There wasn't much to see here. Never had been. Not on the surface. Everything . . . everything had been underneath. What he was looking for had long disappeared, now overgrown with moss and grass, stones and rocks providing a final covering. He sat down, his back to the north wall of the dyke, and opened up this worst part of the legal archive.

The photographs were held in a small album. The thick card cover worn with use had the words *Property of Lothian & Borders Police* typed starkly on it. He'd been through quite a few of these during his short career as a prosecutor in the Edinburgh criminal courts. A career path consciously chosen in defiance of his father and as an attempt to make amends for what he'd done. But less than two years on, it had all gone up in smoke. If asked why, he'd always replied: 'Because the guilty bastards keep getting off.' It hadn't been as simple as that, of course, but it was answer enough. London and the relative simplicities of corporate law – unencumbered by the extremes of human emotional misery – beckoned, bringing considerable rewards. Up to a point. Until a nagging, and eventually overwhelming, ennui had set in.

He blocked that particularly unwelcome memory and fingered the album in his lap, trying to ignore the trembling in his hand. There were about two dozen photos in this, the only surviving album in the archive, of which about half charted the descent into hell. Thankfully, they were black and white. The twisted pale leg and what he knew had been the reddish black gash at the throat looked somehow unreal. Completely unconnected to his abiding memory of that moment when he'd watched the frenzy of police on this spot, an incredible thirty-two years ago. What he now knew to be decomposition had made the face, in particular, look so distorted to his eleven-year-old mind, adding to the night-mares and flashbacks that were to come. Ones that poor Greg had inherited by some osmotic process. Probably from eavesdropping on explicit conversations between Dr Buchan and their mother about events on the island that terrible day. Poor Greg. He'd repeatedly asked what had happened but Miller had refused to respond, claiming soon after that he couldn't remember much. It didn't take long for their mother, and Mhari, and Dr Buchan probably, to variously have a word with Greg and warn him off any further probing. But his little brother's trauma must have been all too easy to see and feel, leaving Greg more affected than he'd ever admitted.

Maybe that was it. In his ignorance of the true picture, Greg's imagination had gone into overdrive, unleashing years of gruesome nightmares. Just like his own. Their poor mother. What it must've been like dealing with them both, *and* his persistent bed-wetting that had begun the first night after the discovery of the bodies. As for the episode on Tantallon's battlements, he'd grown very adept at not confronting that memory. Except in his own nightmares.

Strange, despite her having witnessed so much of his disturbed sleep, he'd never told Nikki the full story of what had happened that day, of what he'd seen, of why he *still* dreamed about it. She'd never asked him about anything, not in recent years. Thinking on it now, it emphasized more than ever the emotional gulf that had always existed between them but which he was just beginning to wake up to. Also, he had wondered over the years if at some point Mhari had taken it upon herself to tell Nikki the grim details of his childhood trauma. He had no evidence of this but he knew Mhari's relationship with Nikki had at one stage been, if not close, then very chummy.

He flicked quickly through the album, moving towards the few images at the end. Oddly, although these ones had no hint of the recently dead – quite the reverse – they unsettled him most of all. The first photograph was fairly straightforward. An overall record of the remains, in situ. Each of the two skeletons lay on their right side, knees slightly bent towards what would have been their stomachs, the hands in front, at breast level, the heads bent backwards, chins up. Out of their grim context they might easily have passed as illustrative plates in some old archaeology tome.

But they were far from that. The close-ups told a more detailed story. Identical in both cases. The wrist bones retained the evidence of the bonds used to tie them together: lengths of halyard rope, familiar to any sailor. The skulls were more than bent backwards. They were thrust back towards the shoulder blades, each mouth gaping, the exposed teeth adding to the impression of a rictus snarl. It was what lay above the mouths, however, that had left him reeling the first time he saw these images. He'd read about this macabre feature of the crimes in the court documents and in some of the more sensational reporting of the case. Seeing it was a different matter. What could then only have been eye sockets had been smothered by thick blindfolds. Blindfolds of packing tape wound around the heads, again and again and again.

While all the previous entries in the album had recorded the disturbing, the cruel, the sickening, it was the final two photos that held the saddest record of the hell that had befallen these girls. Positioned at the back of each victim, and running the length of their curved spines, were the dog leashes. Simple items. But here so full of meaning. He snapped the album shut and lay it to one side on the grass. Had this self-conscious attempt to reignite his feelings about what had happened here made any difference? He had been so careful to keep some sort of track of what he was feeling these past few days. If for no other reason than to strengthen his resolve to clear everything up and move on. But the journey was turning out to be far from straightforward. Initially, all was as he'd expected. The feelings of . . . of what at the hospice? Satisfaction at his father's end? Fear at being in a place of death? And then anger, no, near fury at the will. Irritation at Mhari's self-righteous behaviour. Frustration at Greg's usual indifference to, and abdication of, family responsibility. But then the familiar changed.

Then there was Dad's letter. And then there was Duncan Alexander. And then there was Catriona.

25

She was twenty minutes late. If it was work holding her up, she might have called. And she couldn't have got lost. She knew how to get to the mainland house with her eyes shut. He had half a mind to call her on the mobile number she'd left and cancel. But what difference did it make if she was late? He wasn't going anywhere. Maybe she'd had a change of heart about visiting. Miller hunched down by the fire, vigorously stirring it up with the poker and tossing on another log, setting off a momentary vortex of spitting embers. The last thing he felt like tonight was any company, so if she couldn't come, then fine. The past day or two since his island visit had left him feeling flat and down. The conflicting feelings, the 'what ifs' about his father, sat in his mind like a yawning chasm ready to swallow him up. He'd tried repeatedly to avoid it but he was, quite simply, driving himself mad. The effort was debilitating, preventing sleep, rest, relaxation. He was worse than down. He was reaching desperation. And the fact he had no one to share it with, the loneliness, inner and outer – though, paradoxically, he'd been craving solitude – was perhaps the worst aspect of all.

To add to the hell, clearing out and allocating his mother's and father's remaining belongings had affected him more deeply than he'd expected. He'd given it up for now. The worst moment had been when he'd come across old family photos taken before his father's arrest. He'd put most of them away except a few including Catriona. She might find them amusing, although he couldn't escape the chilling images from the police photo album, crowding in on those in front of him. An unsettling comparison.

He got to his feet, pausing to examine the snapshots he'd arrayed along the mantelpiece. His mother had had an irritating and embarrassing habit when it came to photos. She'd put them neatly in one of the numerous albums she kept, and write cheesy captions beneath each, *and* repeat the same on the back in case they lost their place in the album. The first snap he'd pulled out had the legend 'Beach Belles' and showed a happy, smiling Catriona in a pale, cool dress, leaning against the harbour wall accompanied by a surly-looking Mhari. Possibly taken before a summer holiday excursion to Fidra? Or a beach party? It was an unflattering one of Mhari and he was surprised she hadn't ripped it up years ago. As had been, and still was as far as he knew, her usual practice.

He almost missed the faint tap on the door. He welcomed her in along with a flurry of dead, sodden leaves from the garden, blown in by a rogue gust.

'God, thank goodness the weather's broken a bit, though the rain's back on. The storms have barely stopped all week.' Catriona gave a short laugh, hands clasped in mock prayer. '*Please*. Let us have some respite!'

She shook herself out of her raincoat, casting around for somewhere to put it.

A conversation about the weather! His first reaction was relief. Gone was the brittleness he'd sensed at the funeral. Yes, she'd exhibited a kind of superficial warmth and openness there – just a good bedside manner, he suspected – but now she seemed more relaxed. She was fumbling about in her bag.

'Here. I noticed you were drinking red wine at the funeral. I'm partial myself. Hope you like this one.'

*

She was drinking very slowly because of the car, and he knew he was drinking too fast. They were three quarters of the way through her gift of an undoubtedly expensive burgundy. He'd had most of it *and* a couple of glasses of cheaper stuff before she arrived. She'd spent the first few minutes demanding, in the nicest possible way, a guided tour of the house, saying that she remembered it so well but that she'd never stepped inside it since she was young. That had puzzled him. Hadn't she made friends with his mother in recent years? She had explained that it was an article of faith for his mother that she always meet Catriona somewhere in town. To show the gossips that she wasn't afraid to be seen in local cafés and restaurants. Also, the public endorsement of a friendship with a popular, respected GP was, his mother had apparently told her, a very strengthening experience. This had come as some surprise to him, marking out his mother as a more strategic thinker than he'd ever considered her to be.

Although now feeling more than half drunk, he hoped he was holding it together okay. He'd managed to keep Catriona doing most of the talking by asking as many questions as possible, although she'd given nothing away about her personal life. Well, that was none of his business anyway, although he had to admit that he'd like to know what she'd been doing with herself these past thirty years other than being a doctor. Was she married? Divorced? Children? In this arena she had the advantage of him, his mother having told her all about his family life with Nikki, Emma and Callum. Catriona asked about them but never reciprocated with any similar information of her own. Fair enough. He stuck to what he thought she felt most comfortable with.

'And your Dad? I really liked him. Always so nice to me

as a kid. Great GP. Anyway, I remember Mum telling me on the phone about his stroke.'

She shrugged, still sipping at her first drink. 'Yeah, out of the blue. And not. Dad didn't have the most advisable lifestyle. Drinker, pipe smoker, little exercise and too much driving. Quite typical of his generation of doctors.' She laughed. 'Not too far from my own in fact. Some of the colleagues I've had! Death wish or what! Dad had had a history of strokes, leading to him having to take very early retirement. Eventually, they got the better of him. The second last stroke was a severe one. Very disabling. I was working down in the Borders at the time, living in Peebles. As luck would have it, a GP's position was advertised here about the same time as Dad became really ill. So I relocated. He didn't last much longer after that. He had one more and it finished him off.'

Right. Maybe she didn't have any ties then, to be able to uproot herself just like that. He refilled his glass, veering the bottle towards hers but she shook her head. She seemed to drift into a memory for a moment, her face unreadable, though the mouth set firm. Then she was back with him.

'After that it was your mum. Poor Ailsa. Her heart attack was so unexpected. I'm sorry. It must have been an appalling time for you, with . . . well, considering everything.'

It was probably the wine that was fuelling his boldness but he thought it worth telling her the truth about the recent past.

'Actually, apart from being sad, very sad at her death, that time was remarkably easy in other ways. I considered myself to be orphaned then. My father, using Greg and Mhari, *still* tried to get me to visit him, write to him. I refused. As I'm sure you know, there was a . . . a *contretemps* at Mum's funeral. After that, it was easy. Easy to get on with my life. As far as I was concerned I didn't have a father. Hadn't had since I was eleven. But Mum would always slip his name in somewhere. I mean . . . you may know much of this from Mum herself but I never came back here . . . well, not until she died. I refused. I'd have Mum down to London to see the kids and things, and same with Mhari, and Greg too, when he was visiting friends or passing through London. Then th—'

He faltered and took a slug of the wine.

'Then there was his diagnosis?' She'd finished the sentence for him.

He slid his glass on to the table. 'Yes. And that changed everything.'

'Is that why you came back? To see him for one last time?'

He slumped back deeper into the armchair, the creaking and shifting of the house about them making him feel safe, insulated from harm. He'd always loved it as a child – still did – especially if there was a storm. The house had felt so secure. His very own Tantallon Castle. He looked over at her in the dim lamplight. She leaned forwards to top up his glass, half smiling, waiting for him to reply. In all honesty, he no longer knew what the answer was to anything to do with his father.

'I wasn't going to come back to see him. You may think that callous but I really *wasn't* going to come back. Then . . . then I thought of Mum. What she'd think, what she'd want. The pressure was building up. Mhari had given me a running commentary on everything, trying to make me come up. Greg called a lot too. He came over from Spain and visited Dad a couple of times at the hospice. Anyway, I left it to the last minute. Just hammered up the motorway non-stop from London. Actually I must've been in some bizarre fugue state. Can't remember much of the journey. All I know is that I drove fast and arrived in the middle of the night. Forty minutes too late. But I saw him. It was dreadful.'

'Death is dreadful. It just is.' Her voice was soft, barely audible.

He sat forwards, head bowed, running his hands through his hair. Her tone was even gentler.

'I'm sorry, Mill. I think this is too upsetting for you. I'll go.'

She was getting up but he laid a hand on her forearm. 'No, please. Don't. Things . . . things have become very complicated for me, about my father. My feelings . . . just keep vacillating. One moment this, another way the next . . . and . . . all in such a terrifyingly short space of time.'

He paused, mildly embarrassed by this self-revealing outburst. 'It's all happening too quickly. I don't respond well to change. It's just that I've made what is beginning to feel like . . . well, like a monumental journey. I feel odd. Don't know why. I just do. Frightened, maybe, too.'

26

'Thank you for listening. I've not actually laid it all out like that, rationally, to a third party, before tonight. It's been a great help. Truly.'

Catriona had been a remarkably good listener. He couldn't remember the last time he'd felt comfortable talking, not just about the events surrounding his father's conviction, but his *feelings* about his father, now so torn between extremes. It had been made easier by the knowledge that, during their regular tête-à-têtes, Catriona and his mother had discussed, in detail, the slow path to recovery of the young Miller, and his growth into the successful, highly functioning adult he now was. Or appeared to be – his inner defences were perhaps the most highly functioning part of him. Could she tell? That apart, if he'd known at the time that his mother was discussing him in such intimate terms, *and* to Catriona of all people, he would have blown a fuse. But now he was grateful for it.

The only painful, indeed still terrifying issue which Catriona hadn't brought up, was the Tantallon battlements episode and its aftermath during that terrible first Christmas following his father's conviction. It had been his crisis as a child, his cry for help the psychologist had said, and thankfully nothing behaviourally so severe had ever been repeated. If it had been, he was certain he'd have ended up in a mental hospital. Catriona must have covered that time in her chats with his mother. But she, sensitively, had chosen not to raise it tonight.

He smiled. 'I think it's been so easy to talk about everything because I consider you to be an honorary McAllister family member, if that makes sense? You were around so much in our childhood. Shared so much. It's been good to set things out. In fact, I was thinking of getting back in touch with Russell Sinclair and talking things through with him. I know he's not a well man but he so obviously believed in Dad.'

Catriona accepted her raincoat from him and paused. 'I'm sorry, Miller. I didn't want to say anything when you mentioned him earlier but I'll have to now. Russell Sinclair died two days ago. He was my patient. It came sooner than we thought, sadly. Very sudden deterioration.'

Miller leaned back heavily against the wall of the vestibule. '*Really?* I knew he was ill. What a bloody shame. He would've been so . . . so *encouraged* to know I was taking an interest. Look at this.' He opened the door to his father's old study where he was temporarily housing the box. 'That's it. What he sent me. All that remains of Dad's legal archive. That reminds me. It's got witness statements in it. I need to fish out Lena Stewart's before I meet her.'

'When are you going to see her?'

'Don't know yet. Dunc-the-monk's going to call me tomorrow. He's arranging it.'

He caught her smile at the nickname. Had it sparked off in her the same shared memory? Their childhood glee felt every time they'd used it when his mother's strange and exotic friend came visiting. Simple pleasures.

She'd finished buttoning up her coat. 'Tell you what. Let me know when you're going to see her and I'll come with you if you like. If you want some company, and another mind on things, I'll be happy to do it.'

He felt surprisingly heartened by her offer. He was no

fool. Neither was she. They'd already discussed the fact that Lena Stewart's story may not, in and of itself, mean exoneration for his father. He was also acutely aware that, despite all he'd told her about his changing views on his father, Catriona had not once said or intimated that she thought him innocent. Perhaps she did. But he didn't want to ask. Not yet. He was too afraid that her answer might chime with his rock-solid beliefs of the past thirty years. Just as they were beginning to shift.

'If you'd rather I didn't come th—' She'd obviously read his look as being one of refusal.

'No, no. I'd love you to. It's a really good idea to have another mind on the case, a bit of objectivity. Please, do come. I'll call you when it's been arranged. Now, safe journey home. Where d'you live by the way?'

'Oh, a bit further east from here, up the coast. I've got a cottage. It's my sanctuary. A lovely little two-storey stone-built place along by Canty Bay. Y'know, on the way to Tantallon?'

The spark of that other shared memory stopped them both. She spoke first. 'That day's still with me. I'm . . . I'm just so glad Greg was there. I . . . I froze.'

He shook his head. 'I don't think much about it to be honest.' He didn't know if the lie was convincing or not. All he *did* care about was that he wasn't going to talk about it now. Or ever? He shrugged and smiled.

'I was a pretty mad wee boy, eh? A real nutter.'

She half smiled back at him. 'No, you weren't. You were just very bright. And in a lot of pain. Especially that Christmas. Goodnight, Miller.'

She kissed him lightly on the cheek and was out the door before he could reply. Instead, he offered her a slow wave and turned, a little drunkenly, back into the house. As he closed the door and made his way to the living room he nodded to himself. She'd done it again. When she left, you felt it.

She was glad to be home. Glad for the isolation. Sea, rocks and sand. God, that had been a difficult hour and a half. It was odd, bizarre even, spending time with someone you'd known a lifetime ago. Someone who was thrusting intimacy on you by confiding things you didn't want to but had to hear. Miller was in a bad way. He'd made a brave attempt at self-control but his need to offload had won. Though in some ways, it hadn't been too difficult to deal with. Once she'd sensed his need to confide, it had been easy to distance herself from him. As if he was a patient, relieved to have a sympathetic ear at his disposal. When the floodgates had opened, he'd been unstoppable, bordering on manic in his delivery. All that stuff about re-examining his father's case. Surprising. Shocking even. It was taking its toll on him already. That was clear. And that reference to the Tantallon battlements episode. She wondered how much he really remembered about that. How much detail. What she'd said to him. '. . . *but I suppose it'll be very hard if your dad did do it, eh? Hard for everyone to live with . . .*' But it had only been the articulation of what she knew he thought.

She'd opened her own bottle of red, happy to plunder it without Miller's or anyone else's judging eyes. Christ, how she'd have liked to drink the way he had. With abandon, lucky sod! But she had to drive *and* she wanted to keep in control. It wasn't just *his* past, *his* feelings he was stirring up. There were others', her own included. She stared out of the kitchen window into black nothingness. She was used to it. She never felt afraid here.

She pulled open the table drawer. Russell Sinclair's death

had been a bad one. Yet another bad one. Great pain and fear at the last and too late to witness Miller's transformation. He had asked for her promise again. About the letter. Handed it over during a recent home visit. She nodded. Everything was beginning to have that strange feeling of synchronicity about it. That, in its turn, left her with a gnawing anxiety.

Dear Catriona

I do hope you don't mind me being so familiar with you, but calling you Dr Buchan outwith the consultation room seems so unnatural for someone I remember from when she was a little girl. As you're well aware, I knew your father – a fine man – as was his best friend, Douglas McAllister. At that time I didn't know either of them well. Just a passing acquaintance but I thought of you as two lovely families.

I would never have imagined such decent people suffering two tragedies. The loss of your mother when you were so young must have left your father in despair. Although I gather from Douglas that both you and your father spent a lot of time with the McAllisters so that you were, at times, a kind of extended family. Douglas talked so fondly of your many shared times together.

That a second tragedy should hit the same group of people surely beggars belief. Douglas's conviction affected you all but he was always so grateful for the help that your father offered dear Ailsa, and for the help that you offered her, once your poor father passed on. Those occasional lunches, coffees, general chats, were some solace to Ailsa, I'm certain.

Now I want to ask for your help again. One last time. You have heard me (and your kind father did many a time before that) talk of my dismay over the conviction of Douglas McAllister. I suppose patients bring in all their life's worries to your surgery at some time, not just their physical ailments. I hope I didn't bore you too much when I talked of Douglas. The realization that I failed him, both professionally and as a friend, has persisted over these past thirty-odd years. He, typical of the man, never laid any blame at my door. But his death and my own illness leave me desperate. It's not as if I leave behind some younger, committed, idealistic legal partner who can continue to carry Douglas's torch, albeit posthumously. And sadly, the leading QC who appeared for Douglas is long dead. Although, if still alive, I suspect he would be unable to offer you anything more on the conduct of the case than what I've told you. As for where we stand today? Legally, all courses have run dry. We did try, believe me, but fell at every hurdle.

No. Since Douglas's death, what I really hoped and <u>prayed</u> to be able to do was to somehow convince Douglas's youngest that his father was an unjustly convicted man. Probate issues have meant that I must be in touch with Miller (and his siblings). He is now up here but extremely hostile to any discussion of his father's innocence. However, he's to be here for a while, sorting out his family's affairs. Since he is here I wanted to ask for your help. Enlist some support. I don't feel that I can ask you this directly, and not in the context of a medical consultation. That would be too uncomfortable, for us both, I feel. What I would be eternally grateful for is if you might find the time, the inclination, to talk to Miller. By all means say that I asked you if you wish. I just wonder if a plea from someone younger, someone he knew at the time, might have some effect on Miller rethinking things.

I do hope you'll consider this and not think me presumptuous. I quite simply have no one else to ask who is trustworthy, respected, and who knew the family when their misfortune occurred.

My thanks to you.

Russell Sinclair

Reading through it again, the underlying assumption still struck her. Russell Sinclair had taken it as read that she considered Douglas McAllister to be innocent. She thought back to their recent few words at the funeral. Russell, tea cup and saucer clattering in his frail hand, had apologized for the letter. Said that he was going to have a final stab at talking to Miller then and there. She had reassured him: 'Please, it's perfectly okay. I, of all people, don't want you worried. If you feel you want to talk to Miller this afternoon then go ahead. I'll say hello to him later and see how things go. But don't worry. I *will* talk to him.'

Well, if only Russell Sinclair could witness Miller's near volte-face now. She placed the letter back in the drawer and slid the photo towards her. 'Beach Belles.' Her eye had been drawn to it and the handful of others on show on the mantelpiece. Miller had seemed to welcome the momentary respite from discussing his father, and they'd spent a pleasant few minutes studying the photos, laughing at the most embarrassing captions. He'd offered her this photo, saying that Mhari would bin it otherwise. She propped it up against the wine bottle and sat back, staring at the image until it blurred out of recognition. That day, what they were doing, she couldn't recall. But the atmosphere she could. Though apparently chums, Mhari's three years' seniority had got in the way. That, and her envy. Once she'd left for university, her air of superiority had become even more insufferable. But she never knew the half of it. For someone who considered herself so clever, Mhari had missed so much of what was going on back home. Especially that hellish Christmas with Miller. Just as well.

27

24 December 1974

'Don't you think we should tell someone? My mum, your dad? What about Mhari?'

'Don't be daft!' For once, Greg was paying attention to her. Not playing with some toy or binoculars, or pretending to read a football comic. Anything so he didn't have to look at her. He was going through a shy phase but pretending not to be. The afternoon's events had obviously left him badly shaken. It was a miracle they'd all got through teatime without any of the grown-ups picking up on their mood. She'd successfully persuaded them that Miller had caught a chill on their bike trip and he was allowed to go unchallenged up to his room. As she and Greg crouched on the landing they could see into the bedroom where Miller seemed genuinely asleep now, a thin, limp arm lying across Bella's neck.

'But, Cattie, he's only twelve years old and's just tried to kill himself! We've *got* to tell someone. What if he tries it again?'

She poked him in the shoulder, her own voice rasping but low. 'Keep your bloody voice down! They'll hear you downstairs. Come on.'

She led him into her room, or rather one of Mrs McAllister's comfortable guest rooms which was acting as her bedroom for the next two days. Clothes, sheets of Christmas paper, half-used rolls of Sellotape and shiny stick-on bows made from cheap ribbon were strewn everywhere.

'Jesus, Cattie, what a mess! You'd better not let Mum see the place like this. Crikey, you're only here for a couple of days, why'd you bring so many clothes?'

She began snatching up items of clothing and cramming the Christmas wrapping into a carrier bag. 'Sit down. On the bed there.' She watched him lower himself obediently on to the end of her bed, while she sat back, lounging against the pillows.

'Look, Greg. I don't know why Miller did what he did this afternoon but I don't think we should tell anyone. Mill was begging you not to, all the way home. Think about it. We could get into big trouble for not looking after him properly. God, your mum's in a foul mood at the best of times these days, she'd go spare! Anyway, there's no point. They know the state he's in. I've heard Dad and your mum talking about "getting help" for Mill. Some sort of "expert". They're going to send him to a doctor for loonies or something. Bit scary but it's got to be for the best.'

She frowned at Greg, worried that he'd blurt something out. It would be a disaster if the grown-ups got wind of Miller's latest behaviour. Too many questions to answer.

'The thing is, Miller's not normal, you must see that. I mean, he's not a normal kind of kid anyway. Especially not since your dad's thing. I thought for a minute he was getting over it, but no, and definitely not after today. He needs help. Your poor mum can't cope any more.'

Greg looked on the verge of tears. 'I don't understand . . . I just can't get through to him. He won't talk to me about . . . that . . . that day on the island. Won't talk to me about Dad *at all*. I showed him a letter I was writing to Dad. Said he should add a bit about what he was up to. Say how Bella was, stuff like that. He just ran out of the room and didn't say a word to me for the rest of the day. It's over a year and a half since that scene at Saughton. He just won't go back, won't write. Nothing. Mum wants to try and take us all to see Dad soon. Thinks Mill might go if we're all together. But Mum and Mhari have been rowing about it.'

Greg shook his head, his eyes wide.

'They were at it hammer and tongs the day Mhari came back for the hols. Mhari says he shouldn't go on another prison visit. Said it would be too ... too "traumatic" and may "escalate matters". Y'know how Mhari talks, specially now that she's at uni. You'd think *she* was the psychiatrist. But I think she's right. *I* don't even want to go really. I hate the prison. It's just so, so *horrible. Horrible* place, *horrible* people. But I've got to go. Mum'll make me and I really do want to see Dad anyway because . . .'

He'd faded away and was roughly wiping at the corner of his eye. She took over. 'Yeah, well I agree with you *and* even Mhari, believe it or not. I think it'll be too much for him an—'

'*Awwwwww! Help, help! Help meeeee!*'

They both leapt from the bed, Greg beating her to the door just as they heard the smashing of glass. All hell had broken loose. She saw her dad racing up the stairs two at a time, Mrs McAllister and Mhari close behind. Bella was running up and down the landing barking, almost tripping up Greg as, one hand on the doorframe, he swung himself round into the next bedroom.

Mrs McAllister's voice was screeching. '*Miller! Coming, son! Oh Forbes, quickly!*'

Catriona stood back to let her dad and Mrs McAllister hurl themselves past her, shrugging and shaking her head in reply to Mhari's worried look. Mhari stood beside her on the landing as they surveyed the chaotic scene inside the bedroom. Greg was holding Miller, much in the same position as he had hours earlier on the castle battlements, cradling him to and fro, cooing sounds of comfort into his ear. Meanwhile, his mother was fast reaching hysteria, looking down, both hands to her face in shock.

'Oh! Oh my God! Miller!'

But, as ever, her dad was taking control. 'Ailsa? *Ailsa!* I need your help! Give me that bed sheet for now and go and get my case from the car. Here's the keys. *It's all right. All right!*'

Catriona heard Mhari's intake of breath as she stared, disbelieving, the blood seeping from Miller's gashed hand on to the dazzling white sheet.

The wind, whistling through the hole Miller had punched in the window, was gently ruffling his hair as Greg continued holding him tight.

A Deserted Island

Although, at the time of writing, only a few years have passed since the grisly events on the island, Fidra's day-to-day existence continues. Twice yearly the lighthouse is maintained. This is essential as it is a vital beacon to ensure the safety of shipping in the Firth of Forth. Also, members of the RSPB have been allowed to land and carry out surveys of the locality's birdlife who continue their breeding patterns on the island, oblivious of its recent history.

But even these routine events have not been without note. During the first year following Douglas McAllister's conviction, a number of sensational and misleading reports surfaced about reluctance among the lighthouse maintenance crews to land on Fidra. Ghoulish stories about the men drawing lots to avoid duty on the 'island of horror', and of 'ghostly apparitions' of the dead girls seen by those on lighthouse duty, appeared in a number of press outlets. These claims were later retracted and resulted in two men being dismissed from the crews. The episode both reawakened great sympathy for the dead girls' families, and reignited a fresh bout of hatred against Douglas McAllister. Thankfully, the matter was largely forgotten within weeks.

Fidra, however, has become a deserted island, where not a soul willingly sets foot, apart from the checks to the lighthouse and the occasional RSPB visit. Other than that, the island remains bereft of any human presence. Only its ghosts remain.

Extract from *Fidra – an Island History*, by Duncan Alexander, Whitekirk Publishing, 1st edition, 1978.

28

LOTHIAN & BORDERS POLICE

Witness Statement of Miss LENA STEWART
Date: 2nd July 1973
Time: 12.05 hrs
Interviewing officers: DS Johnstone DC Wallace

My name is LENA STEWART. I am nineteen years of age and live with my parents at 12 Coates Gardens, Aberlady, East Lothian. I work as a nursery school teacher in Haddington.

On the evening of Friday 22nd June 1973, I was with my fiancé, ANDREW BLACKFORD. We had been for a walk on the Lammermuir Hills, south of the village of Garvald. It is something we often do when the weather is fine as it was that evening.

We had been for a stroll for about an hour between approximately 7.30 and 8.30 p.m. We then sat in Andy's car for about half an hour or so talking and having a couple of cigarettes.

At no time up until then did we see anyone else, either on our walk or at the secluded point where we had parked the car. I have marked on an Ordnance Survey map the exact route of our walk and the spot where Andy parked his car. I did this in the presence of the interviewing officers.

At about 9 p.m. we were driving down a narrow road that leads to the B6370 and I noticed to my right the figure of a man climbing up through some bracken. He was probably about 60 or 70 feet away. I believe this man to be DOUGLAS McALLISTER who lives on the outskirts of North Berwick. I know Mr McALLISTER by sight as he knows Andy and I have met him a couple of times when in Andy's company. I have also said hello to him when I have passed him in the high street when I have been in North Berwick shopping.

Lena Stewart
2/7/73

Witness Statement of Mr ANDREW BLACKFORD
Date: 2nd July 1973
Time: 14.20 hrs
Interviewing officers: DS Johnstone DC Wallace

My name is ANDREW BLACKFORD. Everyone knows me as Andy. I am twenty-six years of age and live with my grandfather at 3 Puffin Cottages, Aberlady, East Lothian. I work for HM Coastguard.

On the evening of Friday 22nd June 1973, I was out with my fiancée, LENA STEWART. During the good weather we made a habit of walking on the Lammermuir Hills, especially the area south of the village of Garvald. That Friday the evening was fine and we drove up there in my car.

We had just under an hour's walk between 7.25 and 8.20 p.m. I can be precise about the time because I check my watch regularly. A habit I have, primarily to do with my work. My watch is also set to 'the pips' and checked for accuracy regularly which is a habit also connected to my work.

After our walk, Lena and I sat in the car smoking and chatting. At 8.35 p.m. we set off for home to Aberlady.

I would like to emphasize that up until that point we had seen no one on our walk or during our brief time sitting in the car. On the request of the officers present, I have marked on an Ordnance Survey map the exact route of our walk and the place where I parked my car.

Approximately five minutes after we drove off and as we were travelling down a narrow road leading to the B6370, some movement on my right-hand side caught my eye. It was the figure of a man climbing up an incline. He was wearing dark clothing. I couldn't make out the details of his clothing as this was obscured by foliage.

As I drove on, I could see the man's face and head more clearly. It was still light, sunset being about half an hour away, and visibility was very good. At the closest point he was about 20 yards away. I believe this man to be DOUGLAS McALLISTER who lives by North Berwick. I know Mr McALLISTER as he keeps boats and I frequently see him when I am on patrol as he sails between the mainland and the island of Fidra, where he has a second home.

I am certain that the man I saw was DOUGLAS McALLISTER.

Andrew Blackford
2/7/73

Witness Statement of Miss LENA STEWART
Date: 3rd July 1973
Time: 15.50 hrs
Interviewing officers: DS Johnstone DC Wallace

Subsequent to my previous statement of 2/7/73, I would like to clarify two points.

The times given in my previous statement are approximate. On further consideration, I now recall that Andy [ANDREW BLACKFORD] did have a watch on and I noticed him consulting it on several occasions during our evening together. This was not unusual. Andy is always very conscious of the time.

I would like to clarify that the man I saw on the incline was partly obscured by bracken which did not allow me to see his clothing. However, his face was visible.

I am certain that the man I saw was DOUGLAS McALLISTER.

Lena Stewart
3/7/73 (Witness Statement No. 2)

29

Late September 2005

'I don't think I've ever seen one of these before. The language. It's so archaic. Unnatural beyond belief!'

Miller met Duncan Alexander's smile of incredulity with a nod. 'Oh yes, the language of witness statements was always the subject of great hilarity when I was a law student. Ludicrous. You'll know better than me but I bet Lena Stewart doesn't talk like that and never has!'

Miller, grateful for the bit of levity, took a sip of coffee and looked around the room again. On his arrival at the abbey's guest-house building, Duncan had led him to a high-ceilinged room off the main hallway – the 'morning room' – where anyone staying there could retire after breakfast to read the papers, the Bible, books, or just sit with coffee. The place was empty now, the afternoon sun flooding through the bay windows, warming the chilly air. They were cocooned in vast leather easy chairs with a clear view down the long garden, past rhododendron bushes, to the grey seas of the Firth in the near distance.

He'd been glad, though nervous, to get Duncan's call saying that Lena Stewart definitely wanted to talk to him. Duncan had stressed the woman's increasing anxiety and suggested a visit that evening. But he had, with a gentle though unmistakable insistence, asked that Miller call at the guest house first and talk through what might be 'a difficult encounter'.

Duncan flicked some stray drops of coffee from the sleeve of his woollen habit. 'I don't know if you remember this, Miller, but I attended most of the trial. I thought it important to be there, to help your mother if she needed it. Forbes couldn't sit in for much of it since he was, technically, a prosecution witness, having ... as ... as you know, a key role as police surgeon in attendance on that terrible day. And, friend of the family or no, he was the only police surgeon available to go on the island search that day. He told me as much at the time.'

Duncan placed his coffee cup on the table. 'You'd know more about this than me, but I suppose things are more scrupulous today, legally speaking. But then Forbes had to do what he was told. He was stuck between the proverbial rock and a hard place. In the light of that, of course he was taking a risk helping you all out during the trial. Strictly speaking he shouldn't have had contact. But, he told me that if he'd been challenged, he was simply going to say that he was your doctor and concerned about your welfare. Brave man.'

Miller shook his head. 'It's strange. There are so many gaps in my memory during those weeks of the trial. I do remember us staying the night at his house a lot. I'm not quite sure why. To give Mum a break, I suppose. I remember being allowed in court for the verdict and sentencing. That I'll never forget. The rest? Much of it's a blank. I suppose the shrinks would say it was the mind protecting itself. But ... going back to the evidence of Lena Stewart and her fiancé, what I'm struck by is the crude attempt at dovetailing.'

Duncan was frowning at him. 'Dovetailing?'

'Yes. Remember we're in nineteen seventy-three. The unreconstructed days of dodgy police behaviour. You don't even have to read between the lines. It's obvious that Lena Stewart's "clarifying" supplementary statement is nothing short of an attempt to dovetail perfectly with her fiancé's. As I say, I think it's quite crude and from studying the trial transcript, my father's defence team did try to make something of it.'

Miller nodded at the papers in front of them. 'However it looks like both Lena and Andy Blackford stuck to their guns on what they saw. Also, the time factor was important because if the sighting had been nearer to Lena's original statement, then it would've been nearer to sunset and there would have been a big visibility argument. Probably not enough to get my father off, given the other evidence. But enough to make a dent.'

Here he was, chatting away, analysing evidence in a lawyerly way, trying to appear composed, in control. The truth was that Catriona's visit the day before, teasing out of him some of his true feelings at what was happening, had left him unbelievably vulnerable. He was having a job remaining composed. But lawyer's talk was helping.

He leaned forwards and fingered the one-page statement. 'By the way, what happened to Andy Blackford? My father said in his letter that the couple never married. There's mention of it too in Russell Sinclair's notes.'

Duncan shrugged. 'I've no idea. Long gone it seems. I asked her but I got the impression she didn't want to talk on the phone about him. In fact she's reluctant to go into anything in depth on the phone. She seems a very down-to-earth sort of woman. Wants a face-to-face encounter before she opens up. Reasonable, I suppose, all things considered. Okay, now she's expecting you at seven. She lives just outside Haddington. Shouldn't take too long to drive over there. Why don't I pick you up some time after six?'

Miller shifted in his seat, suddenly uncomfortable. He hadn't expected this. In truth, he hadn't thought through that step. Of course Duncan would want to be there. He'd organized everything. Wanted to know all Lena Stewart had to say. Duncan obviously had his best interests at heart. He'd already cautioned him twice on the dangers of reading too much into anything she might say, even if she had revelatory disclosures to make, it didn't mean his father was innocent.

Duncan was right. Logically. But matters were swiftly overtaking logic. Here he was, sitting with Dunc-the-monk in the place where his mother had found spiritual comfort, maybe happiness, wanting, *needing* to satisfy himself about his father's guilt or innocence. There was no turning back now. As every day went by and he immersed himself up here – the once beloved place of his childhood – he was aware more and more that he wanted a better outcome than the one he'd lived with for the past thirty-two years. The visit to Lena Stewart was just the beginning. He'd risk the disappointment. After all, he'd lived a lifetime of it already.

But what he didn't want was anyone else there. Except Catriona. He did want *her* input. It seemed fitting that if he was going to open up a Pandora's box, then he shouldn't be alone. He should be with someone whose perception of that time was nearer to his own.

'. . . so would that be okay?'

Duncan was pressing him for a pick-up time. 'Eh . . . sorry, Duncan. Look, I've been thinking about this. I . . . I hope you'll understand. I'd prefer to see Lena Stewart on my own.' The lie would obviously be found out the minute Lena Stewart got back on the phone and told Duncan that he'd brought Catriona Buchan with him. But he'd deal with that when it arose. He just didn't want to have to explain to

Duncan what he could barely explain to himself. He wanted only Catriona with him on this journey. A journey he now knew would take him to where he'd least expected. That was all he could say right now. He hoped Duncan would understand.

Duncan gave a final half-hearted wave to Miller, wandered back to the morning room and began to gather the coffee cups and the plate of untouched biscuits. But halfway through he had to give up, flinging himself into the chair which Miller had vacated. The sun had gone and once again the room felt chilled. More white horses had appeared on the horizon now. The wind was blowing in off the Firth. Another batten-down-the-hatches night at the abbey, like that January night in 1975 when he'd eventually drawn the awful truth about Miller from Ailsa . . .

. . . She'd tried the single malt again. Out of desperation. Her earlier defensiveness had now completely given way and she was close to breakdown. The true story of the McAllister/Buchan Christmas had been a far cry from the jolly-against-all-odds time that she'd originally painted. Ailsa couldn't lie even to herself, it seemed. Relating the tale of Miller punching out a window pane had reduced her to sobs. Clearly, the incident had just about broken her.

'Thank God Forbes was there otherwise I'd have had to take Miller to hospital. Then what? Questions. Suspicions. Was I looking after him properly? It . . . it would've been awful. Anyway . . . Forbes said it would heal. Wasn't nearly as bad as it looked. The glass cut the hand rather than an artery or anything. Didn't need a stitch, just careful cleaning and dressing . . . Oh God! What is happening to my wee boy! And what am I doing here? Forbes insisted that I take a break but . . . but it feels so wrong leaving my own little lamb when he needs me. But Forbes says he'll take care of him, of them all. He

says if I don't have a break, I'll get ill. He's offered me some pills but I draw the line at that. I just . . . oh, but Duncan, I can't tell you how bad I feel about Miller.' She'd paused to wipe her nose with a scrap of paper hanky before going on.

'You know Doug has this theory that Miller has taken against him because of what he saw that day. I've told you about his reaction. How Forbes had to medicate him when he got him home. The laddie was so hysterical. Had seen the girl's body before they could get a blanket over her. I mean . . . you don't have to be a psychiatrist to know that what he saw was . . . it . . . was the worst thing for any child, let alone a sensitive wee creature like Miller. But . . . this withdrawal from his father, his refusal to write to him, talk about him. Do you think a . . .'

She'd stopped. But, though plainly nauseous, she finished off the whisky as if somehow it could become a burning emetic, vomiting the unsayable from her throat.

'Do you think a sensitive young child can know, truly know the badness of another person? Can he know if his own father is a monster? Oh God, Duncan, what if he did it? What if he really did it!'

His eyes slewed away from her pleading look. He had no truthful reply for her. Instead, he let the rattling of the wind on the loosened casement be her answer.

For now.

30

He was relieved that they'd opted to take his four-wheel drive. The roads were strewn with tree branches and other detritus as the wind whipped itself up into a frenzy of gale-force proportions. The jeep bumped over yet another obstruction.

'D'you need me to pull in?'

She was peering with a maglite over a crumpled map. 'No. It's okay. The directions Duncan gave you are complicated but ... hold on ... it should be next right ... Langshaw House. There!'

His wipers were working flat out to shift the downpour from the windscreen and still he could barely see anything ahead. Catriona was leaning across him, pointing over to the right a few yards away. Then he saw it. Atop a post, the white-painted wooden sign announcing 'Langshaw House' was dancing wildly on its hinges, as the gale made repeated attempts to wrench it to the ground. The driveway was a bog and the tyres slithered to find a hold. Outside the house a dim light welcomed them, followed, startlingly, by blazing security floodlights that exposed the frontage of the main building and outlined others to the left. Two Land Rovers, a horsebox and a small car were parked up near the front door.

The nerves were picking away at him now. So much – an incalculable amount maybe – depended on this encounter. The implications ... the feeling of nausea had returned, as had the barely resistible desire to flee, just U-turn the jeep and disappear. Forever. Instead, he sat back staring out at the deluge.

'You sure you want me to come in?'

He nodded, not looking at her. He bet she knew something of what was going on in his head. Sensed his reluctance to go on.

He answered unnecessarily sharply. 'Yes, yes. I'm sure. Just, well, it just feels . . . strange . . . but never mind. C'mon, let's do this.'

As he slammed the jeep's door, he heard a high-pitched shout and spun round. A small figure in ankle-length coat and wide-brimmed hat, rain streaming from it, was scurrying towards them.

'Miller McAllister? I'm Lena Stewart. Come wi' me.'

The stables offered escape from much of the elements, although the most ferocious gusts of wind managed to find their way through, setting off the occasional whinnying and loud snorting from one or all of the three horses in the stalls. Lena Stewart had removed her hat and coat, accepted Catriona's presence without demur, offered them both a bale of hay to perch on and started grooming the nervy-looking grey.

'This is Twilight. Bonny but awfy highly strung. She absolutely *hates* storms and the only way to calm her down during them is to groom her. Disnae work for the others, but then they don't really need it. They're much calmer those two. My ex-husband was one for the horses. Got me hooked quick. One of the reasons that I married him. Come to think of it, about the only good reason. Now I cannae live without them. I shall be a mad old wifie one day, if I'm not that already. Just me and my horses.'

He caught Catriona's smirk of wry amusement but looked away. He wasn't enjoying himself. He could sense the little woman's nerves, matching his own. Hiding behind the horse's flank, she was rabbiting on so that she didn't have to make the first move.

'Ms Stewart, I'm v—'

The disembodied voice cut in. 'Just call me Lena. I'll call you Miller.'

'Lena. I'm very grateful that you've let me come here and . . . and . . . that through talking with your niece and Brother Duncan, you've been thinking about what happened with my father.'

A small hand appeared on the animal's rump as she pushed the grey a few steps forwards. She'd stopped grooming and held the rubber curry comb in mid-air.

'Go on, girl. That's enough for now. The storm winnae bite you.'

She patted the beast away, secured the half-door behind it and sat on her own hay bale opposite, cradling the brush in her hands.

'I think I can safely say that, next to my hellish divorce, these past few weeks have been the worst of my life. What a turnaround. When Lizzie first told me that your father was going to be a patient at the hospice I agreed wi' others who told her to leave, or at least take a leave o' absence. In my mind, he was the worst, the very worst. That's how I always thought of him. How I'd been encouraged to think of him.'

She'd refused to take her eyes from the curry comb during this preamble but now she snatched a quick glance at Miller. To see if he was listening? To see if he was upset at this description of his father? He gave her a weak smile and nod to continue. Her voice was lower now. Quieter. Almost subsumed by the louder, complaining creaks of the building and the howl of the wind. He inched his body closer, half turning his head to Catriona, who was sitting stock still. The already weak lights flickered momentarily as an extra strong gust swept the stables, bringing with it a stinging spray of rainwater, hurtling through a wedged-open door at the far end. The grey started kicking at her stall, letting out a half-hearted but unnerving whinny.

'Sssh, Twilight. Cool it, lassie. I must say that it's to Lizzie's credit that she stuck the job at the hospice and didnae take that leave o' absence. Otherwise, well otherwise we wouldnae be here tonight. Are you religious?'

The apparent non sequitur caught him by surprise. But he couldn't lie, so shook his head. She didn't seem interested in Catriona's state of faith as the conversation seemed to draw only him and this small intense woman closer and closer in. Indeed, Catriona had deliberately positioned herself back in the shadows now, sensing perhaps that this was a private, intimate conversation between two people. Only the scent of the horses, their breathing and occasional complaining noises indicated that there was any other living soul in the place.

Lena lifted her head, turned to look at Twilight and went on. 'I *am* religious. More now that I'm older. Maybe that comes to us all. I dinnae know. I was brought up religious, though I didnae pay much attention to it when I was young. But life changes you. What I *do* know is that the stories Lizzie brought me about your father, his suffering, his conversations wi' her, made me look at what happened back then.'

The stable block's lights made one final flicker and gave out, plunging the animals into darkness, obliterating Catriona from Miller's peripheral vision and leaving Lena Stewart in a pale yellow pool from a single surviving lamp, hanging overhead. She seemed almost oblivious, giving the hint of a shrug as she cast her eyes up towards the lights for a second.

'Let me take you through that evening. June, nineteen seventy-three. I was nineteen years old. A young nineteen-year-old as it happens. Poor, hard-working family. Very strict. I worked at a local nursery school, loved kids and was engaged to one of the hunks, *the hunk* of the area. Life was good. Sort of. Andy Blackford wisnae what he seemed. Oh he had looks, a glamorous and respected job wi' the coastguard and was very charming to my parents, to everyone. But he was a drinker and could either be the nicest o' the nice or pretty bloody nasty wi' it. Looking back, I think he was a manic depressive. I've known a couple o' folk in my life who had that illness. I'm sure he suffered from it. I dinnae really think he ever intended to marry me. In fact, I think the whole proposal, engagement, ring-buying thing was done when he was half-cut and on a high.

'Anyway, that evening we were up on the Lammermuirs. We used to go up there a lot. To be blunt, it was the only place we could safely have sex. I might have been young and strictly brought up but I wanted my fun too. I lived wi' my parents and he lived wi' his granddad. The best place to be alone was the Lammermuirs. That evening we'd been out a long time and Andy'd had a few cans. We went back to the car and it was getting dark. We had a couple o' fags and Andy finished off another can. I remember us having words about it. I was going on about drinking and driving. I didnae have a licence then, so it wasnae as if I could take over and get us home if he got completely pie-eyed. Besides, he'd never have let me drive his precious car anyway. Men and their bloody cars!

'So, once he'd finished his can we got going. The idea was for him to drop me off at my parents' and go on home. I think his granddad was going to be out at a neighbour's, so he wasn't in a big rush to get back or anything.'

For the first time she paused and then hurried on as if trying to force the words out before she changed her mind. 'And . . . and then a few days later everything blew up.'

She paused again and he watched as she fiddled away with the curry comb, plucking the coarse grey hairs from it. She now seemed utterly lost in her own thoughts, unaware even of her precious animals. All three were becoming increasingly restive as the storm pummelled away at the four walls around them.

'But, Lena? What *exactly* did you see on the way home?'

Catriona's intervention made him jump. She was leaning into the pool of light, her face looming unnaturally pale and oversized in the glow. Although she'd kept her voice low and gentle, Lena Stewart looked up, shaken out of her reverie. He cursed Catriona, thinking she'd made a mistake. Broken the spell.

But he was wrong. Lena stopped her fiddling with the curry comb and stared at the ground. 'That's just it. I didnae *see* very much. In fact I saw *nothing*. And I'm damn sure Andy didnae see a thing either, despite what he said later. My goodness, he had enough trouble keeping the car in a straight line. There wasnae any way he could've got a good look at a damn thing and it really was getting dark by then. In fact, I'm sure now that it was *later* than I originally said and it was definitely much, much later than what Andy claimed.

'A few days afterwards it all started happening. The police were up to ninety. They had to make a *cast-iron* case against your father, especially after what they'd found in his garden and on Fidra. They had a lot but apparently it wisnae enough. Anyway, Andy was pally wi' the police. Used to drink in the same pub wi' a few o' them. Had contact wi' them through his job. All that kind o' thing. And that's how it all started.

He'd mentioned that he'd been up near the area where that poor lassie disappeared from. Then things got a bit heavy. Some detectives started visiting him, and me too, and ... well ... Andy started saying to me that he was sure he'd seen Doug McAllister on the way home that night and did I no remember? I said that was rubbish, that we didnae see anyone. Then I was at Andy's one afternoon. Cannae remember where his granddad was. Maybe in hospital. But anyway, I was upstairs when these detectives came round and there were raised voices. I crept down to the living room door. They were threatening to tell Andy's bosses about the booze. Said that they would destroy him, that he'd lose his job. Lose everything. They were convinced that Douglas McAllister was their man. *Convinced.* They had loads of other evidence, they said. Just needed Andy, and me, to ... how did they put it? Aye that's it, to "dot the Is and cross the Ts". And that was it. We concocted a story. Not a complicated one but one that would pass muster.'

She was looking up at last, directly at him.

'But I ... I want you to understand this, Miller. I was convinced as well, *convinced* that your father was guilty. Those police were *very* persuasive. So was Andy. It's ... I have to be honest, it's no' really troubled me since then. Aye, I didn't like lying at court. I was brought up not to lie, and certainly not on oath, but I thought it was for ... well, for the greater good.' She dropped the curry comb to the ground, crossed her arms and hunched her shoulders, suddenly feeling the cold. 'But ... oh Lord, who'd have ever thought it, after a' these years? It's coming back to haunt me. Deservedly so I'd say. When Lizzie told me about your father's last few weeks, things he was saying, I started having doubts. The dreams started, horrible dreams about that time. Like a haunting ... I became frantic about wanting to do something and then that's when I spoke to Duncan. I've been badgering him about being able to meet you, talk to you, apologize. I did wrong. Sorry can never be enough. I have to live with that.'

She paused to hug herself even more tightly, a frown flitting across her face. 'But, know this, I'd do anything, *anything* to make things right. I'm sure now your poor father was innocent.'

31

She'd offered to drive and Miller had accepted. The journey had been spent with him slumped in the passenger seat, saying nothing. She'd had the sense and sensitivity to keep quiet. He was more than grateful for that. The plan was to drive to her cottage, drop her off, and then he'd go home to get some badly needed sleep.

He'd wondered if he had imagined Catriona's initial reluctance as she invited him in for a drink before his drive home. Was it just a perfunctory offer made out of politeness, not meant to be accepted? Did she really want her privacy invaded? Or was she sufficiently worried about his morose, uncommunicative state to want to keep an eye on him? Whatever the reason, once inside, she'd seemed relaxed and happy to have him there. Now, in front of her hearth, he too could relax a bit. Or rather, make the appearance of it. The encounter with Lena Stewart had replayed itself a million times on the way back. It was going to become a torment.

He knew he looked, and was, shattered. The drink was probably a mistake. She'd only given him a single shot, but he was feeling it. Better not have any more if it was offered, which seemed unlikely. He shut his eyes, enjoying the warmth from the fire. She'd said something about checking her emails and had disappeared upstairs. He pressed his head into the soft chair back, listening to the storm trying to make its way inside, along with the waves he knew were hurling themselves at the beach a mere stone's throw away.

But it was all in vain. This was a safe home, comforting . . .

He'd almost nodded off. Surprising under the circumstances, but forgivable, given his utter exhaustion. Still, it wouldn't do. He stood up, stretching his arms out and turning his head to ease the painful tension in his neck. His eye caught sight of something squatting in the shadows that he'd missed on the way in. That old sideboard. Quite out of keeping with the rest of her modern furniture. He was sure it was the one that had been in her father's house. He wandered over to get a better look at what was sitting on top of it. The wood-framed black and white photograph of Forbes Buchan had been taken in the summer. It looked vaguely familiar. He'd probably seen it before. There'd been a lot of showing off of photos, swapping snaps, discussing the latest cameras in those days. Forbes was squinting into the lens, in shirtsleeves, his smile twisted and lopsided by the ever-present pipe. He looked pleased with life. Good-natured. Just as Miller had always, well almost always, remembered him. No photos of her mother, though. Too painful perhaps? He gently replaced the frame and noticed the pipe, lying nearby. The same one? Maybe. Dr Buchan had surely owned a host of them in his lifetime. But it looked the same. She'd kept it. Touching. And then, lying in a corner behind the photo, he saw it, catapulting him back to his childhood. It was well before Dad had been taken away. He'd been on a visit to Catriona's house, her voice filled with pride . . .

'. . . It's a nineteen forty-nine edition. The one with illustrations by Mervyn Peake. It's an amazing thing to have. Here, look. Careful, though.'

He accepted it, her fingers cold on his as she passed the book to him like it was the finest crystal.

For my most beautiful Catriona, a special gift.
The world is yours. More vast than Treasure Island!
Your loving Dad
xxxx

Funny. Signed almost like his own dad signed things. He started to flick through the pages. He'd heard about these drawings. At school. Seen some slides of them at a talk in class. He hadn't liked them. The red cover had a drawing on it. A man's face. Coarse-featured, with wiggly hair like worms.

'It's Long John Silver.'

He nodded his reply at her, keeping his eyes on the book. 'I know.'

'Dad gave me it years ago. I don't bring it out very often. I'm far too grown-up for it now, of course, but it's a special edition, you see. Very special, don't you think?'

He was flicking through; each drawing he came upon seemed more disturbing than the one before. There was a horrible one of Long John Silver with a broken bottle, drunk, staring eyes, and a cutlass in his hand; a deformed and ugly Blind Pew almost breaking Jim Hawkins's arm, the boy's face contorted in pain; a full page of the amputee Silver, no trace of the peg leg found in myriad other versions. Just one long, long leg, a stump, and a never-ending crutch.

The illustrations made him feel uneasy. The stuff of nightmares. He closed the book. Managed a smile. 'It's great, Cattie. Great.'

She took the book back, replacing it carefully in its clear plastic wrapping.

'I'm to keep it forever. Dad says so.'

He tried another smile, thankful beyond words that his own father hadn't given him such an abomination . . .

He shook his head. Clever Forbes Buchan. Keep it forever. Good advice. Worth a bob or two maybe, despite his potentially devaluing inscription. This was an absolute classic.

The draughtsmanship breathtaking. Though still disturbing surely, to the very young and sensitive.

'Incredible, don't you think?'

He hadn't heard her come into the room and stepped back from the sideboard, feeling unaccountably guilty. 'Eh, yeah gr—'

She took the book from him. 'My favourite's opposite page one hundred and sixty-two. Jim in the coracle. On the high seas. Look. Isn't it fantastic? And then the next one. Wee Jim swinging from the bow of the *Hispaniola*. Look at his little face. Delightful.'

He wasn't sure he would have characterized it like that. The child looked terrified. But there was something uplifting about her pleasure at this cherished childhood possession, offering a rare, almost intimate insight.

She topped up his glass without asking and he took his seat again feeling suddenly embarrassed, like he'd been caught snooping. But she'd already made herself comfortable in the chair opposite, feet curled under her, nursing her wine. Relaxed. Talking more to the roaring fire than to him.

'So, what about Lena Stewart, then?'

He took a sip of his drink knowing it to be unwise. She must be in no doubt about how the Lena Stewart meeting had left him feeling. But she'd asked the question as if she was talking to a patient. With a distant reserve. A professional enquiry. Maybe she sensed how close he was to breaking point and didn't want a further night of his confidences. Fine. Neither did he. But he was going to have to call on all his self-control to even begin discussing the encounter.

He tried an over-light, casual tone. 'Aye. I've been thinking about her all the way back here. Odd wee woman. Very pleasant. Very earnest. I mean, saying that she's prepared to make a new statement, will talk to anyone she has to, police, legal folk, is quite a thing to offer. Potentially, she's got a lot to lose. But, you know what? I want to talk to this Andy Blackford before I do anything else. If it's true that Lena Stewart can find out a current address for him, then all well and good. She says he's living somewhere around the Trossachs. I think I'm going to have to make the trip.'

'Why? Don't you believe her story?'

'No, quite the reverse. I absolutely *do* believe what she told us. I just want to hear his version. If he'll give it, which is a big "if". Thing is, if he sticks to his story, it's a case of his word against hers. As for the police, I've seen a note from Russell Sinclair saying that the detectives who investigated at the time are both dead. Doesn't matter really. If they'd been alive I've absolutely no doubt they would *never* have made any admissions anyway. Same goes for any of their surviving colleagues. *However*, if this Andy character feels like making good, then legally I could think of putting something together, police or no police. Two key witnesses admitting to perjury's a pretty big deal. There's something called the Scottish Criminal Cases Review Commission that looks again at cases. But, I'd have to mug up on them and my Scottish criminal appellate law. Take advice on the position of posthumous cases.'

He knew that extreme tiredness often cut him off from his emotions. And thank God, it was doing its work tonight. But it was a major fault of his. Hadn't Nikki complained often enough about that? But here he was, thinking like a lawyer, talking like one, and wilfully refusing to let himself *feel* the implications of this evening's events. It was unquestionable that he was having a reversal of opinion about his father. Recent events couldn't be ignored, denied. But wasn't he just galloping a few steps ahead of himself? Already the knowledge, or rather potential knowledge, that his father might be innocent wasn't enough. Now he was thinking of exploring some publicly recognized exoneration. All too much too soon? Maybe. But if his father really was innocent, then all those years, wasted years. His father's. His own. Nursing a hatred so deep . . .

'. . . all right?'

'Sorry, Catriona, what?'

She was frowning. 'I *said*, are you all right?'

He toyed with his glass, turning it round and round on his thigh. 'Yes. And no. I'm . . . I think I'm just beginning to realize the implications of all this. I mean, if, *if* my father was innocent . . . where does it leave me, my beliefs, my decisions about him? I have to be honest, and I made this point to Duncan recently, much of my childhood after the arrest is hazy, if not missing. And I know the psychology around that. Unhappy episodes get edited out. To help us live on after hell. Truth is, my adult life hasn't been spent *consciously* grappling with conflicting feelings for my father. Trying to remember the once loving, caring dad I thought he had been. No, I saw through that and he was removed from my life long ago. My barriers came down. End of story. Yet . . . yet, here I am. Doing this.'

He sat up, frowning, annoyed and embarrassed that he'd started talking about himself, yet again, in too intimate terms. 'But . . . as Duncan pointed out . . . whatever Lena Stewart said, whatever she thinks, it doesn't a priori mean and it certainly doesn't *guarantee* that Dad was wrongfully convicted. It's a hell of a long time since I ever prosecuted in the criminal courts, but that doesn't matter. Most of the population now accept that the police, certainly in the past, have been known to "help" the evidence along to convict the guilty. Belt and braces approach. We may just be in that scenario. You know what I'm getting at? They got the right man, whatever the means.'

He stopped, waiting for her to take her eyes off the fire and look at him. It took her a moment before she seemed to hear the silence. There was a flash of the old Catriona, an almost imperious glance which he recognized from childhood. It meant that she'd been caught out daydreaming, not paying attention. But he wanted her attention now.

'You know, this is something I'm afraid to ask. Of Duncan. Of you. People who have always supported us but who have never actually said what they think about our dad.' He finished off his drink. 'Tell me. What did you, what *do* you think about my father? His conviction.'

Immediately he regretted the question and with it another flush of embarrassment. But it had to be asked, and answered, if he was going to continue to have contact with her, let alone ask for her help.

She had stretched her legs and was sitting up, her glass discarded on the hearth. Was she getting ready to adopt her best bedside manner, preparing to deliver a killer diagnosis? Her face was unreadable. Shut down. But at least she was looking at him.

'You know what, Mill? I take it you want a truthful answer? We're not kids now.'

He nodded slowly, beginning to feel sick.

She shook her head once. 'I don't know what to say. Other than I don't know. I've never known. I've never been one hundred per cent sure of his guilt like you were. Though I'd suggest that your certainty around your father's guilt was very much an emotional response to what you went through, what you saw, at the time. On the other hand, he *was* convicted. Very convincingly. I just don't know. But what I *can* tell you is that I'm more than prepared to stand by you in this. Offer any support you need. And that's as much to honour my father's memory as anything else. He spent a lifetime doing what he could for your mum, and, by default, your father. I know your father felt relieved because he knew that my dad – a man he called his "greatest friend" – was looking after things.'

Her reminder of what a lifeline Forbes Buchan had been to the family prompted another train of thought. Before his father's conviction, his recollection of McAllister family life was well-nigh idyllic, wasn't it? Fantastic home, an island playground, good brother, pain-in-the-arse but really okay older sister, not many friends, in part due to being at school so far away, but there had been Catriona and her dad. Two bonded families. Granted, to the outside world the McAllisters may have seemed, and were, a self-contained family unit. Maybe, by the standards of modern psychoanalytical theory, they had been too self-contained, excessively inward-looking. But they'd all been decent kids, a 'normal' middle-class family, hadn't they? From late June 1973, of course, all bets were off. Any attempt at analysing the McAllister family along lines of normality was futile. Though, given what they *had* all been through, it was nothing short of a miracle that he and his siblings had turned out as well as they had.

Greg was the most well adjusted of them all. Almost spookily so, all things considered. Looking at him now, in youthful middle age, you'd never be able to guess at his true family history. Mhari's overachieving, bossy ways were already well ingrained by the time of the arrest, therefore didn't really count. So, it was just him. Little traumatized Miller who'd grown into what? A man, husband, father, stoked full of suppressed anger and disappointment when his only role model so catastrophically let him down? A man who so lived in his head that he didn't even notice that his wife had been carrying on an affair under his nose for the best part of a year.

And where did that leave *him* as a father? Simple: riddled with shortcomings. For example, how much could he honestly say he'd considered his two little ones these past couple of weeks? Of course he loved them, adored them, but what sort of fathering had he offered them during their lives? If he was honest, he barely, at times, felt fit to be a father, stubbornly holding within him the identity, the *sense* of still being a young child himself. He'd felt that in all walks of his life. As a father, as a husband, as a professional. When carrying out 'important', 'grown-up' duties at work, in court, with clients, in meetings. Everything. It all ended up the same. He felt a fraud. Through and through. In many ways work didn't matter and exactly how much did his crumbling marriage really matter? What *did* matter and what he didn't want to face, couldn't face, was if he'd been a failure and a fraud as a father. The prospect of admitting that to himself was unthinkable. Maybe he was scared of it. Fatherhood. Scared to try and then let his little ones down. As he had been so devastatingly let down . . .

'. . . and I'm sorry if it's not the answer you wanted to hear.'

Her voice roused him. He'd momentarily forgotten where he was. Doing it again. Rambling off into his interior life.

'It's okay, Catriona. It's an honest answer and not as bad as the one I *did* expect.'

'Really?'

'Yes. Like I said. I felt it with you, with Duncan too. There's sympathy but . . . I felt a *doubt* and that's absolutely fair enough. I'm a bit at sea myself in this, to say the least. Look, I need to go. I need some sleep. And Nikki and the kids are coming up tomorrow. I've got to organize the house.'

The mention of his wife and family in her presence felt odd. When she'd visited him a few days ago he'd talked about them quite readily, even floated the suggestion that she might meet them. Then, the conversation had seemed easy, comfortable, although he'd been left mildly frustrated that she didn't reciprocate with any personal information of her own. Why the sudden discomfort? Why no reprise from him of his offer for her to meet his family? He knew damn well why and, despite how emotionally withdrawn, how almost autistic he could be at times, he could sense that she also knew why. Well, his crush was a lifetime ago. He didn't need any more complications now and Catriona, for her part, seemed content to stay supportive but essentially remote. So be it.

They both caught the full brunt of the gale as she opened her front door for him, the wind tearing at their hair and clothes. She shut the storm out again, leaning against the hallway wall.

'My God! Can you get home in that? You're more than welcome to stay here. Plenty room.'

He smiled his thanks, gently easing past her. 'No need. Besides, it's not that bad. I love weather. Don't you remember?'

Her laugh was light. 'Of course I do! That was just one of your many, very fetching quirks. G'night, Mill, and drive carefully. I don't think you're over the limit.' He felt her touch on his forearm. 'And, Mill? I'm glad you're back.'

As he raced to his jeep, deliberately without a backward glance, his discomfort had turned to excitement and, in turn, to worry. How tempting to have stayed. What then? Nothing. Surely nothing. No matter what feelings were trying to break through within him, she was just being — what? Friendly? Supportive? One thing was for sure. The bond that held them in childhood was still there. That realization should have been reassuring.

Instead, he felt more fearful and isolated than ever.

32

Catriona couldn't hear him leave over the noise of the storm. But she watched as his headlights zig-zagged down her potholed and flooded drive, the brake lights blinking their way round the final corner. She pulled the curtains at the front of the living room, switched off the main lights and wandered over to the sideboard. She realigned the book flush with the wall. Miller had never liked those illustrations. Still didn't by the look on his face. She picked up the photo frame and fingered the spotless glass.

She carried it and the pipe with her, sat herself at the dining table by the window, and set both items in front of her. Only the fire offered any light, its orange glow flickering across her father's smiling features.

'*Oh, Dad.*'

There was nothing to be seen outside. The black waters of the Firth were exceptionally noisy tonight. She enjoyed that and wanted to get closer to the outdoors, moving through to her covered verandah that ran down the entire west side of the cottage. Along with all the other little islands, she knew Fidra lay out there in the distance, though not in view. She was thankful for that. Hers was a far more sheltered outlook than the one Miller had from his mainland home; over the headland from him, with only the benign hulk of the Bass Rock breaking the uninterrupted views to the glittering lights of the Fife coast directly opposite. She nodded. Hers was a place of safety. The rest of the world held at a reassuring distance. Unbreachable.

High up to her left, she could make out the faint lights of Whitekirk Abbey. Peaceful, at ease. Behind her, unseen, Tantallon would be skulking atop the headland, withstanding as it had done for centuries this particular blast of the elements. She shivered. Although the glass-encased verandah made the best of any sun offered during the day and held its warmth, there had been precious few rays on offer recently. Reluctantly, she made her way back to the dining table.

She held the pipe, stroking its bowl as she thought through her evening. The Lena Stewart meeting had been nothing short of a revelation. The *connections*. Who would have thought that Douglas McAllister would have been nursed by her niece? She'd never heard of Lizzie Henderson before. She only knew the hospice director and his deputy, a time-served nursing sister who'd been friendly with her father. Then Lizzie gets to know Duncan Alexander through her visits to the abbey as a guest. Just like Ailsa McAllister before her! Connections, connections . . .

'. . . They wouldn't let me go with Doug. Said I could come through and visit him later this afternoon. I'm leaving now. I've left the kids with Mrs Watt but can you go over? And . . . and where's Cattie? Does she know what's going on?'

'She's upstairs doing homework. I'll talk to her later.'

But she'd abandoned her homework and peered down from the top of the stairs. They were standing in the hallway, Mrs McAllister sobbing her eyes out on Dad's shoulder, saying only one thing, again and again. 'Oh God, Forbes, what'll I do?'

They seemed to stand like that for an eternity. Until her father broke the silence. 'I'm afraid things look pretty bad, Ailsa, m'dear.' Dad was looking worried, serious, and what else? Frightened. That made her feel frightened too. But everything would be all right, wouldn't it? Wouldn't it . . . ?

She picked up the photo and pipe and took them back to the sideboard. Slowly she made her way up to bed. As she tried to calm herself for sleep, the images crowded in on her. Miller as man and boy. Lena Stewart and her nervy horses. The Mervyn Peake illustrations. All chased themselves round her head, fighting for attention while the raging weather closed in from outside.

33

'Miller! Will you keep an eye on Callum? I'm going in to organize something to eat. Emma's helping me, okay?'

'Yeah, okay!'

Bloody hell, he didn't know where Nikki got the energy from. She'd just driven four hundred miles with two kids and a Border collie in tow, had taken a lightning tour of the island and house, *and* was now about to cook a meal.

She'd been a bit on the cool side when she'd arrived and pointedly busied herself with the kids who were both tired and overexcited, especially by the boat trip across to the island. But she seemed in reasonable spirits now. He was thankful to her for one thing. She'd done what they'd previously discussed on the phone and laid the ground work with them well, telling Callum and Emma that they were going on a visit to 'Daddy's new secret homes'. Both had seemed to accept this without further enquiry, more engaged with the novelty of their surroundings than how and why they actually came to be there.

He took Callum's hand, Meg trotting happily behind them, her sheepdog's instincts on display as she made occasional forays ahead and back again, herding and checking them as they sauntered down to a mossy, sheltered dip in the land. It was far from warm but the sun had come out to play and the air would do them all good. Everyone, Nikki included, had been directed away from the much deeper dip that was the chapel ruins area. He was happy enough to allow his family on Fidra. It marked the beginning of his attempt to reclaim his island after all. But there were limits.

He set Callum down a few feet away. He seemed happy playing with his favourite toy truck, chuntering away to himself. Nearby, Meg was rooting around in the grass and eyeing any gull foolish enough to get too close. Just like Bella used to . . .

'. . . C'mon, girl! It's dinner time. C'mon! Race you back!'

Catriona, her dad and Greg had gone ahead to help Mum. The three of them, but not Catriona's dad, had been swimming off the West Sands. Mum wouldn't go to the West Sands because you could see Fidra really clearly from there but Dr Buchan said it was okay if they wanted to go. It had been a good day. He'd almost forgotten, sort of, about Dad. Sometimes he forgot and he felt okay. But he'd heard Mum and Cattie's dad recently. Whispering about 'the trial' and what 'an ordeal' it was going to be.

'Ah, who cares, Bella! C'mon!'

He danced across the rocks and grass in only gym shoes and wet shorts, towel slung around his neck. Overtaking him, Bella was barking excitedly as she ran ahead and then stopped to shake the last of the sea water from her glossy coat, spraying him from head to foot.

'Hey! Stop it! You did that deliberately, you naughty girl!'

Back at the house his mum was waving from the back door. She seemed in an okay mood today. Relief.

'I've made you a packed lunch! D'you want your sandwich in here or out in the garden?'

'Down here, please. Bella too! You got her bone?'

'Aye, son. I'll send Dr Buchan down with both your lunches!'

A few minutes later he tore the lid from the Tupperware box, ripping the foil from the sandwiches and tucking in. He was starving after all that swimming. In front of him, Dr Buchan was crouching down, tearing the butcher's paper from Bella's bone. She was circling round him wildly, tail wagging non-stop.

'Okay, okay, okay. Here we go, lass. There.'

Miller smiled as Dr Buchan stood up and walked past him, ruffling his hair. 'Right. I'll leave you two to it. I think Cattie and Greg'll be down in a minute. Give me those wet gym shoes and towel. Enjoy your lunch.'

The sandwich was brilliant. He was finishing off the first half when he heard it. A rough, dry sound. Bella had backed off from the bone and was lying down on her belly coughing and wheezing.

'What is it, girl? Lunch not to your liking today, eh?'

But she was on her side now, the coughing turning to a harsh rasping sound. He jumped up from the grass, spilling his glass of milk all over his leg. Bella had funny foaming stuff at her mouth and her side was going up and down really fast. She was breathing harder than if she'd been running for her ball all day.

'Mum! Mum! Muuuum! Greg! Here! Hurry up!'

Within seconds they were all there. Dr Buchan had taken control and was leaning over her.

'The bastards. Bastards!'

The shock of him using such language was lost as his mum bent over Bella, practically screaming. 'What is it, Forbes? What's wrong with her? Oh, my God!'

Cattie's dad stood up, his mouth turned down. 'Someone's poisoned her. That's what. Poisoned her bone. The butcher leaves your order on the back step often enough, doesn't he? Someone's got to it. Cowards! Can't get at Douglas, so they go after his poor bloody dog. We'll be lucky to save her. I must get to a phone and call the vet. Quickly!'

The shivering had started ages ago but only now did he notice it. Catriona had moved forwards and was taking off her cardigan. Gently, she put it round his shoulders, its warmth – her warmth – seeping immediately into his skin.

Just a whisper. 'I'm sorry, Mill. Really sorry.'

He couldn't remember running away or at what point he'd trodden on the milk glass. As he reached the top of the garden he looked back *at the heaving body of Bella, the others still crowded round her, faces crumpled in shock. He felt the wetness on his foot then. There were at least two big shards sticking in it. He didn't care. He only cared about Bella. Dad's Bella. His Bella. Even the wailing that tore itself from his chest didn't seem to belong to him.*

'No, not Bella! Bellaaaa! Waaaaah . . .'

'. . . Waaaaah!'

'What the? Wh—'

'In God's name, Miller, what are you doing? *Look at him!*'

He swivelled round. 'What? Who? Bella? I heard her j—'

'What you talking about! *Look!*'

Behind him, Nikki was racing down towards him, pulling Emma behind her, with Meg scampering up to meet them, barking loudly. A few feet away, Callum was lying on his front, yelling. Miller sprang forwards but Nikki had beaten him to it. Callum's nose had a lateral gash across it from a rock he'd fallen on.

'*Good grief!* Come on, my little love. Mummy'll take you up to the house. Here we go.'

Miller made a move to take him from her. She turned her back to him. 'I'll manage. I need to clean his wound. See how bad it is. What the hell were you doing? I thought you were watching him! Just, just *get out of my way*! Emma darling? Come with Mummy.'

He stood in the doorway, listening to the shifting of the house as the wind buffeted and the sea fought its way round the island, making the inexorable journey into shore. The waves' rhythmic beat was loud tonight. Not quite the stormy weather of late, but that would return. The weather, the sea, seemed manic, schizoid at the moment. One day this, one day that. Unpredictable, unsettling. Entirely in concert with his own feelings ... but he needed to hold those within himself, hidden away from Nikki and the kids. Emma and Callum would be out for the count until morning. The wee lad's nose wasn't half as bad as it had looked earlier and he'd happily accepted a bedtime story before nodding off.

Nikki, lying naked in front of him, sleek blonde hair fanned out across the pillows, the duvet kicked down to her shins, was sound asleep too. After their row, no, after her *scolding* of him she'd seemed to accept that he wasn't himself. And then they'd become entrenched in a what? A *coolness*, yes that would do. She'd taken a pill, something she'd become worryingly dependent on in her endless quest for rejuvenating and revitalizing beauty sleep. He moved forwards to gently replace the duvet over her and retreated back to the doorway. It wouldn't matter if he rejoined her in bed or not. She'd be totally unaware. There was enough residual light from a nearly full moon to see her by. The perfect body. It never seemed to age. But then that's what drove her. Obsession with fitness. With youth. Their shared passion. Until very lately when he'd stopped training. There was more to life than the body beautiful. And keeping age at bay.

With a final glance at her, he turned and padded down the stairs, Meg trotting halfway up to meet him.

'Hello, girl. Wondered where you were. Thought you were in with Callum. C'mon, then.'

He eased himself into the chair by the glass doors, Meg snuggling up to his bare feet. He closed his eyes, shaking his head. Earlier, he'd hoped that some post-coital closeness would be the best time to explain things. To gauge Nikki's reactions, to prepare her for his new plans about his father. Plans. That sounded a bit grand. Very organized. Wasn't it nearer the truth to say that he was blundering through something he didn't entirely understand? Maybe it was just as well he never got the chance to speak to Nikki. The hoped-for moment never arrived.

The sex between them had been strangely awkward. For both of them, he judged. She had been . . . *functional*. And he had . . . ? Well, he had felt an inexplicable reluctance to engage in any sort of coupling. It was a sensation that disturbed him and drew him back to the problems he'd had after the end of her affair. Was it about the Callum thing? No, she'd got that off her chest by the end of dinner. Seemed to have forgiven him. Was there something not working about his desire – purely physical desire – for her? Hardly. She was stunning. No, this was about something in him *and* something he sensed in her. A distance in her which left him unable to, and not wanting to, tell her more about his father. And feeling more emotionally isolated than ever.

There had, of course, always been limits to what he had told Nikki about his father. Yes, she knew about his conviction, their estrangement, though details had been kept to a bare minimum. But in the heady first few weeks, months and even the first couple of years of their relationship they had both been complicit – happily so it seemed – in burying the issue. Apart from anything else, her well-to-do parents would never have countenanced their only daughter marrying a convicted killer's son. Miller shuddered at those early times and the mockery of their wedding, when those few in the know were briefed on the party line: Miller's father is dead. Nikki's parents were of an age to have memories of the well-publicized case. But his surname alone wasn't enough to reawaken them. He even moved his childhood upbringing from East Lothian to Edinburgh. The entire charade had cast a blight over his wedding and destroyed what should have been a joyful day for his mother too. She'd agreed to the lies but it had always left him feeling deeply, indelibly, stained with shame. If it was now, he'd have told Nikki's snobby parents the truth and they could go fuck themselves if they didn't like it. Or maybe . . . maybe now, he just didn't care about Nikki in the same way any more. He shook that line of thought away. Not now.

But what had happened to him up here recently, what he planned to do, *had* to be discussed with Nikki. His actions *were* going to be pivotal for them both, for the family, and he had no sure idea of how she'd react. He had to explain that he wouldn't be coming home for a while. He'd already decided to ask for extended leave from work. Under the circumstances – bereavement, family matters to sort out and the like – and with his position of seniority in the firm, it would be okay. Frankly, he didn't give a toss if it wasn't. He was sick of work. The problem was if she suggested they *all* stay up here for a week or two. Yes, after the initial explosive fit of temper once he'd revealed his plans, that's the sort of thing Nikki might suggest. The possibility niggled away at him. He'd have to be ready for that. It was the last thing he wanted. He needed to be on his own to do this, whatever 'this' turned out to be. Exoneration of his father? Reconviction? Or, worst of all options, abiding uncertainty with no way of proving matters either way. In that event, he'd have to walk away as if nothing had changed. But he was kidding himself. A major shift had already occurred. The possibility that he'd been wrong about his father had stirred up some, just a trickle maybe, of the feelings for his father he'd had as a child. And if he did let them break through, there lay a pain so unimaginable . . . *but no!* He couldn't face that right now. Just quietly get on with what he was going to do, step by step.

And what of Catriona Buchan's role in what he was planning to do? She'd offered her help. She was here, on the ground. This was her part of the world, like it had been once for him. And might be again? Most of all, she'd been *there*. There at the time. But so had Greg and Mhari. Shouldn't he tell *them* what seismic shifts were going on within him? He'd consistently avoided Mhari's almost daily phone messages these past two weeks. Her fears were over the estate and what he was doing with it. Little did she know! But he'd have to tell her soon, if only to stop her fulfilling her repeated threats to charge down from Fife to check up on him.

He shut his eyes against the thought and forced a smile to himself through the darkness. There was tomorrow. With it, the hell of facing Nikki. But there would be good things too. If the weather held, tomorrow he'd take the kids out on the mainland.

34

Within the split second that it took to happen, Miller realized what he'd done wrong. He had been pushing through the queues at the funfair. Callum, with a brightly coloured, cartoon character sticking-plaster on his little nose, was sitting proud as punch astride his shoulders, tugging at his dad's hair. Emma was clutching his hand, pulling him to the next ride she wanted to try. The shove came just as he was fishing out some coins for the ride. The money had fallen and he'd released his daughter's hand to steady himself and Callum. And then she was gone.

'Emma? Emma!'

Useless. Heavy bass music was thumping out from some deadly-looking ride a few yards to his right, drowning out his shouts. But he had to try again, aware that his voice was sounding more frantic on this attempt.

'*Emma! Ems!*'

He spun full circle. Twice. Above him, Callum was giggling, thinking it was a game. Miller peered through the crowd, trying to see over their heads and then crouched down to get a fix on her little legs. Nothing. The ride! He knew which one she was heading for. The big merry-go-round near the centre of the funfair. He started elbowing aside anyone in the way, ignoring the glares and complaints. Callum's inappropriate giggling heightened his tension as he raced towards the centre of the fairground. He reached it and grabbed one of the workers standing nearby.

'You seen my daughter? Red parka, dark hair. Called Emma?'

'Sorry, pal. 'Fraid not.'

'Jesus! She's gone! I've lost her!'

The man seemed infuriatingly unalarmed. 'Aye, okay. Look, dinnae worry, pal. Kids are always wanderin' off here. Go over tae the far side o' the park. That way. There's a police car stationed there, beside the St John's ambulance. Talk to them, okay? She won't have gone far. On ye go.'

Miller nodded his thanks but Callum had finally picked up his father's fear and started a low grizzling. He reached a hand up to him, tousling his soft hair. 'It's all right, son. All right. We'll find Ems. Stay up there for just a wee minute more, okay?'

He was racing round the back of the food stalls and spotted the police car. It was empty.

'*No! Where now?*'

He spun round too quickly and staggered back, desperate to keep his balance as Callum teetered above him, his grizzling turning to a low moaning.

Jogging back the way he'd come, Miller began to feel completely disorientated. Now he was back near the deadly-looking ride and the centre of the fairground. But which way had she gone?

'Did ye no' find her then, pal? Yer wee lass?'

It was the fairground worker again. Without waiting for an answer, the man raised an oily hand, clutching a walkie-talkie.

'Hold on a minute, pal. I'll contact my brother on the other side of the park.'

Miller patted Callum's leg and tried to make out the unintelligible garble of the walkie-talkie conversation. In a moment the man turned back to him. 'Come wi' me.'

'Have you found her? *Have you?* Where is she? *Where?*'

Miller knew his yell was hysterical, and foolish, because

it had set Callum off into a full-blown wailing. As Miller reached up to bring him down, the man shook his head.

'I'm no' sure. Just come wi' me.'

At last Miller lifted Callum down and held him, allowing him to bury his tiny face into his dad's neck. More jogging and they reached the merry-go-round.

'Is that yer lassie over there? Red parka, you said?'

'Yes, yes! Thank you!'

Miller saw Emma's face break into a smile as she caught sight of him. She began waving wildly, while talking to a girl of similar age astride the horse next to her.

'Hello.'

Miller looked over his shoulder. The woman was smiling at him, taking her eyes off his only briefly, to acknowledge the fairground worker's nod as he faded away into the crowd.

'Is that your little girl on the merry-go-round?'

She was young, a bit tired and harassed looking, but kept smiling as she glanced over at Emma. 'Not the first one to take off on her own, I'm sure. I saw her and popped her on the ride. That's my wee one next to her. Julie. Anyway, I said to your girl that I'd try and find her daddy. The fair's here three times a year and I'm getting to know the workers. The lad who runs this ride was brilliant. As soon as the walkie-talkie alert went, he was on to it.'

She'd said all this while watching the merry-go-round and waving manically each time both girls appeared. Only now did she turn her full attention to him and Callum.

'Is that your wee boy?'

Miller nodded and hefted Callum more securely on to his hip. He had quietened down but was still grizzling. The woman was staring at him, her smile turning to a half-frown.

'Is everything all right?'

Miller was suddenly aware how he must look: frantic, already at the end of his tether, probably dishevelled, and clutching a red-eyed unhappy little boy, sporting a nasty facial injury. He began stumbling into an unasked-for explanation.

'I . . . it's . . . I mean, I was just getting some change out for the next ride. Someone . . . passer-by . . . bumped into me and I let go of Emma. I . . . I'm just *so relieved* she's okay and that sh—'

The woman was scrutinizing Callum's face again as she spoke and began sidling away towards the ride as it came to a halt.

'I . . . I see. Oh well . . . ah, there's your Emma. Bye, then.'

His face was burning with shame as he watched the woman bundle her child from the ride and scuttle away as fast as she could. *Christ, she thinks I'm some kind of abusive bastard!*

'What in God's name were you thinking of, Miller! Did you really believe for one second that you could hide such a thing from me? When exactly *were* you planning on letting me know what had happened? Of course Emma was going to tell me. It's not every day she has to depend on the kindness of a complete stranger! And don't even think of saying it was an "accident", that children are always getting lost at fairs. You're just stuck in that head of yours. Not paying attention! *You're fucking useless!* I don't know how long it's going to take Ems, both of them, to get over this. And all this . . . this *shit* about your bloody father. Christ, it's like some mad fantasy! A hospice nurse, a crazy old woman with horses, a bloody monk, and some childhood friend. The local GP, no less! I would've thought *she'd* have known better than to get embroiled in this . . . this *folly*. What's Mhari got to say about this?'

Nikki had refused to look at him throughout her tirade, instead making a show of checking and zipping up the final holdall before marching towards the car. She'd been icy on their return from Fidra and had spent the rest of the morning busying herself with the packing. Of course he'd been wrong not to mention the funfair incident as soon as they got back. But, coming on top of the Callum episode, Nikki's reaction didn't bear thinking about. Emma had blurted out the story within minutes of her return. He was now doubly guilty in Nikki's eyes. She, quite justifiably, accusing him of deception in trying to hide the incident, as well as breathtaking negligence over their children. *Twice*. He'd run out of excuses.

'Nik. *Please*. I've tried to explain everything the best I can but . . . but . . . fuck it, I don't even know *why* I feel the way I do. I just need to sort this out. I'm so, so sorry about Callum . . . and the thing at the fair. I can't tell you. I'm sorry, just so sorry.'

'It's not me you should be apologizing to. It's them!' She nodded towards the back seat where Emma and Callum were safely strapped in. Both had been worryingly subdued at teatime. Callum, occasionally putting a stubby finger to the plaster on his nose and wincing. Emma, silent as she picked at her food.

Nikki slammed the door on his children and turned to him. 'Look, Miller. You do what you like. We're going home. Know what? It's probably a good idea that you stay here because I don't know you at the moment. Come to think of it, I don't think I've known you for a very long time. It's not just *this*. You need to sort your head out about a lot of things. I hope you can manage to. While you've still got a home, a job, and a family.'

She nodded over to where Meg was snuffling about in the shrubbery. 'Oh, and you can keep *her* with you. We're getting a couple of kittens next week, so the kids won't miss her too much. She's your dog anyway. And by the way, I'd advise you to start looking after yourself. You look a bloody mess. Get a shave and a haircut. You're like . . . like some swarthy Latin vagrant.'

Her anger had left him paralysed, rooted to the spot, as he watched the car disappear into the distance. No wave from Emma, no excited giggle from Callum. Not a glimmer. Jesus, what had he done?

He was still standing on the gravel long after they'd gone. Only the beginnings of a heavy drizzle seemed to awaken him. He slumped down on the bench by the rockery, ignoring the rain as it turned to a downpour, the drops quickly soaking through his T-shirt and running down his overlong hair, soaking his face. Meg jumped up beside him and he wrapped a welcoming arm around her neck.

The tears, when they came, were a blessed relief.

Misery and Isolation

As the dust settled on the terrible events, the McAllister family attempted to get on with their daily lives. It was not an easy task. Despite the trial judge's plea for the family to be left in peace, this was not to be. A close friend of one of the victims' families embarked on a campaign of intimidation against the McAllisters. Ailsa was accosted and threatened and their beloved dog, Bella, was fatally poisoned. However, the vendetta was brought to an end. The culprit, a member of the prison service, had also been involved in threats to Douglas. Ailsa identified the man on a prison visit. He admitted the offences and was dismissed from his position. The family declined to prosecute, hoping to lay matters to rest.

Meanwhile, Douglas McAllister was visited regularly by members of his family, excluding the youngest, Miller, who had been traumatized by an early remand visit and had been unable to go back. This was said to have upset Douglas, who sank into a deep depression after his conviction, knowing that he was unable to see his youngest child.

In recent years, the rest of the McAllisters have been trying to recover. Mhari has completed university, gained a first-class degree and is now studying for her PhD. At the time of writing, Gregor is away at university in Dundee. As it is closer to Peterhead prison than Edinburgh, he tries to visit his father as much as possible. Ailsa continues to look after Miller and keep up her charity and church duties.

The family's recovery was not witnessed entirely at first hand by this author, who for some of that time was in seclusion as a consecrated hermit. Permission was sought to follow other hermits who, throughout the centuries have spent time on Fidra, and to hopefully pray that some of the evil of its recent past could be cleansed. Douglas McAllister readily agreed. Although a man of no firm faith, he had always been generously helpful with this author's researches into the island and had facilitated numerous trips there.

However, Ailsa felt unsure about the proposition, viewing the island as desecrated beyond redemption and Forbes Buchan, acting as de facto caretaker of the island, shared her doubts. Apart from any other consideration, he felt that the visits by lighthouse maintenance crews, RSPB officers, and his own checks on the island would disrupt the isolation that a hermit requires.

Consequently, the notion was dropped and the island retained its air of contamination in the minds of locals.

Extract from *Fidra – an Island History*, by Duncan Alexander,
Whitekirk Publishing, 1st edition, 1978.

35

The first seventy-two hours after Nikki's departure went in a blur. Sleep, at last, had found him. But it was the slumber of someone who could not, *dare* not meet the real world. Unconscious all day, waking only at twilight, and moving around in the dark. Eating and drinking habits topsy-turvy. Inane, all-night TV replacing human contact and intelligent thought. By day four, something – he didn't know what, or why – had changed. A last-ditch grasp at survival?

The trip to the painfully fashionable, overpriced barbers in Edinburgh had helped a bit. He could probably have got the same haircut locally for half the price but he'd set a trip to Edinburgh as his challenge. And he'd met it. But not without difficulty. As soon as he'd boarded the train at North Berwick station, he'd felt the panic, the irrational fear of the agoraphobic. He would have leapt from the moving carriage back on to the platform, and sprinted to the safety of home, if the guard hadn't physically restrained him.

As Miller looked at himself in the bathroom mirror he cocked his head, squinting. It had only been a week, but hopefully his normal shape would soon come back. Not thanks to any boring gym regime. On the Edinburgh trip he'd invested in a quality wetsuit and now, twice daily, no matter how cold and unappealing, he was in the sea with Meg, playing fetch with her new floating ball. It was hard exercise as he raced her for the ball but it did them both good. His nocturnal existence of the past few days had disturbed her too. Being left to wander around the garden at night, her usual routine abandoned, had been wantonly cruel. She was a loving animal and deserved better. Another example of suffering thanks to him. But their swims were making up for it. Something to be thankful for at least. Though he had to face it, every day was becoming harder and harder to get through. At least if he could regain some fitness, that might give him *some* feeling of control over part of his life.

He towelled off and began dressing. A persistent anxiety had settled in following Nikki's departure. She had done what he'd feared, called Mhari, and spat out her anger, puzzlement and worry. Mhari, in turn, had called him. In full bossy mode, her voice nearing the limits of its irritating upper register.

'She thinks you're losing it, Miller. She was in tears. Barely coherent. Told me some appalling story about you losing Emma at the funfair. *And* your practically letting Callum fall off the island! Unbelievable! *And* she tried to tell me some garbled story about you and Dad's case. Anyway, I've agreed to drop everything, at considerable inconvenience to me and the family, may I say, and sort you out. Hopeless. Bloody hopeless!'

He checked his watch as he put it on. She'd be here within the hour. Planning to stay for the weekend. To 'sort him out'. Well, it would take more than that. Antidepressants and a psychiatrist might just begin to do the trick, or maybe he was beyond that too. He sighed heavily. He didn't want Mhari bearing down on him. But there was no stopping her and so he might as well put a brave face on it. He'd spend the evening with her here at the mainland house but tomorrow he'd be gone. He finished dressing and wandered downstairs to sit with his coffee by the big windows. In the short time since Nikki's angry departure he'd been through it all. Her visit had been a disaster. He should never have invited her and the kids. Even before the trouble at the funfair he'd been more than aware that something was wrong. Her remoteness, their strange detached sex, his own feelings of introspection, isolation. Emma's and Callum's presence had lightened him up considerably. But the very thought of them now choked him. Everything was his fault, *his* mess.

Nikki had let him speak to Callum and Ems only twice since they'd left, claiming that they were either asleep or with friends when he called. She had refused to engage in any sort of conversation with him about his parental negligence or the reasons for it. Her tone had gone from distant and remote to patronizing, leaving him with the feeling that he was the third child in the family.

The recent calls had left him depressed and feeling guilty in another way. The memory of that momentary loss of Emma had had him rummaging in the middle of the night through the legal archive, searching for a letter Russell Sinclair had received years ago. It had been from one of the victims' relatives, upset at the periodic publicity that Sinclair had tried to drum up for his father.

> . . . *have you given a minute's thought to how it is for the families? To have lived with that hell for all these years only to have it dragged up yet again. If you are a father, Mr Sinclair, just imagine what it would be like to lose you child, say for five minutes, in a busy street perhaps. Imagine the torment, the sick feeling, the dread. And once you've done that, multiply it by a lifetime. By three lifetimes* . . .

Miller shivered. If he thought his mother and his siblings had suffered each time his father's case was raked up, what must it have been like to see that same photograph of your once vital, alive, precious daughter screaming out from every tabloid rag and television news programme? And that was the point. Although the funfair episode had been unforgivable of him, it had allowed him a glimpse inside the shattered lives of the families of those poor girls. There was, quite simply, a terrible truth underlying the words in that angry letter.

He'd discussed that very point with Duncan and Catriona. He'd felt the need, the compulsion to call them and talk about the funfair incident. Surprisingly, neither had been openly disapproving. He'd felt driven by some emotional masochism to tell them so that he could receive more of the criticism that he knew he deserved. But he got the distinct impression that they felt *he* needed looking after. But he didn't need or merit looking after. In truth, he didn't care much what happened to him. Duncan and Catriona obviously did. He had an idea that they'd been discussing him behind his back. Both had been doing daily 'check calls' to see how he was and Duncan had invited them both to dinner at the abbey when they came back from seeing Andy Blackford. Thankfully they knew where to find him now. Lena Stewart had been as good as her word and called two days after their meeting. There was obviously someone in the Blackford's extended family who she was on decent terms with: 'Let's just say that over the years Andy's got on a lot of people's nerves. Some close to home. Good luck with the trip and let me know how you get on. Oh, and *don't* give Andy my regards.' He smiled at the memory. She was a kind-hearted woman. He looked forward to seeing her again.

He stood up, taking a final look outside. A grey drizzle covered everything, obliterating the horizon and leaving only the ghostly outline of the top of Fidra, giving the eerie impression that she was hovering just above the waves.

Gloomy and oppressive.

36

'So, let me get this right. In the space of, what? Two, three weeks, you've pretty much taken up residence here in the mainland house like you've never been away. Your dog too. You've become best buddies with Catriona Buchan and Dunc-the-bloody-monk, been hunting down key witnesses from Dad's case, lost your daughter at a funfair where she could have been abducted by any sort of maniac, are so preoccupied that your son practically falls off a cliff, and are planning a full reinvestigation to exonerate our father. The latter I'm very pleased about, but for heaven's sake, what has happened to you?'

Miller wasn't going to answer Mhari yet. She could wait. Instead, he stared out of the dining-room window over to Fidra, the blink of the lighthouse hypnotic, leaving him strangely calm after his sister's onslaught. Unusually, for Mhari, she'd drunk more than her fair share at dinner. They were on their second bottle and she was definitely the worse for wear. The increasing incredulity on her face as he'd outlined what the past couple of weeks had brought for him, was almost comical. She couldn't raise her eyebrows any further if she tried, nor screech any higher.

He'd been unable to put his finger on exactly what was setting her off. He had an idea that she didn't like the tables being turned like this. For once their big-sister-little-brother axis had been flipped on its head. He was relatively sober, unlike her, and feeling pretty much in control. Usually her role. She was clearly and oddly upset. Because? Because 'wee' Miller wasn't playing by the rules. Her rules. He was acting out of character. Grown-up for a change. He knew she'd always had him and Greg infantilized in her mind's eye. She didn't like this new version of him, even though they seemed to be reaching agreement after all these years about Dad. He filled her glass again. He may as well keep her off kilter while he set the record straight.

'Okay, number one. Losing Emma was the result of a pure accident. She was nowhere near being abducted. What upset Emma and Callum was the state *I* was in. Granted, it was a nasty, *very* nasty episode but it won't happen again. *Also*, Callum was nowhere *near* a cliff. I admit I was negligent, preoccupied yes, but he's okay. Number two. I am not embarking on a "full reinvestigation" as you put it, of Dad's case. Things . . . well you know, I've told you what Russell Sinclair said, what he gave me.' He nodded to the lidless archive box, dumped on a spare dining chair, its contents spilling over half the table.

'Listen, Mhari. I'm changing my mind and with it my feelings about Dad. Isn't that what you, Greg, Mum wanted all these bloody years? I don't see what's wrong with that. It's what you all prayed for. I'm in it now. Steeped. All this going to see witnesses, taking up with Duncan, Catriona, it's all . . . well I'm trying to be absolutely sure that . . . that Dad really *was* innocent. If I can get to that stage *within myself* then Russell Sinclair will truly have done his work. As for anything else. Any legal remedy? Well, who knows? I'm thinking that through. If I can satisfy myself that Dad *was* innocent then I may well set out on some legal battle. It would be disgraceful not to try and clear his name. And, as far as the families of the poor victims are concerned, they'd need to know that their loved ones didn't get the justice they deserved.'

He'd been looking at his undrunk wine during this mono-
logue and it was only as he paused that he heard her snuffle.
She was crying. Silently. Napkin to her face. He reached a
hand over hers. His anger at her had proved an effective
distraction from his depression but that anger had dissipated
now. She made a pitiful sight.

'Oh come on, Mhari. What's up? I thought you'd be
pleased.'

She looked up, eyes reddened. '*I am, I am! Fucking well am!*
It's just so . . . so hard to believe. To get used to. *Shit!* Why
didn't Russell bloody Sinclair try to involve . . . to engage
you long before this? Before Dad got ill. Oh God . . . it's all
. . . it . . . it just feels all too late. If only Dad could have
known, felt for *one second* that you were . . . might be beginning to believe in him. *It's so horribly cruel, so unfair!*'

She was in a full-blown collapse now, head in hands, glass
knocked over, pooling red wine all over the white tablecloth.
Normally, she'd be up like a jack-in-the-box, fussing, apologizing, tut-tutting at what was just a trivial accident. But she
hadn't even noticed. Her face was buried in the napkin, sobs
racking her shoulders. He rucked up the sodden tablecloth,
pushing it out of her way, and moved his chair to sit closer,
an arm lightly round her. Funny how another's distress could
make you override your own. He *had* to take control. She
was as upset as he'd ever seen her.

'C'mon, Mhari darlin'. C'mon. It's okay now. Don't you
think I haven't been going through these very same thoughts
this past week or two. Particularly these last few days. Nikki
will have told you that she effectively stormed off last weekend. I know I'm really crap at the moment. My head's full
of . . . full of . . . *damn it*, I don't know. There's a sort of
weird, fated feeling to all this. The past few months, no, the
past year or so back home in London has been, well, I won't

go into details, it's been just shit. It's not just Nikki's affair.'

He sighed, shaking his head. 'Maybe it's my age. Maybe it's Mum dying and it took me so long to catch up with it. You know I'd never come back here to this place my entire adult life, until she died, and even then I couldn't get out of here fast enough. Maybe that visit did something, sparked something off. Don't know. It's odd. Months before you called to tell me Dad was dying I'd started having dreams about him again. I hadn't had them for years, *years*. It might even go back to that scene at Mum's funeral. I remember thinking about it for weeks and though I felt anger that day at Dad, I just ended up, over time, hating, absolutely hating *having* to hate. All of it got me thinking even more that perhaps I *didn't* have to. Can you understand? It was a draining, leeching, desperate feeling. Maybe whatever's been going on started there. But Christ, listen to me, trying to psychoanalyse myself, eh? Go on, Mhari, tell me. I'm about as self-aware as Meg over there, am I not? Ah, she knows her name all right. C'mon girl, say hello to us, then.'

Thank God for the dog. He felt relieved to see Mhari sit up and pat her lap, inviting Meg to sit by her. Mhari had never really been one for pets and never paid any heed to Bella in their childhood. But he knew how much animals could be a comfort. More than humans sometimes. Mhari was making a half-hearted effort to rally herself, straighten her matted hair and wipe her face. Be a big sister again.

'I . . . I'm sorry, Mill. For making such a fuss. It was stupid of me.'

He smiled as Meg nuzzled at his sister's hand.

Mhari looked pleased. 'She seems to like me.'

'Well, that's lucky, 'cause I might well have to stay away overnight tomorrow and wanted to ask you to look after her. Give her at least two good long runs on the beach and let her go in the sea. She loves it. If you don't want her around I'll take her with me but it'd be easier if she stayed. That's *if* you're still staying?'

She nodded. 'Yep. I'll stay. For a while. I need to be away by tomorrow evening, so if you're not back by then, I'll make sure everything's okay here before I go. Actually, I could do with some time to myself. So, just Meg and me it is. I'd like to go through this box too. If . . . if that's all right with you?'

He gave her shoulders a final squeeze and moved back to give them both some space. 'Of course. But be warned. There are some gruesome things in there. The pathologist's statements and reports. Worst of all are the police photos taken at the scene. I don't advocate you look at them.'

He leaned forwards again and made her look at him. 'I mean it, Mhari. If you're not used to seeing these things, they're a shock. Also, some of the old newspaper cuttings might . . . well . . . bring it all back a bit. Go easy on yourself and don't try to get through everything at once.'

He'd seen her safe and sound to bed, hoping that sleep had found her mercifully quickly. He doubted he could recall a single instance in childhood or adulthood where she'd been so vulnerable. The evening had turned out far from what he'd expected.

He sat sipping the rest of the wine, eyeing the box. It was right that Mhari should be allowed to go through it. But there was one item that wasn't in the box even though it went with everything there. He knew he'd never show it to her. His father's last letter was for him and him alone. Besides, there had been a number of potentially hurtful aspects to it which Mhari shouldn't see in black and white. Firstly, there was its tone that so strongly implied his father's favouritism towards him, even if his father hadn't consciously known it himself. The pages bled with paternal love. It would've been mawkish and overweening if the man hadn't been writing his dying words. Though, on balance, his father's favouritism would hardly be a surprise to Mhari, surely. Secondly, the surprisingly stern but truthful words about Mhari, her husband and her family – they undoubtedly *would* have been a surprise to her.

He reached over the table and slid the witness statement of Andy Blackford towards him. It was a risky business just turning up on his doorstep, out of the blue. But he had to do it. Catriona would be with him once again. That thought eased his mind. Of anyone he'd rather h—.

The ringing of his mobile made him jump.

Two minutes later the glaring sweep of full-beam headlights appeared as a vehicle wound its way up the drive. He jogged down the hallway to the front door just as the car was pulling up.

Duncan was dashing through the rain, the outside light picking out a worried frown on his brow.

Miller stood back as the big man squeezed past him into the hallway. He was breathing heavily. 'Hope you didn't mind me calling you so late. I . . . I wanted to check you were still up. I'm sorry, Miller. But . . . it's . . . it's Lena Stewart.'

'Lena Stewart?'

Duncan shut the front door behind him and leaned against it, obviously needing its support.

'Aye, Lena. She's dead.'

37

The whisky bottle sat between them.

'Here. Have another.' Miller was keeping his voice to a near whisper, dreading Mhari waking up. 'Please. Just go through it again. Take your time.'

Unbelievable! For the second time in a night, he found himself acting the comforter. He watched Duncan guzzle the drink and, for the umpteenth time, wipe his huge hand across his shaven head and down his face, momentarily pulling his features taut, his eyes staring unseeing at a slumbering Meg by the fireside.

'Like I said, this is all second-hand from Lizzie. She found her, poor lassie. She was due to go over to Lena's this evening and stay for the weekend. Lena had said to call her before she left to make sure that she'd be back. She was apparently going to some horse sale near Dumfries, wasn't exactly sure what time she'd be home. Anyway, Lizzie had been calling her for hours on the mobile and at the home number. No joy. By about half nine she was getting, well, not worried, just confused really. Wondering if *she'd* got the wrong end of the stick. After a while she thought, to heck, I'll drive over to Langshaw House as arranged.

'Well, the first thing Lizzie noticed was that all Lena's vehicles were there. She *had* to be at home. Lizzie let herself into the house. No sign. Only one place she could be. The stables. The lights had blown. They do that from time to time it seems, particularly if the weather's bad. So, it took her a minute to see. Lizzie found her in the stall of her favourite horse. The one you said she was with when you saw her. The grey called Twilight. It looked like she'd been grooming her. Lena'd been kicked in the head, repeatedly. The animal's been destroyed.' He took another stiff slug of the whisky, glancing over as Meg stirred in her sleep, and then refilled his glass. 'It's terrible, Miller. Terrible. I'm sorry . . . sorry for her and for you . . . I mean, what she was going to do for you, for your dad.'

Miller twisted in his chair and glanced through to the bottom of the stairs, still worrying that Mhari might awaken. *Jesus*, of all the things to happen. Though, looking back, that particular animal had seemed unusually highly strung. Poor woman. What a way to go. Your favourite bloody horse. But . . . highly strung or not, she'd seemed so at ease with the animal.

He glanced at Duncan, who had his eyes covered by his hand.

'Duncan? I know this may sound . . . well, you do *believe* it was an accident? I mean, I don't know who might want to harm her but . . .'

Duncan rubbed his eyes and squinted back at him.

'What? Oh . . . I see. No, listen, you can banish that idea. Lizzie's talked to the police. As far as they're concerned there's nothing odd about it. It was an accident. It's appalling but let's keep things in perspective, shall we, Miller?'

'Fair enough. It's just . . . I'm finding it very easy to get things out of perspective at the moment. Can't help it.'

But, and he felt bad about even thinking this way, where did Lena's death leave him and what he was trying to do? Thanks to her, he *did* have a clearer idea of the truth, or *probable* truth, of what had happened that night. But her death made tomorrow's trip to see Andy Blackford all the more crucial. He shook his head. Just when he was edging closer to some resolution about Dad, it seemed to be sliding away from him.

What a hellish mess.

Mhari lay upstairs, already feeling the nauseous effects of the hangover that tomorrow would bring. They were trying to keep their voices to the lowest murmur but it was no good. The noise of a car engine had her up and peering down as the shadow of a robed figure made a dash for the door through the rain. A male voice. The robe ... Dunc-the-monk? Had to be. Why, at this time of night? She didn't have the energy to either creep down and spy on them – God, shades of their childhood! – or to make herself respectable and announce herself. Whatever it was, it had to be pretty bloody urgent if he'd come to their door at half past midnight on a night like this. She'd ask Mill in the morning.

Her mind was staying stubbornly on their evening's conversation. It was so hard to adjust to this 'new' Miller. Everything just tumbling out from him like that. She should be, she *was* pleased, or at least relieved. But also, she was what? Worried? Anxious? It was hard to pin down. Why all that blubbing earlier? God, that had taken her by surprise. Analysing it now, the reason seemed clear. In her eyes, Miller had definitely been repositioned as far as his place in the family was concerned. Yes, it had started with that ludicrous will. A shock ... and a rejection. What had Dad been thinking? But, looking at it now, if he *hadn't* left matters that way, Miller wouldn't be on this road to Damascus experience right now. Could Dad have known that? Predicted that? Could he have known the deepest part of his son – whom he'd not had any contact with for thirty-odd years – so well? That would be uncanny and unsettling.

This thought gave her a stab of jealousy. Maybe father

and son were even closer than she'd ever liked to believe, leaving her, as ever, out of the loop. And what of Greg? Shouldn't he know what was happening here? She'd raised the point with Miller during the evening but he'd said let things be until, and *if*, there was good news to deliver. Perhaps that was right. Let Greg get on with his own peculiar way of life.

And if the news came out good? A full public exoneration? What she wanted? Yes. But where would it leave her deep down? With Neil? With her bohemian friends and colleagues? Some knew all about Dad and were intrigued, impressed even at her attitude to it all. Her whole adult identity had been informed by being Dad's daughter. The eldest child. Doughty stalwart, always standing by him, helping Mum in the absence of the feckless, infuriating middle son and the alienated, unstable youngest. But that would change. *Was* changing. The family history was altering. And with it not just her identity but the entire family identity. *Fuck*. All this thinking, wondering, worrying was exhausting!

It was Miller's doing. Or rather it was their father, operating posthumously through the agency of his favourite child. The stab of jealousy coupled with irritation hit again. Family secrets were unravelling. Dad's doing again. Miller had told her about his last letter to him, though he hadn't offered to show her it. But she couldn't help being satisfied, smug even, over Miller's surprise at her private family knowledge.

'Mum wasn't perfect you know, Mill. All this church and charity stuff. Yes, she was genuine in that but there was another side to her. A kind of zealot side to her. Repressive. That's why we rowed a lot when I was in my late teens. I could sense her frustration, probably unconscious on her part, and she was, probably again unconsciously, envious of what I had ahead of me. I may have been a late developer in the love-life department but at least I had somewhere to go. I was young. Let's be truthful here. Dad was a steady, committed family man. He hadn't had the happiest childhood himself, so he was trying to create one for us. I've got to thank him for that. But maybe he tried too hard to be steady and stable and I'll bet that Mum eventually found him plodding and boring. I mean she was often . . . what was it you and Greg used to call it . . . snippy and snappy? Mum was frustrated. Plain and simple. I noticed, sensed all this, long before she told me about the religious order thing. In fact, I thought she was having an affair. In a way she was. I think it was a kind of displacement. She kind of fell in love with the idea of being so devout. A bit of emotional excitement dressed up with all the trappings and esotericism of the Church. It was a substitute for what Dad couldn't give her. She actually told me quite soon after Dad's conviction about her plans to enter a religious order. I thought she'd been a bit mad round about that time. Mad or callous because, when you think about it, it was an utter rejection of us, her kids and her husband. God before all else. Even your loving family. Scary.'

That she'd known all along about their mother had obviously shocked Miller. When he'd first tentatively raised the issue during the evening she'd met it with a shrug and 'of course I knew'. But she'd been the only one. Greg hadn't known and she'd kept it that way. She had been worried, because she knew how guilty her mother had felt, that it might come out at the trial though, not surprisingly, it didn't. She imagined that her father had never dreamed of using it in court because he loved their mother so much. Not that it would've helped him to any great extent, given the eye-witness testimony that sealed so much of his fate. He hadn't stood a chance.

She sat up, head beginning to ache, and looked out at the blinking lighthouse sweeping its yellow beam across from Fidra. The family. Secrets. Skeletons. Seeping out. They all concerned dead people. Ghosts. But all could have an impact on the living. Would it have been better if Miller had never started his digging?

She padded back to bed and lay down. The biggest worry of all was settling in, promising to keep her awake for many hours. It was a worry that had visited and revisited her over the years and one she'd always managed to keep at bay.

Regardless of whatever witnesses Miller was chasing down now, what Russell Sinclair had tried to achieve these thirty-odd years had all come to nought. Wasn't that significant? So much energy for so little result? There lay her problem. Somewhere, there had always, *always* lain the tiniest lurking doubt about Dad. It was only human to have doubts. Surely? Utterly irrational but always there and seeded, she had been certain, by some small misgiving their mother had harboured. Never explicit – probably barely conscious – and never openly expressed. Only sensed by her and, finally, overheard in a hushed and urgent late-night tête-à-tête with Forbes Buchan. Yet, that doubt had surely in its turn been seeded by the young Miller's own uncertainty. God! It was like some nightmarish, never-ending, cyclical thought. A truth, *the* same truth. Round and round. Same, same. Whichever way you looked at it. Miller thought Dad guilty, so Mum did (a bit or sometimes), so she herself did (a bit or sometimes). Was he? Was Dad somehow manipulating things from beyond the grave?

Almost all of her couldn't believe that. But now, this Damascene conversion of Miller's was threatening to turn her into a most unlikely devil's advocate. Horror of horrors! What if she had to ultimately save Miller from himself and confess her doubts! Warn him not to hope for too much. Not to finish what might be a fool's errand. *Christ!* The cruelty, the pain of it all.

The thought still made her shiver as she crept under the bedclothes, dreading the night ahead.

38

'I'm sorry, Miller. I couldn't leave when I said. Emergency. Here. Peace offering. Will we make it before dark?'

Miller accepted the paper cup from Catriona. The last thing he felt like was coffee. He felt sick with nerves again. He waited as she secured herself into the passenger seat. It was the first time he'd seen Catriona looking harassed, on edge. Bad day? He wasn't sure he wanted to know. His own had been grim up to now. The morning had been a wretched affair, trying to play in the sea with Meg when his heart hadn't really been in it. To cap it all, on his return, he'd found an exceptionally glum and puffy-eyed Mhari at the breakfast table, poring over the archive box's contents. The creased and discoloured photocopy of *The Scotsman* newspaper front page was spread out before her. She had both hands clasped, as if in prayer, placed protectively across the head-and-shoulders shot of their father. It made a depressing scene and he'd had to fend off her enquiries about Duncan's late-night visit with a couple of white lies. He didn't want to discuss that with Mhari. Not at the moment.

He checked the dashboard clock and glanced at Catriona. Her features had already lost their tension and returned to a more relaxed impassivity. He forced some coffee down. 'We're okay for time if there are no hold-ups. It's about a hundred miles to Andy Blackford's place. It should take two, two-and-a-half hours. I've no way of knowing if he'll be in. But Lena had said that he works as a gillie, so if he's not at his home, he'll be out on the land somewhere. We might just have to wait for him. There's no point in worrying about it. We'll find him, one way or another.' He handed her his cup and started the engine.

She was sipping at her own coffee, looking straight ahead. 'I called Duncan myself after we talked this morning. Wanted to know more about what happened. Bloody tragedy. Not that uncommon. Accidents with horses. But you'd have thought she'd have the measure of her own animal. I'm really sorry, Miller.'

He felt her look at him. 'It's desperate. Mainly I'm sorry for her of course. Poor woman. She was, at the end of the day, a decent soul. I didn't hold anything against her for what she did about Dad. She wasn't much more than a kid when it all happened and she thought she was doing the right thing. She had pretty intolerable pressures on her. It's funny. It was only blind chance that brought us together. Now look where that's got her. And ... and I know this sounds a bit mad but I did wonder if it *had* been an accident. Duncan thinks I'm being ... well, a bit irrational, shall we say?'

She offered him back his cooling coffee. 'Yeah, Duncan mentioned that. I think ... how can I put this? I can understand *why* you might think that, the coincidence. But if you're to *logically* follow that line of thinking, where do you end up? I think the truth is that Lena had a lot on her mind. According to Duncan, she's admitted to Lizzie Henderson time and again that she was worried, distraught even, about your father. She probably just wasn't paying attention to a lot of things in her life, that nervy horse included. *And* that's not to say what happened to her is your fault. Blind chance *did* bring you together and despite her death it has helped you. In a pretty profound way. Hasn't it?'

He took the cup, swigged down a gulp and handed it back.

He nodded. 'Oh, yeah, blind chance has helped me. But I have to wonder what good'll come of it. A decent woman's dead. Like you say, not because of what I'm doing but I feel it all the same. I'm . . . well as I told you before, I'm going through my own transition. Mhari's not taking it the way I'd thought. Frankly, neither is Nikki but that's another story. The whole fairground, Emma episode . . . well, enough said. It's not all smooth going.'

He wondered if the mention of Nikki might tempt her to ask more. More about his personal life. But she was staring ahead at an increasingly dull and rainy landscape. It was strange. No stereotypical gender roles here. Quite the reverse. Wasn't it the male who was meant to be closed off, unforthcoming? While she should have been galloping on with a potted history of her life. Not necessarily all the intimate details but something. Any marriage(s), long-term relationship(s), children, all of it? But then she'd always seemed a bit secretive, and remote, in their childhood. Maybe that was because of the age difference. She was a blossoming, well-developed teenager, when he had still been an odd, obsessive anorak with a crush on her. Until afterwards, when he became . . . well, something quite other. A disturbed, moody and damaged child. Most of that damage only visible from the inside.

And what of Catriona's love/sex life? As a child, he'd always wondered, longingly, what sort of boyfriend she wanted, fantasizing himself into that role when he was older. But that particular obsession was short-lived. Dad's conviction had just about rubbed out all and everything in his own life, so the crush was largely forgotten.

Almost.

*

Wet weather apart, the journey had gone smoothly enough. He'd spent the last hour admiring the view and enjoying his own company as she dozed beside him. The sight of her sleeping had reminded him of how, during those long-ago summers, he'd grasped each and every opportunity to spy on her as she slept. Languid and elegant. Loving the heat. Like a cat in the sun. On the beach at North Berwick. On a grassy hillock during Fidra visits. He hoped, no he was sure, that she *had* been asleep, blissfully unaware of his scrutiny. Embarrassing if she hadn't. He'd imagined stroking each downy golden hair on her brown forearms, wiping the light sheen of sweat from the flawless skin of her face, or lying as close as physically possible beside her. But he'd done none of those things. Of course not. Looking back, it was a pre-pubescent fascination. Sexual yes, but an unconscious one. Innocent. Harmless . . .

It was time to rouse her.

'Hey. Catriona? Hello-ho? We're almost there.'

No response. She was obviously exhausted from work and he was regretting bringing her. It looked like she should be spending her weekend sleeping, not haring off with him to the damp Trossachs. He sighed. He just couldn't take the responsibility of one more person. Last night it had been comforting Mhari and then dealing with Duncan's shock about Lena, as well as his own. This morning it had been Mhari again, and now he had a knackered Catriona on his hands. For Christ's sake, he could barely look after himself right now. But, then again, Catriona *had* offered to help him, *had* given him invaluable support already. The least he could do was appear a bit more amiable.

'Catriona? Look where we are. Balquhidder. D'you know it? It's lovely. Even in this weather.'

The eyelids flickered and then she was stretching out her

long legs, trying to stifle a yawn. 'God, have I been asleep all this time? Sorry, Mill. I'm absolutely shattered. Putting in too many hours. Might be good for my patients but not my health. Balquhidder? Yes. I know it. Beautiful loch near there.'

'That's right. There it is! Loch Voil. Small but spectacular in its own way. Looks like the trees come all the way down but you can get right to the water's edge this side. Good for picnics.'

She laughed. 'Maybe! But not in this weather. D'you need me to map read or something?'

He shook his head and leaned forwards, his head practically over the steering wheel, peering through the rivulets that the wipers couldn't keep up with. 'No. Lena gave very specific directions. I think it's next right. His place is just at the entrance to the track. Might be a little but-and-ben or something. Called "Calair End". It's apparently his own place, not tied. Although he works as a gillie, I think it's only occasional. When he retired from the coastguard he moved up here and bought his own place apparently . . . ah, here we are.'

It was more than a but-and-ben. A sizeable whitewashed three-storey stone house stood before them, the front garden offering neat flower beds surrounded by a low wooden fence. He parked up at the front gate.

Catriona was pulling on her coat. 'How d'you want to play this? Assuming he's in of, course. Not much sign of life that I can see. I'd have expected some sort of madly barking retriever to bound out at us.'

He agreed. 'Mmm. Looks a bit too quiet, though there seems to be land extending from the back of the house. He might be there or anywhere on the estate, I s'ppose. I'm not sure what estate he works on. Presumably nearby. Anyway, let's give it a try and knock on his door. I'm just going to be straight with him. If he kicks us out, too bad.

'But what I'm *not* going to tell him is that Lena's dead.'

39

'Yer a bit bloody late, aren't ye? I read that yer faither's deid. I dunno why yer botherin' me wi' all this rubbish.'

It was the third time Andy Blackford had said that they were late. Miller was tiring of it though relieved that they'd even been allowed through the front door. Allowed to sit at the rough-hewn wooden table in the vast kitchen. They'd only had to hang around a few minutes. He *had* been out on the estate, and there *had* been a barking and distinctly unfriendly dog, now thankfully shut in another room somewhere. With deliberate rudeness Blackford had poured himself a huge whisky – something he did a bit too regularly by the look of his over-ruddy features – offering them nothing and taking generous slugs. Miller didn't think Blackford was actually drunk when he'd arrived home but he was on to his third large one in ten minutes. He'd seemingly accepted their lie that Russell Sinclair had passed on his address to them, having intended to contact Blackford again. A convincing untruth since Russell's notes *had* made clear that years before he'd been in contact with Blackford at his previous address. For his part, Blackford had invited them in, despite an initial look of unease. But it was best to be wary. There was something in the man's shrewd expression to caution Miller that Blackford took in much more than he let on behind that boozy exterior.

Miller studied him again. He bore no relation to the memory he had from childhood. His recollection of Blackford then was of a smiling muscular man, waving from a boat as he and his father were toing and froing from Fidra. And then there was the more sombre image. Blackford sitting in the public gallery, hearing the verdict. Uncomfortable in formal clothes but ruggedly handsome, just about tamed into a suit and tie, having delivered his killer evidence days earlier. How different a picture he presented now. He was very thin, almost wasted. The once black hair, styled in a ludicrous retro Elvis bouffant, was more than peppered with grey. The face was raddled by drink, making him appear at least ten years older than his actual fifty-eight. He'd plonked himself down with his ancient, mud-caked wellingtons too casually placed on a nearby chair, and was leaning backwards, his head facing up to the ceiling in a parody of boredom and nonchalance.

'I dinnae care whit Lena says. Silly cunt never did know whit time o' day it wis. Your faither was up that fuckin' hillside that night. Am tellin' ye, okay?'

Miller sighed. They were getting nowhere. With Blackford staring pointedly at the ceiling, he took the opportunity of looking at Catriona and mouthing a silent 'you try' at her. She half smiled and nodded, shuffling her chair forwards as Blackford clinked the inside of his signet ring against the whisky glass, the sound unnervingly loud in the airy room.

'Mr Blackford. Lena told us about a day when she was at yours. Some detectives were there. They were saying how they were sure Mr McAllister was their man. But they just needed a bit more evidence. To "dot the Is and cross the Ts" is how she said they put it. D'you remember that day?'

He clearly did. The eyes darted from the ceiling to Catriona and then back again. Silence. Miller raised an eyebrow at her. *Go on!*

'See, Lena says that the police were putting pressure on you to say you saw Mr McAllister. She says that you, both of you, *knew* you hadn't seen anyone on that hillside at all but that the police were *forcing* you to say it was Miller's father.'

At that he booted the spare chair away, toppling it over and launched himself across the table at her, his breath whisky-sour. '*Rubbish! Absolute fuckin' shite!* How could they force me? I am my own man! Naebody forces me to dae anything. *Nae cunt!* Now, ye'd better be on yer way. *Go on, get the fuck oot o' here!*'

He was pushing his own chair back with more than a hint of violence, when Miller cut in, his hand raised to hold him off.

'The thing is, Andy. Lena says that the police were blackmailing you. Tell what they wanted you to tell or you'd lose your livelihood, lose everything. Ensure that you never worked in another responsible position again. Because they were going to shop you about your drinking. Simple as that. She heard that, Andy. And she's going to make a formal statement saying that she did *and* that it was *you* who pressurized her to lie in court. You'd better get used to the idea. It's all going to come out. It's serious to lie in court, however long ago. You can go to jail for it.'

Blackford was refilling his glass yet again. Then he glared at Miller, bobbing a single nod sideways in Catriona's direction. 'Tell her tae leave. *Now.* I'll no talk to ye if there's anyone else here.'

She was glad to be outside and away from the Neanderthal atmosphere. The rain had reduced to a minimal drizzle. She could've waited in Miller's jeep but she needed the air. She breathed deeply, thankful for the beauty of Loch Voil and Strathyre Forest beyond, fast fading in the setting sun's rays. She wandered out the gate and across the road to a clearing by the lochside and began tossing pebbles, ruining the water's glassy surface. What the fuck was she doing here? It wasn't necessary to nursemaid Miller on these visits. Certainly not this one anyway. That had become clear. She wasn't helping get anything out of that dolt Blackford and anything Miller *did* extract, 'man to man', he'd tell her about. But as far as Blackford was concerned, even if he did agree to tell the truth, how credible a witness would he be? His currency as a witness would surely already be devalued from his first perjury. That would also have been true for Lena Stewart though, overall, she was a far more credible prospect. In addition, Blackford's obvious lifelong drink problem would compromise him, wouldn't it? It was tricky all round really. Trickier than Miller knew, poor devil.

Miller. He had the evangelical zeal of the newly converted. Where would he stop? Lena's death was a blow. Of course she herself was a witness to what Lena had said. Duncan and Lizzie Henderson too. But surely that would be legally meaningless, sound and solid citizens though they all were. Their evidence would be second-hand, not from the witness's mouth. Still, he'd go on. She knew his tenacity and stubbornness would leave him wanting a legal, publicly avowed exoneration *if* he became certain of his father's innocence. And that was fast becoming the case. Yes, he'd be doing his damnedest in there to get Blackford to make admissions *and* to make them formally. That was never going to happen, no matter what that shit Blackford said. Miller's crusade was going to leave him more disturbed, more damaged than she'd remembered him from childhood. There was no way of stopping him. She'd have to let him take his journey. See where it led. She didn't know all the contents of the archive. He'd said that she should take the box home for a couple of days and have a look. Of course she wasn't a lawyer but he'd said that didn't matter. A fresh, intelligent mind on things might help spot something he'd missed. That was unlikely. Although she needed to have a look all the same. But he had to be destined for failure, or thwarted expectations at least. Though this time there were other ways to manage him. Not just the pat on the head and some chit-chat about ornithology of thirty years ago.

'Oh, Miller.'

She flicked her last flat stone and admired its eight-bounce skim. Behind her, she heard him calling her name. He must have finished with Blackford. Or, more likely, vice versa. With a final glance at the rippling waters, and with a familiar feeling of dread, reluctantly she turned back.

It was time to deal with Miller's disappointment.

40

'It all went okay, I reckon. I really think I might be able to get somewhere with him. He'll see us, well, see me again, in the morning, but I want you to come with me. I need to plan how to play it with him. With luck he might be sober then and . . .'

Catriona sighed. Ever since they'd left Blackford's house, Miller had been making the same claims. Trying to convince her, and although he'd never admit it, convince himself. She switched off from him and cast her eye around the hotel dining room. It was the best they could find in the area with a couple of rooms spare. Despite the time of year and the weather, the area was chock-full of weekend tourists. Still, the food was quite good, though she craved the welcome solitude of her own home.

'. . . he said he knew things, "things no one else does". He said there . . . and he put it like this, "there probably was a stitch-up", but he wouldn't *exactly* admit outright about lying. But I think somehow I can bring him round.'

She put her fork down and sighed. 'But, Miller, you said he wanted money. To talk any more. That's . . . that's just crap. It undermines anything he says. That's if you were foolish enough to give him any. Even him asking. Well . . . it's all a bit dodgy really, don't you think?'

'What? You mean you don't believe him at all? He said enough to make me satisfied that he's a *fucking liar!* He didn't see my dad that night. Lena didn't. *Plain and simple.*'

She reached over to touch him lightly on the arm. 'Okay,

Miller. *Okay.* Now please, you're raising your voice. Disturbing other people.'

She took another glance round the room. In truth, only one other couple was staring and whispering, no doubt mistaking Miller's outburst for some lovers' squabble. But she had to calm him down. He'd spent the entire return journey babbling on as they stopped at various hotels and B&Bs in an increasingly fruitless search for overnight accommodation. This reasonably sized country house hotel near the village of Callander may have seen better days but there were vacancies. The driving round and round had added to her exhaustion. That and Miller's running commentary on events. He'd obviously had a difficult time with Blackford but was recounting it as if he'd had a roaring success and had come away with a sworn affidavit admitting to the lies that had been told. She was beginning to wonder at Miller's state of mind. Blackford had made admissions, or hinted at them, and that was what was crystallizing Miller's belief in his father's innocence. The tide was obviously turning. Had turned. Now he wouldn't let it go.

She watched as he made a half-hearted attempt to rally himself, raising his glass to her. 'Sorry, Cattie. Let's change the subject.'

She returned the toast with a smile. 'Okay. What subject d'you fancy?'

Dinner over, Miller finished off his second cognac and nodded to the waiter for another. Catriona was long gone, pleading exhaustion and the need for an early night. He was sitting alone in a blissfully deserted lobby bar by a huge window, looking out at nothing but blackness. He was pissed. Not blasted but pretty gone. But he felt better. Blackford was a lying bastard and he was going to prove it somehow. He'd admitted lying when they were one-to-one, though still maintaining the 'yer faither could have done it' argument. It had been a half-hearted attempt, though. He could see it in Blackford's eyes. Something akin to guilt there. Possibly. Hopefully.

But what was it with Catriona? She had opened up. At last. She *was* normal after all. *Had* experienced the usual ups and downs of intimate relationships. However, he was becoming more and more irritated by her softly-softly approach to what he was doing. It was obvious she didn't want him to get hurt, to disprove one part of the evidence only, far down the road, to find that it didn't change anything about Dad. It was also increasingly obvious that she still retained some doubts about his father's innocence. But was she being overly careful because of the hurt it would cause him? Probably. Nice to know she cared. Very nice.

She'd lightened up during the meal when he'd changed the subject *and* talked about herself. No, she hadn't ever married but she'd had a couple of long-term relationships. One with another GP that had seen her making a home in the Borders, and which split up when she returned to East Lothian to nurse her father.

All in all she'd been pretty forthcoming about herself, amusing even, saying that she'd make the worst wife ever because she was a workaholic and liked, no *loved* being on her own. Loved being alone in her cottage at the sea's edge, only the waves and gulls for company, admitting that as she got older she craved solitude more and more. He wondered why. Maybe the quiet, relatively solitary childhood life with only her and her father had fostered the need for privacy, to escape from the crowd. She'd even said she would love to live on a place like Fidra, away from humanity. He knew the feeling.

Miller nodded his thanks as the waiter placed the cognac on the table. He looked at his watch. *Shit!* He should've rung Nikki. It was too bloody late now. Up in his room, the mobile would be red hot as she tried to track him down. He'd promised to phone her today. Callum and Emma were with her parents for the weekend. Ominously she'd said that there were things they needed to discuss. *Fuck, fuck, fuck!* He wouldn't be surprised if all this was enough to drive Nikki back to that wanker she was seeing before. Or someone else. Bloody marvellous. Another affair.

He shouldn't have been so caught up with dinner and Catriona. She didn't really look like she was enjoying it that much anyway. Had he been a bore? Talked too much about himself, about Dad. At some unidentifiable point she'd seemed to go off her dinner, drifting away into an inner world, merely nodding, giving out the odd, polite, 'Mmm, yes,' before retiring to her room. He picked up the brandy balloon and slung his jacket over his shoulder. Time to go.

Upstairs, he dug around in his jeans pocket for his room key and made a couple of unsuccessful swaying attempts to slot it in, while juggling the brandy glass and his jacket. Then he gave up and turned round to look at her door. Opposite rooms made it tempting. Too tempting. Just one ever-so-soft knock? See if she was awake? Apologize for being such a poor dinner companion. She was just across the corridor. One step, two steps. He raised his fist. But before he could do any more, the door clicked and opened.

'I heard you rattling about with your key. You all right?'

The room behind her was in darkness. She was standing squinting at the corridor lights, both hands raking through her sleep-tangled hair. Her left breast was almost fully exposed by the half-open silk dressing gown.

And then she stood back, holding the door open for him and allowed him to press his hand against her slim, warm waist to steady himself as he slid past her.

41

A boiling hot shower and a shitty instant coffee hadn't helped much. His head had an axe, no two, in it. He fumbled about in his washbag. Yes! Two crumbled aspirin still in their blister pack. He knocked them back with the last of the filthy coffee and sat on the edge of the bed rubbing his temples. He pulled his boots on but the effort was too much and he fell back on the bed, lolling across it sideways.

Fuck. How could he face her? The image of her standing half-naked in that silk dressing gown, breast exposed, still persisted. But it was quickly washed away by the images that had haunted his fitful sleep throughout the night.

The feel of her skin through the silk was warm as he brushed past and into her darkened room. Somehow she relieved him of the brandy glass and his jacket without him knowing. He heard the click as she closed the door. Immediately he'd turned to her. Brought his body and face close to her. To kiss her. And? Touch that breast maybe?

'Come here.' She'd put her hands on his chest. But not to kiss him, not to touch him. Merely to guide him to the easy chair in the corner of the room. And then a lamp was switched on and the spell broken.

'You need to drink lots of water. I'm going to make you some coffee too.'

She'd force-fed him three glasses of freezing cold tap water, after disarming him for the second time of the brandy glass, as he made a last-ditch attempt to throw its contents down his throat. But she'd been too quick and too sober for him and chucked ten quids' worth of the best cognac down the toilet. He couldn't remember drinking the coffee. If he had, he wouldn't have tried making it this morning. And then he remembered her coaxing voice and his big hand in her little one as she led him out of her room, across five feet of corridor to his own door.

He'd found himself in crumpled shirt and jeans, face down on top of his bed. It was still dark. What a fool he'd made of himself. She'd been long gone, hadn't she? Long gone and probably furious. It had only been his drink-fevered imagination plaguing him throughout the night. He knew it hadn't been real but he'd kept feeling the warmth of that exposed breast as she leaned over him, kept hearing her voice as she floated back out the door.

'I'm not going to bed with a man who's pissed. However much I want him.'

If only she had said that. If only . . .

What a fiasco. As he made his way downstairs he tried to thank his lucky stars. Whatever he thought Nikki might be doing, and she probably wasn't yet, there was no excuse to try and follow suit. It was just his paranoid fantasy. But, imagine if anything *had* happened between him and Catriona. He'd never cheated on Nikki. Never. Had seldom, if ever, been tempted. Most of the women he came upon through work or the gym were too hard, too brash. Too like Nikki? Jesus! What was he doing? Should he just pack up and leave? Go back to London. Accept that, yes – maybe, possibly – Dad was innocent but then maybe he wasn't. Perhaps he *should* sell the whole estate, like he was going to do before . . . before he got sucked further into this mess. Pretend, as he had done for most of his life, that nothing had happened. His dad was dead. End of story.

But he knew he was kidding himself. There was only one way to go. Onwards. He just hoped to God that he'd not alienated Catriona. Whatever his feelings for her, sexual and otherwise, he'd most definitely *have* to forget them. The childhood crush of old was rearing its head again. He'd thought she felt the same, but again, that was only his misguided fantasy. Presumably some therapist or psychologist could make much of his predicament. Here he was, chasing through his family past while pointedly ignoring and being careless of his own family in the present. *Enough!*

The nauseating breakfast smells of bacon and kippers drove him through the lobby, quickly past the restaurant, and into the snug bar to sit down away from the general bustle. Some real coffee was on the hotplate and he slumped into a corner booth, with a newspaper, trying to ignore the inanity of some trashy morning programme blaring out from the TV over the bar. But he couldn't concentrate on the paper. He had to work out what to say to her. To apologize.

He closed his eyes and leaned back his aching head. The TV was grating, booming out some godawful local news jingle. He was just about to ask the barman to turn it down when she appeared. Half smiling but a bit brisk.

'Hi. Here. You left your jacket in my room last night. Have you had breakfast? Because, if not, I think you should. But you'd better hurry. It's late. I'll drive you over to Blackford's. But don't worry, I'll leave you both alone. I'm more than happy to play skimmers on Loch Voil rather than step inside the lion's den. Let's go.'

He had to admire the way she'd dealt with his embarrassment.

'I'm glad you stopped by so that I could sober you up. I was feeling the wine a wee bit myself. Glad I didn't stay for the brandy. Mind you, that stuff in the rooms they call coffee's probably what gave you the headache. It's poison! Sorry to ply you with it. Anyway, you're looking better after some proper breakfast. Doctor does know best on this occasion. Gird the old loins for the meeting. Y'know I think Blackford's a real sod, Mill. I hope he's not leading you up the garden path.'

He nodded, thankful again for her help and her tact over last night. She'd clearly decided to dismiss the episode and concentrate on today's events.

She pulled up just short of the house. Blackford's place had the same empty air as the day before. Miller looked at her and shrugged.

'Here goes. See you in a while.'

She was halfway to the lochside and already searching for suitable flat pebbles to play with when she heard him.

'*Catriona!* Cattie, wait!'

She watched him scramble down to join her, something white flapping in his hand.

'Look. It was taped to the door.'

The A6 squared graph paper looked like it had been torn from a school exercise book. Folded in two, it had 'TO McA' scrawled on the front. She flattened out the page. Pencilled block capitals ran across the page, from before the faint pink margin line on the left, to the very right-hand edge. Dark, indented, like he'd been pressing too hard, there were sporadic multiple underlinings scarring the paper. It looked like the work of a demented, angry child.

DID YOU THINK I WAS GOING TO TALK AGAIN. YOU HAVE A NERVE TURNING UP HERE. YOUR FATHER DID IT. HE DID IT. I WILL NOT SPEAK TO YOU AGAIN EVER. GO AWAY. I AM LEAVING HERE AND THERE IS NO WAY YOU WILL FIND ME. SO FUCK OFF.

She looked back at Miller's pale exhausted face. He seemed ready to cry.

'What am I going to do, Cattie? I really thought I could talk him round. Just get him to tell the truth. He more or less admitted it to me yesterday. That he lied. Just like Lena said. This ... this ... "your father did it" shit. *Why? Jesus!*'

He'd collapsed on to the muddy bank, face buried in his palms, shaking his head again and again. She perched down in front of him, placing her hands gently on his knees.

'Come on, Miller. Let's get you home. Blackford is a bastard. A real shit. He's been playing around with you.'

At that, Miller snapped his head up. 'But he said it, more or less. That the police had made him lie. *He did!*'

'Okay, okay, okay. I believe you. Lena told us as much. But ... I ... I just don't think Blackford will ... well, come up with the goods. He's probably frightened, behind that tough-nut exterior. I mean look at his life. Sheer isolation. He can hole himself up here away from the world and drink himself silly every day without answering to anyone. The last, very last thing he wants is the past knocking on the door. I don't know if he really is leaving or has just run away for a while but ... basically, he's not Lena. I'm sorry, Mill.'

He was beginning to worry her. Still slumped on the muddy bank, staring over her shoulder, apparently unseeing, to the calm waters of Loch Voil, he'd started shivering from the damp air. She had to get him home. She tried gently to pull him to his feet but his solid bulk resisted.

'I can't leave it like this, Cattie. I just can't. But without Lena I've got nothing. Nothing.'

He darted a confused, desperate look at her and then back to the water.

'But then maybe Duncan was right. Even if those two lied, were made to lie, it doesn't matter.'

She gave his hand a soft squeeze as the first tear ran down his ashen cheek, his head nodding with emphasis.

'You see, Cattie, maybe the greater truth stays the same.'

Fear and Guilt

For those readers familiar with the first (1978) edition of this book, you will remember the words of the presiding judge in the case. If it were judge Lord McLeish's intention to keep Douglas McAllister incarcerated until his death then he succeeded. That is, apart from the final taste of 'freedom' that Douglas was offered by being released into the care of St Baldred's Hospice, near to his East Lothian home. Even this most basic concession to common humanity had to be hard fought for by his family and friends (this author included), his solicitor, and the hospice director.

Now, more than thirty years on, following Miller McAllister's aforementioned inheritance of most of the family estate and the awakening of his interest in his father's case, a buzz went around the locality about what Miller was doing. In any small place word travels rapidly, and more so when it concerns the region's most notorious criminal event.

This author has picked up a range of views on the topic from those living in the area. Sadly, many, if not most of those who will give an opinion, are very aggrieved at any attempts to re-open the case.

It seems that Miller initially wanted only

to satisfy himself of his father's innocence, following a lifetime's belief in his guilt. But now, as his belief in his father's innocence grows, this goal is no longer enough. A public exoneration and overturning of the verdict appears now to be the desired outcome.

Miller has expressed growing guilt at his refusal to believe his father's lifelong protestations of innocence and is adamant that he will do all in his power to reverse the verdict. However, at the time of writing, there are those who remain fearful that such a mission may well end in unhappiness, if not worse.

Notes for 'Fidra - an Island History Updated'

42

Duncan checked the dining room for the last time, nodding his approval. The table looked good. But the lighting? Too gloomy with just the wall lamps. Were there enough candles for the table? He flicked the overhead lights on. No, far too bright. Those were for when they had a full house and someone was doing a reading. Or for the darker winter mornings so guests could see to eat.

He retreated to the doorway to get a better look. Maybe setting things up in here was a bit over the top. The place was simply too big. Even this smallest table, albeit dressed beautifully in dazzling white linen *and* by the blazing log fire, seemed adrift in the mass that was the refectory. But he couldn't use any of the abbey's other facilities. Women weren't allowed in them. And further, this place afforded perfect privacy, being physically some distance away from the abbey proper, and being currently devoid of a single guest. Yes, privacy. If it were known that he was acting as host to Miller McAllister and his supporter Catriona Buchan, some in the abbey would be dismayed. Disapproving. Notions of forgiveness apart, there was still a significant minority who held strong views about the McAllister case. Nothing that reached the abbot's ears. They weren't brave enough for that. But the patchy, though persistent, atmosphere of disapproval was sufficient to tell him that not everyone was in agreement with his ongoing contact and dealings with the family. Thinking back, Ailsa's retreats to this place had also fostered a silent and brooding opposition from some members of the community. But that was a long time ago and, frankly, now he was past caring.

He moved forwards and poured himself a small glass of red wine from one of the two glass decanters placed centre stage, careful not to spill any drops on to the brilliant white tablecloth. He pulled a chair away, marring the effect of the ensemble, and placed it nearer the fire. He checked the clock. They'd be here in twenty minutes, weather permitting. Only the strongest of gusts could be heard through the thick walls of the building, sometimes making themselves known by wafts of smoke erupting from the fireplace. But the windows were another matter. As leaky and rattly as those in the bedrooms, the rain was tap, tap, tapping away, niggling at his thoughts.

He stared at the quivering flames, replaying the telephone conversation of last night. Catriona had answered. At Miller's house.

'. . . yes, Duncan, thank you, we're still coming. Eh . . . Miller's still out. Walking his dog. 'Bout half seven'll be fine.'

'How'd it go? With Blackford? Any joy? You found the place all right? Lena's directions okay?'

She was sounding strained and he had that unmistakable feeling that someone else was there. Miller, of course. Not dog walking. But he wouldn't or couldn't talk.

He seemed to wait an age for her eventual answer. 'Found him okay? Oh yeah, yeah. Look, Duncan. We'll see you tomorrow and talk about it all then, okay? 'Bye.'

Although strained, she had sounded her usual confident self. Duncan tried to recall her in childhood. She had seemed distant but also remarkably assertive and self-assured for a girl who had been brought up with no mother – or at least a mother who had died before she could remember her – and without the influence of siblings. Perhaps that was it. Forbes had brought his only child up to stand on her own two feet, especially since he was so caught up with his work. Duncan had liked and admired Forbes but he had to wonder if the self-sufficiency he'd fostered in his daughter had developed into something bordering on arrogance or conceitedness. That had been his first impression when Catriona had returned, in recent years.

Duncan smiled at the thought. Ailsa had vehemently disagreed with him on that. Got quite fiery about it. Understandable, since Catriona had been such a valuable companion for Ailsa in her last year or two of life. Maybe he was being unfair. Had he been jealous of Ailsa's easy friendship with her? And now Catriona was doing Miller good too, wasn't she? There was no doubt that she had an influence over him, always had, though especially now in his current vulnerable state. The lad obviously still thought a lot of her. Duncan wondered how far Miller's affection would go, had gone . . . but that was none of his business.

The chimney coughed out a billow of smoke, breaking his chain of thought. He moved out of its way, the high-pitched scraping of his chair on the stone flagging unnervingly loud in the vast refectory. He felt unwell. The headache had gone on for two days now, leaving him sick to the stomach. The last thing he wanted to do was eat, or cook for that matter. But some fresh fish with salad should be plain and tolerable enough. He leaned forwards to replenish his glass. Enough of this stuff usually made him feel better and it would help him face tonight. Work on the new edition had left him tired, listless. The new edition. What a waste of time. He shook his head. The pointlessness of it! What to do? Prayer was beyond him. Sleep beyond him. And confession and thus forgiveness.

Wearily, he reached inside his habit and drew out the ragged unstamped envelope. *Mr Douglas McAllister, Prisoner SG5567, HMP Peterhead, Aberdeenshire.*

6 February 1975

Whitekirk Abbey
East Lothian

Dear Douglas

On my last visit some months ago, you were thinking back over the evidence that convicted you. I too have been doing the same. As you know, I attended most of your trial. I witnessed the welter of evidence ranged against you. It seemed, no, in fact it *was*, a tidal wave set to engulf you. Although Ailsa and Mhari, in particular, expressed doubts at the time, in the heat of the moment of your conviction, I believe that the legal team Russell Sinclair put together on your behalf could not have done much other than they did. Russell expressed his absolute despair at the end of the trial and I tried to put his mind at rest. He has nothing to reproach himself for.

I can make no guess as to how you are finding the move to Peterhead. Ailsa tells me that you are in a special 'lifers' unit' and is relieved since it means that you should be safer from attack there. Ailsa is suffering a lot and that saddens me. But she has faith. *Real* faith. Enough to put some here in the abbey to shame . . .

One in particular.

The bell rang out twice, echoing its shrill peals around the room. He folded the pages away, safely hidden from view.

His guests had arrived.

43

'Well you can see for yourself, Duncan. He's devastated. Thing is, I reckon Blackford was a no-go from the start. An aggressive alcoholic, playing fast and loose with Miller's desire to clear his father's name. He asked for money, for goodness' sake! A chancer. Absolute chancer. Though he hardly seems to need it looking at his house. Apparently he kept boasting to Miller about how he'd bought and sold boats and "made a mint" when he left the coastguard.'

She shrugged. 'Maybe he's spent it all on drink and was looking to Miller to be his next soft touch. *The nerve of the man!* Now look at Miller. In a mess. With Lena gone, he's got nothing. Nothing that'll stand up anyway. Lizzie can say what Lena told her, as can we, but it's not the same as a sworn statement from a witness. Poor Mill. He's had it. That . . . that *sod* Blackford!'

She continued gutting the sea bass with expert, vigorous efficiency. Duncan looked on. Her face was taut with concentration and the obvious annoyance she'd just expressed at Blackford. She'd arrived in a tense mood, a downcast Miller trailing behind her. She delivered the bald, disappointing headlines from the Blackford encounter, including Miller's agitated state throughout the trip. She seemed genuinely furious on Miller's behalf, displacing that ire by practically ordering Duncan about in his own kitchen and taking over the food preparation. His initial reaction had been to pack them both off to the dining room with aperitifs but he knew she wouldn't have that. She needed to offload on to him. His second tactic had been to let her get on with it and offer a listening ear.

He managed a smile as she continued her frenzy with the fish.

'Maybe you should've been a surgeon, eh?'

She returned his smile, obviously relieved that he was trying to lighten the mood. 'Maybe. I was never one to be squeamish, not even as a child. In fact I used to be quite the angler. Though Miller could never abide it. Thought the fish felt pain. Always worried about something. Just look at him now. Nothing's changed.'

Duncan finished wiping down the worktop and faced her. 'Still . . . I *do* understand Miller's feelings about Blackford. But, what do you think of what he said?'

She had the taps on full pelt and had to raise her voice as she sluiced out the fishes' body cavities, tissue and blood cascading down the waste disposal.

'I told you earlier. I wasn't there for the "admissions". But think about it. Blackford couldn't very well deny what Lena had said, so yes, I'm sure he did just about say he'd made it up. Which I'm sure he did. Fairy stories, the whole thing. From both of them. But Miller'll never prove it. Not now. Not without Lena.'

She flashed Duncan an anxious look as he leaned back against the worktop, head shaking.

'Aye, poor Lena. What a tragedy.'

Catriona raised an eyebrow. 'Yes, indeed. But I saw that animal at close quarters. Granted, I'm no horse expert but it was a nervy beast. Very nervy. An accident waiting to happen?'

She bobbed her head towards the dining room as she towelled off her hands. 'You know, you'll have to help me, Duncan. I'm worried about him. I can't help feeling . . .

feeling . . . well, that there's something about how Miller is right now that reminds me of when he went off the rails as a child. You weren't around for that. But I saw it first-hand.'

He nodded. But she wasn't the only one who'd been given that privileged insight into Miller's damaged childhood. He'd heard about it at close hand also. Chapter and verse. From Ailsa.

Duncan stared again at Miller. The lad had grown more and more morose, continually raking his hair, and staring at the tabletop, talking more slowly than normal, almost trance-like.

'Okay. Even if, *if* I can track down Blackford again, I accept he won't say any more. I do. But where does that leave me? Leave Dad? They were my only hope. There's . . . there's nothing left. *Fucking* nothing.'

Miller looked up, momentarily embarrassed.

'Sorry.'

Duncan held up a hand. 'Don't be daft. I've heard far, far worse expletives from some of the folk who stay in this place. So please don't bother yourself about that. As for what's left. I don't know, Miller. I don't know enough about your father's case legally. But look, maybe, *maybe* you might have to consider just settling for belief.'

'Belief?'

'Yes, and I'm sorry to pull the religious analogy here, a bit corny, I know. But you might have to settle for *believing* your father to be innocent without any proof. Or any further proof. I mean, isn't it what you *feel* that counts more? Think of the distance you've come in your feelings about your father in this short time. *Incredible.* Yes, it's wrong that your father has that appalling stain on his character, and yes it's wrong for the families of the victims not to know the truth. An—'

Miller shoved his glass to the side, almost toppling over the port bottle. 'And what about who *did* do it? Killed those poor girls. What about him?'

Duncan felt Catriona's eyes on him before they shifted pityingly back to Miller. He had been ready to answer but she was taking over and moved nearer Miller, simultaneously placing a comforting hand on his forearm and sliding the port bottle out of his reach. Duncan heard her sigh to herself. She obviously wanted no repetition of the Callander episode. In his current emotional state Miller would need only one drink over the odds to lose control. Duncan echoed her sigh. It was time for some straight talking. Catriona needed to back him up.

She'd moved even closer to Miller, trying to get him to meet her eye. 'Look, Miller. It's not your or our job to go around trying to convict other people. Who would know where to start? Certainly, if you want to go and talk to the police, tell them about what Lena and Blackford said, then fine. Do. I doubt they'll thank you for it. And I doubt they'd start some big new reinvestigation. But what do I know? You're the lawyer. If you feel you want to go down that road, then you must. But frankly, I'm with Duncan. Can't it be enough just to *believe* that your father is innocent? After all, that's what the rest of us, your father's supporters, and your family have done all these years. Don't you think it would've been enough for your dad. He just wanted you to believe in him. That's all anyone ever wanted.'

But he was shaking his head. '*It's not enough! Not enough after all these years. All my doubting. It won't do!*'

Duncan sipped his drink and watched as Miller sank forwards, laying his forehead on the table in a gesture of utter dejection. Catriona shrugged and raised an eyebrow in a 'what next?' expression.

He had no answer for her.

Duncan closed the door and turned to her. Between them they'd managed to get Miller to the nearest bedroom.

'Is there anything you can do for him? Medication or something?'

She frowned. 'Let's wait and see. This might be a blessing in some ways. Get all that thirty-odd years of hell out of him. I'll keep an eye on him. I might have a word with my colleagues. We can always have him taken on as a temporary patient if things get that bad. Don't worry.'

He offered her a curt nod back. 'Very well. Thanks. Now look, you might as well stay too. The weather's filthy anyway. It'll take you an age to get back. See on the other side of the stairs and through that door? That's the female quarters. Bedroom at the end's made up. Basic toiletries there too. I'm going back to the abbey but I'll see you in the morning for breakfast.'

Five hours later he let himself into the building. He avoided the creaking fifth step. The door of the end room – Ailsa's room, as he always thought of it – was open. Just a bit. The wind was attacking the windows and whistling down the unused fireplace.

'Catriona? Hello? Cat—'

He nudged it open further, the creaking faint but audible to anyone inside. There was enough light from the hallway to see that the bed had been used but she was nowhere to be found. There was silence from the entire landing, bathrooms included.

He made his way down the stairs and through the

connecting door, doubling back up to the first floor of the male quarters. Just as he turned the corner, he heard the click of a door. She was barefoot. In T-shirt and jeans. No bra. And her hair was tousled.

She smiled nervously at him. '*Je—!* Oh, you gave me a fright! What you doing up? It's still the middle of the night. I was just checking on him. Exhaustion's won. He'll be out for hours. I'm going back to bed. See you later.'

And then she was gone. He placed a hand on Miller's door handle and then thought better of it. Instead, he stood for a moment, thinking back to their arrival. Tense, anxious. Miller certainly. But together. Close. Yes, they'd arrived looking like lovers. Surely they were?

He wandered down the draughty corridor, hunching himself inside his woollen habit, hands up sleeves as he walked. The shivering in his body would hold off no longer. But it was more than the cold his body had to answer to. He padded down the last flight of stairs, ears straining for any sign that either of his guests were abroad. Doubtful. Miller was surely unconscious by now and Catriona had looked completely spent, probably already asleep.

The door to the dining room was open a fraction. Had he left a candle burning hours earlier? Probably. He was getting absent-minded these days. Hardly surprising. He flexed his right hand. It felt clammy and cold, the trembling worsening by the second, as he creaked the door wider. Two candles *had* been left burning. He moved forwards to snuff them out with dampened forefinger and thumb, the acrid smoke floating upwards, stinging his nostrils. Wearily he made his way to the front door. Time for another stormy dash back up to the abbey.

And another futile attempt at prayer.

44

The sky was eye-wateringly off-white. Cloud cover so low it was practically on top of him. Lying on his back, the waves cradling him so gently, Miller could almost fall asleep. Apart from the cold, of course. It bit through the best wetsuit. So what? At this moment he didn't give a toss if he was carried right out to the North bloody Sea, and he could wave good-bye to Fidra as he went. Right now, who'd care? Apart from Meg, of course. He knew she was waiting patiently on the beach, ball at her feet, tired out and ready to go home for her breakfast. Just a wee while longer, girl, a wee while longer. These last few days he'd spent most of his time with her. Alone at the mainland house. He had a notion to take her to Fidra and just dig in. Hide away . . .

He closed his eyes, the brightness trying to break through the lids and, ears submerged, he listened to the crackles and hum of the sand, seaweed and pebbles stirring beneath him. He liked the sound of underwater. Otherworldly. Comforting. But he'd started to shiver. He breathed deeply. If he stayed in here long enough, early hypothermia would kick in, and he'd become sleepy. Nod off maybe. He could almost do that anyway, the motion of the waves was so rhythmically reassuring. He let the idea of being swept out to sea run around his head. A favourite game from childhood. He'd drift further and further away from a panting and confused Bella . . . no Meg, *Meg* on the shore. Then, between his flippered feet he'd see the top of Fidra and wave cheerio. If he wasn't mown down in the shipping lanes of the Firth, the current would suck him into the depths of the North Sea. His body might pass over and through those strangely named places he'd used to stare wonderingly at on the atlas. The Long Forties. The Devil's Hole . . .

He opened his eyes and blinked against the light but he knew it was more than that bringing the tears. He wiped a dripping hand at them. Salt water on salt water. *Christ, what a state.* A breeze had kicked up and was really cutting into him now. He noticed the air above him was getting hazy. A haar was creeping its way in, adding to the chill. He moved his legs a few strokes. He was getting too cold but he was reluctant to move. No, relax those muscles. Relax. The water will hold you. He often thought that being in the water was like flying. Gravity so altered it seemed as if he were completely weightless. And when he was snorkelling over some abyss, he fantasized that he was an astronaut space-walking over a new, strange-looking planet. Oh God, if only he *was* on such a planet. Away from everything and everyone. He'd had enough of it all. Hide away. Was that going to be possible? Unlikely. There'd already been a flurry of calls. Mhari, checking on him. Greg too. 'I've had one of Mhari's letters.' She'd really gone to town on 'Miller's extraordinary conversion. Seems quasi-religious to me. Real road to Damascus thing. Remarkable!' He and Greg had had a laugh about that. Greg, though, had been fascinated by his volte-face over Dad. Wanted the whole story. The Lena/Blackford angle had really interested him. 'Just fucking bad luck, Mill. That's all. Life sucks and all that.' Good old down-to-earth Greg. But, between the lines, he'd got the distinct impression that Greg wanted it all to die down now, so everything could get back to normal.

Mhari, on the other hand, had the bit between her teeth. She'd pushed him on the legal side of things. Was there really nothing else he could do? In truth, he had no answer. He'd had all these dreams of full exoneration but these past few days had left him depressed, rudderless. Utterly demotivated. He'd made a fool of himself with the police. Twice. He'd rung up about Blackford, only to be driven off the phone. 'Mr Blackford is an adult, at liberty to go where he wants, live where he wants. He's clearly not a missing person since you say he left you a note announcing his departure from the area. Further, if he has anything to say about a long-closed case, we'll listen to it. But until such time . . .'

He'd then gone to Edinburgh. Been allowed to see a fairly senior detective. An older man, who knew of the case at the time. 'These days we do take the idea of miscarriages of justice seriously but I have to say, Mr McAllister, there's nothing in what you've said that will prompt me to take matters further, despite your claims about the eye witnesses and your rather offensive and unsubstantiated accusations against the investigating officers at the time . . .'

Even Lizzie had tried to do her bit and talk to the police. Useless. All fucking useless. Maybe he could go through the archive again? Hire some specialist to help him? But no, he was tired. So tired. And what about the kids? Nikki? At least she was talking to him now and letting him speak to Callum and Ems. They sounded great. Asked when he was coming home. Soon. Had to be soon. To use Nikki's overworked word of late, all had surely become folly. His family was suffering. And why should he perpetuate more family hell? The devastation of his own childhood and the position he'd taken over his father, so obviously wrong now, shouldn't, *couldn't*, be allowed to infect a second McAllister generation. Enough *was* enough. He had to lay all this to rest. Or, maybe there was a better way, in the long run. Perhaps it would be easier, kinder to everyone, if he just let the currents take him away . . .

He sighed and turned his floating head out to sea, freeing an ear to the air. Then he heard it. Meg's barking. He swivelled his head the other way, over the bobbing waves. With a lurch of alarm, he saw that he'd almost got his morbid wish. He'd drifted way too far from the shore and Meg had noticed it. *And* the mist was thicker than he'd realized. What the hell was he thinking of? He had to get back. Meg's silhouette was running up and down the shore, still barking madly, desperate for his attention.

Behind, a tall, ethereal figure was marching its way towards her.

45

He set out on a powerful front crawl, cutting through the waves as fast as he could, fighting against the restraining tangles of sinewy seaweed and the tiredness in his cold, weakened muscles. He'd stayed in too bloody long. If he was trying to kill himself, he was doing a good job. He hauled himself with arm-crippling strokes through the last dozen yards, arriving breathless into shore.

The ghostly figure of before was all too real now, and reassuring. Catriona, wrapped up in a heavy coat and sand-caked winter boots was hurrying towards him.

'Come on, Miller! Time you were out of there. Good Lord, it's worse than I thought! You're blue with the cold!'

He stood up, and in the last couple of feet of water, tried to remove his fins. He managed one but he felt a surge of dizziness and a strong wave toppled him. Catriona was running in to help, oblivious to the sea water soaking the hem of her coat.

'*C'mon now, Mill!* That's it . . . I've got you.'

He felt Catriona's surprisingly strong arms pulling him upright and dragging his body the last few yards on to the sand, Meg now encircling them, overexcited by all the activity.

Catriona, clutching his dropped fin, was looking him up and down, clearly worried at the uncontrollable shivering running through his body.

'Have you *any* idea how long you've been in there? Come on, we're going back to my place.'

*

He'd been there most of the day, a day that had turned into a minor medical emergency. Now he lay on Catriona's sofa, under two duvets, warm at last. Her story had been straightforward. Although it was the weekend, she'd been at work, catching up on a few things. From her surgery window, she had a clear view of the Firth of Forth, and had become used to seeing him go down to the beach for his daily swim. By the time she'd finished work and was packing up to go home for a quiet Sunday lunch, she was astonished to see him still in the water. Meg was running around, clearly distressed as she watched him drift further and further from the shore. She'd rung a colleague – another devotee of open water swimming – asked him the approximate temperature of the water at this time of year, advisable times for immersion and suchlike. That had been that. She'd walked to work so had no car and had to tear down to the beach on foot to haul him ashore, bundle him and Meg into his jeep and burn rubber to get him to her house.

She'd plied him with fortifying snacks, hot drinks, and even went to his house to fetch some clothes for him to wear after the long, warming bath she'd insisted he soak himself in. She'd made no attempt to interrogate him about what he'd been doing floating there for so long. But it was clear that she was concerned about his mental as much as his physical condition.

Lying on her sofa, with the light gone and Meg sleeping by the blazing log fire, he could hear Catriona moving about upstairs. He felt strangely euphoric but he wasn't fooled. The high was the same effect you got any time you survived some form of near miss, physical or emotional. No, whatever he'd been doing out there today, it had been profoundly worrying. And what made it worse was that he had been largely unaware. Granted, he'd had thoughts, fanciful ones, of floating away to oblivion, but it was just his mindset. He didn't mean it. Yet, his actions said otherwise. He'd given himself a fright. And what about his family? His siblings? At this rate, the next funeral they'd be attending would be his. How selfish.

More guilt. And now his actions had brought worry to Catriona. Even more reason to give it up. Be thankful for what he'd got. That was a lot, wasn't it? He could make his peace with Dad now. With the past. Who would have considered *that* possible a handful of weeks ago? He eased himself up and stood, unsteady for a moment, before shuffling over to place another log on the fire.

She appeared in the doorway and gave him an approving tilt of the head.

'*Well*, you look better than you did a few hours ago. Though still far from your usual self. How you feeling? You've been dozing for ages. Both of you.' She nodded towards Meg.

He moved over to a nearby chair and slowly lowered himself into it.

'I'm feeling okay. Look, Cattie, I want to thank you for he—'

But she was holding up a hand. 'Please. Don't, Mill. I just want you to promise to look after yourself a bit more. Okay?'

He nodded, thankful that she didn't want to have some dramatic post-mortem on events. He couldn't have taken it right now. He had many reasons to be grateful to her. Tact and timing were two of them.

She moved towards a darkened area of the room.

'Okay, now you're feeling a bit better, there's something I want to show you. Over here.' She switched on a light.

He followed her. The closed archive box sat on a table. Only one item lay beside it. A slim, blue solicitor's notebook.

The kind used for taking notes in court. She gestured for him to sit opposite her.

'Have you been through these? The whole bundle of them?'

He nodded. 'Yeah, pretty much but Sinclair's wr—'

She nodded back and finished the sentence for him. 'Russell Sinclair's handwriting's appalling. Yes. I don't blame you for not wading through it all. But I'm pretty good at reading bad handwriting. I am a doctor, after all! And I picked up on this late last night. Insomnia. Needed something to do. Look at this. It's a record of Blackford's appearance in court. I checked back with the trial transcript. It's not complete. Blackford gave evidence over two days. The transcript in the archive box doesn't have everything. That's why you missed this. Now, Russell Sinclair obviously went back over his notebooks during the years. There's an annotation beside his entries on Blackford's evidence. It's in different coloured ink and it looks fresher.'

A Blackford/EiC/X/XX

RE: Dropping off Lena Stewart: '. . . sometime after 9 p.m. and then went home and had an early night [NB *uncorroborated] due to early morning coastguard shift the next day [NB corroborated] . . .'
[*Uncorroborated. Live-in grandfather away in hospital during this period].

Then in blue biro, a more legible scrawl.

NB – do timings re: E Ritchie. Check B/ford's whereabouts for Galbraith and Bailey.

She broke into his thoughts. 'What's EiC, X, XX?'

He looked up at her, still fingering the notebook.

'Evidence in chief. That's the main evidence, before the cross-examination by the other side. X is cross-examination, XX is re-examination by the lawyer who called him in the first place.'

She frowned. 'Okay. But you see where Sinclair's coming from here? Problem is, I can't find any other follow-up. Maybe the times didn't fit. For any of the girls.'

Miller shook his head. 'But wouldn't . . . no, I suppose not. I was going to say wouldn't Sinclair have gone down this road early on? But not necessarily. My father's letter said or implied that Russell Sinclair leapt upon any and all alternative theories over the years, as the prospect of a successful appeal faded away. Looking at Blackford was probably just another of them. Christ, he probably looked at everyone. But I should check those books more thoroughly.'

She took the notebook, placed it back in the box and slid it towards Miller.

'I have. It's left me cross-eyed but I've done it. Blackford's the only one Sinclair's annotated in that way. I checked on a couple of things myself. He would've been twenty-two when the first girl went missing. He joined the coastguard here when he was twenty-one and before that was in the merchant marine. All ships, boats, water – and time on his own presumably – certainly when he got to patrolling for the coastguard. Plus a dark alcoholic side. I can see Russell Sinclair's logic.'

Miller shrugged. 'I'm not sure. If there's no follow-up. Probably an empty theory. I think I'll sleep on it.'

Twenty minutes later, he'd finished his last warming drink. He heaved the archive box under one arm and walked towards the front door, searching along the coat hooks in the hallway for his wetsuit and fins.

'I'll come over in the morning to pick these up. Why don't you keep Meg for the night too? She's out for the count. And, she'll keep you safe. She's not a bad guard dog. Sometimes.' He opened the front door but she moved forwards and brushed past him, clicking the door to again with her back.

'Course Meg should stay. I wish you could too.' She took a step towards him. 'After all, you're not a man who's pissed tonight. Are you?'

It took a moment for him to get it. He hadn't dreamed it. *She had said it!*

Gently, she put a cool hand to his cheek. 'But . . . no . . . it . . . it wouldn't be any good. Not right. For either of us. I think I know what you've been feeling, Mill, and I'm just catching up. But we need to leave it at that. I'm sorry. I probably shouldn't have said anything but I . . . I just sensed . . . oh God, I'm crap at this.'

He put his hand over hers, astonished that she was opening up to him. *At last.* Slowly, she moved out of his way, gave his hand a final squeeze and re-opened the door, her voice taking on a self-consciously jolly tone.

'It'll be lovely to have Meg but you shouldn't worry about me. Worry about yourself. Take care.'

He managed a farewell smile and headed out into the cold. The earlier euphoria had long since drained away. Though the feel of that gentle hand on his cheek, and those whispered words, had lifted his heart, but only momentarily. He had to face it. He was seriously out of control. Becoming more and more like the childhood Miller. And that left only one familiar feeling.

The overwhelming sense of impending disaster.

46

Another night of angry weather. Another night without sleep. Although, for Duncan, the two weren't causally linked. He'd lived through too many stormy autumns in this place and survived with the bare minimum of rest for most of his life here, what with the early morning prayers. Just as well it was low season for the guest house and he had fewer responsibilities. Because he wasn't functioning. He'd slaved away trying to get everything done before he left. Nearly 3 a.m. and here he was, holed up again in the guest-house office with the inevitable bottle of whisky. It had become his refuge. The bottle and the office. About the only place where he could think, work, write.

The envelope was in front of him. Again. *Mr Douglas McAllister, Prisoner SG5567, HMP Peterhead, Aberdeenshire.* Page two was where it really began.

Ailsa also holds a lot of guilt in her which she has discussed endlessly with me. She says that she has asked for forgiveness from you and that you have given it. She also asks for forgiveness from a higher authority and I hope that she will be granted it.

But whatever actions she berates herself for, they can be as nothing compared to others'. Guilt that haunts is, in some ways, punishment enough for wicked acts. Apology to those affected, and prayer - if prayer is

still a possibility - to one's God may be far
from enough. But it has to be a beginning.
    And I want to begin by apologizing to you,
Douglas.

For a moment he stared at the expanse of fading pale blue,
where the rest of the words should have been. He had half
a mind to find a pen and finish it off. Thirty-two years late.
Instead, he clasped both hands over the page in a conscious
emulation of prayer. He had to face it. That was as far as he
would ever get now. Emulation. This wretched letter? Would
he ever, really, have completed it and sent it? Of course not!
But he'd kept the thing. To be unearthed from time to time.
Then buried again for years. Existence and contents denied.
Now, with Douglas's death and Miller's reappearance on
the scene, here it was once more. One last time. Matters
were approaching their final resolution. There could be no
doubt. He folded away the pages and placed the envelope
in his desk drawer, keys jangling as he began to secure the
lock. But why bother locking anything now? He pulled the
laptop towards him. Time to get down to work. There was
much to do. But the memory nagged at him. Of what was a
final visit? No, not final. That had been reserved for the
hospice visits a lifetime later. But the last, realistic chance
he'd had of making things right . . .

*. . . He'd opted to drive to Peterhead. A cold, misty, grey day. His
dread increased with every hard-driven mile. The preliminaries had
taken a bit longer than usual. Staff shortage, he was told at the front
gate. But, too soon, he was inside and directed to a specific numbered
table. Different drill from Saughton. Security and atmosphere tighter
all round.*

Douglas had lost weight. A lot of weight. Duncan was surprised.

His limited knowledge of prisoners and prison life had left him with the idea that stodgy food and lack of exercise usually made the long-term incarcerated put on weight. But not Douglas. Either he wasn't eating or the stress was making him shed weight. More likely, both. He'd developed the 'prison tan' though. A ghostly pallor that was more startling because of his black hair. Although even that had greying streaks at the temples now. Another new physical feature. Another sign of stress. The telltale charcoal shadows under his eyes completed the picture of torment.

Looking at Douglas, he felt like throwing up. Had to grip the sides of his chair to stop himself from jumping up and fleeing from the room. The miserable, stuffy room, with only a few tables occupied by couples in desultory, mumbled conversation. Forty-five years of this! Unbearable!

'Ailsa's sent a few things up with me. I've checked them in at the gate. Things to eat. A couple of books. Toiletries. Not sure what else. So. How . . . how you managing?'

To his surprise, Douglas had pulled out a tobacco tin and started rolling the thinnest cigarette, staring him in the eye, a half-smile on his face. 'Aye, Duncan. After a lifetime's abhorrence of the filthy habit, I've started. Well, you've got to do something in this place to while away the time, and it forms a kind of social bond between prisoners. And *baccy's* currency in this place, believe me. As valuable, if not more so, than the cash you keep in your wallet. Anyway, how's Ailsa? And the kids?'

Douglas hadn't answered his question. Why should he? It was pretty obvious how he was managing. Best leave it for a moment. 'I've not seen much of the kids. Ailsa's been at the abbey. Forbes "prescribed" it for her. She's a bit like yourself. Getting a wee bit on the thin side. They not feeding you in here then, Doug?'

His attempt at lifting the tone had fallen flat. Douglas was fiddling with his lighter, frowning.

'And Miller? My wee lad.'

The dreaded question. 'Like I say, Doug, I've not seen much of the kids but I'm sure Miller's okay. When Ailsa's been at the abbey Forbes has been looking after him and Greg. Catriona's there too. And . . . and yes, I'll send him your love.'

He leaned over to press a reassuring hand on Douglas's arm, caught the disapproving glare of a nearby warder, and sat back again. 'Listen, Doug. I'm sure your laddie will come round. It's just the shock of . . . of everything. Give it time.'

He regretted the word as soon as he'd uttered it. Time! Idiot! Douglas certainly had enough of that to spare. A silent nod in return. A slow grinding out of the cigarette end. 'How much has she told you over the past year, Duncan? The lot, I suppose?'

His own silence had said it all.

'It's bloody ironic. She confides in a monk more than she does in her bloody husband . . .'

He could still feel the heat of that anger now. Anger which they both recognized was really directed against the system, not at a misunderstood but still passionately loved wife. Forty-five years of hell before him. How could any man withstand that? He knew he couldn't have. Come to that, he couldn't stand much of anything any more. What was there left? No prayer, no faith, no joyful, loving human contact. Just deceit, lies, torment. All torment. But he had been a different man in his youth. Had used these past thirty years to try and make amends with humankind. Had stayed in the order. Had tried, *tried* to live the best life he could. But he'd never asked for forgiveness. Because asking for forgiveness meant confessing to wrong. And that had been unthinkable. Until now.

He clicked the laptop into life. Time to use the sleeplessness profitably for once. He shivered. The empty guest house seemed to stir around him as the wind picked up outside. From upstairs, he could hear it rattle and whine its way through the casements in the empty, darkened rooms.

As it had done year after hellish year.

Belief into Certainty

Although Douglas McAllister must have hoped –
perhaps eventually prayed – each day of his
incarceration for some miracle that would
expose the truth of what happened to destroy
his life, it never came. Not in his lifetime.
As fate, and God, or the Devil would have it,
it took his own terrible and painful death to
start the train of events that would lead to
the truth.

Miller, now certain of his father's innocence, had reached that awkward and frustrat-
ing juncture where he *felt* what he believed
to be the truth but was unable to prove it
and turn it into knowledge. This fine dis-
tinction may seem more fitting to some theor-
etical philosophical discussion but is wholly
understandable. Miller was always, from a
boy, inquisitively interested in so much.
Equally, he had always wanted definitive
answers to his questions.

Those who wished to help him, tried to
encourage him to accept what he felt and what
he believed, and to let matters rest. All
Douglas McAllister ever wanted was for his
beloved youngest child to believe in him.
During his final troubled days at the hospice, where I visited him, he drifted in and
out of morphine-induced sleep. When he did
float back to fleeting lucidity, Miller was

the name on his lips. Along with Ailsa's, his wife. His two most beloved people on earth. 'Make Miller believe. Make him see the truth.'

Those repeated mantra-like words are with me forever, eating into my days, flooding my sleepless nights. Well Miller does believe. But he doesn't know the truth. And there are several truths to be known from all those years ago.

Notes for 'Fidra – an Island History Updated'

47

LEAVIS, LINDSAY & MCCOLL
SOLICITORS

7 November 2005

37 St Andrew's Crescent
Edinburgh
EH1 0PP
Tel: 0131 507 2534

Dear Mr McAllister

RE: Your late father, Mr Douglas Cameron McAllister

As agreed when we met yesterday, I am now formally recording the
latest results of my dealings with the relevant authorities regarding
the conviction of your father and our attempts to achieve posthumous
exoneration for him.

In addition to that given by you, I have taken statements from: Dr
Catriona Buchan, Ms Elizabeth Henderson and Brother Duncan
Alexander, concerning what Ms Lena Stewart reported to them or
reported in their presence about the evidence she gave at court in
1974. There are one or two details outstanding that I wish to clarify
and I would be grateful if, when Brother Duncan returns from his
retreat, you would ask him to get in touch.

Contrary to the promising initial assessments made by me on hearing
of Ms Lena Stewart's intended change of evidence, her death has

left me far less sanguine about our prospects. That, coupled with the refusal of Mr Andrew Blackford to meet with you again, and the note he left you apparently recanting whatever admissions he made to you during your recent conversation, leave your father's case severely compromised.

I have passed the statements on to the relevant authorities, and following lengthy conversations with them, it is clear that they are reluctant to take any action at this stage. It could be argued that this position may be nothing more than administrative obstinacy, in that they are unwilling to even consider that a miscarriage of justice has taken place in your father's case. I get the distinct impression that there are some senior investigators and officers who are resolute in their belief that he was guilty. However, there are others more forthcoming and I have to say that my dealings with them, to date, have been very open and above board. They have intimated that if any further information is unearthed, for example if Mr Blackford reappeared and gave a sworn statement changing his evidence, then the position might be altered. However, I gather from you that this is an unlikely prospect, although please bear in mind that a change of heart by Mr Blackford would not, *on its own*, be enough.

Overall, the outlook seems rather bleak and we must discuss further what steps you next want to take. I have to reiterate my original advice which I discussed with you yesterday. There are other elements in the case against your father that were overwhelming. I do not need to rehearse them here. Any effective attack on his conviction must take account of them. What is clear, is that there can be no rush to consider quashing your father's conviction for some considerable time, if ever.

On your request, I have forwarded copies of this letter to your brother
Gregor and sister Mhari.

Yours sincerely

James McColl

48

He stood out on the freezing balcony of the mainland house, staring at Fidra, the letter lying crumpled at his feet as the wind threatened to suck the white ball through the bars of the handrail.

Catriona moved forwards and picked it up, smoothing the paper out again on her thigh.

'Mill. Come on. Come inside. Please.'

Arms ramrod stiff, fists clenched by his sides, he wasn't moving a muscle. Catriona reached out a hand to touch his back and then retracted it again before making contact. Somehow, she felt like she'd be stung, burned by the force of . . . of what exactly? His anger? Disappointment? Sadness? At this moment he was unreadable. Shut off. Out of nowhere, Meg brushed past her legs and sat by his side, looking up at him, eyes plaintive. He placed a gentle hand to her muzzle, held it for a moment, and then pointed for her to lie down.

'We're going out there. To Fidra. Me and Meg. Just the two of us.'

He moved both hands to the balcony rail, his shoulders hunching, back still facing her, his voice a monotone.

'I know you've been wanting me to take you over there. I will. Just not now. I've decided. It's time for a clear-out. A new start. Whatever else, I'm going to do something with the island at last. I'm thinking of allowing the RSPB greater access. They've been wanting to put bird observation cameras on the island for a while now, like the ones on the

Bass Rock. And I've got someone from the archaeology department at Edinburgh uni coming over in a couple of days and someone from Scottish Heritage. I'm thinking of allowing excavations. I came across a bit of correspondence in the files from years ago, involving Russell Sinclair and your father. The experts wanted to do some preliminary research work. On balance, I think it was considered a bit distasteful. Still a bit too soon after the event. But I want to open a new chapter now. It's time to honour, respect the island again. Get it cleansed. An exorcism, if you like, before I finally decide what to do with it. I want to do it on my own. I hope you'll understand.'

Her answer was a whisper. 'Of course. Of course.' This time she took a step towards him. Lightly kissed his cheek. 'I'll call you later.'

Silently, she backed away and let herself out of the house, leaving the crumpled letter on the hallway table.

The loading was almost finished. He was travelling light. He slung his bag in the back of the boat along with the archive box and a bag of Meg's dried food. She hopped in after them.

The crossing was going to be choppy and cold. Fine. Just what he felt like. North Berwick harbour was quickly lost behind him as the haar moved in more speedily than he'd expected. No matter. He could do this journey blindfold with no instruments *and* find his way to anywhere on the island with his eyes shut. He once made a bet to that effect with Greg. Insane but never followed through.

Meg huddled into his legs and he stroked her soft ears. He was grateful beyond words for her loyal, reassuring company. 'That's it. Snuggle down.'

He wondered if he was now at a lower ebb than he had

ever been during these past two years. When he believed his father to have been unquestionably guilty, when Nikki was shitting on their marriage, and when his mother had died. During that time he'd gone to the doctor's and been prescribed a mild antidepressant. He'd never told Nikki, since she'd somehow have seen it as 'unholistic', unhealthy even. He didn't care if chattering-class wisdom saw it as papering over the cracks, masking the real causes of psychic pain. Well, sod it, he knew the causes. All of them. He just wanted some relief. The drugs had helped. He wished to God he had them now. Instead of the couple of bottles of wine and hip flask he was carrying over. That and some unappetising and unhealthy meals-for-one to put in the new microwave. Better not let Nikki know he was eating that trash, not looking after himself.

'You won't tell, will you, girl?'

Would Nikki care? They were more distant than ever now. He didn't think she'd considered the possibility of him having another woman. And there wasn't really another woman. Catriona and he had settled into a comfort zone of sorts, a briefly acknowledged mutual feeling, probably more powerful on his side, but not to be acted on. She was there to help him through this hell. She'd said as much, and then after that? Friendship? He dearly hoped so. At last there was someone he could trust with his dark memories.

Though, in fairness, he'd never really given Nikki the chance to help him with the past. And rather than trying to help now, she was withdrawing. And worse, she was withdrawing the children. He wasn't going to let that continue. Not once he'd sorted things out. *Sorted*. That was a laugh! The meeting at the solicitor's office and McColl's subsequent letter had just about finished him. The end of the road. Drawing of the line. Irony of ironies. Here he was.

After a bloody lifetime of denial, and then driving himself to the limit to make up for what he'd done to Dad, to the whole family, it was all pointless effort. Now no one seemed to be listening. Well, no one who mattered, who could change things. Not the police, not the solicitors.

Might as well face it. He'd come a long way since that hellish night at the hospice. Tried and failed. What a waste. He'd been a wretched son, the cause of untold anguish for his mother. A difficult, moody husband. Deeply inadequate father.

And now everything was ruined, thanks to him. He'd handled Blackford all wrong. Had been too gung-ho, aggressive and scared him off. Now, what with the solicitor's opinion, all was lost. McColl was more or less saying Dad still looked guilty. Fuck it, maybe he was! It was always what Catriona and Duncan had thought even though they didn't want to say it to his face.

Speaking of Duncan, *he'd* even abandoned him now, leaving a terse phone message saying that he was going on retreat for a while. Miller had wanted to know more and thought twice before calling him back. Duncan's odd, troubled tone had almost made him think otherwise. The ways of spiritual men and women were beyond him and the last thing he needed was another human drama to deal with. But it was okay. Duncan wasn't answering, so he'd left a friendly enough message saying he hoped the retreat went well and that he might be interested to know that the chapel ruins were going to be examined professionally. Something for his next book on Fidra?

He'd also had a mind to call the solicitor and have it out with him. *'If you think Dad's guilty then fucking well say it in plain English, damn you!'* But again, he'd thought better of it. He just didn't want to hear it. While he'd had his head buried in the witness issues, there was all the other damning evidence. Maybe he'd just been cherry-picking, not seeing the whole picture. The solicitor's letter had given him a reality check, a bitter reminder that demolishing his father's case involved more than just uncovering two lying witnesses. Duncan had warned him of that weeks ago. He wished he'd paid more heed. Further reason to berate himself.

'It's all *crap*, Meg. *I'm* complete crap!'

The jetty was in view now, seeming to float towards him out of the haar. With a sickened shake of the head, he guided the little boat in.

Time for the finale.

49

'Okay, then. See you next week and if those tablets don't do the trick, ring up the surgery. I'm always happy to have a word. 'Bye now.'

She guided the elderly woman out of the room with a smile and then shut the door, praying the heavy sigh of relief was inaudible to those outside. She was glad to see the back of the last patient. A difficult case, true, but that wasn't the reason. She looked at her reflection in the small wall mirror and shook her head. Yes, Dr Catriona Buchan was exhausted. Couldn't find another sympathetic smile even if it was tortured out of her. The rest of the afternoon would be easy, though. It was her early-finish day, to catch up on repeat prescriptions, reading and writing of reports, correspondence and the like. Tasks that required only part of her mind to be on duty. The empathetic, sensitive demands of dealing with patients weren't necessary. A relief.

She checked her watch and moved over to the surgery window, opening the blind fully. She spotted it immediately, in the distance. One small boat making towards Fidra. It was him. He said he would be on his way by now. She could just about make out his silhouette, hunched down against the wind and spray, cutting a ghostly figure as he disappeared into the haar.

He was in a bad way. Despite his professional background in the law, he'd admitted to harbouring unrealistic expectations of what could be done with his father's case. With no Lena Stewart and a hostile and now non-existent Blackford, of course matters were pretty much hopeless.

She was staring at the point where he'd disappeared into the haar, imagining she could still pick out the wake of the tiny boat. A mess? Quite probably. If Miller had retained core characteristics from his childhood then he was likely, *very* likely to do something destructive, self-destructive, that he'd regret. With another heavy sigh, she moved from the window and sat down wearily at her desk, wondering how she was going to get through the afternoon.

As usual she was the last to leave the surgery. She punched the security code in and made her way across the deserted car park. She had a world of reading to do and cursed as the bundle of medical journals slithered from her grasp in her fumbling quest for car keys. The night was damp and chilly enough without having to scrabble around on the ground for the bloody journals.

From a side road, in his darkened car, Duncan watched as she gathered up her belongings. Would she be going home? Probably, if she had what looked like a pile of work with her. He sat back, closing his eyes as her brake lights gave their final flicker before turning the corner. His head was killing him. All the travelling, lack of sleep, tension. He'd be pushed to estimate the mileage he'd done. Up to Caithness. Now back again. Recent memories were continually vying for prominence, like waking dreams, pushing in on his consciousness as he'd driven mile after punishing mile. He squeezed his eyes tighter shut as if that childish action could blot them out, banish them.

The nursing home in Caithness had been, for some unfathomable reason, stuck in the middle of the bleakest moorland imaginable, a few miles from Wick and any form of civilization. Anyone responsible for consigning a relative to the place deserved to burn in hell. As expected, his garb, his credentials as a holy man, were unquestioned, universally accepted wherever he went, particularly in that still God-fearing part of the world. She was a handful of years off her century. Worn out physically but nevertheless compos mentis, though her local accent was well-nigh impenetrable. But that hadn't mattered. She could give him what he sought. More, much more than he'd expected . . .

The flash of passing headlights roused him. He'd almost dropped off. Time to go. Time to plan.

She'd hoped that the hot chocolate would offer her some memory of childhood comfort. It sat inside, cold, barely touched, as she stood out on the verandah, listening to the sea, hugging the book to her stomach. *'It's your special gift, sweetheart. You look after it, always.'* Today had been one of those days. Hating being a grown-up. Hating responsibility. Frightened of tomorrow. She shrugged to herself and turned back into the house. Maybe she just needed a holiday. A real break. On the other side of the world maybe. Or, maybe she should leave here. Soon. She wandered back into the living room and replaced *Treasure Island* on the sideboard, nodding at the photograph of her father. Don't be frightened. Tomorrow would be better.

50

Miller had awoken to a cloudy but dry day on Fidra that, in part, lifted his mood and strengthened his resolve for what he planned to do. Yesterday's haar may have cleared but he was merrily creating his own.

He'd positioned the bonfire at a deliberately high point. Like a beacon, glowing and billowing out over the Firth. A funeral pyre. Set to lay everything to rest once and for all. He knew he was saturated in the stench of smoke, his face glowing from the fierce heat he'd set up, stinging his skin in contrast to the biting air.

Certain items he'd left until last. The police photographs had just gone in, melting the victims' images into further disfigurement. He waited as, one by one, they bubbled and disintegrated.

'Not long now, girl.'

He watched as Meg kept well out of the smoke's trajectory. Atop a hillock above him, lying on her belly, alert but unsure. As ever, he knew she'd sensed his mood today and was biding her time until it passed. As it would, with the eventual dying of the embers. Two more items to go. The Russell Sinclair letters had gone long ago, as had a copy of the will. That act had seemed strangely unsatisfying, strangely empty of the longed-for catharsis. Instead, he was filled with an underwhelming sensation bordering on pointlessness, and with it, helplessness.

Now it was time for that wretched front-page cutting. Almost immediately the flames attacked the smug-looking, or was it just professional, head-and-shoulders shot of his father. Gone! Black ashes. Nothing else. Time for the last. His father's letter as penned by Lizzie Henderson was meant to go in ceremoniously, page by slow page. But somehow, at the last minute, he faltered and flung the entire thing in, still within its crumpled envelope, and watched as the flames, infuriatingly, took their time over its destruction.

He turned from the fire and with a final burst of energy began a heavy stamping to flatten the archive box, jumping up and down as the seams gave way, leaving a crumpled mass underfoot. He was bending down to begin tearing the cardboard into more manageable strips when he first felt the heat and then the pain near his left hip. Looking round he saw that the hem of his jacket had caught alight, flames licking their way up towards his waist. Frantically he began to rip the jacket off, throwing it away from his body, and then running after it to stamp out the flames.

'*Fuuuck!*'

He knelt to inspect the damage. Some scorching to the waistband. Luckily, the denim had been heavy and resisted most of the flames. But the reason it had ignited was obvious: some patches of oil were clustered around the burned area, probably rubbed off from the boat.

'*Fuck it!*'

He marched back to the fire and flung the jacket towards the centre of the flames.

'*Go to hell, bastarding thing!*'

He backed off from the bonfire, his heart still pounding from the shock of finding himself on fire. *Jesus!* He could have been burned alive! He lifted his T-shirt and saw a reddening of the skin near his hip but there appeared to be no actual burning. He lowered himself on to a rock and covered his face with hands reeking of smoke. A deep, agonizing paper cut had bled its way down from finger to palm, but he made no attempt to clean it. The first sobs came in quick succession as he pressed his fingers against his eyes to stop the tears.

'*No, no, nooooo! Oh God, help me. Help meeee!*'

A whimper from Meg made him look round, wiping his eyes.

'Fuck this. Okay, girl, let's finish the job.'

He took a deep breath and jumped up, striding back towards the fire and tearing the flattened cardboard box and its lid into six almost neat chunks. He watched the pyre catch for the last time.

'There. Finished.'

Then, just on cue, Meg kicked off, jumping up, barking manically. She was even brighter than he thought. A celebratory display from her. Perfect timing. All done. But it took him less than a second to recognize what the rumpus was really about. Despite the wind, his ears had picked up the engine noise too. The boat was close. He must have been so caught up with the final fuelling of the bonfire that he'd missed it. He checked the flames. He'd surrounded the fire by wind breaks, so it should be fine if left unattended for a while. He needed to see who the hell was invading his solitude. It wouldn't be Catriona. He'd explicitly said that he wanted to be alone.

He clambered down the incline, Meg bounding ahead, and made for the jetty. He had never seen the man in the wheelhouse before. Only as the boat was manoeuvring into the landing area did Miller see another head bob up, as the passenger left the shelter of her seat, the face almost obscured by the hood of a bulky waterproof.

'I'm sorry, Miller. Really sorry. I called Catriona. She said you were here and didn't want to be disturbed. I tried to call in advance but your mobile's off. I *must* speak to you. *I must!*'

Her face looked grave and the whole tableau had more than a hint of déjà vu about it, hurtling him back to Duncan's arrival only a few short weeks ago.

He sighed, anxiety once more beginning to pick away as he reached forwards and grabbed her gloved hand.

'It's all right, Lizzie. Come ashore.'

51

Miller watched as Lizzie sipped at her coffee. She looked chilled to the bone.

'. . . my brother-in-law is the sailor in the family. Please, don't worry about him. He wanted to stay on the boat. Keep an eye on things. It's choppy out there. But he'll get me safely off. Don't worry. He knows all about the tides.'

Despite the drama of her arrival, she seemed reluctant to explain her presence, instead enquiring after his well-being. He knew he looked a mess. Reeking of the bonfire, covered in smoke smuts, and his overwhelming stress now permanently scarred into his face. For her part, she looked older than he remembered. But maybe that was due to the obvious lack of sleep, evident in the dark smudges under her eyes, and there were definite lines of strain around the mouth and jaw. Join the club. Though they'd talked on the phone, he hadn't met her since his father's funeral. Even then she'd had to introduce herself. He simply hadn't recognized her outside the hospice setting of that dreadful night. Thinking back, he wondered why he hadn't contacted Lizzie recently. He'd left all that to Duncan, who was close to Lizzie after all. But he should have tried, especially after Lena's death. Why had he kept away from her? He knew the answer. In his unconscious mind she was tainted for being the very catalyst that now left him feeling so dissatisfied, emotionally drained. Unfair – irrational, certainly. The least he could do was give the woman a cup of coffee and some of his time.

He sat back, rubbing a temple, desperate for a proper night's sleep. He looked again at the letter she'd been cradling since she sat down.

'What you got there?'

She shifted in her seat and placed her cup back on the table. 'It's Duncan. I've been contacted by one of his oldest friends in the abbey. Another one of the brethren. I've met him quite a few times when I've been staying at the guest house. He dropped me a note at the hospice. Here.'

Dear Lizzie

I have been worried for some time about Duncan and I know that you have become a friend of his this past year or two, so I feel that I can ask for your help. I'm not sure exactly what's prompted me to take the actions I have but I'd like to call it more than instinct, divine guidance if you like. Recently, I am sure Duncan told you that he was going on retreat. He mentioned it to me, rather surprisingly, only on the morning of his departure, saying that he'd tell those who needed to know. I have to say he seemed very subdued, troubled even, but I didn't pry any further, trusting that his retreat would help him.

I made one or two enquiries here and have since discovered that Duncan asked for permission to leave the abbey at very short notice. This was granted because the guest house is closed at present and because Duncan cited 'an urgent spiritual crisis'. I have since checked with the retreat centres that Duncan has used in the past. He has not been there. Some discreet ringing around on my part has been of some use. Duncan has apparently been an overnight visitor to a seminary in Caithness. I don't know if there is any family connection to this visit, since I was of the belief that Duncan has no surviving relatives and hails from the Borders.

I feel slightly uncomfortable about prying into what Duncan is doing but I am worried, very worried. Duncan has had one or two ailments these past couple of years, and I hope and pray that there are no serious health issues with which he is wrestling but feels unable to share with me or others here. I hope that I am wrong. There is no way of contacting Duncan. The abbey guest-house mobile is lying unused in his office.

The worst part of my prying has yet to be revealed. I admit that I have been into Duncan's sleeping accommodation and his office at the guest house. I have found some notes that relate to Douglas McAllister. In particular, Duncan seems to have been recently interested in an Andrew Blackford, a witness in Mr McAllister's case, I believe. As I think you are aware, Duncan's championing of his cause was not universally popular in the abbey, then or now. I know that you are deeply involved in these matters and I would ask that you please let me know if you think they have any bearing on why Duncan has effectively disappeared.

I am going to say nothing to any of the others here for now. But, if by any chance Duncan has confided in you about what he is doing, even if you cannot divulge it, please let me know that he is well.

My best to you,
Brother Michael

Miller looked up at her. 'And? Has Duncan said what he's doing?'

She shook her head. 'No. Nothing. I got a message on my home phone to say he was going away "for a while" is how he put it. I'm worried. But, that's why I'm here. Surely if he's looking at your father's case, he'd have told you? Particularly if he's going after Blackford.'

Miller frowned. 'No, nothing. He just announced that he was going on retreat. "For a while" is how he put it to me too. I've no idea where he is, but if he's gone after Blackford I hope to God he's careful. That man's trouble.'

Lizzie shifted uncomfortably, yet again, in her seat. 'There's something else.'

He watched as she rummaged inside her waterproof. 'I was so worried that I went to see Brother Michael. He ... well ... he let me into Duncan's office at the guest house. I'm ashamed to say that I did considerably more prying than Brother Michael. Did you know that Duncan was writing another book on Fidra?'

Miller shook his head as she nodded and went on.

'No, me neither. I found some handwritten notes in a folder marked for transcription, on to his computer presumably. They were in a file called 'Fidra – an Island History Updated'. Remember that first little book he wrote had a bit about your Dad's case? But it was really more about the whole history of the island, the old monastery, all that stuff. Well this material I've come across seems to be going into greater and greater depths about your father and your family. Here. He's given the notes a title. Rather dramatic actually. 'Fear and Guilt.'

She was handing the pages over to him. 'Dear old Duncan. He certainly seems to be rather worried about something.'

Duncan watched Lizzie's boat carry her away into the night. He was thankful for the cover of darkness, snow and the howling wind. He could slip his craft into the north cove undetected. Earlier, he'd spied on Lizzie from a safe distance. Through his binoculars, he'd monitored her urgent arrival as she'd leapt ashore, helped by a puzzled, annoyed-looking Miller. What was wrong with her? He'd find out soon but he couldn't worry about that right now. He had work to do.

There would be all the time in the world to do what

had to be done. No question of Miller venturing out on the island. Not tonight. Not in this weather. The earlier sleet had turned to snow and was whiting out visibility to an alarming degree. No problem. He knew the island as well as anybody. The horizontal sweeps of snowflakes stung and bit at any exposed flesh on the scramble up to the chapel ruins. But once there, a dip in the land would provide shelter, cover from prying eyes too, as if it were needed in these conditions. A final haul over the last ridge and a quick slither down into the hollow. Blissfully quiet, wind-free, deceptively cocooning. What a place. This was where the eleven-year-old Miller had seen the worst, the very worst. Time to move over to the blocked-off area. Slide the backpack off. If he needed any tools, they were in there. As was the camera.

Miller felt guilty almost shooing Lizzie off the island. Though he appreciated her visit, it had more than a bit of overreaction about it. If Duncan had buggered off somewhere without telling anyone where he was, that was his business. If he was planning some sort of gloomy, rather overpersonalized update of a book, so what? Except he wished he'd mentioned it to him. Duncan's pessimism about his father's case was hardly a surprise, especially now. Further, it was doubtful that his pessimism, as expressed in the notes, was the cause of his troubled state. Like anyone, Duncan no doubt had his own demons to deal with from time to time. Good luck to the man.

He'd tried calling Catriona back but she was on voice-mail. Then *she'd* got hold of him. What a palaver. But she'd made him laugh with a silly joke she'd heard at the surgery. Under the circumstances, that was something. That had lifted him. He hadn't wanted to bother her with any further obsessing about what he was doing, but nevertheless, he'd given her a brief outline of Lizzie's visit. She'd sided with Lizzie a bit, making the point that Lizzie knew Duncan well, so probably had a point, but that there was no use worrying yet. No use worrying about anything, so he should just enjoy his 'little bit of hermit time'. That had cheered him even more.

Then Nikki had rung. Nightmare. It was plain they were reaching the point of no return. Now Nikki, who was so obviously sensing his distance, was urging him to return, claiming to have missed him. But all he wanted to do was talk to Emma and Callum, hear how they were doing, promise them he'd see them soon. Promises he vowed to himself he'd keep.

By the time he recognized Mhari's number coming up, he'd let voicemail deal with it. Her message was characteristically terse.

'Miller, I don't know where you are. I've tried the mainland house. No answer. Now you're not answering the bloody mobile. Great! I've a mind to drive down but the weather's filthy up here in Fife. We've had an early snow. At least a foot of it and it's heading your way. Please ring as soon as you get this. Oh and Greg's gone AWOL too. I want him to get the next flight over here. Shit, this family. It's beyond me! Anyway, I've taken the liberty of speaking to that spineless lawyer McColl. We've got to do something more. Simply got to.'

Bang! She'd just hung up. No farewell niceties. As per. So, Mhari was picking up the role of Dad's main cheerleader again. Well, she was welcome to it. He'd call her later, when he felt like it. All he wanted was to be undisturbed here for at least a day. With a shake of the head at his infuriating sister, he strolled to the kitchen for a well-deserved drink.

He nodded to himself. It was turning into a night just like the first one he'd spent here after Dad died. Déjà bloody vu all right.

52

Everything around was in darkness now. Just the fire for light, the sky dropping snowflakes into the flames. Lovely. But the box wouldn't empty. Paper, after paper, after paper. Magically replenished as he fed the fire.

'It never empties, Bella. See. This letter from Dad must be a million, no a billion pages long. A trillion! Like all the blinks of Fidra's lighthouse and more, eh? Endless pages.'

'So why're you trying to burn it, son? It took me a lifetime to write it. A whole lifetime.'

He spun round to his left. Dad. Standing on the edge of the bonfire. In his pyjamas! But . . . but there was something wrong with him. He was yellow, and skinny, and old, and ill, and dying, and holding a red rose.

'Lizzie took days to write that out for me, laddie. You shouldn't burn it.'

'No. You shouldn't.'

Mum! Moving out of the darkness to the edge of the bonfire, next to Dad. Young. Happy? With what? What was that she was holding? A big white bundle.

'What's that, Mum? Wh—'

She moved closer to the fire, the flames flickering off her features. But she looked old suddenly. Old. Wizened. But smiling. No, grimacing. No, crying. Silently sobbing.

'The lost girl, Miller. Look, Eileen Ritchie. All swaddled in a white blanket.'

'Yes, the lost girl, wee Miller. You found her.'

Duncan? Robed. Hood up. Stepping into the circle now. Taking the white bundle from Mum.

'The lost girl. Your *lost girl*.'

'I have one too.'

He swivelled to his right. Catriona! Fourteen. Smiling. Oh so pretty. In the 'Beach Belles' dress.

'Yes, I have one too. A lost girl. Jacquie Galbraith.'

But what was Duncan . . . and Catriona too . . . what were they doing? The blankets. Pulling them back. They're all red. Bright red!

'No!'

Duncan smiling, his hood down now. 'Oh yes, wee Miller, too many lost girls. Now, Catriona! Now!'

With perfect timing, the two bundles, bloodied to saturation, thrown high above the flames. In slow motion, circling down, down, down, like the helicopters off a sycamore tree.

'No! Stoooooop!'

'Yes, Miller.' *In unison. All of them. Dad, Mum, Duncan, Catriona.*

'Bella! Fetch girl. Fetch!' *In unison again.*

And there she was, launching herself into the flames, her strangled yowls of agony ripping through the darkness.

'Bellaaaaaa!'

'Bella! Oh Jesus, oh, what? Where ar—'

He felt Bella's, no Meg's, it was *Meg's* front paws on his lap as she whined and then began a battery of short, sharp barks.

'*Shit!*'

His foot had caught the half-tumbler of melted ice and vodka dumped on the floor before he'd passed out from utter exhaustion. He needed some water. Now. He staggered through to the kitchen, the nightmare still half alive, and gulped a pint of freezing tap water down in one. Then splashed the same amount over his face and the back of his neck. Meg was at his feet, licking the droplets from the floor.

'Air. Need some air, girl.'

The observation platform had a covering of snow, gathered in shallow drifts. Meg followed him out, her nose plunging immediately into the flakes but as quickly retracted with a shake of her head and loud snuffling. The sea seemed strangely silent but it was out there. In the blackness. He shivered. He had on only a thin T-shirt and hooded sweatshirt. Still, he didn't care. He had to wake up. The dream. *Horrible.*

He scuffed some snow off the handrail and leaned against it, the iciness under both palms a welcome, awakening sensation. Why had he been so rash? He could never get that letter back now. *Never.* The fact that he knew its contents pretty much by heart didn't matter. He'd done it again. Dismissed Dad. Tried to negate, nullify, deny, destroy his memory.

'*Oh Christ, Dad!*'

He grabbed a handful of snow and rubbed it into his face and stubbled chin, head shaking. He'd need some psychiatric help before long. In truth, he probably needed it now. Everything felt out of control. Every wretched thing.

'*Fuuuuuck!*'

He flung his yell as far out to sea as his lungs would allow. Then a flashback from the dream had him running for his coat. The bonfire! He'd forgotten all about it! The snow should have put it out, the windbreaks contained it. But he had to check.

'*Right.* We're going for a walk, girl. I need to get out of this house anyway. C'mon!'

If the tides had allowed it, he'd have cast off and sailed away. But no, he'd have to stick it out until the morning. He didn't want, daren't risk any more sleep, any more dreams. He'd check the fire, and, if necessary, walk himself and Meg ragged around the island until daybreak. He marched through to the hall, Meg still at his heels, and grabbed his parka, her leash, one of her chew bars and a torch. As an afterthought, he doubled back for his hip flask.

He was set to get through the night now.

53

He'd not been outside for two minutes before he knew he'd made a mistake. Not only was it freezing but the wind was whipping the snow into blizzard conditions. He looked back at the yellow glow of the porch light. It was far from welcoming. He didn't want to go back to the house. He felt hemmed in there.

'Oh, come on, Meg. I need to check that bonfire. Then maybe we'll do a couple of circuits anyway. Let's go.'

He smiled as Meg let loose a bark of anticipatory pleasure. She wanted to be out of the house too. Fine. Peas in a pod. They made a quick sprint up to the site of the bonfire. As he'd expected, the ashes were cold now. No need to worry but it had been an unforgivable oversight, demonstrating – as if he needed any reminding – his distracted state of mind. Okay, fire check done, it was time to do the clockwise circuit. Away from the house, down to the left to the narrow part of the island, and then back round via the lighthouse. If it got too blowy there was always the dip by the ruins for shelter.

The flurries were sheeting across his vision in near-horizontal waves, hardened icy flakes striking his chin with a stinging force. Ahead of him, Meg was cowering out of their way. This wouldn't do. He couldn't see an inch in front of his face.

'Right! Up to the ruins, girl. There's always a bit of peace there.'

But which way to go? They were already higher up than

he'd realized. Best to approach the hollow where the ruins lay from the north side. He patted his thigh to bring Meg to heel and they inched forwards. He orientated them by the position of the lighthouse but the conditions were making distance deceptive. Suddenly, he realized that they were on the cliff edge above the hollow. Too near, far too near! *Bloody fool!* He should have realized. He directed Meg to the leeward side. Christ, she could've been blown over the cliff and into the sea with the next gust of wind. The waves were welcome to take him, but spare her at least. He felt the snow and scree move underneath him and struggled to keep his balance. There was no safe way down to the shelter of the hollow with conditions underfoot so precarious. They'd have to work their way around the hollow and then climb back up to shelter that way.

It took longer than he thought but they'd made it down. Now time to go back up again but by a safer route. He began the frenzied scramble up the incline, his boots slipping on the snowdrifts that had made a home in the rock crevasses. Beside him, Meg picked her way round them. Then, through the lines of sleet, he could see the edge of the dip. Excellent. A quiet sit-down. Try to clear his mind. Enjoy the storm raging around them. Dad had rarely let him come over to the island in the winter. Those times were a novelty and all the better for it. Brilliant fun, especially in extreme weather, be it thunder, lightning or blizzards. Dad had been okay about him sitting close to the ruins if it was just for shelter. And it had been great to sit in the hollow with Dad and Bella, or just with Bella, listening to the angry world outside.

The only problem now was his hands. The cold was biting through his gloves and making it hard to keep hold of the hip flask. He stopped, head and torso bent against the wind, and unscrewed the cap. A quick couple of warming gulps and then he squirrelled it safely back inside a pocket. Just a last few feet to shelter.

'*There!*'

He heaved his body over the edge of the hollow in an ungainly movement, and slithered down to the nearest corner, envying Meg her ability to leap safely into it with a couple of well-judged bounds. He reached the bottom and lay back on the grassy slope, laughing, his mouth open, to catch the stray flakes of snow that dared to find their way into his sanctuary. His mood had immediately lifted. They were safe! Meg began a frantic snuffling in his ear, her soft head and icy nose nuzzling against his cheek.

'Hey, hey, hey. It's okay. We did it. C'mon. Come here.'

He grabbed her by the neck and began her favourite wrestling game. But she contorted herself out of his grip and started up her staccato yelps of playful joy.

'Okay, you win!'

He rolled on to his right side and began to sit up. It was then that he noticed the change opposite. Completely used to the dark now, his eyes picked out the alteration in the profile of the blocked-off area by the ruins. It was glaringly obvious. He felt for the torch in his parka pocket. This warranted a closer look. Some stones from the dry-stane dyke had been moved. A lot of stones in fact, lying in a pile to the right. And? What was that behind? Wood. Splintered wood. A door? Wall? Meg had picked up on his inquisitiveness and was trying to push past his legs to forage ahead.

'No! No, Meg. Stay back.'

But she was whimpering now, obviously excited, having picked up on a scent or a noise.

'Right.' He fished her leash out from his inside pocket and clipped her on to it, securing the rest of it around one of the stones. 'Sorry, girl, but I want to have a look first. Just sit down and wait. Sit!'

This time she obeyed. He rewarded her with a chew bar and a pat and then turned back to the splintered wood. It was a door of some sort, definitely a door.

He frowned and pushed. It gave about two feet. Enough to get through. He squinted at what the torch beam had highlighted. The beginning of steps! What had been going on here? This area had been closed up for all . . . well for all that time since the . . . since *that* day. This was exactly the spot where he was going to allow the university people to have a look. But they wouldn't have been here ahead of him, breaking and entering? No way. With a final look at a pining Meg, he slipped through the gap and made for the steps.

54

He was now in almost complete silence, the wind down to a whisper. The powerful torchlight played around the walls as stray snowflakes drifted inside, fluttering across its beam. He'd not been allowed to attend court on the days when the trial described the whereabouts of the bodies. But he'd read enough of the court papers, and picked up from the correspondence between the university academics, Forbes and Russell Sinclair what lay beyond the 'blocked-off area'. Even before Dad's arrest it had been known as a place that was out of bounds. Dangerous ruins. Unstable. His dad had been very clear about it to them all. *Keep away.*

He felt oddly excited. His childhood attempt to break in with his brother had never got this far. Now here he was invading the one place he'd never set foot inside, on an island that he knew every inch of. He also felt his anger rising. Someone had been here, meddling. Why? Well whoever it was, would be long gone. No one in their right mind would want to be stuck tonight on a freezing Fidra. Apart from himself, of course, and he was far from being in his right mind at the moment. Cautiously, he sidled down the uneven steps, ancient and roughly hewn out of the ground. He stumbled on the last one and had to put a steadying hand to the jagged stone wall. His nose caught the faint scent of earthy, stale air. Then he was inside.

A room? Chamber? Hard to know what to call it. Three sides, obviously windowless. Small. Cramped. But not empty. An old, vaguely familiar easy chair was positioned in the right-hand corner. The narrow, metal-framed bed, also familiar, lay across the far wall. A low, long table had been fitted in next to the chair, flush with the side wall. A dartboard, and six darts with yellow and red plastic flights clustered around the bullseye, took up the left-hand side of the far wall. Slung out on thin steel rods embedded into the walls were four battery-operated camping lamps. They were old and obviously defunct. But the fifth was a new, modern one. He switched it on, swivelling it downwards. It cast its strong circular light on to the table below.

Some were in albums. Closed but with titles. Some had been framed. A medley of four photographs seemed to be the favoured sequence. The sense of familiarity of the faces struck him. Almost, for a moment, he thought he knew them. Had passed the time of day with them. But they were faces he'd seen in other photographs. In newspapers. In police albums. With no flesh. Alison Bailey. Jacqueline Galbraith. Eileen Ritchie.

He was finding it hard to take in, to believe what he was looking at, to piece it all together. He shook his head in disbelief. Forget the precise clinical delineation of their injuries as recorded in the pathologist's report, positing what most likely had happened. Disregard the impassioned outrage of the prosecution speeches, captured in the dry record of court proceedings, theorizing on what they may have suffered. Here was the truth. Before him was the pictorial record of how these three girls became ghosts.

Ghosts of Fidra.

'Catriona'

It is an irony that Catriona Buchan, named
after the sweetheart of the hero of R. L.
Stevenson's 'Kidnapped' and its sequel,
'Catriona', should now be so close to Miller
McAllister. The young Miller who revelled in
the works of Stevenson – most notably 'Treasure Island' because of its Fidra connections
– could, I'm sure, never in a million years
have known how the cards would fall all these
years later between himself and Catriona.

The deep scars of his childhood trauma have
left him craving the support and understand-
ing of those who were present during the terrible events of 1973 and 1974, Catriona being
one of them. It is my belief that his
revisitation of his childhood past has left
him unstable and unbalanced. He also appears
to have, I hope temporarily, cut himself off
from his wife and children and, unknowingly,
sunk into a revisitation of his childhood
isolation from which it's questionable he
will ever return.

He will need all the help he can get to make it
through an immediate future that I am certain
will be filled with pain and regret. But there
will be resolution. Of that there is no doubt.

And justice of a sort. At last.

Notes for 'Fidra – an Island History Updated'

55

It was as if there were two of him. The cool, rational, sensible Miller. The one who gathered up the stack of albums, the handful of framed photos, even switched off the lamp. The one who raced up the steps two at a time, grabbed Meg's leash, unclipping her so that she could join his fleeting dash through the blizzard back to the house.

Here was the other one. Hands shaking so much he dropped cube after cube of ice into the sink as he tried to fill a glass with the remnants of his hip flask. The flask had cascaded from his fingers and landed with a heart-stopping crash on the tiled kitchen floor.

The hellish pile was sitting where he'd thrown it. In the middle of the dining table. Unexamined, beyond what he'd seen out there. He stood back, keeping his distance. Meg was by the fire, keeping hers. From him. From the table. No need for any word or gesture of instruction. She knew. He ventured a step or two towards the table and stopped. Then took one step back. Ice in his glass was rattling as his left hand refused to stop its palsied trembling. The fire spat as another log cracked from the heat, and the wind slammed the snow against the windows in wave after relentless wave, drowning out the sound of the sea below.

He finished the drink in one freezing gulp, the shock of it almost inducing vomiting, and adding to his shivering. He swallowed the nausea away. Just a few steps forwards and he was there. He turned the framed photographs face downwards and reached a shaking hand to the albums. Like their old family albums. Cloth-covered tartan ones, each of a different tartan, its name helpfully supplied at the bottom left-hand side, picked out in embossed gold writing. Their tartans. Or ones they could lay claim to. *Could* have laid claim to. The greens, blues and reds blurred in front of his straining eyes. And there, dead centre. The legends.

'*Eileen – Garvald Lovely.*' '*Jacquie – Dirleton Queen.*' '*Alison – Yellowcraigs Beach Belle.*'

Beach Belle.

He forced himself to open the first one. Black and white. Four white-edged, rectangular prints per page. Each held by red, triangular photo corners. Like holiday snaps. His family's holiday snaps. Not quite. He thumbed through every page, each more quickly than the last until the images ran together like a rudimentary cartoon flick-book. A macabre cartoon book. Though there was no trace of animation in these images. The girl was dead. Not long dead perhaps but utterly lifeless. Posed naked, spread-eagled, legs and arms sprawled in a mockery of post-coital bliss. The gash at the throat gaping, blood pooling on either side of the delicate neck. Album two was the same. But colour now. Some of the tones leached out by time. Though garish enough. The reds clear. The fear, the horror, the torment clear.

'*Eileen – Garvald Lovely.*' The last one. The most recent. Could he? He dragged the album towards him. Closing his eyes, index fingers and thumbs ready, he prised it open, roughly halfway. Just one look. To check. His eyelids twitched as he forced them open. Four pictures. Colour. Set out the same. The final gaping-throated image staring back at him.

He thudded the album shut, pushing it away from him with such force that it toppled over an empty glass on the other side of the table. He felt Meg sit up and then, in answer to his glance, she slunk down again by the fire. How had the police missed this? Had he been wrong? His memory mistaken where it had happened? The place was ancient, had the air of long-term neglect. Thirty-two years of neglect? Ever since his father had been taken away? But in that case . . . had the police not searched enough . . . ? Missed it? *No, stop it! Absolutely not!* None . . . surely none of that was possible? Yet . . .

What to do, what to do, what to do? The mobile! He patted his jeans' pockets. No. His parka! He began frantically slapping every pocket, rifling each one twice over. Nothing. He ripped the coat off, flinging it on to the chair back and sat down, both hands rubbing his aching eyes. He'd been getting too distracted, careless. Forgetting things. Didn't he stuff it in his parka in anger after listening to Mhari's last message? He thought so and now it was probably lying outside under a ton of snow. Lost during his stupid cavorting with Meg!

Her single bark made him jerk his head back, his eyes disbelieving the vision behind him.

56

'What in God's name is going on, Miller? I saw the fire. It was going for hours! What's that all about? And Lizzie . . . she rang me again at the surgery. Said you were . . . well, looking dreadful. Bless her, she got her brother-in-law to bring me straight over. You're not answering your phone? All the mess with the ice on the floor? And what's that on the tab—'

'Nothing. *Nothing!*'

He hunched his body over the albums, like a child shielding his classwork, but they were all, mercifully, either face down or tight shut. He stood up, scraping the chair back so roughly that it toppled over with the weight of his parka. Clumsily, he wrestled it upright and made a vague gesture with his hand, while simultaneously switching off the light above the table, plunging the horror into a welcome darkness.

'Why don't we . . . sit, eh . . . sit by the fire? C'mon, Meg, make room, girl. Please, Cattie, have a seat.'

Still in her damp raincoat, she sat herself down in the easy chair opposite him, quickly glancing around. Trying to take in the long-faded familiarity of her surroundings? The happy memories of before. So long ago . . .

'Good grief, Mill, you look terrible.' She moved over and crouched in front of him, taking his head in both her hands as she looked into his eyes and felt around his neck. Next, she took his pulse and then retreated to her chair, a worried frown on her face.

'When did you last sleep? Properly, I mean.'

He shrugged, the gentleness of her touch had him near to breakdown. 'Don't know. I . . . I, eh, was just going to turn in. I'm sorry, you're right, I'm a bit under the weather. I'm sure I'll be better tomorrow. Let me show you where you can sleep. There's the small room at the top of the house. Remember it? I'm sorry that I can't just take you back, take us both back until the morning but . . . oh well, I just think th—'

She held up a hand to stop his stuttering progress. Was she going to remonstrate with him for his rudeness, his obvious desire to get rid of her? 'Look it's fine, Mill, really. Why don't we all have an early night? We both need it, and probably Meg too.'

He tried to return her smile but instead rose, almost painfully, out of his chair and wandered to the bottom of the stairs, gesturing for her to follow. 'Remember the room? Two flights up. The bed's made up and I'm sure there's a towel. Put the heater as high as you like. I'm going to clear up here. See you in the morning.'

He nodded towards the first landing. 'I'm in Mum and Dad's old room. I'll take Meg in with me so she doesn't come scratching at your door. She's liable to do that with people she likes, so I'll keep her with me. Goodnight.'

He watched as she made her way slowly upstairs, removing her raincoat as she went, and giving him a puzzled backward glance. 'Just give me a knock if you need anything, Mill. Please.'

Immediately she was out of sight, he sprinted back to the dining table, keeping the overhead light off. He bundled up the albums, whispered for Meg to follow, and made for his bedroom, taking the steps two at a time. Above, he could hear Catriona padding across the hallway to the second-floor

335

bathroom. He shoved the bundle under the bed and eased himself down on to the mattress, elbows on knees.

He had to go back out there. Had to. See, understand what the place was. The legal archive was all gone. Burned. He cursed himself. The files had contained maps and diagrams that he'd ignored. Now they were destroyed. And the police photos. They hadn't shown enough of the main area. What *was* the chamber? Not the same place as where the girls were found. Or was it? The archive of horror? But it couldn't be. It would all have been cleared by the police. *What was happening?*

Reluctantly, he stood up.

'Stay here, girl. Stay.'

Silently, he closed the bedroom door on Meg and crept down the single flight of stairs. Grabbing his parka and torch, he let himself out the front door, looking up at Catriona's darkened window before bending almost double as he launched himself into the blizzard.

57

He'd bent down to her level, inviting her over with a slap on his knee. 'Good girl, Meg. You've met old Duncan before. Now, come on. That's it.'

Miraculously, she'd stayed quiet, responding to the ruffling of ears and scratching of the chest that he was offering her. But then he was good with dogs.

'You're no use at guarding at all, are you? Just a big softie.'

Now his eye caught the corner of an album. Slowly, he slithered them all out from under the bed and sat on the floor, back to the wall, patting for Meg to sit with him.

Selecting the one he wanted, he scanned through what he already knew was there, the photos flickering across his vision. Then, from inside his habit he withdrew a similar tartan-covered book. Page after page. Black ink, some faded, some fresher. He fingered through until he'd found what he wanted. One entry per page. Neat. Ordered.

Beach Belle
Wednesday, 12th November, 1969

Alison had a boxer puppy. Just eight months old, she told me. Called Lucy. Alison knew she was down on the beach later than she should have been. It was deserted apart from a couple of figures so far in the distance that they looked like matchstick people. The winter night was just about upon us. I said I'd escort her back up to the road. She wasn't far from home then, she said.

Lucy came bounding up, surprisingly obedient to Alison's summons. She was a perfect pedigree specimen; brindle body, four white socks. I patted her and asked if I could give her a chocolate button or two. 'Of course. She'll love you forever.'

She clipped Lucy on to her lead and we made our way across the dunes and through the spiky grass. I didn't want to throttle the breath out of the girl too far from the car. Or too near. Just in case. But it was dark now. No one was going to see. I unleashed an interested but uncomplaining Lucy, bundled her mistress over my shoulder, and left the beast to forage in the sand for the scattered chocolate buttons. A couple of minutes later as I was getting into the driver's seat, I thought I heard her whining carried to me on the wind.

I can't really blame myself for making a mistake on my first outing, but I did. I thought I had Alison secured away from prying eyes before her final journey to Fidra, when I heard a voice.

The most unexpected witness had arrived. I had to trust that my excuses that 'the lady's not well, she's having a lie down' would suffice. They did, up to a point, though from that moment on I had effectively recruited an accomplice, whether or not they knew it or could admit it to themselves.

Dirleton Queen
<u>Thursday, 10th February, 1972</u>

She told me her name quite readily. She trusted me, you see. Obvious why. The dog was a cairn terrier. Friendly. I patted it and said what a cold night it was and asked her where she lived. Jacqueline, or Jacquie as she said to call her, told me that she lived about fifteen minutes away. But always brought Tam to the outskirts of Dirleton village for his walk. She said that although he was a small dog, he needed his exercise and a *good mile each way was just what he loved. I asked if I could give him some chocolate. 'Just a wee bit, then. Thank you.'*

I said it was a bit quiet and dark these winter nights and didn't that scare her. She'd shrugged and said it was 'really safe around here and anyway, when you've got a dog, even a wee dog, you're safer. Folk think it might bark or bite them.' I almost laughed out loud at that, and as if to mock her foolish words, the dog started to jump up at me for more petting and attention, thus making her feel even safer.

Tam hadn't complained. He'd let me remove his unconscious mistress to the car, put her in the back, cover her with a picnic rug, and he just stood there throughout it all. A few feet away watching, ears pricked up, tongue lolling out, almost smiling at me. I unclipped his leash, patted his little head, and said my goodbyes with more chocolate. As I was driving away, I checked my rear-view mirror. There he was, wandering into the middle of the deserted road. Only then did he seem to get it, and I saw his head rise and jaws open as he started to bark.

This one I did all on my own. No other living soul knew, saw, witnessed. What a feeling!

That was enough for now. Gently, he closed the book, trying to stifle Meg's rising whimper as, above them, both could hear Catriona stirring. She'd made it to the island just in time before the tides had made landing impossible. Good. Just what he wanted. He gave a single satisfied nod, eased himself to his feet and moved over to the windows. White-out. How Miller would ever find his way out and back from there, he didn't know. But whatever he was doing, he was wasting his time. Here was where he should be.

58

The torch had proved worse than useless. A two-inch visibility was all that it would allow. He switched the damn thing off and put it in his pocket. Childhood boasts of being able to navigate his way around the island blindfold were getting a bitter rebuttal tonight. He couldn't risk it. One mistake and he'd break a leg or go over a cliff. He'd have to go back. Should he wake Catriona? Tell her what he'd found? No, he didn't want to inflict that on her. Not tonight.

He turned round, head bent to his chest, the wind whipping at his hood.

'*Fuck it!*'

The icy flakes kept hitting him in the face, forcing him to shut his eyes every second step. But the pale yellow glow-worm of a porch light was ahead. Faint but there. At last! He had to keep the noise down and hope to God Meg wouldn't hear him and kick off with some welcoming barks.

He fought against the wind to close the door without slamming it and stood in the space between the inner and outer doors, listening. Nothing. No Meg going crazy upstairs. No Cattie padding downstairs, that characteristic frown creasing her lovely face. Sighing, he unzipped his parka and eased off his boots. The stairs were institutional concrete ones, no need to worry about creaking. He reached his bedroom door already offering Meg a reassuring whisper.

'It's only me, girl. Sssh. Only me.'

He felt her absence immediately. Not just the lack of her scrabbling to get up and greet him, or the lack of a high-pitched yelp, not even her breathing. He just knew within a millisecond that she wasn't there. His eyes took longer to adjust from the light downstairs, to see what lay on the floor. The albums were strewn across the carpet, a handful of photos loosened from their hinges, as if they'd been shaken. One album was missing. The whole scene had a look of urgency, even near-violence to it. Catriona!

Her door was wide open, the bedclothes rumpled, an indentation on the pillow. Her raincoat slung over a chair. But no other sign of her. Gone!

'*Catriona!*'

He ran along the top landing, kicking every door wide with his stockinged feet. Nothing. The first landing. First bedroom, second bedroom, bathroom, even cupboard. Nothing. He leapt the final four steps down to the ground floor. The observation platform. Impossible on a night like this but it had to be checked. The glass doors were shut tight, only darkness outside and a few stray clinging snow-flakes visible on the glass. Something else too. Meg! How on earth . . . ?

He slid the door to let her run in and quickly shut the storm out again.

'Where is she, girl? Where?'

Only one place left. Outside. *Outside!* He crammed his feet back into his boots, grabbing his parka from the floor where he'd dumped it. The torch, the torch! Yes! Still safe in a pocket, though useless for the ever-worsening conditions.

He reached for the door handle, readying himself for the full blast of the elements.

'Miller. Wait.'

59

The disembodied voice was made flesh as soon as he stepped out from the pitch-black dining-table area, more ghostly than ever in the dark woollen habit.

'Wh ... what? For fuck's sake, Duncan! What ... what *you* doing here? Lizzie's worried sick about you. She came over here, practically in tears. She says you've not been on retreat. She's frantic ab—'

'I know. I saw her leave.'

Instinctively Miller found himself taking a step or two back from Duncan as he approached. The man looked terrible. Almost ill. He'd lost weight around the face, leaving it strained and exhausted. 'What d'you mean you saw her? How long have you been here? Why didn't you tell me? Just stay where you are.'

He felt Meg at his heel picking up on his growing anxiety. 'Did you put Meg out on the platform? In the snow. Where I couldn't hear her in all this weather. Catriona wouldn't have done that.'

Duncan had ignored his plea to stay put and was still moving forwards, both hands raised. 'I had to put Meg out for a minute because I wan—'

Miller let his parka drop to the floor, leaving his hands free. '*Stay* where you are, Duncan. *Stay back!*'

'Miller, will y—'

He didn't give Duncan time to take another step and threw himself head first at his legs. The rugby tackle landed both of them in the fireplace. Miller fell painfully on his right shoulder but managed to grab a poker while grappling with Duncan's heavy bulk. In a second Meg was up, barking manically, dancing around them both, joining in their 'game'. He ignored her as Duncan slipped his grasp and shoved him away, backing off to the French windows. With a final leap forwards, Miller hurled himself at him, hearing the glass shatter before both fell through it. He could feel the shards biting through his sweatshirt, impaling themselves in his back and aching shoulder as he hit the metal flooring of the observation platform. Meg was yelping, not so happy now, as she started to pick her way across the shattered glass and snow that had drifted into the room. He lay paralysed. The snow was swirling around his nose and mouth. He tried to sit up and saw Duncan, now in possession of the poker, standing above him. He lay back down and Meg was on him, licking his face.

'*No! Stop it! Enough!*'

He pushed her away and managed to make it to a sitting position. The wind was creating a whirlpool of the snowflakes around him but it was waking him up, numbing his pain. Duncan had retreated into the centre of the room but wasn't taking his eyes off him. Very slowly, he stood up, the shattered glass scrunching under his feet. His back must be injured, maybe badly lacerated. He could feel the warm wetness of blood. Gingerly, he tried to reach a hand round. It was difficult. His right shoulder and arm were stiffening from the hard landing. What he could do was remove his hooded sweatshirt. He unzipped it and shrugged it off. Holding it up, he could see the glass blades poking through it, the holes bloodied. He tossed it to the ground, and staggered forwards to face an obviously injured Duncan swaying like a drunkard before him.

The clatter as the poker was tossed into the fireplace rang around the massive room.

'We won't be needing that.'

Miller felt Meg cower close into his heel as he too swayed, leaning back against the shattered doorframe, remnants of glass cracking underfoot. The sound of the sea and the wind were loud but Duncan's deep tones were carrying over them.

'I want, I *need*, you to calm down, laddie. I mean it. *Calm down*. You can hardly stand anyway. You'll need your wounds tended but they'll wait for now. Where's your whisky? Kitchen?'

Miller ignored him. 'Where's Catriona? *Where?* If you've harmed h—'

Duncan held up a badly cut hand. 'I haven't touched her. I wanted her here. I called Lizzie just after she left you. I'm sorry she was worried about me but she said that she was going to call Catriona and get her over here to see you. I would've suggested the very same thing myself. You'll need her here. She's out on the island but she'll come back. I think she must have realized that you'd gone out and tried to follow you. I didn't expect that but, like I say, she'll be back. There's no visibility. She can't go far.'

Miller's head was spinning with yet another worry. 'But . . . she'll freeze and . . . oh Christ, no . . . she's been in my bedroom! The photos, albums!'

But Duncan was shaking his head. 'No. That was me. Meg was making a bit of noise up there, so I had to quickly put her outside for a moment. I didn't want to alarm Catriona, let her know I was here yet. I needed to see you first but I had to check out something on the island before that. I didn't expect you to be out there too, not in this weather. But look, you've nothing to fear from me. I just want to talk, *calmly*, to you. *Now, where's the blasted whisky?* I don't know what kind of pain you're in but mine is just

344

about more than I can bear. I need kitchen roll, or a towel or something too.'

Miller felt Duncan's eyes on him as they weaved and stumbled their way to the kitchen. A selection of bottles was crammed into a crevice between the sink and fridge. Wordlessly, he handed Duncan a quarter-full bottle of Scotch. Next, he wrenched open the freezer door and grasped the vodka.

He trailed behind Duncan who was wrapping loop after loop of kitchen roll around his bleeding hand. Suddenly he stopped in the middle of the main room. Miller followed his eyes as repeatedly he darted looks at the front door and the observation platform. Despite his attempts to calm things down, he seemed jittery and hyper vigilant.

'What the fuck is it, Duncan? Who are you looking for? Is there someone else here? *Who?*'

He didn't answer, instead limped over to the corner where the dining area was in darkness. He flicked the wall switch and the table came to life. What looked like one of the albums lay face up. And, centre stage, stood a state-of-the-art digital video camera, its shiny silver body glinting under the subtle low lighting.

'Sit.'

'What's going on, Dun—'

'Fucking sit!'

The shock of the expletive left him biddable and obediently he lowered himself on to a chair. The dining area was offering some shelter from the elements pouring through the broken glass doors on the far side of the room, but not much. He might as well be naked for all the protection his thin T-shirt was giving him. Simultaneously, he took a swig of vodka in a vain attempt at some inner warmth, as Duncan threw back yet another anaesthetizing mouthful of Scotch.

The blood was seeping through and disintegrating the cheap kitchen roll as he reached over to the camera.

'This is a legal document of sorts, if I'm not mistaken. Watch.'

60

Duncan manipulated the small but bright LCD screen display and then switched off the overhead light. The bluish glow played eerily on his features as, obviously in pain, he sat down. A muffled, low-level conversation could be heard. Duncan and who else? Male or female? Hard to say. The screen had turned to a greeny-blue blur. A close-up of something. He could hear Duncan's voice more clearly now.

'Thank you. Thank you. Yes, please shut the door.'

The picture wobbled and then came to rest. A blanket! Two spindly knees encased in a thick woollen blanket. Then, tilting slightly upwards and somehow fixed into position, the gaunt, deeply lined features of a very old woman came into view. Duncan's voice was crystal clear now . . .

'. . . The date is the tenth of November two thousand and five. I am recording this at the Achairn Nursing Home, Caithness. I am with Jessie Carmichael who has some things she wishes to say. Jessie?'

There was the sound of dry coughing as the old woman's throat seemed to momentarily constrict, the wrinkled elongated neck throbbing like some triumphant diving bird demolishing its prey. Then, she lifted her previously drooping eyelids and stared directly into the camera. The face may have been weathered and aged but the eyes held life. Miller shuffled his chair closer to the tiny playback screen.

'Thank . . . thank ye, Brother Duncan. Through these many, so many dark years of my life I have been waiting for someone like yersel' to turn up. Ye've either been sent by the Devil to fool me or by the Lord himsel'. I hope it's Him above. I've tried living a good life.

I have. I hope I've managed that, apart from this one terrible secret that I've held all these years. A lifetime.'

More swallowing followed by a short but rasping cough.

'Not long before my son died he broke an estrangement wi' me of nigh on thirty years. For a mother, any mother, to say that she is glad that her child went before her must surely sound wicked. Aye, wicked it may be but in my case it's true. What I gave birth to, grew into a Satan of a man. He was his father's son, of that there can be nae doubt. And like Satan he had all the charm in the world. A seducer of people. But it hadn't always been like that. As a child I had never been able to protect my son from his father. The beatings, the humiliations he suffered. I tried to protect him. I was his whipping boy more than he ever realized. But still, my son went deep inside himsel'. Became a loner.

'So, it was wi' some sadness but mainly relief that I saw him packed off to university. I fretted mysel' sick about him but knew it would be the making or breaking of him. The big change came after his first two years. He was home on a visit. I heard the sound of shouting downstairs in the living room. There was my brute of a husband cowering in the corner and my boy standing over him with a lump of firewood! His father's head was bleeding badly from one blow as my boy threatened another, maybe fatal? He just kept shouting, "I'm the master now! I'm the master now! Your bloody worm has turned!" He even looked different. Older. Stronger, inside and out. His clothes were different. Fashionable. Most of all, he seemed confident, powerful. I should have been relieved. Instead, I was terrified.

'He raced through university and started his career in Edinburgh. I thought he wasnae going to take a wife. He'd never mentioned any women but then out of the blue he met someone from around here. She'd lost her own parents and was, I'm sure, looking for somewhere to belong. She was a good quiet girl, younger than my boy and bowled over by his attentions. I was hopeful. But his father was far from that and his word was law. My husband emerged from a period of silence

that had lasted since their last fight. There was another war of wills between father and son. Another fight. The outcome was no surprise.

'His only child, who he'd hammered into his own image, had, in his turn, broken him. My husband clung on to life for a year or so, once again shutting himsel' up in his room, barely uttering another word to me. To say I welcomed his death would be an understatement. One way or another my son killed his father. I was grateful. A wicked thought but true for all that.

'My son's courtship and marriage happened in a flurry. Again, I hoped this would be the making of him. I was even more hopeful when, within a year, they'd started a family. I had my first grandchild. But my hope was cruelly short-lived. Although she tried to hide it, I could see the fear, the unhappiness in my daughter-in-law's eyes. And my grandchild was an equally unhappy, unsettled baby. Under the surface of that young family, lay a dark truth. To my horror, my son had taken over his father's work, dealing out the abuse to his wife in the way his father had so unjustly punished me. The Devil's work indeed. I ca—'

'Jessie? Are you okay. D'you need some water?'

Miller strained to hear the almost incomprehensibly strong Caithness accent as it started up again, louder, more confident this time.

'I'm fine thank ye, Duncan. I need my eyeglasses and the . . . the book please.'

More muted mumbling as the skull-like head turned from the camera and then appeared back in focus, the eyes enlarged by huge spectacles far too big for the delicate bony face.

'I'm feeling a wee bit tired now, Duncan, so I think I'll just do what I said I would. Read from the last thing my son sent me. The last contact I ever had wi' him after nearly thirty years . . . I can manage thank ye. I can read perfectly well. I did spend all my life teaching Sunday school. I know how to read out loud properly. I'd rather do it this way. After all, his presence on this earth was in large part my doing. God forgive him, me, the whole family.

'Now. This book I have here has lots of bits and pieces of his in it, lots of crossings out and then he's written much the same again. But I'll read from what I think he wrote last. It has a title. "Fidra's Archive."'

A final swallow and then she was ready, head bent forwards.

'"To have a room pulsatingly alive with memories is one thing. To have an island to oneself is quite another. To have both is paradise. It took a bit of organizing and planning. But it was worth it. I have my memories here. My archive. That's good enough, I suppose. I have the furniture, the precious photos, my jottings. I enjoy my jottings. Reading them too. Again and again. Sometimes I rewrite things. See how memory has altered over the years and compare. No one will read them except me but it's part of the pleasurable process. It keeps my mind active even though my body is far less than that. Keeps the events alive, sharp as if they were yesterday's. I've been thinking about my youth this past week. It's been making me a bit angry, a bit malcontent. Time to put it all down again.

'"I had tried to put much of my family life behind me. My cold, cheerless upbringing. I'd plotted my escape early. Nothing else to do. No friends, no brothers, no sisters. Just schoolwork. Studies. And the Bible. It was the first and only time there was ever a glimmer of something approaching approval. 'So, ye want to go to the university then, laddie. Aye. That'll do.' But it almost didn't happen. He was chary about letting me go. Worried about 'the influence of drink and loose women'. That was a laugh. Loose women. He'd made me terrified, beyond imagining, of the species.

'"But wiser minds prevailed in the shape of the minister and a couple of his fellow kirk elders. The only men he'd listen to. Then I was off. My mother seeing me on to the Edinburgh bus, tears streaming down her weather-blasted face. Father, stock still, unmoved, like a piece of granite beside her. She'd feel the heat of his fury back home. She'd shamed him in public by her display. Even though the only people there to see us were the bus driver and one old crone of a passenger accompanied by her mongrel.

'"Unsurvivable. That's what university felt like. I was a laughing stock. My old-fashioned clothes, my social ineptness. Once again no friends, just studies. Those first two years I soared away to the top of the class. Making me even more unpopular.

'"But then something happened. A Cinderella story, an ugly duckling story. I changed. Maybe it was my academic success. Maybe it was being away from that miserable family abode. My visit back there after my second year was going to be short. At first there had been ructions when I said I wasn't staying for the summer. Instead, I was going to work away from home. But I won that small though significant battle. I think that was the beginning of my father turning in on himself. A period of his silence and Mother's equally wordless endurance had begun.

'"I don't remember ever actually feeling happy during my time of 'freedom'. Just nervous, excited, challenged. I had a job delivering beer to local pubs. 'Just a delivery job,' is what I told my father. If he'd known my cargo, he'd have come to fetch me from Edinburgh and taken me back, never to leave again. As strict a Presbyterian as it was possible to get. No drink, no fun, no women, nothing. Except a skelp round the ear, a heavy punch or worse for me, for Mother. No pleasure for us. Only for him and only on Saturday nights, as his faltering and animal grunts informed me, my mother, presumably gritting her teeth beneath his weight, praying for it to be over. But never a word of complaint and if I ever tried to side with her on anything, she would walk away. Leave me alone. She didn't want me as an ally. She didn't want me. So it was. So be it. Rejection complete.

'"To rebel, eventually, against it all was surely natural. But I more than rebelled. I'm far beyond analysing what my life has been. At the very least, I consider that I was pre-programmed for what happened later. My own early encounters with women, for example, 'loose' bar women that I'd meet on my summer job, were dismal affairs. They mocked, taunted me for my inexperience, awkwardness, ignorance. Then they felt my anger. My father's anger, if you like, since I felt like *him, felt as if I was him when I did it to them. After half an hour with me there was no more mocking. No possibility of them telling. I grew to enjoy the fearful looks they gave me. They knew my vows of retribution were not empty, idle threats.*

'"But by the end of that summer I had come to a conclusion. Experienced women were a danger. Not worth the effort. Far easier to look to inexperience and innocence. That's how it began.

'"And here I am at the end of my life with my memories and a few totems and souvenirs to give life to them."'

He was aware of Duncan's bandaged hand resting on his shoulder as he reached over to pause the image on the screen. The bloodied palm was then raised to halt any utterance. The cold. It was freezing in the room now and the storm's rage flooded through the broken window into the silence left by the pausing of the film. He watched, his shoulder and cuts strangely numb now, as Duncan heaved two dining chairs over to the broken windows and piled them up, cramming them into the space to reduce the levels of wind, snow and noise invading the room. Limping painfully back towards the table and reaching into the darkness for something, Duncan switched on the low lighting. Just enough to see by.

'Miller. I need you to look at this book. This'll help you understand the rest. There are three entries at the back. Just look at that one now. Please, son. Please.'

Garvald Lovely
Friday, 22nd June, 1973

The dog was called Angus. Bigger than the others. A golden retriever. I cursed myself for not having any chocolate on me. But then I wasn't, as it were, on the lookout that evening.

Not on a summer evening. I genuinely was on a walk. Had a fair bit on my mind. Needed to clear my head. It was a good spot to be alone, although I think I heard a car cruising by at one point.

Eileen was jumpier than the others. Was initially suspicious when I literally stumbled across her sitting in a sunken, sheltered area. I think her nervousness was partly to do with the fact that she was in strange territory. She said she normally didn't take Angus this far from home but the weather had been fine and here she was. I sat down beside her and she seemed to be comfortable enough with that.

Angus was out of sight when I touched her. As with the others, there was no question of any noise coming from her lips. I was about to bundle her up, unconscious but very much alive, the dog leash safely in my grasp.

I returned frantic from Fidra that night. Although the island was safe as houses for my purposes, I had made a mistake. The dog leash! It had disappeared. Was it lying out there on the island in clear view, dropped by me, to be discovered on the next family outing? Or, had I lost it nearer to home? High and low I searched. High and low. Only later in the day did my 'accomplice' relieve my worry with a few devastating words.

'It's okay, Dad, I've dealt with the dog leash.'

61

Duncan's eyes were locked on his. He was near to tears.

'Okay, Miller, son?'

The jumbled pieces of data were entering his brain, his thoughts, but he was having difficulty converting them into logic. It was like the terrifying paralysis of a waking dream. Aware but incapable. Of action. Of speech. Of free will to do anything.

Duncan was reaching over to the camera.

'I'm sorry. Just a wee bit more of this. It's important . . . it's painful but you *have* to hear it . . .'

. . . Once again, the screen flickered into life. A trembling claw of a hand grasped the glasses from her face as she looked off camera.

'Duncan? I . . . I think that's enough of that now. I hope ye have what ye need. I give this book into yer own safe keeping. How thankful I am that I didn't destroy it, though many a time I've been sorely tempted.

'I'll need a wee lie down and maybe a nice cup of tea soon. I've only a few more things to say. But they're the most important of all. About the book . . . perhaps he sent it to me as an explanation, an excuse maybe. If so, that makes me angry, ashamed. But that shame is nothing compared wi' the shame of my silence these past years. All the suffering, the injustice. If I was trying to give an excuse and I cannae, it would be the love of my grandchild.

'It's a pitiful tale. My daughter-in-law died after a short illness. My infant grandchild was left alone and vulnerable. My wretched son said he couldn't cope. His job left him little time and he was happy to

bundle his child off to me from an early age. I had hoped for a change in him after losing his wife. But I couldn't say how her death affected him. We remained largely estranged. What I can say is that I think of his dear wife as a kind of saviour and martyr. I think she kept his worst instincts at bay but when she died, he looked again to the outside world and then all was lost. He was on the slippery slope to becoming the murderous monster he turned out to be.'

Another painful cough and she croaked on.

'My greatest fear, other than the worry that he might beat my grandchild or treat her harshly, which it seemed he didn't, was that she would feel rejected by all this sending away. Every day she was in my care I would tell her that her daddy loved her but that he was very busy with his work and so it was best she stay with me sometimes. In that I believe I served her well. By the time she started school and needed the stability of staying at home, only seeing me during holidays, she had become very attached to her father. Over the years I realized that I'd done my work too well. She became too attached. For my son's part, he seemed satisfied with that state of affairs. He had control. She lived an isolated life with him. In addition, there was the occasional babysitter, and superficial friendships with those in the locality. The McAllister family featured in her chatter as her best friends, her only friends really. And it was what she told me about the McAllister family in nineteen seventy-three, when she was just fourteen, that horrified me. And led to my unforgivable lifetime of silence and my estrangement from my son.

'But the seeds of it all had been sown years before. She'd told me about things in her chatter that I'd ignored, not seen the significance of. But by seventy-three I got the message. I vowed silence to my son if I never saw him again. Although my door would always be open to my beloved grandchild. But . . . I . . . Brother Duncan? I'm too weary now to go on. You have the truth. I'll leave it to you. All I'll say is that I adored my grand-daughter. I've done unforgivable wrong. But how could I let the wee soul down as long as there was breath in my body?'

Silently, Duncan switched the camera off. Miller sensed a movement behind him, before he heard anything. Or maybe it was Meg's head rising from her paws, or Duncan's sharp intake of breath that alerted him. Swivelling round in his chair, he peered into the darkness as the figure moved from the shadows at the bottom of the stairs until it stood on the opposite side of the table, between him and Duncan.

'The special present. That's why he gave it to me. He couldn't be sure how much a ten-year-old saw or would believe. Somehow he made me know it was secret but that it was all right too. But the book was my reward for seeing and not telling. I don't know how he'd got her back. The first girl. Alison Bailey. In his car I assume. He'd paid off the babysitter, put me to bed with a goodnight kiss. I don't know when I woke up. But something wasn't right. I wandered about the house. Past the room he always kept locked. His darkroom. Not allowed there remember, Miller? Off limits. Nasty chemicals. And other things. He was in the basement playroom. You know the one? The little bed, big comfy chairs, the dartboard.'

Her low monotone was droning on. A different voice from usual? Now solely addressed to Duncan, it seemed.

'I believed him. The lady was ill and had to see her doctor. Needed a lie down. On the little bed. Of course she did. I turned on my heel, blew a goodnight kiss at him, went back to bed and slept like a log. Slept, sleep-walked through the next part of my childhood. But not for long. He got careless after the second girl, careless around the house. I got into the darkroom one day. I wasn't sure what I was looking at but he caught me and said it was another sick, sleeping lady. But she wasn't sick or sleeping. Later, I could put a name to her: Jacqueline Galbraith. At the time he told me I wasn't to worry. But he knew I knew ... what did I know? I wasn't sure but I knew something wasn't right. But Daddy said it was okay. I believed him again, almost. I had to. I shut it all out.'

Her blank gaze had moved from Duncan to the far wall, her voice flat, quiet, almost too soft to hear above the wind still whistling through the broken windows.

'By the time of the last girl he'd started leaving me in the house alone at night, if he had to go out on an emergency call or something. No babysitter needed any more. I didn't care. I was safe in Dad's big house. I can't be sure what it was that was different that night. Maybe my own sixth sense. My room was as far away from the garage as possible. But something woke me up. I moved silently through the house and looked out of the upper landing window. It gave a clear view down to the area outside the garage. I saw him by the car. So what? That was my usual response. Off to deliver a baby. Off to diagnose someone's acute appendicitis and get them taken to hospital and save their life. Giving life. Saving life. That's what Dad did. No one else's dad could do that. No one's. Then I saw him bundling her in and he was off, away down the drive. I tip-toed down the stairs to the door that connected to the garage. I found the leash in the shadows on the gravel of the driveway.

'I was always nagging Dad for a dog but he said that it was too much of a bind what with all his house calls and looking after me. Anyway, he said, there was always Bella I could play with, borrow, walk. Bella. Lovely Bella. That's what gave me the idea. The leash had to go. Had to. I knew that. But where? I had to get it away from the house. I washed it down under the tap by the garage and wrapped it in a damp rag. No trace of anyone on it any more. Then, I put my coat on over my nightie and wandered the, what . . . five-minute walk? To the McAllisters. One, two, three!

Over it went into their garden. They had a dog. It played in the garden. Problem solved.'

Miller didn't even have time to stand up. The rancid, stinging bile of his vomit exploded on to the table, spraying over the photos, over the black slanting script of the notebook. There was little in his stomach but vodka. It was enough. He kicked back his chair, throwing himself head first towards her, his stomach smearing through the pooling liquid.

Both hands were digging into her thin shoulders as if he'd snap them.

'*Why? Why? Whyyyyyyy!*'

He felt fingers grappling at his own painful shoulders as he was thrown bodily back into a chair and pinned down. Duncan's contorted face was an inch from his own sour breath.

'*Miller. Stop it. Get a hold of yourself. Now! And Meg, lie down! Go on!*'

The slap across Miller's face stung and he felt the wetness from Duncan's bleeding hand on his cheek. He looked up. Duncan was standing between him and Catriona, trying to remould the saturated kitchen roll round his hand.

'Just tell him what else you've got to say. *Tell him! He's got a right to know!*'

She inched backwards until she reached the wall and put both hands behind her, one leg bent as if she was posing for some celebrity photo shoot.

'I didn't think about what kind of leash you used on Bella. I really didn't. I just thought no one would notice it. I . . . I think Dad was going to go and get it back from the garden when we came back from the trip to Fidra. I know he didn't really want to go on the trip because of it but the McAllisters were meant to be his best friends and it would look odd if he'd refused. And in another way the invitation was useful. If others were going to be on the island he needed to be there because of what he'd done with the girl's body. But he didn't have to worry. The rules about the out of bounds area were strict. But ... as we got back from Fidra that weekend ... those police at the harbour steps ... well, I knew then it was too late.'

'*Too late? Too late! It was just the beginning!*'

He felt the weight of Duncan's hand on his sore shoulder again, keeping him pinned.

'*Wait, Miller! Wait!*' He nodded at her. 'Go on.'

She moved her arms to the front, wrapping them around her waist as she shivered in a thin pullover.

'I ... I ... I can't explain. It's like telling a lie. Once it's started ... you have to go on ... *oh, Duncan! I can't, I can't!*'

A slow motion movement, sliding down to the floor, her body wracked by silent sobbing. Duncan was moving forwards, roughly pulling her to her feet and thrusting her into a nearby chair, ignoring the shaking and weeping.

'Right. Sit where you are, Miller, and listen to me. If *she* won't tell you, I will. Lena Stewart was very concerned about you going to see Andrew Blackford. She'd had no direct contact with him for many, many years, but through his extended family, she knew he was liable to drunken outbursts of violence. She'd rung me on the day you were meant to see him. I wasn't sure what to do. I had some knowledge of Blackford in the past as I was acquainted with his grandfather and I thought Lena might be right. On the other hand I didn't want to call you and cause you more worry. I decided to drive up there myself. You'd been and gone but Blackford was there.'

Duncan shook his head at the memory. 'All I can say is that if you thought Blackford aggressive when you met him, my encounter was much more fraught. Your visit had managed to put, if not the fear of God into him, certainly something like it, and he was worried. The news about Lena's intended change of evidence had him rattled. Anyway, I eventually got him to calm down and we had a relatively civilized conversation about what he was going to do. During the conversation, we ventured over the old territory of those years ago, and he *in passing* made an astonishing remark. He said that on the night of the Eileen Ritchie disappearance he'd seen Forbes Buchan up in the Lammermuirs. Not at the spot where he and Lena claimed to have seen your father. No, at some point Lena had walked on ahead of him back to the car, and he'd seen Forbes in the distance. Blackford thought no more about it but did mention it when Forbes came to make a home visit to his grandfather soon after. He merely mentioned it to make conversation. There was no question of Blackford seeing the local GP as anything other than a good man.

'Forbes Buchan was clever. He must've seen the danger and reacted very quickly. He said that he'd been on his way to an assignation with "a lady friend" and that since the lady in question was a married woman, he'd need to keep mum. All of that wouldn't really have had me pricking up my ears, except for the last part of their conversation. Blackford, probably thanks to being full of drink, had pushed his luck a bit and began trying to find out who the "lucky lady" was. For some reason, perhaps not surprisingly, since the two families mixed so much, Blackford suggested the lady friend was your mother.'

Miller jumped as Catriona leapt to her feet.

'*No!* That wasn't true. *It wasn't!* He wasn't having an affair with anyone! *Rubbish! It's lies!*'

Her face was crumpled from the earlier crying but

was now being replaced by fury or something wilder, much more disturbing. She was emitting a low whimpering now, surely near to full mental collapse. But Duncan was ignoring the signs, merely pressing her back into her seat before he went on.

'Forbes Buchan made no attempt to correct the impression that he was having an affair with your mother. But I was stunned. I had to ask to use Blackford's bathroom at that point, such was my shock. I stood by that grubby latrine racking my brains. Forbes wasn't having an affair with Ailsa. That was impossible.

'Because I was.'

62

Duncan's crushing weight was back on him this time, but attempting a reassuring squeeze as he threw a threatening look at Catriona, to keep her in her place.

'Sssh, Miller. *Listen.* To call it an affair is . . . is . . . well it was much *less* and much *more* than that even though we only had one precious night together. We'd attended a charity event up the coast. It went on late, the weather was bad, and she had to stay the night. It happened the winter before your father's arrest. It was completely unintentional, I promise you. On her side anyway. We agreed to try and forget it and be friends, confidants. I . . . I felt wretched. My supposedly wise counsel and spiritual care for your mother was, at the end, utterly self-serving. I'm sorry, Miller, but . . . I *loved* your mother. Wanted to spend every minute with her. It was a mess. It's *I* who has to answer for much of your father's, your family's hell. If I hadn't encouraged Ailsa, seduced her with the cloak of my devoutness, then maybe, just maybe we wouldn't be here now. *Please, just wait.* I'll explain.

'Ailsa was with me *that* evening, discussing her decision about leaving her family and entering an order. So, this passing comment by Blackford had me puzzled. Why on earth would Forbes have lied about something like that? Why? It left me confused *and* suspicious. It also threw up reminders of other elements of his behaviour that I hadn't properly registered at the time. For example, *why* he refused every offer from me over the years to help with the maintenance of the island. Why he seemed so firm about not letting me establish a hermitage there in the face of your father's wishes.

'Once I'd seen Blackford, I left, offering to support him through whatever might happen with a reopening of your father's case, but I urged him to go away for a while. However, he *had* to keep in touch with me, which he has. The fact that he chose to leave you the note he did, effectively toying with you, shows you the sort of man he is. But I believe he *will* now tell the truth, though we no longer need him as we have Jessie's testimony.

'It was common knowledge that Forbes Buchan had a surviving mother in Caithness. Jessie Carmichael. That's her maiden name. She reverted to it after the husband she hated died. I saw her at Forbes's funeral a couple of years ago and we shared a few words. She was easy enough to find. I don't know what, if any, religious beliefs you hold, Miller, but my encounter with Jessie will stay with me as unarguable proof of God's existence until the day I eventually meet my maker. It was as if she and He were just waiting for my arrival. A day later and . . . well, Jessie died a few hours ago.'

'*No! God no! Grandma!*'

Miller felt Duncan release his shoulder and move towards Catriona. Her face was a twisted sneer as she tried to get to her feet. For a moment Miller thought Duncan was going to strike her. Instead, he stood in front of her, not touching her, but daring her to rise. She kept sitting but her arms were flailing as she repeatedly punched at Duncan's stomach.

'You . . . you fucking *knew* but you didn't tell me! *You interfering bastard!* How *dare* you go and see her, interfere, about her, about Dad! You don't understand. No one can! How *dare* you judge anyone? *You fucking hypocrite!*'

Miller watched as the pummelling continued. She was a

strong woman. It must have been hurting Duncan. Miller tried to stand up to help him but he slumped down again, feeling sick. He could barely move, speak. Eventually, Duncan grasped both her wrists and held them aloft in what must have been an agonizing grip.

He was shaking his head at her. 'I asked the nursing home to ring me first if her condition worsened. She was in a bad way when I made that film two days ago. When I received the news, I told matron that I would tell you myself and she was not to ring you. You see, I don't know what kind of peace your grandmother will find now, but the only way to forgive her for her lifetime's silence is to see that she did it for the love of you, Catriona. The dawning horror in nineteen seventy-three, as you blurted out what you'd done with the dog leash, and how that connected to seemingly irrelevant stories about your father from years before, just about finished her there and then.

'Once she'd made her pledge of silence to your father, she hoped, prayed, over the years, that you would somehow forget and then never spoke of it again. It was only at his death a couple of years ago, when Forbes sent her the record of the archive that he'd set up, and which he'd been living through, that she discussed it with you again. *Enough*. She'd had enough. She wanted to go to the authorities at last. And yes, Miller, it would have been in time for your father to see exoneration in his lifetime. For your dear mother to see it too. *Just*. But no. Catriona forbade it. Said it was too late. Too much time had passed. What good would it do? She tried to take the archive writings but Jessie kept them.'

Duncan let her wrists drop and backed away from her.

'You know, Catriona, you can perhaps be forgiven your childhood actions, but nothing, *nothing* can forgive your self-serving adult ones. What I believe is this. I think you befriended Ailsa to see if you could get access to Fidra and root about to find and then remove the archive. It's clear from his writings what the archive was for. Your father set it up soon after Doug's conviction. Whatever his reasons for being the monster that he was, wherever his urges to destroy those young girls' lives came from, and it'll take a cleverer man than me to work that out, your father knew he had to stop. By God, he must've thought he had nine lives! I wonder how happy he was when he saw how the cards had fallen against Doug. He knew he was safe. He had nothing to fear from you. Ever. You may have largely disappeared from his life during your adult years, but he knew you'd not do anything. To do so would harm him, you, and your grandmother. No, as far as you and your father are concerned, you were stuck in your *folie à deux*. Anyway, with Doug gone, he could have Fidra back as his playground with exclusive access. If he couldn't follow his urges, he'd play them out in Fidra's archive. He'd recreate the hell-hole bit by bit, at his leisure. And then he could settle down and enjoy it. Replaying it all again and again and again. As his own health failed at an early age, this activity became his "work". But after his death the risk of discovery was all too real.

'When your friendship with Ailsa failed to give you access to Fidra, I think you tried the same with Miller, using his childhood fondness for you. When, to everyone's surprise, he started believing in his father's innocence and the eye-witness issue arose, you began to make a plan, all the while appearing sympathetic to Miller and his cause. Accompanying him to see Lena and Blackford, *and* trying to lay suspicion on him for good measure, hauling Miller out of the sea when he was near to breakdown. You learned well from your father how to play the good Samaritan. All to get to the archive. And you've been in it. The telltale new lamp attached to the ceiling gave that away. When I arrived, it was clear someone had recently broken into it before me. You'd hidden your access well, but you'd been there and tried to seal everything back up until you'd decided what to do. What *were* you going to do? Set a fire? Try to remove everything before Miller allowed access? Throw the furniture into the Firth of Forth? Burn the albums? You took a chance, one that you wanted to avoid. You couldn't risk anyone seeing you go out there. Miller didn't want you to come here until he'd made the place clean again. Exorcized the past. But tell me, Catriona, tell *us*, when were you there? *Speak!'*

Though her voice was faltering, she practically spat the words at him.

'*You . . . you're not my judge and jury, never will be*! I don't *have* to tell you anything . . . but . . . I came out here two nights ago. Helped myself to Miller's boat. I saw how things were going with *him*. He was *that* far from a breakdown. He'd been muttering on and off about having the ruins excavated. I had to see what was there. You've no idea how long I'd waited to get out there. Ailsa had forbidden me. Didn't want me "sullied" by a visit. Hah! That was a laugh! But I *couldn't* be seen going out there. Christ, she was up day and night looking through her bloody binoculars. She told me as much. Just like Miller! Perfect, if she saw me sailing out there! It was too risky. And then Miller wouldn't take me! It beggared belief! After everything I'd done, I still couldn't get out there. But I didn't care any more. *He* was losing it. I *had* to go and see what was there. And . . . and I did. By God, I did! And then I resealed the place and yes, of course I was going to try and destroy everything . . .'

Miller thought he was about to vomit again, the hint of

retching tugging at his stomach, but he managed to get the words out.

'*Damn you, Catriona, tell us what else, what else! Tell u—*'

The tears started just as Duncan stepped forwards and took over.

'I think, no I *know* you were responsible for the death of Lena Stewart. I've spoken at length again and again with poor Lizzie Henderson. She knew Lena well, knew how she was with her animals. Initially she accepted the police verdict that it was an accident. But then she thought more about it. How at ease Lena was with her animals, even the highly strung Twilight. She simply didn't, *doesn't* understand how it could be an accident. Nor do I. Whatever happened to you in childhood I . . . I find it hard to excuse what you are now. I've seen much wickedness, evil even, in my time. Ever since you came back here, Catriona, I have felt a deep unease when in your presence. You may have fooled Miller, and his mother and others. But I have *never* been happy around you. Miller was the one who was supposed to be the odd, strange child. *And* he was, in an endearing way. You, you have always been something different. I'm no psychoanalyst, so I don't know what made you the way you are. I don't know what life was like with just you and your father for all those childhood years. Or why you kept quiet. I'm utterly bereft of explanations. But there is *one* thing I do know. I'm far from convinced by your description of tossing the leash into the McAllister's garden in a panic-stricken moment. Far easier to throw it in the bin, surely? Why wipe it down and wander along the road in your nightclothes?

'From talking with your grandmother, I now believe that there was another reason. You wanted to cause trouble. You *hated* Mhari, you *hated* Ailsa. Both got a lot of attention from your father. The two families were too close for your liking.

I think that you have a deeply possessive, envious side to your nature. One I think that was created by living in such unhealthy isolation with your father *and* by being complicit in such horrific secrets. And I've noted that possessiveness again in recent years when you claimed ownership of Ailsa, offering her a listening ear, and then Miller, but using rather different charms. No, your wicked act with the leash was not the simple reflex reaction you'd have us believe.'

Duncan shook his head. 'You were fuming at the attention your father paid to Ailsa and Mhari. But he was a charmer. Whether it was trying to save the day when Bella was poisoned, or being the perfect family doctor and loyal friend in times of trouble. And you didn't like any of it. So, out of childish spite, you led everyone into a nightmare way beyond your control. Your envy caused this nightmare! *You are despicable!*'

'*No! It wasn't like that! It wasn't! Listen to m*—'

Duncan took a step away from her, his bloodied hand raised to stop her.

'*Well? What was it like? Have you nothing else to say except weak denials?* To me? About the last redemptive hours I spent with your grandmother. To Miller? Who has, I suspect, loved you as girl and woman. Nothing to say to either of us? You owe some words of explanation to Miller. From childhood until now he has suffered beyond description because of you. As have others. I intend to have Russell Sinclair's body disinterred to find out why he died months earlier than expected. But most of all I want to know about Lena. *Now tell us!*'

Miller's waves of nausea were returning as he caught Duncan's look – of apology? Reassurance? Suddenly Catriona kicked her chair back and moved halfway across the room, hands held high as if in surrender.

'I went back to talk to her. I was frightened. I wanted to stop her. To ask her to be careful about giving Miller false hope. Told her there was more to the case than her evidence. It was an awful night. Raining, yet again. Stormy. I'd parked down on the main road and watched from the cover of some shrubbery in the driveway. She'd arrived home just after dark. She'd maybe been indoors for ten, fifteen minutes. I was working up to going to talk to her. Then I spotted her. She was making for the stables.

'She looked in on each of the three horses and stepped into Twilight's stall. I had just called out and walked into the stables when the lights flickered again and blacked out completely. Both things, me arriving and the blackout, must've terrified the horse. The animal was snorting and kicking at the stall door. Lena was calling to me, trying to get me to help her out of there. The hoof blow to her head was enough to down her. She was unconscious. I backed away. I couldn't get in there. What could I do? I heard another few thumps and . . . and oh God, a horrible crunching sound! When the lights came on again, I knew she was dead. But . . . there was nothing I could do. *It was an accident, for God's sake! It wasn't my fault!*'

The shaking in his body had worsened. He saw Duncan fling him a worried look. A look of warning too?

'It's all right, Miller. All right.'

'No, Duncan. No. It's not!'

He scraped his own chair away and stood, legs shaking, facing her, his voice low and tremulous. 'And what about Russell Sinclair? That poor man. He was right! Right all along!'

She was shaking her head so quickly it looked as if she was having a fit.

'*No! He was in pain! It wasn't my fault. He asked me, pleaded!*'

369

'Not your fault! Nothing's been your fault, has it? Not Dad, not Russell, not Lena, not me! Fucking hell, you practically had me throwing myself off Tantallon when I was *this* high! Fucking around with my mind even then, you cunt! Nothing your fault? *Daaaaaamn you!*'

The momentary surprise he glimpsed in her eyes at his gut-wrenching yell disappeared just as quickly. She moved swiftly to her left and ran for the front door. Within a moment she'd disappeared, snow pouring through the entrance as Meg followed, her bark carrying back to them on the wind.

63

'Where can she go?' Duncan was shouting at him above the noise of the wind.

Miller shook his head. His fingers were having trouble zipping up his parka and the pain in his injured shoulder had returned, more searing than before. But the nausea had gone.

He threw a reply back to Duncan as he headed for the door. 'There's nowhere she can go! The tide won't let us off for a few hours yet. She can't get on to my boat. Where's yours? The north cove?'

'Yes!'

'Well she's got the same problem there! Meg will have followed her. We'll find her that way. *Meg! Meg!*'

But where was she going if she couldn't get off the island? Or was she running away at all? Maybe she was just panicking. Meaningless flight. Whatever her plans, she couldn't get far. Conditions were atrocious. The blizzard had thickened since earlier. His peripheral vision caught the sweep of the lighthouse beam on the other side of the island, seeping yellow into the whiteness of the snowfall. Then his ears picked up something other than wind and sea. Meg!

'Duncan! She's at the ruins! Stay close to me or you'll get lost and go off a cliff!'

Thanking his lucky stars – and his childhood obsession – that maybe after all he *could* negotiate this island blindfolded, he picked the quickest way up to the ruins.

Duncan had raced ahead, the wind tearing at his habit,

snow covering his torso. His hands were cupped to his mouth.

'Catriona! Come back to the house with us. Now! You've got to come back!'

She appeared over the north lip of the hollow. Barely recognizable. The wind was tearing wildly at her already spiky hair and tugging at her thin pullover, icy deposits settled in its creases. Meg bounded away from her, back to Miller's side.

He saw Catriona move her lips as if to shout a reply. And then she was gone.

'Duncan! Stay here in the shelter with Meg. Wait here!'

He scrambled up the snowy incline. No sign. Moving forwards at a slow painful jog, his back was burning now with the cuts, his shoulder stiffened into near uselessness. There was only a second's warning before he realized he'd misjudged the distance. Like earlier, he was too near the edge of the cliff, below lay only a sickening drop. The sea was competing with the elements to deafen him. Then he saw her! Standing, arms by her side, staring sightlessly out to sea, buffeted by the wind as she teetered on the cliff edge. She had to be standing in the very footprints he'd made a short while ago, or what remained of them.

'Get her, Miller. Catch her!'

Duncan had ignored his order to stay put and was slithering and sliding his way up towards him.

'No, Duncan! Stay back. It's dangerous! I'll go on!'

His boots scuffed the edge of the cliff and once again he felt the scree shifting beneath him. He couldn't keep this up for much longer because of his shoulder. One last heave up the incline and he'd be behind her. As she turned towards him, he made to grab her right arm, missing it by a millimetre, the force of his lunge setting him off balance and sliding back down the incline. He looked up, peering through the snow as again he scrambled his way towards the cliff edge. It took two last retreating steps from her, as she seemed to lean backwards into the gale. For a second it appeared to hold her in mid-air, her left hand raised. In appeal? Terror? Farewell?

By the time he reached the spot where she'd stood, the foaming waters of the Firth had already closed over her.

64

Triple Murderer 'Undoubtedly Innocent'

'Severe blow to the Scottish criminal justice system'

The Scottish criminal justice system was in turmoil last night as it was confirmed that one of the country's most infamous murder convictions was a miscarriage of justice.

An East Lothian man, Douglas McAllister, was tried and convicted in 1974 for the murders of three girls, dating back to 1969. In recent months, Mr McAllister's son, Miller, 44, a London-based lawyer, has been looking into his father's case.

James McColl, a leading solicitor who appears regularly in the Scottish criminal courts, and who is acting for the McAllister family, said that the conviction would be quashed due to 'crucial new evidence' recently coming to light. He went on to comment that, 'Mr McAllister was undoubtedly innocent. This is a severe blow to the Scottish criminal justice system.'

Lothian and Borders police refused to comment saying that it was 'too early to give any considered analysis of what has occurred'. However, unnamed sources within the force are said to be 'dreading the consequences of this case'.

Full story, page 4: Another miscarriage of justice – the scandal of the Douglas McAllister case.
Editorial, page 24: Crisis in our criminal justice system.

65

'I don't know how you can bear reading and rereading these things. They make me feel sick. I mean it. The hypocrisy. Broadsheets *and* tabloids. Bastards. All keen to convict and torment Dad given half the chance before, and now bleating on about what a terrible injustice he's suffered, baying for a posthumous quashing of his conviction. *Bastards!*'

Classic Mhari in full flow! He cast another look around the bright room, the morning sunshine streaming through the new glass doors. Last night was the first time the three of them had sat down for a meal together in the island house since childhood. He'd thought of it not as a celebration dinner exactly. Too much to be regretted. For him anyway. But it was the marking of a major turning point. The evening seemed to go surprisingly well. Mhari had cooked in good humour, while he and Greg had set the table. Then she'd grabbed a private moment with him.

'So, what about you and Nikki? The wee ones?'

'I don't know, Mhari. Not yet. We've been talking a lot but I still feel . . . well, there's a distance. We've both agreed to take time out. She's with Callum and Emma at her parents' house for the summer. They'll have a great time. I'm popping to see them each week. To reassure them everything's okay. I don't want them hurt. I miss them so much. But . . . Nikki and I will have to decide eventually what we're going to do. Clear the air one way or another. I tried to explain my actions. But I don't think she fully understands them. I'm not sure I do myself. We'll just have to see.'

He heard the sound first and was out the front door making his way to the jetty in seconds. The now familiar living figurehead, outlined against the sun's rays, bent slightly forwards into the wind. The strong arm that grabbed his own, catapulted him back to that first meeting.

'Good to see you, Miller. May I come ashore?'

As they secured the ropes, he sensed Duncan pause in mid-crouch and look up.

'You sure it's okay for me to be here, son? With the others?'

He gestured for Duncan to join him and they both sat with legs dangling over the jetty, feet almost touching the water.

'Of course it's okay. We'd never be where we are today without you. Dad would appreciate that and . . . as for Mum. Well, I'm sorry about that. For you I mean. We can't help who we fall in love with. Though your conflicts must have been very painful, between your faith and your feelings for Mum. You mustn't blame yourself for anything. There's been too much guilt, too much soul-searching. And . . . it's difficult for me to say this about my own mother but Mhari made a very insightful point about it all. She said that she wished you *had* had a proper affair. It would've made Mum happier. She thought Mum was frustrated with her lot and maybe she was. I don't know. Whatever the truth, it's too late. We can't change things.'

He stood up and gave a helping hand to Duncan. 'Come on, now. We've got something we must do, haven't we?'

'Are you ready?'

They both nodded back at him. Mhari looked ten years

younger. Lightly tanned, a slimming cotton dress billowing in the easterly breeze. *Beach Belle*. Greg, in linen suit, a laser of sunlight bouncing off his sunglasses, looked as if he'd walked out of the fashion pages of a men's magazine.

'Are *you* ready?' A reassuring chorus.

He nodded, lowering his head to smile at Meg and ruffle her soft ears. He tilted his face upwards. The sky was at its bluest, visibility crystal clear. Atop the headland, Tantallon stood imposing but benign in the afternoon sun. Along the winding coast, past the sandy coves and the sun-reflecting windows of the houses at North Berwick, to the endless golden ribbon that was Yellowcraigs beach, all was calm, sultry. Like every perfect summer's day he'd ever known here. From this highest point on Fidra he could see a distant regatta, yachts and dinghies with their dazzlingly coloured sails, speckling the waters of the Firth of Forth. Above, the gulls pealed out their plaintive cries. Or were they laughing today? Perhaps. It was a perfect day.

He turned back to his brother and sister. Pulling it out from the pocket of his shorts, he smoothed the paper against him, trying to stop it fluttering in the gentle wind blowing up from the sea.

'I wrote this a while back. It's the letter I would've, *should've* sent Dad when I heard he was dying. I wonder if he can still hear it.'

He stood up as straight as he could.

'"My dearest Dad. There are so many things I wish you to know. The most important is that I will always be limitlessly proud to have had you as my father. Th—"'

It was then that he faltered. His eyes squinting against the tears, his body swaying, the dizziness of grief threatening to topple him.

'It's okay, Mill. Okay.' He opened his eyes and saw Greg

in front of him, reaching a strong hand to his shoulder. Mhari took two steps forwards and put cool fingers to his cheek.

She smiled. 'Come on, Mill. Let's do it. All of us. Together.'

In silent concert they moved forwards to the cliff edge and took their positions in a ragged semicircle.

'C'mon, Duncan. You too. Please, come forwards.'

Duncan, hands clasped loosely in front, gave a solemn nod, took a few steps but stopped short of joining the family group.

Mhari held the urn out in front of her and all three moved into a tightening circle to hold it. Miller gave the slightest nod. As the white granules glistened and glittered in the sun on their long journey down towards the waves, he reached out a now steady hand. Like sand trickling through his fingers, the chalky white residue welcome on his palm. And, just for a moment, he thought he could hear the laughter of all those summer days. Hear the laughter. Hear the joy.

'Remember, Dad. I'm aye yours.'

If you enjoyed *The Reckoning* look out for

The Reunion

Sue Walker's stunning debut novel

Now out in paperback

*Seven people. Separated by time. Joined by a terrible secret
that won't stay buried.*

Twenty-six years ago in Edinburgh, seven teenagers
spent a year together in an experimental home for highly
intelligent but dysfunctional adolescents. They all left The
Unit. But it never left them.

Innes Haldane has spent years forgetting those dark
days. But when a message on her answerphone brings it all
back, she's forced to face her past and two very recent
deaths . . . What happened that could be terrible enough to
still hold the seven in its thrall?

And what bloody reckoning awaits them all?

READ ON FOR A TASTER

I

Half seven. Early home for a Monday night. Keys and shopping were dumped at the kitchen door, and she wandered over to open the living-room windows. Let some of the precious, hint-of-spring air from Primrose Hill wash into her home. The answering machine blinked once. She hit the message button and turned up the volume, heading back to the kitchen for a well-earned, ice-cold glass of white from the fridge.

The hesitant, familiarly deep voice boomed throughout the house.

'Innes? Innes, it's Isabella. Isabella Velasco. I . . . I . . . Don't ask me how I got hold of you . . . I . . . we live quite close, you know, would you believe? God, you sound just the same. Just the same! Look . . . please don't be angry . . . I need to talk to you . . . see you. Can you call me as soon as you can? My number is seven fi—'

She smashed a bleeding hand on the stop button and threw herself into the window seat, blind now to the beauty of the evening outside, watching instead the blood dripping its way on to the rug beneath her. She staggered to the kitchen for a tea-towel to act as bandage, ignoring the broken glass on the floor, the overturned wine bottle by the sink.

Back at the phone, she put trembling fingers to the message button. And played the tape back. Six times.

To make sure that she wasn't in a nightmare.

2

She'd always preferred the suited, smart, self-contained, corporate cases to the individual, down-at-heel, outwardly sad ones. Like the man sitting before her this morning.

'So, if you'll just hand over all your credit cards, the cheque books and your debit card, and sign here.'

She watched as he took his great rough paw – a builder's hand and irreplaceable tool of his (former) trade – and signed his financial affairs over to her, for at least the next three years. Not for the first time did she scent the mixture of a Dutch-courage-stiff-whisky and too many cigarettes for eleven in the morning. The man's hand shook slightly. It had to be the worst day of his life. And she wasn't enjoying it much either. It had been some time since she'd had to deal with a 'client' face to face. She eschewed, indeed forbade, in her hearing her junior staff using their preferred 'punter' for those sorry souls who found themselves in this building. It was disrespectful, she told them.

She decided to close the interview with this particular sorry soul. 'All you need to know about your bankruptcy and dealings with the Official Receiver's Office is in this leaflet. We have a lot of staff long-term sick at present, so I'll be handling your affairs for the time being, although that will change when my assistants get back. Any queries in the next few weeks, my number's written at the top there. Next to my name. Innes Haldane.'

She gathered papers and stood up, directing the man

from the interview room towards the lifts, nodding at his mumbled thanks.

Back in the privacy of her office, she poured herself a cup of over-stewed coffee, allowing herself a couple of minutes to glance at the mayhem that was mid-morning Bloomsbury, five floors below. Buses and cars nose-to-tail. Tourist hordes heading for the nearby British Museum, in much the same formation as the traffic. The never-ending hum of pneumatic drills, buzzing up their vibrations from street level. Perfect! She had the beginnings of a killer headache already.

She turned away and sat down heavily at her desk, surveying the lists of tasks for the overworked day ahead. She ran tentative fingertips over the two-week-old scar on her left hand. The wine glass had cut deep. Funny she'd never felt any pain until hours later.

She shoved the memory from her mind – she was good at that – and turned to her diary. She was beginning to heartily despise this job. True, it wasn't to be sniffed at. Dealing with the debtors of the world in the ordered, usually distant way that was incumbent on a senior member of the Official Receiver's Office was structured, clinical and, at her level, very well paid. Though the junior-staff absences meant she'd be having quite a few face-to-face encounters with clients. Too close for comfort perhaps. During this past year or so she'd already forced herself to admit that she was becoming less and less able to cope with the 'people side' of her job. And that was maybe why she enjoyed her seniority. The more paper-pushing and remote decision-making, the better.

Three hours later she allowed herself a stroll to the British Museum courtyard, taking one of the last vacant benches, warmed by the sunshine. She pulled her sushi box and a copy of the latest *Ham & High* from her bag, checking her watch and generously allotting herself precisely twenty-five minutes for lunch.

A scan-read of the local paper was all she usually made time for, but today, for some unknown reason, she found herself lingering on the news section. On the third reading, she was sure there was no mistake.

Swimming-pool death – inquest date set

The body of a woman was found floating in the swimming pool of the Belsize Sports Centre last Tuesday evening. Staff were alerted by a young mother who had attended her regular women-only swimming lessons.

The dead woman has been named as 42-year-old Isabella Velasco, of 12 Belsize Park Square, a Scots-born, leading dental surgeon working in various practices across London and a university departmental head. Both her wrists had been cut and there had been a significant loss of blood. The pool is now closed for the foreseeable future, as police and sports centre staff examine the area.

A police spokeswoman refused to confirm reports of suicide but stated: 'We are not looking for anyone else in relation to this incident.'

An inquest is to be held at St Pancras Coroner's Court on Friday morning.

She was having trouble keeping her breath even and steady, and stood up, only to teeter back down, her head light and dizzy. She pulled out her mobile, punching in the pre-programmed number for her secretary.

'Emma? I . . . I'm going home. I feel . . . I think I'm

coming down with something. Cancel all the meetings, will you? No! No calls whatsoever at home for the rest of today.'

She moved cautiously through the museum crowds and headed for the taxi rank by the front gates. Within a minute she was cocooned in a cab and heading home.

To think about the woman she had never called back.

3

Any journey past the arches at King's Cross was guaranteed to be dreary. Those sinister, darkened caverns, immortalized in countless grim TV thrillers were, in reality, as uninviting as they were portrayed. No matter the weather. And today? On foot in London, March rain? Her mood was well in keeping with this gloomy morning of damp chill. She'd had two days to think about coming here since reading the devastating news in the paper. Forty-eight anxiety-filled hours of little sleep and much obsessive thinking. And still she wasn't sure that she had made the right decision.

But curiosity had won out over nervousness and, as quietly as possible, she took a seat at the back of the room, praying no one would take any notice of her late arrival or wonder at her reasons for being there. Verdict: suicide. The usual suspects had given evidence. including an insuffer-ably patronizing GP who had recently prescribed 'the deceased' (never 'my patient') paroxetine, for panic attacks – 'It's a member of the Prozac family, you know. Very effective usually' – and suggested that 'the deceased' take time off. A suggestion apparently ignored, since subsequent evidence had made it clear that Isabella Velasco had continued her various practices and lecturing in dentistry. That had made Innes smile. Like herself, Isabella had grown into a workaholic.

She gazed at the sombre suits and faces of the assembled court, her mind numbly trying to take in the proceedings. Forcing herself to concentrate, she momentarily tuned in as an eager young police detective addressed the coroner, referring frequently to his notes. 'Yes, sir, I made extensive inquiries into Professor Velasco's background, both personal and professional . . .' She tuned out again, sparing herself the catalogue of people spoken to, lectures given by Isabella in the past months, etc.

She looked down into her lap, where both hands lay palm upwards. The wine-glass scar was fading now. She dug a fingernail in it. Testing. Just a bit of tenderness left. She moved her fingers to her wrist. Her pulse was racing. Like she'd run a mile. She did her breathing exercises. Breathe in and hold for eight seconds. Exhale for eight seconds. She'd learned how to do this unobtrusively, anywhere. On the bus, in the theatre, even in meetings. Short of openly using a paper bag to breathe and re-breathe into – something she found herself occasionally having to do in the women's toilets at work – she knew that this was the most publicly acceptable way to avoid her hyperventilation panic attacks.

Isabella had suffered from panic attacks too. That haughty, uncaring GP had said as much. Isabella had been on medication for them. As had she herself. Funny, sad parallels. Not surprising, given their shared paths in early life . . . *no*! She'd tried not to think about all that for so long. For much longer than the few weeks since Isabella's wretched phone call. Jesus! How that had just about killed her! She'd never believed it possible. That voice from the past. Or had she really been so surprised? Somehow, hadn't it been just the dreaded outcome that she'd expected? How can you hide from the past for ever? Particularly *that* sort of a past. You can try to hide it from yourself. From your loved ones – if you have any, that is. Then what d'you get? Panic attacks. Failed marriage. Failed relationships, full stop. Failed life. No, that was going too far. Much too far.

She'd lied to her therapist for the best part of the last eight years about *that* part of her past. But it was adolescence, wasn't it? It was a normal, 'off the rails' episode, surely? Why hide it? No, that was self-deluding nonsense. Lies. All lies. To herself. To everyone. And here she was. Sitting in shame. And in fear, fear of discovery. At the inquest into the death of someone she'd . . . she'd what? Shared so much with? Been true friends with? Been ill with . . . She nudged the memory away, drifting back into the young detective's orbit. What he was saying took her breath away.

'Yes indeed, sir. We did find some initially interesting evidence in Professor Velasco's personal life. A new acquaintance. A Mr Danny Rintoul, of Calanais on the Isle of Lewis, in the Western Isles of Scotland. I gleaned evidence from her credit-card records that she had paid numerous and lengthy visits to the Hebrides since last year. I found details of Mr Rintoul in Professor Velasco's address book and in her personal organizer, and there was evidence of frequent telephone communication between them. However, it seems that Mr Rintoul died, drowned off the coast of the Scottish mainland at the beginning of the year. Although an inquest delivered a suicide verdict in his case, I have no reason to believe the events are linked. I also have no evidence to offer as to how Professor Velasco and Mr Rintoul met or knew each other, since no friends or acquaintances of Mr Rintoul ever recall meeting Professor Velasco . . .'

She thanked the gods that she'd chosen to sit on an aisle seat at the back of the court – an unconsciously executed precaution against exactly this sort of eventuality. She followed the ladies' signs and fell into the last cubicle. Although all three were vacant, she always preferred the added security of the end one. Fumbling in her jacket pocket, she pulled out the paper bag, scrunched the neck of it between hooked thumb and index finger, and blew into it. In and out. In and out. Five times. Then relax and repeat. She leaned back, the cistern ice-cold on her neck.

Danny! Danny Rintoul! Isabella had been meeting him! But the witness said he was a 'new' acquaintance. How was that? Had Isabella tried to get in touch with him recently too? Why? Why Danny? Dear Danny Rintoul. Dead too. Drowned too.

She closed her eyes, the paper bag crumpled, forgotten, in her lap, and pictured again that first day. The place lay beyond the comfortable suburbs of the western outskirts of Edinburgh. It was a Sunday. July, 1977. In the middle of that feverishly hot summer . . .

SUE WALKER

THE DEAD POOL

Coming in Autumn 2007

Morag Ramsay can remember little about the day a year ago when her boyfriend and her best friend were bludgeoned to death on the banks of the Water of Leith. Which is unfortunate because Morag has spent the last few weeks in prison on remand for the killings.

The death happened at a deep, natural pool known as the Cauldron, and after her arrest Morag is quickly dubbed 'The Witch' by her fellow prisoners.

Now, due to lack of evidence, the charges have been dropped. But Morag cannot escape the continued whispers hinting at her guilt. Or the authorities' determination to one day bring her to trial.

Then a stranger, Kirstin Rutherford, appears on her doorstep desperate to discuss another mysterious death at the Cauldron. Together the pair rebuild Morag's fragmented recollections in the search for proof of Morag's innocence – or guilt . . .

ANDREW TAYLOR

A STAIN ON THE SILENCE

You can run from a guilty conscience, but you can't hide . . .

James wasn't much more than a child when he had an affair with Lily. And now, twenty-four years later, Lily confesses to James that their affair led to a daughter, Kate.

And Kate desperately needs her father's help: she's wanted for murder.

But there is no room for murder in James's life. He has a wife, a good job, a nice house in the country . . .

As Kate comes crashing into his world, so she lights the fuse under his ordered life. Because James has also been keeping a secret – a very dark and deadly one . . .

A Stain on the Silence **is an unputdownable psychological thriller that will keep you guessing till the very last page.**

'Told at a cracking pace . . . a very readable, fast-moving thriller' *Spectator*

JIM KELLY

THE MOON TUNNEL

From beneath a wartime POW camp near Ely, deep in the Cambridgeshire Fens, a man crawls through an escape tunnel. But he won't emerge until fifty years of peace have passed . . .

When he does, unearthed by archaeologists seeking a Saxon burial tomb, local journalist Philip Dryden knows he has a mystery to solve. First, the man appears to have been shot in the head – and second, he was breaking into the camp, not out.

While the police treat the body as a historical curiosity, Dryden digs deeper – and soon unearths a corpse of much more recent origin …

'Superb. Kelly excels and has produced another story rich in plot and character, with a bit of history as well' *Publishers Weekly*

'Kelly writes with obvious affection about the Fens, which make an eerily atmospheric background to a deftly plotted mystery' *Sunday Telegraph*

DAVID LAWRENCE

COLD KILL

Like a lamb to the slaughter . . .

Winter. Crime scene: a London park at dusk. DS Stella Mooney stares down at the brutalised body of a young woman.

From the shelter of nearby trees Robert Kimber is watching events . . . watching Stella. Next morning he walks into a Notting Hill police station and confesses to the murder.

It's a fast clear-up – just what the AMIP 5 squad wants this close to Christmas. But Stella has her doubts about Kimber's guilt.

So if Kimber didn't commit the murder, who did?

Someone without conscience or pity. Someone who will tap into Kimber's disturbed mind. Someone who needs an apprentice for the dark business he has planned . . .

'A chilling, complex psychological thriller' *Daily Mail*

'Stella Mooney [is] a tough cop who is head and shoulders about most of her rivals in his crowded field . . . a superior thriller' *Sunday Times*

He just wanted a decent book to read ...

Not too much to ask, is it? It was in 1935 when Allen Lane, Managing Director of Bodley Head Publishers, stood on a platform at Exeter railway station looking for something good to read on his journey back to London. His choice was limited to popular magazines and poor-quality paperbacks – the same choice faced every day by the vast majority of readers, few of whom could afford hardbacks. Lane's disappointment and subsequent anger at the range of books generally available led him to found a company – and change the world.

'We believed in the existence in this country of a vast reading public for intelligent books at a low price, and staked everything on it'
Sir Allen Lane, 1902–1970, founder of Penguin Books

The quality paperback had arrived – and not just in bookshops. Lane was adamant that his Penguins should appear in chain stores and tobacconists, and should cost no more than a packet of cigarettes.

Reading habits (and cigarette prices) have changed since 1935, but Penguin still believes in publishing the best books for everybody to enjoy. We still believe that good design costs no more than bad design, and we still believe that quality books published passionately and responsibly make the world a better place.

So wherever you see the little bird – whether it's on a piece of prize-winning literary fiction or a celebrity autobiography, political tour de force or historical masterpiece, a serial-killer thriller, reference book, world classic or a piece of pure escapism – you can bet that it represents the very best that the genre has to offer.

Whatever you like to read – trust Penguin.